I0760285

GODS AND MONSTERS

TERRA SOLARIS

JAIDEN BAYNES

WITH INTRODUCTION BY PROFESSOR JOHN COLARUSSO

First Edition, 2024
Published in Canada

ISBN 978-1-998753-26-0 (ebook)
ISBN 978-1-998753-27-7 (paperback)
ISBN 978-1-998753-30-7 (hardcover)

For questions and comments about this book, contact us at books@baymarpublishing.com.
Visit www.baymarpublishing.com

Dedication

This book is dedicated to my Grandma Nellie.

Contents

Act 3

Act 4

Act 5

Acknowledgements

Special thanks to Professor John Colarusso for consultation and advising as well as sparking my interest in the wonderful world of comparative mythology.

Introduction

When we think of myth, we usually think of it as depicting gods, heroes, and people in general at a remote past where all is hazy and things now impossible came true. But what if this neat linear sort of olden times was wrong? What if the beings we read about in myths occupied time lines that slid along with ours? What if they were a living part of our world?

This is the sort of time depicted by Jaiden Baynes, where the Greeks are not ancient, but in fact are interplanetary, the Graiacs. Where the gods are not remote memories, but tangible inhabitants, sharing the set of planets with the immortals and people in general, that is "Greek" people. The time lines are not one after another in a long sequence, but are parallel and have "slid along" and have brought the gods of Ancient Greece now together with humans.

What sort of planetary systems would these be? What would be happening? Well, this triad of beings, a ranking recalling the three social strata of Proto-Indo-European, the mother culture of the Greeks and many others, would do what any rational social beings would do: wage war. Here the Titans battle with the Olympians, and humans, immortals and the ordinary are swept along into a series of searing and vivid encounters. The result is a dramatic world that reflects the Greek original in spirit. I can only imagine that Homer, if his time line were aligned with ours, would be envious.

John Colarusso
McMaster University

"The strong do what they may and the
weak suffer what they must."

Thucydides

"It has been said of the world's history hitherto that might makes right. It is for us and for our time to reverse the maxim, and to say the right makes might."

Abraham Lincoln

"I think it only makes sense to seek out and identify structures of authority, hierarchy, and domination in every aspect of life, and to challenge them; unless a justification for them can be given, they are illegitimate, and should be dismantled, to increase the scope of human freedom."

Noam Chomsky

Prelude: Might Makes Right

My generation, the firstborn immortals, had no explanation for our origin. To be honest, nobody investigated such a thing because we didn't care much about where we came from. The point was that we were there. What was more important was that we were different; we were better than the swarms of weakling mortals that were breathing our air. They outnumbered us a million to one, but they were superfluous.

We were Powerful with a capital P. Not simply potent in the abstract sense but rather overflowing with that which made reality mercurial and the impossible possible. True Power was what allowed us superior beings to bend the Kosmos to our will and manifest our desires.

A weakling's strength was restricted by their mere muscles, but with Power, mountains or molehills were equally insignificant. Weaklings would envy the birds or look to the stars. With Power, flying to them and beyond was mere child's play. Weaklings feared injury, growing old, and dying, but those born with Power had no fear of death: Power could reverse all wounds and perpetuate our existences forever in our primes.

Those with Power were rightfully worshipped as the first gods by our lessers. But back then, I was too young to fully appreciate what that meant. Rather than understanding the significance of receiving worship from those beneath me, the only part that interested me was the fear they had of my Power. The adults didn't dare tell me what to do when I could erase them without any effort. All were beneath me.

Many other Immortals fell prey to delusional feelings of compassion or community and joined the tribes of the first humans they encountered. That life wasn't for me, though. Without an equal in sight, I struck out on my own to see what the rest of the planet was like. I sensed Power emanating from beyond the stars: from the other beings on distant worlds. I could've easily taken to the stars with my Power, but I had an eternity to explore, so why not start small?

A little less than a year into my wandering… she appeared. I remember I'd just killed a lion for some lunch, barehanded and without any effort, might I add. That was when she presented herself to me. With brilliant bright blue hair and eyes like a daytime summer sky, a little girl who looked about my age approached me. The community had sent people after me before. They were worried I'd get hurt if left on my own—the irony.

Anyways, at first, I suspected she was another one of them. Doubly so after she began to go on and on about how that fool Ouranos and the others were worried about me. So, I gave the usual spiel about how I didn't need their help and how I would survive just fine on my own.

If anything, she was in more danger. I could usually sense how much Power someone had from a glance, and she didn't have any! I left to keep exploring the planet alone, but she kept following me. I told her repeatedly that I wasn't going back to the tribe, but she still followed behind me with monotone demands that I come back with her. She was so emotionless; it was creepy looking. Pretty cute but still creepy.

When words didn't scare her off, I tried some good old intimidation. Even as a child, I had the highest level of Power on the planet, probably the whole Kosmos, so a flash of that would've scared most people off.

Yet even after I let it blaze out, she wasn't scared at all. Getting a bit annoyed, I gave her a small push to rough her up a little bit. I was thrown away instead, even though she didn't move a muscle. Even if, for a second, I could tell she was hiding at least as much Power as I had.

Justifiably perturbed, I tried to murder the little girl. That didn't go so well. For the first time in my young life, I was beaten. There was somebody stronger than me. She proved herself to be beyond the scope of my Powers. I was furious that I lost, but ultimately, when she bent down and helped me back up, my little heart skipped a beat.

Begrudgingly, I had to acknowledge her as the victor and returned to the tribe with her. It was amazing: so much had changed in the year I had been gone. The Stone Age savages had built a village, learned to grow food, assembled the planet's entire population into a grand central settlement, and much more.

From hunting and gathering, humans had progressed into an agricultural society. It was all thanks to them: that girl and her weird siblings, the Solaris clan. They arrived on Graia only after I'd left and had gathered the diaspora together. They reconnected not just the different people scattered across the planet but the various peoples across various worlds.

Each one of these mysterious visitors was stronger than I was, but they weren't there to rule… just observe. The creepy stalkers helped us build and grow as they watched and recorded all. Over time, they became less alien-like, developing their personalities and quirks as they dwelt among us humans. At least, that's what the simpletons saw. I always figured they just did it to win the idiots over and fit in to study us better. They were whatever helped them blend in best. Either way, they at least became easier to talk to.

But most of them didn't interest me. She was the only one I cared about. She spent most of her time in the fields, so I decided to join her. She was picked as a member of the warband, so I joined, also. She helped run the society, so I took an interest there as well. Across all functions of society, where she went, I followed.

She said she loved all humans equally, but I could tell… I was her favorite. Nobody else had what we had. Just as she followed me everywhere before, I made sure I spent as much time with her as I could. Relentlessly bullying her didn't seem to phase her, so I went with other ways of getting her attention. When I got old enough to stop thinking it was because I hated her, I realized that she was the one woman I loved.

She was the only being in the Kosmos worthy of my love. After all, such a superior being… such a powerful being, demanded such love and devotion. The others interested me far less. Not just her siblings but the other weaklings that flocked to them.

Given my strength, I quickly gathered my fair share of followers. Many lovers as well, but they were all just there to pass the boredom while I worked my way up to being worthy of her.

In the community, the adults raised us as best they could. What's more, the arrogant, bossy kids who tried to shepherd the rest of us fancied themselves our parents. Ouranos and Demeter especially fussed over me as if they were the ones who'd birthed me. They weren't all that strong, but they were genuine and loving; I hated them both.

The others were pacified and weakened by their pathetic sentimentality. They grew up finding their place in our little proto community, using their talents and strength in service to those weaker than them. If I had their lives, I would kill myself.

No, I was meant for much greater things. Even she told me as much. I was special. She taught me many of her miraculous powers and praised my intellect with each successful new skill I mastered. It was ecstasy. Eventually, once I grew enough in Power, she would see me as an equal.

As powerful as she was beautiful, everyone knew of the awesome Power of my Goddess: Terra Solaris.

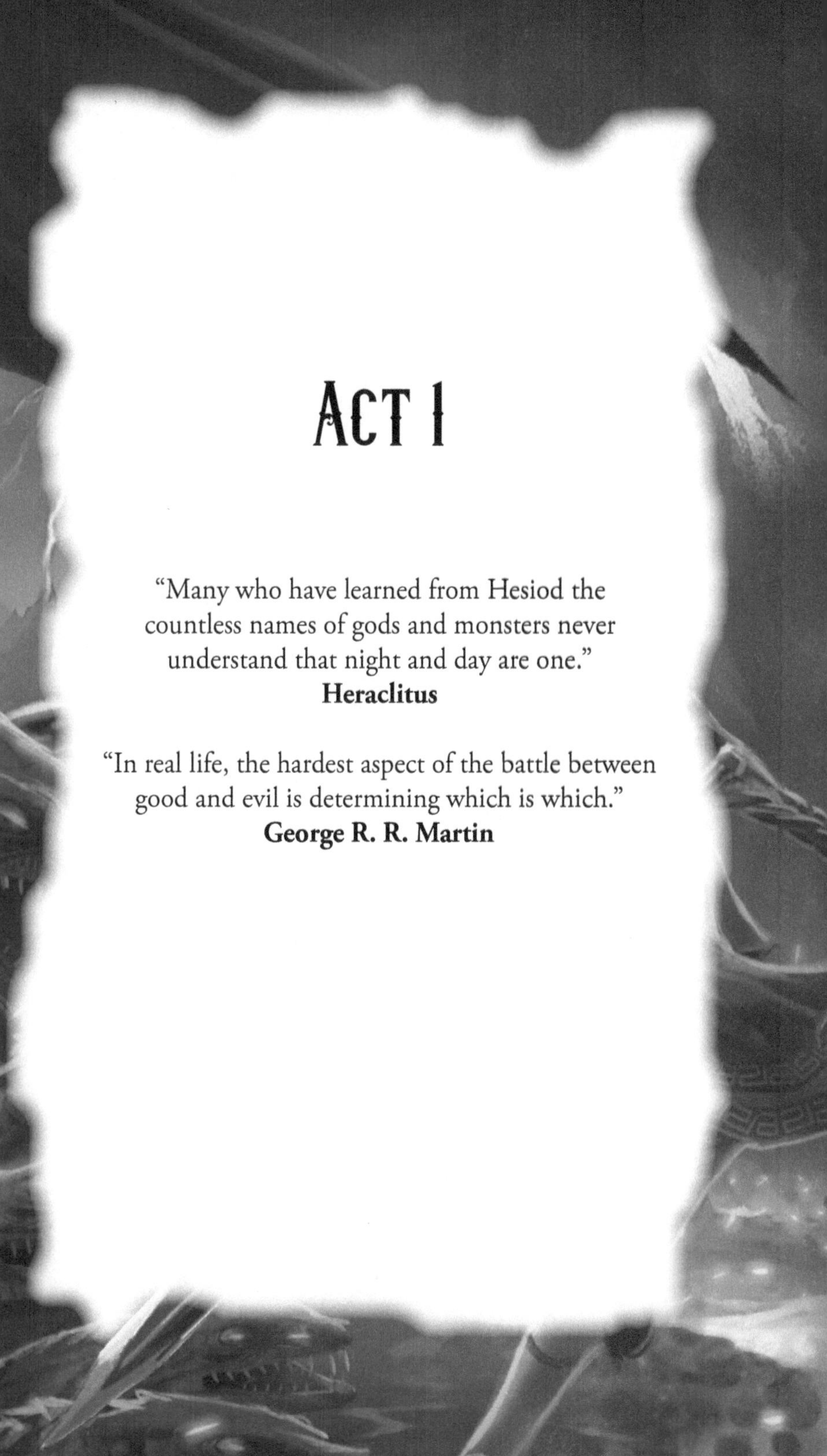

Act 1

"Many who have learned from Hesiod the countless names of gods and monsters never understand that night and day are one."
Heraclitus

"In real life, the hardest aspect of the battle between good and evil is determining which is which."
George R. R. Martin

TALE 1

Night and Day

"Terra… what are you?" a young boy named Typhon demanded of the little girl that stood before him. Terra, the one in question, turned around as her otherworldly sky-blue hair and eyes were silhouetted by the literal other world in the sky.

The portal in the heavens above that had beckoned it here closed and hid the Divine Sphere from view once more. The warband of young gods watched in awe as Terra, the small, harmless-looking girl, had just called upon its celestial Power to annihilate an entire army of Monsters that had threatened the tribe. She did not attack them; she simply erased them all from existence en masse.

Power was the divine flame that allowed its wielders to change reality itself. To differentiate Power, the reality-warping force, from power in the abstract, the P is capitalized to make it a proper noun. Power was beyond anything in the natural world. No natural force under the stars, not even the stars themselves, could oppose the reality-breaking ability that Power afforded these immortal gods. They could only ever be threatened by one another.

Those with Power could destroy entire planets and move so quickly that light would blush. Those without Power could never truly comprehend them… or oppose them. Truly, this showed they were supreme over all others.

But even with all that said… no other immortals fought like Terra. Even the other so-called immortal gods were stunned; she was on a completely different level. It was impressive to many, but it stuck with young Typhon, who finally had to ask directly, "Terra… what are you?"

"I am Terra Solaris, a member of the tribe just as you are." An equally young Terra replied. Her answer itself was odd; last names had not yet been invented in the Stone Age.

"No, I mean, what are you actually?" Typhon asked again.

"I do not understand your question. Please elaborate." Terra tilted her head to imitate the human body language of mild curiosity.

"You know what I mean. Humans are either immortals who have Power or mortals who don't. However, while you have Power, you aren't like the rest of us immortals. Are you a human?" Typhon asked.

The Goddess of nature did not reply. She only stared at him with blank, robotic apathy. Gods could wield Power, but so could Monsters, and that inhuman look wasn't doing her any favors.

"Stop looking like that, it's creepy!" Typhon complained.

"That is a mean thing to say. While I do not care about this body's physical appearance, such words might be considered insulting to others," Terra said, doing her best to feign offense.

"Hey! Don't go trying to change the subject again!" Typhon grew frustrated by the girl's usual tricks.

She was so annoying and so creepy. Cute, but creepy. In prehistoric times, the little boy Typhon stuck to his childhood crush, Terra, like glue. Every day, every free moment he had, Typhon was bugging her about something. Sometimes just to talk or play like kids did… but most often, he was interested in fighting.

Despite the girl's small size and soft appearance, she was undoubtedly the strongest and most terrifying being Typhon ever encountered. She didn't fight the way the others did. To others, Power was seen as a magical and unexplainable blessing, but to her, it was… something else.

One could hardly say Terra fought at all. Moreso than her emotionless persona, Terra's odd way of using Power was what made Typhon suspicious of her origins. Her siblings claimed just to be a group of mighty first-generation Immortals like him. But then, how could they be siblings?

Plus, even though she was a kid, she talked like a grown-up… a weird grown-up. No, even the grown-ups asked her questions. She was a smarty-pants know-it-all who had an answer for everything. How to best plant their crops, how to cure various diseases, why the sun would rise and set each day… she knew it all. While Terra would answer any questions people posed, other than personal ones about her and her siblings, Typhon's questions focussed on a very specific subject.

"Tell me, Terra… how would I become the ultimate warrior? How could I become even stronger than you?" Typhon asked her one morning.

"Why do you want to know?" Terra asked.

"Terra, you should know me by now. You don't need to ask." Typhon sighed.

"After analyzing your personality, it is inadvisable to give you such information without some assurances," Terra answered.

"Like what?" Typhon scoffed.

"Before answering your query, I require a statement confirming your intent is not to harm anyone except in self-defense. It would be unfortunate for everyone if you misuse this information. Do you agree not to do that?" Terra explained.

"Of course, I wouldn't hurt anyone with what you teach me. Who do you think I am?" Typhon lied as easily as he breathed.

"Very well, I shall help you become an ultimate warrior," Terra replied.

Typhon began to smile to himself. Obviously, that question was just a formality. She must have wanted to give him the answer from the start!

So, Typhon continued to train to become the ultimate warrior under Terra's watchful eye. In parallel, he continued challenging her to sparring matches in the hopes of finally overcoming her.

One early morning, the two sparred after finishing their harvest for the year. Still having his sickle from farming, Typhon used it to fight and became quite adept at using it in combat. But that was not his only weapon. Typhon developed the ability to turn weapons into autonomous attack drones. His early weapons were discarded flint tools, old and unused weapons, as well as any sharp farming equipment he could get his hands on.

On top of that, Typhon created flaming eye beams that destroyed anything they hit. Maybe then Terra would finally join all the other girls in complimenting their unique and alluring color.

"Correction: they are not flaming eyes," was, of course, as much as he would get from the emotionless weirdo, "You are actually firing particle acceleration beams that cause anything they touch to reach the Planck temperature, and thus evaporate."

It didn't matter how often she scientifically explained them; it obviously didn't make sense to the young caveman. Typhon didn't understand what any of that meant on a theoretical level, but as a fighting genius, he could do it, nonetheless.

The boy was a fighting prodigy with both Power and skill beyond most full-grown gods. Nonetheless, Terra easily defeated him. She offered him tips and advice for how to improve, just as she always did. Typhon knew in his heart that he was still subservient to Terra and felt shame.

"Damn it! I still need to get stronger!" Typhon growled. Even after everything she taught him about, his mind always returned to that idea.

"Typhon, we have already discussed how Power isn't everything. I have presented you with a myriad of ways to improve as a fighter beyond brute strength. You pursue them all to great success, and yet… why are you still so obsessed with raw Power?" his puzzled mentor inquired.

"It's because… I hate being weak. I hate it when you look down on me. I need to become strong enough so I can do whatever I want!" Typhon grumbled.

"But you can do anything you want right now," Terra replied.

"Not everything." Typhon sighed, much to Terra's confusion. Seeing Terra's confused look, Typhon became flustered.

"You wouldn't get it! You're so strong you could kill me in a second if you wanted!" Typhon grumbled.

"No, I could not," Terra robotically replied.

"Don't patronize me. I know you're holding back whenever we spar. If you used half of the abilities that you taught me, I'd be finished." Typhon rolled his eyes.

"That is not what I meant. I could not kill you because you are an interesting specimen." Terra did her best to try and smile.

"Of course. If I don't get stronger… I'm just another hairless ape next to you. A lower level of life that deserves only contempt!" Typhon cried.

"I have never said any of that about you. Why do you think that?" Terra asked.

"Because… if the situation was reversed… I'd say that," Typhon admitted.

"Why?" Terra asked again. Typhon slowly turned to her, betraying a bit of frustration. Rather than answer, he employed another technique he learned from the knowing one.

"You hold conversations a lot better than you used to. But I'm still just a 'specimen of study' to you, aren't I?" Typhon sighed.

"You are not. You are my friend, Typhon. I am concerned about your mental well-being." Terra did her best to show some emotion. Typhon was taken aback. She really was doing her best to communicate with him. Now, he was just more upset. It was adorable but also upsetting!

"Damnit. I don't know if it's worse that I'm just a toy to you… or that you'd be so willing to patronize me by coming down to this lowly level. A human has no right to be friends with a god. The weak do not deserve to even be in the presence of the powerful. That's why—" Typhon declared but stopped short. He was blushing a little because he knew that if he kept going, he'd say something embarrassing like, "I need to get stronger to stand by your side."

"If that is the case. If the strong do get to decide, then I decide that we are friends." Terra beat him to the punch with the cheesy one-liner. It was horribly corny, but to young

Typhon, that was the coolest thing he'd ever heard! He turned beet red and had to look away from Terra.

"Typhon? What is the matter? Your heartbeat has increased dramatically. Are you alright?" Terra asked with concern.

"I'm fine! Don't touch me!" Typhon jumped in a panic when Terra reached out to comfort him.

He was still too young to communicate his feelings properly. Typhon would just act petty and annoying to keep Terra's attention. Typhon needed to show her- to show himself that he was worthy of her undivided attention. In Typhon's mind: she was his everything, so he should be her everything.

One part of Terra having a life outside of Typhon came from the fact that she never slept. Typhon, feeling entitled to know what she did at all hours of the day, decided to stay up late and find out what she did.

At the tail end of the Stone Age, people still tended to go to sleep not long after the sunset. The knowing one, ever the watchful observer, helpfully told Typhon once that it was three hours and twenty minutes after sunset, precisely was the average time humans went to sleep. Thus, Typhon knew exactly how long he had to wait before sneaking away from the rest of the tribe. After waiting until most people either left or dozed off next to the great public hearth, Typhon decided to move out and find what Terra was doing.

He found her in the woods before an assembly of countless animals winged, clawed, and hooved. Yet before her, all the beasts were docile and orderly. Some presented their young to her or tried to earn approving pets and scratches.

Terra commanded their adoration and respect just as she did among the tribe. She treated animals as if they were people. Or did that mean… she treated people as if they were animals? They squawked and growled and meowed at her, but Terra did not open her mouth to reply. Instead, she just looked at them, and they seemed to understand her response just as intimately as she seemed to understand them.

Typhon was enthralled: those with Power could communicate mentally like that, but everyone knew that animals neither had nor could use Power. Terra must have had some kind of unique ability to interact with their brains (or hearts, in his primitive understanding) directly. As Typhon moved closer, he rustled some foliage and startled the assembled creatures.

They saw this intruder as something fundamentally different to the goddess they admired. Terra stilled the beasts and peacefully dismissed them. Typhon walked over, impressed by the display.

"So, it is true. You can control the hearts of others, can't you?" Typhon asked.

"I can connect with the minds of others," the knowing one answered while subtly correcting the Stone Age misunderstanding.

"That doesn't answer my question." Typhon chuckled at her evasive answer.

"I have the skill you described. But I was not using that. I see it as rather invasive, even on animals. I was just sending a message for them to heed, not forcing them to do so," Terra explained.

"Really? What were you discussing with those beasts?" Typhon could hardly believe what he was asking.

"Some children were harmed by bears recently. I simply communicated that to avoid further conflict or injury, all dangerous creatures should all be on their best behavior and steer clear of humans. I directed them to some other suitable habitats where they will both be safe from our hunters and not risk harming any of our people," Terra revealed.

"If the beasts were giving us trouble, I could've dealt with them." Typhon grinned as his flaming eyes began to glow.

"No. That was the exact kind of outcome I was hoping to avoid. In terms of destructive capacity, the tribe could hunt them to the last. The problem is that they also don't understand the unintentional consequences that would cause." The nature goddess posited.

"Sure." Typhon couldn't have cared less. He was much more eager to get back to Terra's power over both mind and matter.

"Anyways, can you teach me that control of the mind?" Typhon excitedly asked.

"Why would you want that ability?" Terra asked.

"Well, you just showed it can… avoid conflict. Without having to fight at all, it is a power over peace." Typhon's sweet smile concealed his devious intent. Terra stared at him blankly for a few moments.

"No. I am sorry, but I will not do that," she finally concluded.

"But why not!? Like a snake hypnotizing its prey, I could disable any attacker!" Typhon cried before realizing too late that he'd made a Freudian slip.

"Snakes cannot hypnotize their prey. That is a myth," Terra instinctually corrected the misinformation. Oh good, she was focusing on that.

"Either way, I am not teaching you mind reading and control. I have placed severe restrictions on my use of the ability and cannot be certain you would use it responsibly," Terra explained.

"But why restrict yourself? With it, nobody could stop you!" Typhon grinned.

"That is the point. Nobody could stop me, so, unfortunately, I must be responsible for not using my Power unethically. Simply, I must be sure not to exert my will over others in ways I would not want others to do to me. It makes sense to treat others how you would want them to treat you," Terra replied. "Therefore, applying discipline and respect for others is essential."

Typhon looked disappointed. What was the use of all that power if she didn't enjoy it from time to time?

"Back to my point, to avoid conflict, such excessive measures are unnecessary. The potential for abuse outweighs the potential benefits." Terra finished her refusal.

Typhon grew upset. She was growing more and more tight-lipped with her secrets as she grew. She was growing and changing generally; why couldn't she be as gullible as she used to be? Either way, Typhon, as per usual, projected his own thoughts onto Terra. This wasn't really a rejection. She was really telling him that such an ability was unnecessary for him to become the ultimate warrior. He had to focus on raw Power itself.

So, he grew in Power and sought stronger enemies to singlehandedly conquer. No man under heaven was a challenge for him. Even as a youth, he slaughtered them like animals without a second thought. But Terra despaired when she saw all those he had killed in battle.

Typhon reminded her that they were enemy raiders from another tribe that had come to attack theirs. As part of the warband, not only was it their job to repel invaders, but they could do so with impunity. Around the Universe, the unaccountable tribal warbands had earned a reputation for savagery and brutality.

"We can be better," Terra rebuked him. "That strength you love so much can be used to protect. If you can protect yourself and others without having to kill, you should. You were not killing out of self-defense; it was completely unnecessary. We both know that they weren't a threat in the slightest. You have to be better! We all do! With great power, there must also come great responsibility!"

Typhon was stunned by her exclamation. That was the most he'd ever seen her emote. She really felt strongly about this "no killing" nonsense. Or maybe she was just testing him?

Terra brought Typhon and the rest of the warband to go and apologize to the tribe that had their warrior youths killed in the battle. Rather than conquer them as was customary, she offered the enemy tribe their protection. That fool Ouranos just went along with it! Typhon felt humiliated. Everyone else slaughtered to their hearts' content! Why was their tribe's warband the only one that kept to such silly oaths?

Terra's care for these weaklings was utter madness. But as her inferior, he had to respect her wishes. For now. Yes, that had to be it: she was teaching him that so long as he bowed to another, he was vulnerable to any outrageous whims. She must have been further encouraging him to surpass all others! As such, Typhon toned down the murder. Since he could not test out his strength on human beings, he picked fights with Monsters.

So, as he grew in age, he also grew in Power and sought out stronger Monsters to singlehandedly conquer. He would have his followers; the Titans, stay back so he could take all the glory for himself. He was happy to find that Monsters were much stronger than most humans anyways.

Then, one day, it got him killed. Typhon made a big show of slaying the beast before the tribe to earn their praise. But as he stood to gloat and pose, his hubris kept him from realizing that the creature was still alive. In its last moments, the Monster fired a focused beam of pure Power through Typhon's heart!

Not only did it physically damage him, but it also knocked loose the rest of the boy's Power reserves! Immortal regeneration was predicated on using Power to repair their injuries. Once they were without Power, they were just as mortal as a normal human.

The Monster didn't need to destroy a planet or even a star to kill him. It just needed a small blast through his defenses. So, the young man named Typhon fell over, dead. Terra wept. Refusing to lose him, she performed a great miracle before all in assembly. After all, he was only "mostly dead". By sharing some of herself with that mere human, he was allowed to live again because she became his life force.

From then on, Typhon noticed he had grown even more Powerful. He was no longer just a very powerful human… he was divine. Terra had chosen him! She must have wanted him to be her equal. No matter how much he battled, his reserves of Power would not be exhausted. No matter how much damage he took, he could recover as if nothing had happened. His eyes had been opened, and he had knowledge of the secrets of the Kosmos.

Even with Power, human perception was limited. Power allowed humans to see the world at speeds faster than light and electricity-based brains could interpret, but that Power based vision was still limited to a recreation of three-dimensional light-based vision. This was something completely different; this was how Terra saw the world.

Yet rather than having a revelation of the beauty of nature and a greater appreciation for life, the Universe, and everything, Typhon had a different perspective. Upon seeing how small and insignificant humans were in the wider world, he didn't come to see life as precious… he only saw it as small and insignificant. This twisted Overview Effect could only be literal for him: Typhon now saw himself as above it all.

After his apotheosis, Typhon's ego only grew. Now, he had what he always wanted. At the height of his arrogance, he challenged Terra to another battle. He was defeated in short order. Typhon thought he could die from embarrassment.

"Come on, don't be silly. You can't die at all anymore," the flowery goddess giggled and smiled sweetly at him. Typhon was taken aback by her beauty and adorably genuine laughter. Then, his brain caught up with him and processed that she'd just read his mind.

"How did you know I was thinking that? I never said anything." Typhon nervously pointed out, "You said you don't read minds!" He felt horribly violated by the idea, especially given the kinds of thoughts about Terra that usually occupied his mind. Though, he didn't for a second consider that doing the same to anyone else would be just as invasive.

"I am not reading your mind. Our case is a bit different now. Our Minds themselves are connected. Even if you don't intend to, you might send me some of your thoughts and feelings. Congratulations, you have unintentionally discovered our new empath connection," Terra explained with a genuine smile of pride.

Upon seeing how shy that made Typhon, Terra readjusted her perspective and employed proper, non-supernatural empathy to decide on what to do.

"You see now why I don't establish mental links with others. I promise that from now on, I won't view your thoughts, even if you accidentally send some my way. A person's mind is their ultimate possession, and you have your right to privacy," Terra reassured him, for which an uncharacteristically shy Typhon thanked her.

She sat beside her friend, and the two chatted for a while. After all, if they were now connected, it only made sense that they get along. That was why Typhon was so devastated when she left to explore the rest of the Kosmos without him.

TALE 2

Theogony

Back when the Kosmos was still very young, peace reigned, and Ouranos ruled the region of it that would later be known as Graia with a gentle hand. To those he shepherded, he was often called Father Heaven.

Spread across countless habitable planets, humanity simultaneously began a march of progress from the stone age into early civilization. Father Heaven was beloved by all, and his sanctifying holy nature returned that love with divine blessings. Like his female counterpart Terra, he was as kind and gentle as he was mighty. Even now that she had left with her siblings to explore the rest of the Kosmos, Ouranos could protect his precious children from any threat.

But in the comfort of that ancient communal utopia, the early human warriors felt like they'd been left behind. To clear out the monsters and fend off invading tribes, warriors were essential. But paradoxically, the warriors had helped finally bring an end to the need for war. As the migratory cave folk settled down into sedentary zones and began farming, there was no longer a need for conflict with other people. Ouranos' diplomacy reduced conflict in general. And fending off Monsters was handled by the gift Terra had left:

the Hekatonkeries. These autonomous anti-Monster drones dispatched them without the warriors even needing to lift a finger so that Graia would be safe even in Terra's absence.

Increasingly, the warriors felt that there was no longer any need for them. Ouranos desperately hoped they would be able to adjust to living in peace and was happy to find that many successfully did. Unfortunately, while most veterans of the old age eventually adjusted to civilian lives and found their new place in society, others longed for the old days.

"Ouranos is a fool! He has turned his back on us, the warrior caste. We make his peace and enforce his laws but we have been used up and discarded in favor of the foolish rulers and weak producers. The rulers would have no authority without our enforcement and the producers could not protect the fruits of their labor without us standing guard. We warriors have become humiliated: we are caged lions ruled by ungrateful sheep. They needed us warriors more than we warriors needed them!" a charismatic authoritarian rallied his fellow soldiers.

These ideas were nurtured and magnified by a certain strongman leader with ambitions of his own. The military lifestyle instilled deference to power and authority in soldiers that played right into his hand. The charismatic authoritarian seduced and manipulated warriors across the Kosmos into his common cause.

"Neglected warriors of the military caste, come and follow me! I shall return you to your former glory. I shall make you great again. I alone can accomplish this!" was what he declared before his brothers and sisters in arms.

"Brothers and sisters, my fellow Titans! Heed my words. To return the warriors to our former glory, this putrid peace must be shattered, and the world must be returned to an age of bloodshed and war. This is the dream I offer." The wily autocrat called on the warriors.

They swore an oath to him as the Titans, and he swore an oath to them as Typhon, their god and king.

Ouranos' son Typhon had disappeared not long after his Goddess left Graia to explore the rest of the Kosmos. But when this prodigal son returned, his homecoming was not cordial. Typhon returned with vengeance to wage war against his father and claim the Kosmos for himself on behalf of the warriors.

Typhon took control of the Hekatonkeries, and the guardians of humankind became their destroyer. The Titans' evil army spread death and destruction across Graia before finally besieging the old capital itself.

As the army of Titans besieged the central farming city that had grown on Graia, Ouranos barred their way. The entire army did not approach a step further now that Father Heaven stood on guard. Yet from above, Typhon descended before his troops and faced Ouranos down without a hint of concern.

"Typhon, my son… how could you do this?" Ouranos demanded.

"Do not patronize me, weakling. I haven't changed at all. If you've been too stupid to see that I hated you from the start, then you brought this on yourself. Taking me under your wing, treating me like your own son… how humiliating! Before I can be king of the Kosmos, I require that this humiliation be rectified!" Typhon roared before Ouranos and his cowering children beyond the city gates.

Ouranos despaired that not just Typhon but many of his other children from the first generation now sided against him. They were now the terrible Titans that sought to plunge the world into war and strife. Nonetheless, Father Heaven had to put a stop to this wayward rebel. The two prepared to face each other in single combat.

In battle, Ouranos wielded a most unusual weapon: a giant wheel known as the Kosmic Ring. The wheel, like most other divine weapons, was made of Adamant: matter infused with Power that granted it supernatural properties. The foremost property of Adamant was the ability to kill Immortals by nullifying their regeneration. His insignia was the Ouroboros, a snake eating its own tale. His armor was the bright sky, wrapped in the embrace of the clouds.

Against him, Typhon used a humble farming sickle. His insignia was also the Ouroboros, but while Ouranos' was but a single snake, Typhon's took the shape of two snakes overlayed in the symbol of Infinity. His armor was the darkness and the void draped in the starry heavens.

So began the contest for who would reign over creation. Typhon struck first with the swing of his sickle, however, Ouranos did not fret. Typhon found himself back where he started and ran back toward the sky Father to attack again. He was stuck in an endless loop.

Right out the gate, Ouranos had employed his ultimate attack: an artificial mini-Universe known as a Microcosm. Microcosms were artificial Universes that sufficiently powerful and skilled gods could create as realms where their divine powers were absolute. Within their realm, the god that created it was essentially unbeatable.

Ouranos had trapped Typhon in the Microcosm: Aionios. It was an otherworldly realm where time was stuck in an endless now. While the rest of the Kosmos progressed normally, Typhon existed in a state of perpetual re-enactment. This way, he would be unable to harm anyone else.

The other Titans were intimidated. Their father, Ouranos, had grown even more powerful since Typhon left. As the god of eternity, he could bend time into a loop. Yet Typhon, too, had grown, and his mastery over time allowed him to escape in no time at all. Ouranos' Microcosm crumbled, and Typhon walked free in the real Kosmos once again.

"I must warn you against trying to beat me at my own game. There is only one god of time, and that is me." Typhon scoffed.

Typhon retaliated by showing off his power to stop time in the real world! Unlike other warriors who favored the emerging trend of creating Microcosms to serve as their domains and ultimate attacks, Typhon's playground was the Universe itself, and in it, he had as much control as most did in a world of their creation!

Time was stopped, and all were motionlessly defenseless before the true god of Time. Typhon casually walked over to his father and prepared to slit Father Heaven's throat with his sickle. Though time was frozen, Ouranos struck first by swinging the Kosmic wheel! The surprise attack sent Typhon flying away from the sheer force of the blow!

When time returned to normal, it was Typhon who was on the ground and Ouranos who stood resolutely. Ouranos' flock cheered for him. Father Heaven would not let the evil Titans harm another soul. But Typhon stood back up and did not have a scratch on him. He simply leaped forward to attack again with his sickle. Ouranos met him by swinging his Kosmic circle. The two weapons met and created a massive blast that threw both deities back.

"You are a weakling and a fool, but that weapon of yours is indeed impressive. I think I'll add it to my collection." Typhon grinned.

Ouranos was confused by what he could mean, but Typhon just responded by opening a dark portal behind him. Out of the black abyss came his fleet of divine tools that he had stolen from his victims. The divine weapons all began to orbit Typhon. Ouranos was horrified: he recognized them all from many of his other children.

Before coming to slay him, Typhon had killed almost every single god that called Ouranos father. If they did not pledge fealty to Typhon and become a Titan, they were dead. Their divine tools were added to Typhon's growing armory, which lay inside the dark dimension he'd opened to summon them.

Once Typhon figured that he had withdrawn enough weapons to kill Ouranos (easily over 30 divine weapons), he closed the entrance to his armory. Ouranos readied himself as Typhon listed off each tool and who he'd killed to get it.

"Yes… so many of your lambs that were sent to the slaughter. Let us see which of your children will get the honor of having their weapon kill their father?" Typhon chuckled to himself after finishing his cruel taking of inventory.

"Do not sully my children's legacy by touching their weapons with your bloodstained hands! I will not countenance their tools for defending others being wielded by a villain!" Ouranos grew angry at his taunting.

"Wield? Who said anything about wielding them?" Typhon asked with a wicked grin.

Instead of wielding the divine weapons with his hands, Typhon controlled them using telekinetic commands so that they would attack their target remotely. At once, all the weapons aimed at Ouranos and were fired off to skewer him! With great swiftness and skill, Ouranos swatted them all away with his divine wheel. But that was all a diversion. Typhon leaped forward to again aim with his sickle.

"My sickle will be the weapon that kills you, Ouranos!" the prodigal son roared with demonic laughter.

And yet the sickle shattered on contact with Ouranos! His bright and fluffy clouds were, in fact, impenetrable. A frustrated Typhon hurled all the weapons he had plundered from Ouranos' fallen children at him. Each bounced off or shattered on contact as well. No attack under heaven could hope to ever reach him. And it was Ouranos' turn to counterattack. Throwing his ring into the sky, it began to expand until it became the very sky above them. Once again, Father Heaven trapped his rebellious son in another powerful Microcosm: The Floodgates of Heaven.

Typhon found himself in a place that looked just like the planet Graia during a rainstorm. But that ring of Heaven was still ominously floating above in the sky. The floodgates of the heavens were opened as the rains came down, and the floods came up, but Typhon was undeterred.

Ouranos' son stood, looking to the heavens as the raindrops fell on his head. Shockingly, the drops of "water" were each as heavy as a continent and punched holes in the ground as they fell. When the raindrops fell on them, stones and mountains would crumble under their weight, but the mighty Typhon was not harmed.

"My son, whom I loved… these drops are my tears. Know that even after all you've done, I will mourn you when this is all done." Ouranos' voice echoed through his realm.

Typhon expected an attack stronger than mere raindrops; but then, the clouds began to clear. As the sky opened up, it was revealed to be a starry nighttime. The roof of bronze was held in place as the many stars glinted and glowed. Then the stars began to fall from heaven: piercing arrows aimed directly at Typhon. He had survived a rain of water, but how would he fare when the stars themselves came falling down?

"Fool. As an ultimate warrior, you should know Microcosms are no concern of mine." Typhon declared before waving his hand to destroy the Microcosm again. It did not work. Looking to the sky, Typhon saw Ouranos' ring of heaven and quickly concluded that it was somehow anchoring and protecting the Microcosm from Typhon's usual means of dispelling. Fine, he'd just destroy it and then tear the Microcosm down. But first, there was the matter of the raining armada of flaming projectiles he'd carelessly let get so close.

With his sickle and fleet of other weapons, Typhon deflected and shot down Ouranos' many projectiles before they could hit him. But each shot from Ouranos was so powerful that it would blast apart each divine weapon it crashed into! The stars were so numerous that Typhon exhausted his supply and needed to withdraw more from his portal armory. Even then, he was not worried. The rain of Ouranos kept coming down, and Typhon exhausted every last weapon he had plundered!

Things were looking bad for Typhon. A barrage of hundreds of projectiles was closing in on him. But Typhon didn't even flinch. To reload, the king of the Titans simply compelled each of his toys to reform and return to his side to be fired again. With this endless recycling of arms, Typhon shot down each of Father Heaven's attacks. The night sky lit up with the explosion of a million and one spectacular collisions.

Then, coming into view came an entire galaxy! As the starry heavens zoomed down, it compressed into a ball of pure Power that was so dense and so fast it could not be stopped by any attack Typhon hurled at it. Unable to stop the attack, the Titan was helpless as it crushed him to the ground. After a few seconds, there was an unsettling silence.

Then, Typhon destroyed it with flaming eyes! He stood up, enraged. While Typhon was off guard, the wheel of heaven shrank back down around his body and held him in place! Typhon was back in the real world, but the full force of that artificial one now wrapped around the god of time. Typhon was completely trapped as Ouranos strode forward.

"My son… I will give you one last chance to repent and end this war without further bloodshed," Father Heaven offered his son.

Typhon's only reply was, "Burn," as his flaming eyes blasted Ouranos away. While Father Heaven was recovering, Typhon built up his Power and shattered the ring of heaven! Whenever he seemed to struggle or be on the verge of losing, he would simply bring forth more and more Power.

Ouranos' celestial ring reassembled, but this time as a weapon under Typhon's control. Now, the heavens themselves were his to command. Typhon mercilessly battered Ouranos with his own weapon. The ring was so mighty that even Ouranos' heavenly robes could not protect him. Ouranos children cried out in concern for the father. Revitalized by his resolve to protect them, Ouranos stopped Typhon's attack with his bare hands and reclaimed his weapon.

Typhon swung his sickle, and Ouranos swung his ring! The Divine ring shattered Typhon's sickle, but Ouranos felt uneasy since the weapon was no longer fully under his command. Again and again, Typhon reformed his sickle only to break it in a clash with Ouranos. Then, Typhon smiled. Once he lured Ouranos into a rhythm, Typhon changed things up and caught him off guard.

With the swing of his sickle, Typhon tore his father's holy robes to shreds all at once and drew blood! It was only then that Ouranos noticed that his son was now wielding a different sickle. He'd lured Father Heaven into a false sense of security with a mundane everyday sickle before revealing his ultimate weapon.

Forged by the Cyclopes whom Typhon had captured and enslaved, Typhon's Adamant sickle was on par with the divine wheel. With one slash, the mightiest divine tool in Graia had been bisected. One slash from Typhon had cut through Ouranos' sword and shield both. This was Typhon's true weapon that he only brought out when he was serious. Nonetheless, Father Heaven refused to give in and reassembled his weapon before preparing to attack again. Typhon only laughed.

As the fight progressed, he was getting stronger. Now, it was Typhon who was shattering his opponent's weapon in each clash. Worse yet, glancing blows were slicing through Ouranos' armor and wounding him.

"Weapons of lesser caliber cannot puncture that armor of yours, but when I get serious, it becomes child's play," Typhon reminded the horrified Ouranos.

Ouranos leaped into the sky, and Typhon followed after him. The two battled in the skies above, swooping and diving about with world-ending blows exchanged between them. Ouranos refused to let any harm come to his children and fought with all that he had. However, now that Ouranos was weary and stripped of much of his powers, Typhon had the upper hand.

Even his weapon was not fully under his control. As his stamina was expiring, Typhon's seemingly endless supply was only matched by his endless growth in strength. Seeing his victory as imminent, Typhon began to laugh maniacally. Toying with the Sky Father, Typhon mocked him.

"Is this the height of your skill? You call yourself a god as if you are in any way comparable to me!? I am ashamed that I ever followed a weakling like you!" Typhon monologued as he had Ouranos on his heels. With each shockwave and cry of fear from the watching people, Typhon saw Ouranos looking to them with worry.

"Those, worthless mongrels down there mean so much to you? They are nothing but chaff next to mighty gods like you and I!" Typhon again mocked him.

"They are living beings. A father does not let strength determine his love for his children. If you can't even understand this, then I must redouble my efforts to keep you from power!" Ouranos replied.

"Only the mighty can decide. Being a king of heaven means nothing if you are not a warrior. A god must be king and warrior both… a thing that YOU clearly do not understand." Typhon laughed.

Ouranos defied him mightily and battled with all that he could. Their clash shook the heavens, but with each passing clash, Father Heaven grew weaker as the usurping demiurge grew stronger.

Ouranos' children pleaded and cried for him. All were united in their belief and support for him. Typhon saw this and grew crueler. As Ouranos was wounded from their battle, Typhon didn't even bother attacking him. Instead, he fired his flaming eyes down at the spectators! Without hesitation, Ouranos swooped in to save them and was shot out of the sky.

Father Heaven fell to the ground and lay defeated and on the verge of death before all his weeping children. Typhon descended with a haughty laugh, presenting their pathetic god to them. After defeating Father Heaven, Typhon assembled all those who followed Ouranos and publicly humiliated and emasculated their father before them.

With his sickle, he castrated Father Heaven before all to see and then threw his severed genitals over his left shoulder. Typhon was sure to humiliate Ouranos before his flock and move them to despair. After making them swear fealty to their new king, Typhon severed Ouranos' head and so killed him. With Father Heaven's power added to his own, he became even mightier! From now on, the leader of Graia would not be a shepherd; he would be a dictator.

TALE 3

Typhon and Terra

It was only far too late that Terra came to learn of a villain spreading his evils across the Kosmos. She and her siblings had long since left Graia to explore distant lands. While Terra was among the distant peoples of lands untold, she heard tell of a massive and evil Empire approaching.

Terra took it upon herself to take down this villain. She returned to Graia and singlehandedly fought her way up the Tower. Blasting the doors off the hinges, Terra declared that she had come to defeat him. But then, Terra's face quickly twisted with shock and horror.

Sitting on the throne was an equally shocked Typhon! The evil King of the Titans was eagerly expecting another foolhardy hero who had come to try and defeat him: he'd never expected an actual god to be the one storming his tower. Though he was as shocked as her, he was not horrified. He was overjoyed!

"My goddess… words cannot describe how much I've missed you." Typhon smiled genuinely at Terra. Terra tried to reply, but words failed her. She couldn't speak because her mind was still racing to try and process all this. It was like losing contact with an old delinquent friend and reconnecting, only to find out they'd become a fascist dictator.

"I must apologize for the sorry state of things. My grand Empire is still a work in progress. I was hoping to have conquered the whole Universe before showing it off to you," Typhon awkwardly admitted. "But since you're here, let me give you a tour of what I have so far -of my tower, at least."

The shattered Terra convinced herself to hear him out. Surely, this was all a misunderstanding that he could clear up if he explained it. She could not speak, and so simply nodded to comply. So, Typhon led Terra around his divine abode.

He showed her the horde of wealth and treasures stolen from other lands: priceless artifacts that were sacred to other peoples were mere trinkets for him. He showed her the room where all his slave women were kept. Upon seeing Terra's horrified reaction, he, of course, reassured her. "No need to worry! Now that you're back, I will dispose of all of them. They were mere substitutes in your absence." He said as if that were the problem.

Then he showed her his trophy room. Unlike the treasures and gold of foreign lands, this was more akin to an armory. On his wall were mounted the weapons and armor of all the gods Typhon had killed. Then she saw it. Walking over to the wall, Terra felt the displayed Kosmic Ring of Ouranos.

"Ah, Ouranos. I actually broke a sweat putting him down. But he was one of the first to fall. After how much stronger I've become since then, he would be child's play to kill now. And I'd happily do it again. He was… one of the most delectable kills I got to savor." Typhon licked his lips.

He thought back to the power and domination he achieved by cutting down the man who raised him. At the sight of this, Terra broke down and wept, much to Typhon's confusion.

"How could you do this? What made you like this!?" Terra screamed at the very confused Titan.

"My Terra… all this, I did for you," Typhon responded plainly and, in so doing, speared Terra's heart.

"You never saw me as an equal before. It was because I was too weak. That was what you were trying to tell me! You left me behind because I wasn't worthy of you! That's why I knew that I had to first prove I was the strongest before I would be worthy of you. So, it was obvious: I would conquer the Kosmos to prove to you that I am the strongest being in creation. With the Power that you have given me, I have no doubt that I can dominate all things! I can do all things through my Goddess who strengthens me." Typhon explained his twisted ideology.

Terra felt a chill the moment he had reminded her that she was the one who gave him this superhuman strength. She was the one who had brought him back to life when the Kosmos had sought to rid itself of this great evil proleptically. This was all her fault.

"Each battle, I've grown stronger and stronger. Each weakling I cut down nourishes me even more! Soon, very soon, I promise that I will stand atop the Kosmos with you as equals: the king and queen of the Universe!" Typhon declared.

"My goddess! I love you!" Typhon confessed to Terra while clasping her hands. As evil as he was, Typhon was genuine. In his twisted mind, he did all this to impress Terra. It was that obvious fact that hurt her the most.

"Why in the Kosmos would you ever think this was what I wanted?" Terra wept as she pulled away from him.

Typhon was confused. He loved her, but he could not perceive her as a being with thoughts and feelings distinct from his twisted ideal. Terra was Power, and Power was a gift from Terra; therefore, strength must have been what she valued more than any of those weaklings. No matter how many times she told him otherwise, Typhon could only ever see Terra as a natural force that justified him. She was his goddess: he was doing her will. Of course, his Goddess believed whatever he believed: he was right.

Terra had enough and pushed him away. She cried and cried and screamed as the full of horror of this scenario hit her at once. Typhon froze when he saw the disgust and confused wrath on Terra's face. He took that about as hard as Terra had taken the revelation of his evildoing. In parallel, Typhon had a mental breakdown right next to her. The one he loved more than anything else had rejected him. If she was capable of saying that she hated him, she would have. Her oldest childhood friend Typhon, the one she'd grown up with and shared so much with, was gone. She had to forget him and face this new creature.

Then, Terra snapped back to attention as Typhon began screaming insanely! The whole tower shook as his madness and wrath externalized themselves.

"Why, Terra! Why would you do this to me!? How could you do this to me!? Everything I've ever done was for you!" Typhon ranted. Terra instinctively tried to calm him down, but this only enraged Typhon further.

"Pity! You still look down on me with pity in your eyes! I'm a god, Terra! A god! Stop looking at me like that, like one of those lowly human creatures!!!" Typhon screamed.

"But Typhon… you are a human." Terra pointed out. Whatever was left of Typhon's sanity snapped. He began to laugh and laugh in a snap manic break.

"Humans! Yes, this disgusting world of lowly humans! They're a distraction! How dare you choose the world over me! Fine then, I'll just have to remove the competition! Yes, this is just a test! I have yet to throw off these human shackles fully! Once I've done that! Once I have even greater power, you will revere me! I will look down on you with those piteous eyes." Typhon screamed at her.

Sensing that the others were in danger, Terra snapped her fingers and so teleported everyone else in the tower away to safety. Now, it was just the two of them, alone in chilling silence. After Typhon's loud outburst, Terra took a moment to collect herself and just let out a dejected sigh.

"Power this and Power that… you're obsessed. I gave you this obsession, Typhon. But as I give, I can also take away," Terra warned. With a wave of her hand, she cut Typhon off. His fellowship with her was severed, and his divine status was obliterated. Typhon at once lost all of his Powers and was once again a man of flesh and blood.

His body was weakening, but in that higher state, in the part of him that existed beyond, Typhon desperately tried to resist falling back down to mere humanity. He saw himself falling, cut loose from the Celestial Sphere that tethered him to the sky. He was going to lose his connection to his goddess forever.

Typhon screamed as he plummeted from that sacred place, away from the limitless power he adored more than life itself. But then he saw it, a second dot not unlike Terra's majestic blue. This ringed glowing divine orb was suspended upon nothing, just sitting there. The other Celestial Spheres were occupied: Power with a soul to govern it, but that one was new. What was more, it was unoccupied.

Typhon cried out to it, praying that he would not be forsaken. Through that, Typhon established a connection with the Ringed World. In the real world, just as soon as Terra had removed Typhon's powers, they were restored! By giving him access to that higher plane at all, Typhon was able to grow to new heights! Then, since he already had a foot in the door and his other upon a celestial foothold, Typhon reopened his connection to Terra by force.

He didn't fully understand how, but Typhon now had two divine patrons and was even more powerful than ever before! Terra was horrified! This had completely backfired. Typhon bellowed; he had two Solaris beings at his back: he was not just the strongest man but the strongest thing in the Universe.

Beyond a boost to his raw Power, his understanding of all things now rivaled Terra's, thus making him all the more dangerous. His eyes had been opened, and he had become as a true god. In exchange for all the data in Typhon's puny human mind, this new Celestial Sphere granted him a glimpse of something very interesting.

The shockwave of Typhon's ascension blasted the roof off his tower, revealing a hole torn in the sky that allowed that ringed world to look down upon him in real life. At once, Typhon summoned his weapons to his side as they orbited around him, just like the ringed world he'd seen in his vision. Terra flinched, looking up nervously at the Ringed World.

"Saturn!!! Stop this! It is not safe to trust this man with your Power! You won't receive any data at all if he destroys this world!!!" Terra pleaded with the prenatal planet in the distance. Yet unsurprisingly, the Planet did not reply.

Then again, Terra couldn't even stop herself from emotionlessly heeding his calls. Her sibling didn't know any better… but what was her excuse? That lifeless rock in the sky just received requests and outputted Power accordingly. That disgusting thing… she was just as guilty in helping Typhon.

"It's too late to stop my ascension. Saturn was much more straightforward with me than you were. Now, I've been enlightened to what you really are." Typhon chuckled. Terra stepped back uneasily.

Typhon opened a ring of portals around Terra and fired weapons at her from all sides. Terra dodged them all effortlessly, but this time, Typhon could actually see how she did it. He could finally appreciate what exactly he was up against. Excited by the prospect, Typhon's demonic Power flared out!

"Listen here, Terra. I am a god. I will make you mine, no matter what. Now I just want you all the more!" Typhon pointed at her as his new enhanced powers burst out. Leaping to attack her, Typhon did battle with Terra. Unsurprisingly, Typhon was the one who found himself thrown from the tower. Crashing down on the ground outside his fortress, Typhon cackled to himself. Terra teleported to be right in front of him, ready to continue.

"Of course… even now, as my raw strength dwarfs yours, you're still invincible. That is why I love you, Terra!" Typhon screamed as his sacred flame burned hotter.

Pushing his newfound Power to its limits, Typhon tore open a portal in the sky above and revealed the ringed world he had seen in his vision. Terra was horrified. He didn't know how to use the Smite, did he!?

Terra raised her fists, ready to continue fighting in that insultingly human way. Typhon didn't bother blocking or dodging those attacks. As a transcendent being, he no longer cared what happened to his crude three-dimensional form. The mangled, crumbling body that danced on Saturn's puppet strings continued his tireless assault. Terra flinched, disturbed by the sight of Typhon caring so little about the damage she dealt.

"Stop fighting me like a human, Terra! It's beneath you!" Typhon roared while firing off his barrage of weapons and flaming eyes. Terra slapped and diverted the weapons with her bare hands before deflecting Typhon's beam back at him.

When the smoke cleared, only a burned skeleton remained of her foe, but he began reassembling. He wasn't even regrowing a body of flesh and blood anymore. On the outside, it looked human, but internally, she saw he was starting to look more like…

Whatever humanity was left of him was long gone, and Terra was visibly disturbed by this. Typhon just scoffed at her concerns. She must've just been surprised to see a mere former human approaching her level.

"I've seen through you, Terra. So, stop pretending to be down to Earth…" the enlightened Typhon began, much to Terra's shock. "A being like you will forever be out of this World!"

The dragon pointed past Terra, the woman, and instead fixed his gaze on the distant blue Planet. Terra turned pale; how much did he know?

"Yes… I see through that trick. For some reason, you are afraid of your Power. That is why you chose me to rescue you. Only an equal that can see you for what you are can save you. By giving your Power to me, you have enabled me to free you from your foolishness!" Typhon declared.

"No, that isn't what I want!" Terra shouted before looking back at herself in a moment of doubt.

"I will destroy the mundane chains that shackle you and release my Goddess so that she can be all that I know she can be! Human beings, human morals… such things are beneath the domain of gods. Stripped of those, you can finally be yourself. You can return to the way you once were. I shall return you to your shattered glory. As your chosen one, that is my goal." Typhon insisted.

"I never said any of that! Why won't you just listen to me!?" Terra cried. Typhon was silent for a moment as looked down on the woman.

"I understand now… that persona that you test me with is not the result of your own flaws. As a perfect being, you can only reflect humanity's flaws back at itself. That mask you wear is your indictment of humankind. Weak, unsure, cowardly… that is your assessment, and that is why humanity is putrid. How genius: how did I never see it before? Truly, you work in mysterious ways." Typhon chuckled to himself. Terra was right there, yet he spoke for her in complete confidence.

Up above, Saturn and Terra began to glow brightly, answering Typhon's request for more of its divine light. The Goddess was Powerless to stop him from using her own Power against her! With this explosive growth in might, Typhon's body proportionately grew to match. This was Typhon at his peak: his Titan form.

He became a writhing, ungodly mass of darkness that cast a shadow on darkness itself. He was a monster among monsters. Any who laid eyes upon it felt an emptiness within their very soul, matched only by the absolute void of the creature.

Beyond its lack of texture or visibility, the writhing mass still managed to be grotesque. The shifting and ever-evolving creature was often described as resembling a mass of snakes wriggling and worming about.

To perceive it via any sense: sight, hearing, smell, or touch, was sensory overload. Every part of the creature emitted fire and made every kind of noise known to the immortal gods. Later descriptions would later say Typhon had 100 demonic snakes writhing about his body, but that was for artistic purposes. In truth, no human that had the misfortune of perceiving him could count them all.

If one looked at the unknowable dragon for too long, they would be driven insane by the primal fear of the being from beyond. Terra and her siblings could better glimpse the beast that could only exist within the third dimension in small parts at a time.

They would simplify its description for others like so: each "snake" tendril on the beast had eyes containing the demonic flames of Typhon. At the center of these ominous tendrils was a figure resembling a human- at least a human torso with wings on its back. He had humanoid arms, but his hands and fingers were many dragon heads. Below his thighs was an army of yet more snakes, and above his neck, likewise. Yet in the middle of the writhing, mass burned two larger eyes of demonic fire, and the smoke of those flames produced flowing "hair" that was toxic to life.

In size and strength, he surpassed all the offspring of Earth. Nothing more terrifying could be perceived in all the Kosmos. In fact, it made no sounds no matter how it moved or interacted with reality, despite what witnesses would swear. What they heard was actually a symptom of their growing insanity as their brains tried and failed to attach properties of anything under the sun to this wholly unfamiliar menace. In exchange for the power this state granted, Typhon was finally as ugly on the outside as he was on the inside.

"Come, my goddess!!! Now I have become a being worthy of you! Show me that you are still worthy of being my equal!!!" the dragon bellowed at the tiny goddess in an eldritch voice that rippled reality and drove any human that heard it mad.

In the face of such a threat, Terra had to get serious. To match the looming Saturn in the sky, Mother Earth manifested herself as well. The Planet hovered above the battlefield and began to glow as it heightened Terra's Powers just as much as Typhon's had been!

To turn the tide, Terra created a weapon of unmatched power: the Sword of Dehmos. None had ever seen its equal. She did not require a forger or smith to create this blade. For her, with her divine will, Terra simply brought it forth into existence. That sword was just as much Terra as the humanoid body that wielded it. The heavenly body Terra up above, the holy sword Terra that was a simulacrum of her Power, and the person Terra in the flesh… all three aspects were gathered as one.

"Yes… the warrior aspect has revealed itself. See? Already, I have begun returning you to your former glory." Typhon hissed.

"I now have your undivided attention in Mind…" Typhon motioned to the Orb in the sky, "Body…" Typhon looked to Terra, the woman, "And Spirit." Typhon looked not at the Sword but rather at what dwelt inside.

Terra flinched, looking at the Divine Construct in her arm. Calling upon that rejected aspect of herself made the goddess tremble. Yet Typhon trembled as well. Even in that monstrous form, he felt a primal fear as pins and needles stuck all over his body.

Even glimpsing merely bits of sacred light that slipped through the cracks of that three-dimensional container, he could tell that Terra's Weapon was worth more than every other weapon in his armory combined. She truly was the ultimate prize.

"Such a spectacular sight. To think you could become even more beautiful, my goddess." Typhon snickered while leering at the weapon without a peer.

As a man, Typhon wanted Terra's body. As something more than a man, he could understand that the most important thing was that Sacred Realm that loomed above. Yet Typhon was first and foremost a warrior. More than his desire for the flesh or Power in the abstract was the warrior's covetous, almost lecherous fixation on that Sword.

"I won't manifest it for a second longer than is necessary. If it weren't absolutely necessary, I would not have summoned it at all." Terra sighed, not even wanting to look at it anymore.

"If it is too heavy for you, give it to me. That's what you want, isn't it? If you fear using your Power, entrust everything to me and find peace," Typhon asked in a deceptively sweet voice.

"You really should have tried that trick… before saying everything else," Terra growled with fierceness in her eyes, unlike anything Typhon had seen before.

Typhon was overjoyed to be the first foe that had demanded Terra's full Power of her. As he let out an ear-piercing roar of joy, countless plundered weapons shot forth from his writhing mass. Teleporting them to himself from all across the Kosmos, Typhon's supply of divine armaments seemed to never end!

Among them, Terra saw so many familiar sacred tools; leading the pack was Ouranos' divine wheel. Her friends' prized possessions torn from their cold dead hands were now careening towards her by yet another she'd loved yet lost. Terra steeled herself and stood, undeterred. Without moving an inch, she dodged each and every projectile. With her blade drawn, she could compel reality itself to make them miss.

Terra was unharmed, but the projectiles that missed all doubled back to try and impale her from behind. Without a hint of fear, Terra turned around and swung the Sword of Dehmos once. Instantaneously, the force of the single strike recurred countless times and diced all the weapons into atoms. Typhon froze in utter adoration for that Power.

That thing she held in her hands wasn't just a sword. Even he couldn't fully tell what that shining weapon before him existed as. All he could tell was that it was beautiful; it was beautiful because it was Powerful. How he longed to wield it; how he longed to wield her for himself.

"Yes! You are truly a worthy opponent, Terra! You exceeded even my wildest expectations! My goddess is the only benchmark by which I can measure myself!" Typhon screamed as he laughed. Then he calmed down alarmingly quickly and menacingly grinned at the unnerved Terra. With a thought, Typhon teleported all of his Titans to his side and surrounded Terra.

"In exchange for finally showing me all that you are, allow me to finally show you all that I am!!!" Typhon declared as all at once, the other Titans transformed into their terrible Titan forms as well. All of them manifested Typhon's powers from within themselves, strengthened even further thanks to his new connection to Saturn.

Terra felt their daunting presence; already powerful warriors overflowing with boosted Power from Typhon. No… all that Typhon had to give was drawn from her and Saturn. Each of those monsters was also of Terra's making.

The Titans were all upon her and attacked ferociously from all sides! Yet, the bigger they were, the harder they fell. Terra battled all the Titans at once, tearing them down one by one with her great strength.

As Terra was the goddess of nature, she had control of both the land and the waves. Yet, Terra's control of waves was not merely about water… it was control of the entire grand wave-equation that was the Universe. With one swing, Terra could hit all her foes. If her attack from the left was blocked, her foe would simultaneously be hit from the right! In the same way that she could dodge anything, with her blade drawn, she could hit nearly anything. If there was a possibility of it happening, she could make it so.

With a single strike, Terra could blast apart the entire giant body of the Titan, leaving only their mangled true human body. However, just as quickly as she defeated them, they rose back up to continue the fight. As Terra found that their numbers were completely replenished, all the Titans united in letting fly the flaming eyes they'd received from their leader.

Terra responded by deflecting their demonic flames right back at them! All the Titans fell around her but again began to regenerate. Terra knew that it would go on forever like this. Nobody was powerful enough to defeat all the Titans at once while Typhon was among them. If she could get them alone, then maybe she would have won, but the king of the Titans was not so easily dispatched.

Unlike his compatriots, he was the one enemy she failed to fell even once. Terra was still unhittable, but even the Sword of Dehmos was only enough to wound the beast, not kill it. After all, Terra was fighting Typhon, herself, and her sibling at the same time. It was her fault he was so strong.

"Aren't you proud, my Goddess!? I trained, and I followed your instructions! You taught me to fight, you gave me the Power to fight, and this is the result! I am the archetypical ultimate warrior, as you described it! Just as you are- just as I always dreamed!" Typhon attacked her with everything they had.

Terra was on her heels as she tried to fend him off at the same time as his evil army. She remembered as children; she allowed the young Titans and their leader to all spar with her. Back then, they were playfighting and training… but this was to the death. All her dearest friends who weren't dead were currently trying to murder her.

But moreso than any of the others, Terra specifically couldn't stand fighting Typhon like this. She kept seeing flashes of his innocent face and hurting her own heart whenever she hurt his body. She couldn't bring herself to kill him. She couldn't do anything right!

Now, he had not only the boost she gave him but also access to Saturn's infinite Power supply. Unlike most fighters who had to regulate their stamina, Typhon could be on full blast at all times. Terra couldn't fall back on just waiting him out until he tired out.

Fighting with all these restraints on her was a losing battle. After successfully evading a flurry of attacks, Terra landed on the ground and closed her portal in the sky. She sheathed her blade and let out a defeated sigh. Typhon's invincible goddess was conceding!? The Dragon began to roar with laughter as his disgusting form shape shifted to return a head and arms to him. With these more humanoid features, he spoke to the tiny goddess.

"Surrender to me, my goddess! I have grown to become a being on your level. Come now and be my queen, that we may rule over all our lessers!" Typhon bellowed.

"Congratulations Typhon. I cannot defeat you. That is true," Terra admitted. Typhon felt an uproarious elation that he could hardly contain!

"But…" the goddess continued, "I do not submit, and I will never join you."

"My love, stop playing hard to get—" Typhon began to hand wave her rejection.

"I don't love you, Typhon, and I'm not your goddess. No means no. You are now my enemy." Terra cut him off.

Typhon froze with the same terrified, mind-breaking reaction Terra had earlier. Then he snapped.

"NO! You don't mean that! That isn't how this works!!! You're being crazy!" Typhon screamed. The elation crashing into the rejection drove him mad: a spiking god complex crossed with an angry stalker who couldn't take "no" for an answer.

"Damned woman! You led me on!" Typhon snarled as he reverted to its true monstrous state. Then, all at once, his countless snake heads let fly a truly terrifying number of flaming eye beams.

"You filled my head with dreams!" the serpent spat venom that was toxic to life and melted all that it touched.

"You watched me pour my heart out and rejected me! Will I never be good enough for you!?" Typhon ranted and roared while thrashing his countless tentacles and serpentine appendages about.

As even that failed to hit Terra, the demon's frenzy only grew wilder. Firing a cacophony of flaming beams from all over his body, the chaotic onslaught carved up and burned the landscape. Even his own allies had to flee and hide as his wrath lashed out and destroyed all. Terra effortlessly dodged each beam by teleporting away, yet she did not fight back any longer.

Instead, Terra looked around at all the death and destruction of nature around her and wept. His newfound strength had made the man ignore just how much natural beauty he'd trampled underfoot. That arrogant, whiny human's tantrum wasn't hurting Terra; he was just carelessly destroying the home she gave him.

"We now stand as equals! I cannot defeat you, and you cannot defeat me! We are peers at the pinnacle of existence!

Now, stop testing my love and submit to my Power!" Typhon roared as the explosive tantrum continued.

"It doesn't matter how strong you become, Typhon. You cannot use Power to force someone to love you!" Terra cried.

"But that is where you are wrong! I will grow further in Power. Then, even you cannot reject me. You may answer incorrectly as often as you want, my dear. Eventually, you will be mine." He hissed as his broken mind began manifesting his madness into reality.

"I'm sorry. I guess I never truly understood you. For that, I'm so… so… sorry. Back then, I thought I was just assuming the best of you… but really, I was only projecting onto you as you do onto me." Terra reflected. The beast was not listening. His mind was made up, and his only capacity for growth was forever limited to his strength. Seeing this, Terra accepted that words would get her no further.

"Goodbye, Typhon. I must retreat now, but I leave you a declaration of war. When I return, I shall have a champion and an army of all creation to oppose you. This world does not belong to you!" Terra declared.

Typhon, enraged past the point of being able to speak, fired every attack he had at Terra all at once. Yet, in the last moment, Terra disappeared, escaping the blast to go and do as she had warned. His days of ruling were numbered.

TALE 4

Warrior King

After usurping the first generation, the Titans made their home inside a great Tower known as Tartarus. It was a black tower made of Adamant that, although destroyed in his battle with Terra, was quickly rebuilt by his very slaves she was trying to liberate.

From this seat, Typhon had made war with the many civilizations of humanity. But the warrior king Typhon was a conqueror and not an administrator. In many ways, the title was oxymoronic. He brought many territories under his control with might alone and ruled only through fear. Naturally, this led to many rebellions. But rather than accept this as a shortcoming of the warrior mindset, Typhon convinced everyone that this was a good thing.

Typhon was bored with statecraft and instead saw his ideal civilization as a kratocracy: a world where power alone mattered. The fact that a militaristic ruler only brought further violence instead of order was a good thing, actually.

In that sense, many argued that Typhon did not rule at all. Not that he minded. Many complained that as a warrior first, Typhon could never be a true ruler. By contrast, Typhon felt he satisfied his role as ruler rather well. Typhon intentionally ruled through fear alone to foster resentment. Rather than trying to prevent coups, he welcomed it. Those with enough power to defy him would serve as good entertainment. He waited on his throne for some foolish hero with more courage than strength to attack. This way, he had eternal wars to keep himself entertained and in shape. He ruled to war and warred to rule.

Thus, the Star Empire always barely held together under the pull of its internal contradictions: Typhon's desire for endless wars both at home and abroad versus Typhon's desire to rule over a vast number of subjects. Then, one day, this contradiction of goals became too much to bear.

The hero who had emerged and united the people against him was none other than Typhon's goddess, Terra. She had singlehandedly stormed Tartarus tower and given Typhon a declaration of war. She was raising an army, a champion to dethrone him. Typhon relished the challenge!

These so-called gods of this Olympian alliance were the cowards who had fled or hid when his reign began. There were a few gods who had their own resistance movements beforehand, but even they were never strong enough to interest him. Divided, they would fall, but united, they made war with the Titans and pushed them back.

But the most offensive detail of the revolution was this: it mostly comprised of mortal men. Typhon's army was made up of the best of the best: the elites of every land under his domain. The rag-tag Olympian forces allowed anyone to join. The weakest fool with a hero complex could enlist and throw themselves at the Titans as the gods' cannon fodder. Truly, they prioritized quantity over quality.

But that alone did not upset Typhon. It made them a bore to slaughter, but the part that truly disgusted him was that when he fought them, they were not Powerless. The gods themselves were so desperate that they were sharing their Power and strengthening the mortals so that they could fight on their level.

The average infantryman of Olympus was a hundred times more numerous than Typhon's forces but a thousand times weaker—such foolishness.

While ideologically repulsive, even that was not enough to explain Typhon's wrath. It was the specific fact that his goddess was taking part in such foolishness herself. Typhon's goddess sharing her sacred essence among the wretched masses made the king sick. For that alone, they all deserved to die. Whatever weak thing violated Typhon's goddess deserved to die. Her Power was for him and him alone!

Even with all of Olympus' powers combined, Typhon only considered Terra herself to be a threat to him. Nevertheless, others among the Titans were more concerned with this developing revolution right under their nose. They saw the fact that the number of rebelling subjects was constantly increasing to be a cause for concern in and of itself.

If everyone was fighting against them, then who was remaining to slave away and produce everything that the army needed to function? Typhon would scoff at a smith who picked up a sword to fight. The Titans were more concerned that he was no longer making their swords.

When the gods liberated the divine weaponsmith Cyclopes, Typhon only scoffed that they were weaklings anyways. The Titans had weapon shortages by week's end, and the weak soldiers of Olympus became armed with stronger Adamant armaments that could even the odds.

The Cyclopes, whom the Olympians had emancipated from the Titans, forged powerful weapons for their liberators just as they had been forced to for their captors. The god of the forge, Hephaestus, led them, and they created tools of unmatched Power, surpassing even their older relics. Jupiter's Thunderbolt Sword Keuranos and Neptune's Trident among them filled many-a-Titan with great fright. The age of the Titans had entered its twilight!

"The she-viper still cannot be found?" Typhon demanded of his generals after the latest onslaught of bad news.

The strategy meeting of the Titans went silent. Nobody wanted to disappoint their wicked master further. Finally, Krius, the most devoted of Typhon's troops stood up to break the bad news.

"I am afraid not, my lord. Jupiter's rebellion is severely restricting our communication and information networks." Krius explained. Typhon was given pause.

"After his latest victory, Jupiter has gained incredible popularity among the rebels, and many more planets are aligning under him as their leader." Krius moved to the next point.

"Jupiter is their leader?" Typhon asked in utter shock.

"Yes, that is what we have been able to determine, sir," Krius repeated.

"Jupiter is their leader… and not my goddess?" Typhon asked in utter disbelief. Why wouldn't the strongest warrior be in charge?

"Yes sir. However, fortunately that means that if we focus our efforts on removing this rebel leader, we can break the morale of-" Krius began.

"Jupiter does not interest me. I leave the small fries to you all. I am only interested in conquering my Goddess, Terra." Typhon hand-waived his general's plan.

The Titans (except the ever-loyal Krius) weren't exactly thrilled by that answer. Typhon wasn't the Machiavellian genius they originally followed.

"Jupiter doesn't interest you anymore? Then what does interest you, Typhon?" a protest arose from among the Titans. All eyes turned to Atlas; Typhon's treacherous second in command.

"The Titans formed around Typhon the warrior king, not Typhon the hopeless romantic! This tunnel vision for the woman has been a disaster for the war effort! Typhon has wasted valuable resources on culling and purging his own subjects rather than properly responding to the crisis our empire faces! And for what? Just to hurt Terra's feelings?" Atlas slammed the table.

Fire flickered in Typhon's eyes at the mutinous tone in his second's voice.

"It is time for a change! For the sake of the Empire, I nominate myself the new leader of the Titans! If I were in charge, nobody would dare rebel against us. I will do in two days what Typhon has failed to do in two years!" Atlas stood up.

Atlas had been making such treacherous boasts behind Typhon's back for years, even before his decline. If the cowardly traitor was so bold as to make these claims before the king, things must've been really bad. An example needed to be made.

The fires in Typhon's eyes burned as hot as stars before blazing out and engulfing Atlas!

At once, the flaming eyes of Typhon blasted Atlas across the room! The inferno left the treacherous second in command on the verge of death as he slammed against the wall!

"Atlas, I keep you around for your brawn and not your brains. However, even I can only tolerate so much foolishness. Remember your place or the slaves will be scraping what's left of you off my walls," Typhon coldly said.

"Of course, my master..." Atlas wheezed as his bones and skin slowly regenerated.

"Would anyone else like to question how I run my empire?" Typhon asked of the other Titans with fires still blazing in his eyes. The room was silent.

"Good." Typhon scoffed as the half-dead Atlas hobbled back to his seat at the table. That was that.

Any questioning of Typhon's authority was suppressed by fear and terror. The Titans had no choice but to listen to his orders because he was the strongest. Power was all that was needed to rule, right?

The rest of the meeting involved him further plotting and organizing his extermination of as many powerless mortals as were not absolutely necessary for the empire. If she loved them so much, he'd take them all away! Those that distracted Terra from who she should be loving deserved to die! If he could not break her body, he would break her heart!

Nonetheless, as soon as such words were given, onto the scene burst the very people's protector that Typhon spoke of. Diving down from the heavens into the villains' throne room atop the tower, the goddess caught all the Titans by surprise! Typhon smiled at the sight of his queen Terra's return to him. But she came wielding the weapon of the people: the Sword of Dehmos.

Terra went right for Typhon with her Holy Sword and clashed with him amid all the others. Those weaklings whom Typhon wanted to rule over had a protector. She was not their leader or ruler as Typhon had expected her to be. Instead, she was their sword.

This was the duty of warriors that Typhon and his Titans had long abandoned. It was the key they'd lost. Now, it was their natural enemy. The gods and titans wielded all matter of weapons and powers, but through the ages, none rivaled this. Even the mightiest warrior and holiest god trembled at this truth: when people worked together, nothing they planned to do was impossible for them—many a tale told of the warrior caste enslaving the productive one. Yet behold a moral inversion! For the first time, the maxim was being reversed, and the revolution of the common people had the warlords on the retreat!

After all, Empires that waged war on the whole World didn't tend to last very long.

TALE 5

Mind over Muscle

The Titans noticed that ever since Typhon's rejection by Terra, he had been… unwell. During the entire war, he was erratic and angry. The problem was getting worse and worse. As the war dragged on for ten years and the Titans were beginning to lose the war… Atlas was no longer the only one ready to start pointing fingers.

"Something must be done about Typhon. At this rate, he will cost us the war," Metis announced to her fellow Titans in a secret meeting.

Of course, Typhon, Atlas, Krius, and Dione were not present. Dione was loyal to Krius and Krius to Typhon. And Atlas, for all his backtalk and insubordination, couldn't be trusted to lead ants to a picnic, let alone carry out a successful coup against the most dangerous man in the Kosmos.

"Typhon is no king at all," Metis declared.

The other Titans couldn't help but silently agree. Lovely Metis was known as the wisest of the Titans. Even if she was far from the most powerful, the others had to agree that she was overflowing with an asset that most of their ranks were sorely lacking: intelligence. Thus, if Metis said anything, even Typhon would pay it heed. She alone was the one who could criticize him and have the clout required to call him into question (at least when he asked for it).

"But Metis! We are a kratocracy. He is stronger than we are, so we must obey him!" one of the Titans declared.

"That is quite literally a child's logic. Surely, we are all now old enough to see the foolishness of such thinking, considering where it has gotten us." Metis dismantled him verbally.

"Moreso than Typhon's incompetence, he has chosen a fool like Atlas to be his second in command. Atlas was chosen just because of his physical strength, and time after time, his insubordination and general ineptitude are never truly punished. You must all agree that Typhon's ideals and obsession with power are to our detriment," Metis continued.

Metis was right again. She was always right. Of course, there was the matter of her being a spy for the Olympians, but the Titans were not yet aware of this fact. Metis saw the writing on the wall long before this. As such, she much preferred to spend her days in Jupiter's embrace rather than the tottering Typhon.

Now, after years of preparation, she was going for her ultimate scheme to destroy the Titans from within. Metis had come to learn of a weapon that Typhon intended to use to take Terra out of the war. The Maw of Typhon was a Microcosm that could contain beings of incredible Power. The mightier the prisoner, the stronger the seal.

This device was created by Typhon and his mad scientist Koeus to trap not only Terra but all her Solaris siblings. What was even better was that while they were trapped in it, Typhon could use their powers as his own, becoming unstoppable. He had learned that his strength increased dramatically the more of Terra's kind he added to his collection and so now planned to swallow them all and feast on their divine strength!

But… why trust him with it when they could make his power their own? The Titans were amazed. Whoever took the weapon for themselves would be invincible. Who exactly would get that power was left intentionally vague.

Metis insisted that she had no interest in the power. Thus, the greed of the power-hungry Titans independently ran wild. In the days leading up to the final plan, Metis whispered into each of their ears. She told each Titan how she, in her great wisdom, could only see them as the new leader of the Titans. Only they could finally crush the Olympians and rule the Universe as Typhon had failed to.

All according to plan. She convinced the Titans of her plan… with some details left out. And they, in turn, convinced Atlas of the plan with even more details left out. As far as Atlas knew, he would be the one to inherit Typhon's Power.

Behind his back, the conspirators snickered that he would be sharing Typhon's fate. Only a fool would assume that they would come out on top when all was said and done. Metis couldn't agree more.

So, Atlas lured Typhon out to a location where he insisted that Terra was waiting.

"Perfect. With this ultimate weapon, Terra will be mine. Whether she liked it or not. Then we will finally destroy the Olympians and regain the Kosmos!" Typhon disturbingly grinned. He held in his hands a decoy.

"Right on schedule." Atlas rolled his eyes.

"Be silent or be silenced," Typhon growled at his lackey's backtalk with a threatening flaming glare. Atlas knew to comply. Typhon never killed Atlas for his insubordination… but he did come close on more than one occasion.

The two Titans went to the abandoned temple where Terra was supposedly hiding out. Around the corner, Typhon was overjoyed to see her gorgeous face, but quickly, he realized the deception. It was Metis, not Terra.

"It's over Typhon! Get him!" Atlas cried.

"Traitor! What are you on about!?" Typhon seized his second in command and demanded answers.

At the same time, Metis fired up the sealing weapon and began to suck in Typhon! As soon as Atlas began cheering, he noticed that he was being absorbed as well.

In a flash, the seal was successful, and Typhon was trapped alongside Atlas. Metis and the Titans returned to Tartarus Tower to celebrate. Yet, as Metis held onto the sealed Typhon, suddenly, the tension between the remaining Titans flared up. Koeus insisted that he should rule since it was his invention. Others pointed out that Typhon had done most of the work.

As expected, they began to fight among themselves. Things became even more violent when Krius and Dione returned from the wild goose chase Metis had sent them on.

Quickly putting together what had happened, the two fought fiercely to free their leader. In the chaos, Metis slipped away to inform the Olympians that the plan had worked. The Titans had been so easily duped, and now, they were all but finished.

Krius noticed her retreat and gave chase. Fighting with Metis to free his master, Krius gave it his all. In the struggle, as all the other Titans descended on the scene to fight over the sealed Typhon and gain his powers for themselves, all turned on Metis, who had before insisted she didn't want the Power.

Things became even more tense when the Olympians appeared to back her up. The united Olympians beat back the infighting-ridden tyrants but tarried too long. The seal began to weaken, and in all the confusion, Typhon freed himself (and also Atlas)! This seal was meant for the Solaris family, and trapping two humans in it was foolhardy. Even with Typhon's demi-Solaris nature, the seal wasn't meant for him, and so he was freed.

Typhon's mind was fuzzy, but the single thought that boiled to the top was an unyielding rage against Metis.

"Metis!!!" Typhon roared with flaming eyes.

No, burning her to death with his fiery glare was too kind. For this treachery, Typhon was going to Smite her! However, he then noticed that his ability to use the Solaris Smite had been lost! A strange side effect left him temporarily weakened! In the chaotic battle that ensued, Metis again slipped away, evading her furious former master.

The uncoordinated and ambushed Titans were losing badly. Even though the plan worked, and he was weakened, most gods steered clear of their mightiest foe as he stampeded across the battlefield. For unrelated reasons, Terra also did not make a B-line for him. Instead, she was backing up several weaker gods that still struggled with the mightier Titans.

Rather uncharacteristically, Typhon dashed right past her. For once, Terra was not the number one thing on his mind. Typhon's rage boiled with a desire to get his hands on that treacherous schemer, Metis! Woe to anyone who would take the warrior king's precious power from him.

Dashing across the battlefield, the mad Titan finally found the target of his wrath. Metis hid behind Themis, her fellow former Titan and co-conspirator.

"Metis! Themis… I should've known you two were in it together. Very well, then you will die together!" Typhon screamed while practically foaming at the mouth.

Themis was a great deal stronger than Metis, but even she trembled as their former boss appeared before them. Typhon swung his sickle, but the mightiest Titan was shocked to find his blow parried by the revolt's leader: Jupiter.

As Jupiter came to Metis' defense, the King of the Titans snarled at him. Metis ran to his side, holding onto his arm in fear. Themis ran to his side to defend Metis, but Jupiter just smiled.

"Stay back, girls. I'll handle this," Jupiter confidently declared.

"Jupiter! Don't be a fool. That woman will betray you just as she betrayed me!" Typhon pointed at her with a look of death in his eyes.

"We're nothing alike, monster. Don't project your failures on me; just accept that I'm better with women than you are," Jupiter boasted with Metis on his arm, "She may fear you, but Metis loves me."

"Well, I hate Metis! I hate Themis! And I'm not very fond of you either!" the ruler of the Titans roared before swinging his sickle to try and slice the Titaness in two. Jupiter parried his attack for a second time. Metis got behind Themis, and the two kept their distance as the king of the gods squared off against the king of the Titans.

"It's just you and me, Typhon!" Jupiter declared in the heat of battle.

"Then you'd better get some help, boy." The Titan scoffed. The two dueled with their signature weapons: thunderbolt sword against sickle in a monstrous godly display of superhuman prowess.

Jupiter was Terra's older brother, and in terms of raw Power, he was stronger than her. However, lacking in skill and overflowing in arrogance, he was hardly a match for Typhon in the past. In most of their previous battles, it wasn't even close: Jupiter always needed backup from his siblings.

But this time, the king of the Titans grew frustrated at his newly weakened state. Now, even Jupiter was giving him trouble. In a rage, Typhon blasted Jupiter with his flaming eyes before taking some time to assess his predicament.

His troops were struggling and panicked while he was too weak to turn the tide. This battle was a complete failure. Deciding it was better to lose the battle with the hope of still winning the war, the Titan king gave the order to retreat.

While he was distracted with that order, Jupiter snuck up behind him and struck him with a blast of his thunderbolt. Typhon fell to the ground and dropped his sickle. As Jupiter loomed above him with his weapon raised, Typhon tried to rewind time to gain better footing. As he feared, he learned that in this newly weakened state, he could not rewind time without his weapon.

He willed his weapon into his hands at the exact moment that Jupiter impaled him with his sword! Typhon was dying as the divine lightning roasted his body inside and out! After defeating mighty gods like Odin, Lugh, and Indra, was he going to lose to Jupiter of all people!?

No! At the last moment, Typhon's sickle rewound time to the instant he escaped Metis' trap. With his memories retained, he at once ordered the Titans to retreat rather than let them lose then and there. The gods were confused, except for the Solaris siblings, who cursed that he had successfully rewound time. They alone remembered the battle that they had so nearly won.

The Titans began to flee as they were ordered, but Typhon hesitated to follow his own command. With his pride wounded, he pathetically looked back at his goddess in hesitation.

All of this had been to grow more powerful and ascend to a being of her level. But in his focus on Power, he was easily outwitted. Now, he was further from his goal than when he started. And now, that look of pity she gave him hurt more than any physical damage he suffered.

While he was hesitating, Jupiter bolted over and sent the Titan flying with a mighty slash. His anger blazed, but rather than turn around and get the last hit in, the tyrant swallowed his pride and fled to preserve his Empire. He couldn't stand to embarrass himself in front of Terra any longer.

The Titans were forced to retreat to Tartarus Tower, leaving their precious ultimate weapon in the hands of Metis and the Olympians. Upon their return, Typhon was enraged at his treacherous minions.

While Atlas was just fine, Typhon had been considerably affected by the sealing device. He could no longer use his Smite: the secret ability of the Solaris. More than that, he had also lost his ability to rewind time without his sacred sickle or even transform into his Titan form! Finally, Typhon's memory was fuzzy as a result of his imprisonment. At first, the Titans thought they were in the clear, but Typhon could quickly guess what had happened.

"Atlas! You led me into this trap!" a fuming Typhon lifted his second in command by the throat.

"I was betrayed just as you! Honestly, the others betrayed us both!" Atlas pointed at the others. Typhon turned to his supposedly loyal allies with furious flames in his eyes, and the other Titans cowered.

"Do not blame us, lord Typhon! The woman! Metis tricked us. It is her fault!" Koeus desperately pleaded.

"It's Metis' fault? Then this is also Metis' fault!" Typhon screamed as he blasted every Titan except for Krius and Dione with his flaming eyes! Even Atlas was hit by the attack.

"Krius and Dione, my most loyal attendants, you have done well." Typhon sat on his throne. Krius couldn't help but blush at the compliments from his dear leader.

"Master..." Dione began in haste, "While that is all well and good, what is to be done to the disloyal?"

Typhon sat down, puzzled by what to do.

"Treachery is not to be tolerated! As traitors and fools, that torture is just the beginning of their punishment!" Typhon roared.

And yet he did not kill a single one of them. Unfortunately, Typhon couldn't fight the gods alone, and so, at this point, he was stuck with them! Worse yet, the Titans were finally starting to realize that.

"Do not fail me again, or I will remind you all exactly why my Power is feared across the Universe!" Typhon bellowed out an empty monologue. After what had just transpired, it didn't even have the same ring to it. After such a grand defeat, trust in their "almighty leader" began to waver. Typhon threatened them that they had only one last chance to prove their loyalty to him: win in the next battle!

TALE 6

Rise of the Olympians

The Olympian Alliance pushed the enemies of humanity back to their home base: the Graiac home planet. Reclaiming this seat of power from the villainous Titans was paramount for ending their stranglehold on Graia. Mighty Jupiter led the charge as the Olympians besieged the Titans for the epic final battle.

On that day, it seemed all of creation had gone to war. The two armies converged, empowered by their patron deities and ready to fight to the finish. Though more dazzling than any of the thousands of thralls that clashed in army combat below were the duels of each side's most powerful generals in the skies above. One by one, the gods triumphed over the terrible Titans. Yet, even as nearly all his generals fell, Typhon remained. He wasn't nearly as strong as he was at his peak, but after a bit of recovery, he was a great deal stronger than he was when Jupiter could face him alone.

Even among the Solaris clan, only Jupiter and Neptune stepped up to battle him. Anyone else throwing their lives away in the face of such an unstoppable force would just be making him stronger. It was an Olympian policy that only gods of Jupiter or Neptune's level were supposed to engage

Typhon in battle… or at least that's what it was supposed to be.

Despite Jupiter's orders to the contrary, a third god with more determination than Power joined them: Hades, the god of the dead. The low-level god was nowhere near as strong as Jupiter or Neptune but wasn't willing to just sit on the sidelines and watch like everyone else. Typhon didn't care either way.

As the three gods attacked, Typhon would block and dodge Jupiter and Neptune but sometimes didn't even bother responding to Hades. Hades' pathetically weak attacks were like the buzzing of flies to him: completely incapable of even drawing blood or bruising the Titan. With the wave of his hand, Typhon moved to vaporize the weakling, and yet, Hades deftly dodged the attack as if he'd seen it a hundred times before.

"You idiot! You're just getting in the way!" Jupiter barked at Hades as soon as he landed a safe distance from the Titan.

"We have to finish him now while he's worn out before he regains his full strength! If he has time to recover, there will be no beating him!" Hades replied.

"Can't you tell he's already recovering! He's almost as strong as before!" Jupiter grumbled.

"No. While his raw Power has been recovering from the seal, his special abilities seem to be weaker. He has been using the same weapons on us without summoning any more to his side. I don't see any of his favorite weapons in play, and the ones he has are being launched conventionally rather than fired through portals. While his other attacks have become fiercer, they lack his usual variety. In exchange for brute strength, Typhon seems to be losing his strategic options." Hades observed out loud.

"Who cares!?" Jupiter yelled at Hades, having stopped listening halfway through.

Typhon, seeing the two had the nerve to be talking mid-battle, moved to slay them. As he attacked, Neptune parried him at the last second! The Titan snarled before trying to attack again. Neptune was such a pain to fight, even when Typhon was at full strength. He didn't have time for him right now. Neptune, like Terra, moved with a flow that made him all but impossible to hit. Instead, it was Typhon that was launched back at the end of their scuffle.

"Any day now, you two," Neptune called out to Hades and Jupiter.

Unwilling to lose the exchange, Typhon released a burst of his Power to try and intimidate his foes. It worked. Even at a fraction of his usual fighting capability, the king of the Titans still sent a primal and overwhelming fear through all who sensed his presence.

Undaunted by that show of force, Hades, Jupiter, and Neptune prepared to go back in for the next round. Stormy Jupiter wielded his lightning blade as well as his Aegis shield. Neptune diverted Typhon with his trident, a large fork-like weapon that amplified his control of the waves. And Hades wielded a spear with two spikes instead of one that was known as a bident. Typhon was very obviously eyeing all three to add to his collection.

As the three gods encircled him and attacked from all angles, Typhon was able to fend them off with his god-killing sickle and fleet of weapons. Even as he'd parry and repost one's attacks, he was able to skillfully move to blocking or dodging the follow-up of the others. Nevertheless, as impressive as that was, even he could never find an opening to counterattack. Like the war at large, this close-quarters duel was locked in a stalemate of sorts.

His foes' weapons were great, but he seemed to have an advantage in the number of tools and lives. All around, as many of the battles settled, the other gods despaired. They had won their battles but did not dare approach the clash of the mightiest of divinities. Typhon was so powerful! Yet, Hades saw something else.

"Jupiter, Neptune, can you two confirm that Typhon hasn't shifted time at all during this fight?" Hades asked while dodging Typhon's attacks.

"Why does that matter?" Jupiter grumbled.

"He hasn't," Neptune spoke over his brother while saving him from one of Typhon's eye blasts.

"If he can't summon more weapons or rewind time… if he finds his refuge only in raw Power, then I think I know how we can beat him." Hades plotted.

"We're on the battlefield! Stop talking!!!" Jupiter yelled at him before calling down a blast of lightning that forced Hades and Neptune to leap back for safety. When the explosion died down, Typhon had only a few scratches on him, and only for a moment.

Whatever damage had been done to Typhon was quickly undoing itself as his body and armor both had a frightening power of perfect self-recovery. An unkillable, ever more dangerous foe like that terrified even the gods! At least, that was what he was sure to project.

While his external wounds healed quickly, Typhon's reserves of Power still awaited repair. To buy some time as he finished recovering, Typhon decided to go on the offensive. He fired off his fleet of weapons like heat-seeking projectiles, which dogged the three gods no matter where they went and forced them to dodge rather than punish his weakened state. He needed time to process this new battle data and evolve accordingly. Hades deduced as much.

"We're getting nowhere!" Hades cried while just barely dodging between two simultaneous spears.

"You're getting in the way! If you get your weak ass killed, you're just going to make him stronger!" Jupiter whined while spinning around and batting away the weapons that surrounded him.

"Exactly! He doesn't want to show it, but he's low on weapons and options. Either because of his low reserves or because the seal's effects are growing contrary to his increased Power!" Hades tried explaining. Jupiter didn't hear a word of it.

"And what in my name is taking Terra so long with Atlas anyways!? If you want to be useful, go and get her! She's a much more valuable ally!" Jupiter cut Hades off.

"It's not all about brute strength. I have a plan of attack!" Hades turned to Neptune as the brother who was more willing to listen to him.

"I have a plan: attack!" Jupiter rushed ahead without the other two despite their protest.

He deflected and dodged past the hail of weapons as he rushed Typhon with his sword drawn. Typhon just grinned with his half-regenerated head. Thunderbolt Jupiter zipped up close, striking the demon with a flurry of slashes. He was able to get a few scratches in, but not before Typhon snatched the blade out of the air and held it in a tight grasp. Slowly, Jupiter noticed a corrupting dark mass spreading over his blade and trying to absorb it. He had to pull it free only to realize a hail of spears and swords was coming at him!

"How many times do we have to save you from this!?" Neptune sighed before leaping in and slicing Typhon's hand off to stop him from absorbing the thunderbolt. Hades simultaneously created a shield out of Adamant that held the blades off for just the split second the three gods needed to get out of there.

Typhon wasn't ready to leave that exchange empty-handed and so reached for Hades' bident while he was distracted creating the shield.

"I'll be taking this." Typhon's eyes began to glow with demonic fire as he tried to take over the weapon as he did Jupiter's. But to his shock, it just crumbled to dust. That wasn't Hades' divine weapon. Just like the shield he was creating; it was a mere construct made of those strange black crystals Hades produced.

As the three landed with enough distance between them and Typhon to catch a breath, they noticed that he had already regenerated from Jupiter's failed assault in no time at all. It was as if he'd never been hit.

"Jupiter, how many times do we need to tell you an uncoordinated frontal assault won't work!" Hades cried.

"Go know yourself! At least I'm strong enough to damage him." Jupiter took umbrage with his lesser, ignoring the hierarchy. In ancient times, "to know" was a euphemism for sleeping with.

"Not everything is about raw Power Jupiter. Now, if you're willing to listen, Hades has a pretty promising plan. But it needs all three of us to work." Neptune cut in. Jupiter, after looking at his still recovering sword, finally let out a sigh and decided to listen to the weakling's little trick.

Meanwhile, Typhon wasn't going to just stand around and let them chat. After taking a bit to recall his weapons to his side, he fired them off all at once! The three gods split up, dodging around the Titan while slowly closing the distance.

As they darted around Typhon, dodging his remote-control weapons, they had a private meeting of the minds to strategize using Power signals. Typhon couldn't hear them but, fearing exactly this, decided to interrupt. He dashed towards Jupiter, the most powerful of the trio in terms of raw strength. He was an idiot, but if his powers were to be used by one of the others cleverly, it could be troublesome.

Then, to the Titan's utter shock, the hotheaded Jupiter abandoned the chance to attack directly in a fight. Rather than meet him in a straightforward duel, Jupiter leaped back and took to the air. In his place, Neptune dashed in and attacked Typhon with his trident.

Typhon and Neptune clashed with their divine weapons and shook the battlefield. Though he wasn't as Powerful as Jupiter, Neptune was a much more skilled warrior, and his superior fighting form made him much more of a challenge. Whipping his blade about with fluid and efficient motions gave Typhon little time to try and snatch it for his own.

This was a lost cause. Typhon needed to get some distance again and reset the battle to its previous status quo. In an instant, Typhon's stolen weapons were upon the god of the waves, only for Jupiter to shoot them out of the sky with lightning. Now, he didn't have cover to fall back to, and so Neptune's attacks continued in coordination with Jupiter's lightning strikes.

Typhon could instantly tell that they were up to something. At once, the god of the sea focussed all his Power directly into attacking Typhon with a brutal flurry of trident slashes and stabs as Jupiter did his best to keep the weapons at bay. Typhon called his weapons down, but Jupiter again struck them down from a distance.

However, as the last thunderclap sounded, Typhon realized something. While he was distracted by Neptune's frontal assault, Jupiter had been building up charge for a bolt that was much more powerful than any of the others he'd used so far. That massive buildup of Power completely captured Typhon's attention for a moment.

"Eyes on me, Titan! I'm supposed to be the distraction!" Neptune growled before impaling Typhon from behind! Neptune was not only the god of the sea; he was also the god of planetary quakes. The blades of his trident were known for their incredible power over tremors and seismic activity. In fights, that meant anything he hit with the three-headed spear would vibrate uncontrollably and shatter along its fault lines. And yet, Neptune was shocked to find Typhon in one piece.

"You'll have to do better than that." Typhon grinned as Neptune finally realized why his attack failed. Right before he was about to be stabbed and shattered, Typhon had used his shape-shifting ability to open a hole in his own body intentionally. The trident had gone through him, but without stabbing him, so the divine attack did not connect! Typhon further employed his power of shapeshifting to make his body reverse itself so that his back became his front and vice versa. Though he didn't move, Typhon went from facing away from Neptune to now having the sea god in his sights again.

"I appreciate your charitable donation to my divine armory." The Titan quipped as his body closed around the pole of the trident, safely avoiding the dangerous spikes. Typhon then seized the trident with his hands and tried to pry it from its master's grasp.

Neptune and Typhon engaged in a fierce tug of war over the trident. However, Typhon called his other stolen toys to his side in the hopes of forcing Neptune to abandon his weapon or be turned into a pin cushion.

But they didn't come. Typhon looked around in utter confusion. None of his weapons were responding to his orders. After Jupiter struck them down, sure, a few would be temporarily out of order… but he hadn't noticed that some of them never came back online at all. The reason his weapon throwing was failing to hold Neptune off was that their numbers had been dwindling from the start. But how!? Had Jupiter's bolts gotten stronger?

No. Just then, Hades removed his helmet of invisibility as he held one of Typhon's plundered spears in his other hand. The bident wasn't the weapon Hephaestus made for him! That unassuming helmet of invisibility was. Fittingly, Typhon had overlooked it.

Typhon desperately tried to will that last spear to his side, only for Hades to coat it in a thick layer of black Adamant as he had secretly done to all the others! The weapon fell to the ground in a thick brick, which kept Typhon's command signals out as well as took it completely out of play.

He was so weak that Typhon had forgotten to consider him with the distraction of Jupiter and Neptune. None of his attacks could harm Typhon, but he seemed to have an endless supply of tricky powers made specifically to annoy the king of the Titans. Manipulating Adamant was a rare ability, even for the gods. Who would've guessed he'd been hiding a power of invisibility as well? No wonder he couldn't even detect him sneaking around once the overpowering presence of Jupiter and Neptune held his attention.

Typhon only ever remembered his strong opponents. In previous battles, he'd defeated Hades so easily that he never paid him any mind. But Hades remembered every battle and analyzed that past information to concoct this winning play.

While Typhon was distracted, Hades was able to encase the weapons Jupiter temporarily disconnected and keep them from rejoining Typhon's fleet. One of the most annoying powers had been neutralized. But the plan wasn't over yet. While Hades was lacking in destructive power, all that Power Jupiter had been charging up wasn't just for a distraction.

"It may not be a fancy, high-concept power like you're used to... but every fighter knows that fighting multiple opponents at once is a worst-case scenario. It is time to remind you why!" Hades declared.

Typhon turned around in horror to find the gigantic thunderstorm that gathered overhead was ready to strike. Neptune held the Titan aloft with his metal polearm pointed directly to the heavens as a perfect lightning rod! Jupiter then hurled his thunderbolt down and struck Neptune's trident, blasting the king of the Titans apart! There was nothing but atomic dust left of him after that. Neptune put his weapon down and nodded to his brother. Jupiter landed next to his partner in crime with a thunderous laugh.

And yet, they didn't even have a moment to relax before they felt his dark Powers reviving. Even from that destroyed state, Typhon began willing himself back into existence. As the villain's body began reassembling itself from nothing, Neptune and Jupiter moved to strike again.

Yet even without a head, two gleaming eyes fired hellish flames at the two. There they were: the flaming eyes that spelled total annihilation for anything they hit. Jupiter and Neptune each blocked one of the eye beams with their sacred weapon but were still thrown back.

"Not bad for my goddess' minions. You can hold my interest at least." Typhon scoffed to himself as he took the time to regenerate further.

"Oh, look at that, the plan failed! What a shock." Jupiter complained as he stumbled back to his feet.

"No, it didn't! Now we can fight him without needing to worry about the long-ranged diversions!" Hades cried. But Jupiter, refusing to give Hades a victory, just turned to Neptune in annoyance.

"Damn it, Neptune! It could go on forever like this! Can't we just Smite him with our—" Jupiter began to grumble as he grew frustrated. Before he could finish speaking, terrifying and palpable waves of wrath began emanating from Neptune and sent a shiver down his brother's spine. For a second, he looked scarier than Typhon.

"Jupiter! Don't be an idiot. We've sworn never to do that. You know the risks!!!" Neptune snapped at his brother and, for a second, looked at him with even more anger than he did at Typhon. The thunder god honestly looked a bit hurt at the biting response.

"It would not make a difference." Typhon grabbed all their attention, "Every time you kill me, I just return even more powerful! By all means, help me regain my full strength even faster!" he roared as true to his word, that dark Power of his spiked.

Just as Hades assessed, Typhon hadn't fully recovered his stamina yet, but he had to burn through what he had left to finish these pests off. The terrible Titan shifted strategies and sought to break the weakest link first: Hades. Hades made up for his weakness using his elusive power of perfect invisibility. Amplified by the helmet, he was almost undetectable. Nonetheless, Typhon quickly adapted to his cloaking and was able to see through his illusion, even while fending off the other two gods.

Even though Hades was invisible, Typhon charged directly at him with killer intent. However, the unseen one surprised him yet again. Using his peculiar ability to create Adamant, Hades began producing massive amounts of it all at once in the shape of a giant Monster!

It was a horrible, bony demon with a horned skull for a head and a gigantic bident. Its Adamant "bones" were, in fact, stone and minerals generated in the shape of human anatomy. The beast's bones were protected by thick and metallic Adamant armor that coated and covered everything beneath the exposed, horned skull. This mineral Monster with Hades as its core was the stuff of nightmares, befitting the lord of the dead.

It was not a frozen statue; in this form, the dark-haired god could move just as naturally as in his own skin and fought fiercely with increased Power. Controlling the beast safely from the inside, Hades' Adamant could move and fight as ferociously as any Monster encountered out in the wild.

Piloting this beast, Hades took Typhon by surprise and struck him with great power. Even in this powered-up form, Hades still lacked the other two's raw Power, but paired with the element of surprise, he managed to do some damage.

The surprise of this ultimate form knocked Typhon off guard as the trio of gods pressed their advantage. Hades batted Typhon across the battlefield with his bident, Neptune smashed him down with his trident, and Jupiter crashed down into him with his divine bolt of lightning. Over and over, the three attacked their foe without restraint in perfect synchronization, ensuring he had no time to recover or counterattack.

The three gods fought in tandem, reinforcing and covering for each other in ways that reminded the tyrant of the power of teamwork, which he'd long discarded. Despite the odds, the three Olympians battled and repeatedly killed Typhon. Even the immortal gods would know death if their regeneration was overwhelmed, or their brains were destroyed. But the terrible Titan had become something much more than a "mere god" and would always spring back to life as if nothing had happened.

However, while blood loss meant nothing to him, the amount of his Power being dislodged by being hit with his opponents' own was of concern. Without the Power to regenerate himself, even Typhon would die permanently. The heavier the hit, the more the gods weakened him. At any given moment, the king of the Titans was being hit by at least one of them. Then, all at once, the attacks stopped. A dazed and punch-drunk Typhon stumbled around, confused as to why he finally had a moment to breathe. Then he felt the massive build-up of Power being pointed directly at him.

Jupiter, Neptune, and Hades united their strength and blasted Typhon with all their powers combined! The three beams of Power melted Typhon to dust, blasting out large amounts of his Power reserves.

"Your blast was still the weakest. Mine did the most." Jupiter was sure to let Hades know like a petty child. Hades just rolled his eyes.

After a few moments of waiting for him to come back, the trio could have a moment to breathe. To preserve strength, Hades exited the giant Monster and caught his breath. Before long, the three watched as the smoke reformed into the body of Typhon. But notably, this time, he was on his knees, gasping for breath. It seemed even the god-slayer had his limits.

Now, he found himself completely helpless as the three gods descended upon him from all sides. He'd gotten so much weaker as the war dragged on. In his prime, he'd have won already. But as his foes were upon him, the weary and battle-worn Titan was faced with a new fear for the first time. Was he about to… lose?

No! With a mighty roar, Typhon refused defeat and let fly his flaming eye beams of death! Jupiter and Neptune were each blown away as Hades panicked. Rushing Typhon alongside Jupiter and Neptune in such a desperate moment made sense… but running in alone without his Monster form… was something else.

Typhon roared as he directed all his wrath at this worm whose very existence defied his ideology. Hades froze in terror when he sensed Typhon inches away from him with his sickle ready to cleave him in two!

Yet, in a flash, it was Typhon who was thrown back as if his attack had hit him instead. Hades opened his eyes in amazement to find he was still alive. Jupiter and Neptune were wounded but stood up just in time to see their savior in shock. The three gods marveled at the massive presence that passed them and fearlessly stood before Typhon.

Sacred Terra, sister to Jupiter and Neptune, walked forward, past the group and towards Typhon. Terra had no trace of joy on her face and had silent melancholy, further emphasized by her manifesting her godly Powers in their full glory. Her expression was so out of the ordinary, and her readiness to do battle so apparent that her brothers kept from approaching her.

Typhon was nothing but pulp after she had saved Hades from him. Of course, even from that, he could recover. It was much slower than his recovery from most attacks, but Typhon fully regenerated soon enough and smiled at the sight of blue-eyed Terra. His dear goddess had arrived.

"It's great to see you, my darling goddess." Typhon reached out to her. Terra looked at him with a mixture of pity and disgust. It was a new and shocking look from one who was normally so serene and kind.

"Typhon, I was just talking with Atlas…" Terra began.

"Atlas is a follower of mine. I hope he didn't hurt you too badly, my dear." Typhon chuckled as he got to his feet.

"He tried to kill me." Terra gritted her teeth.

There was a long silence. Before the war and before the Empire of Typhon, when he was merely a man of flesh and blood… many of the gods and the Titans had coexisted.

They had grown up together but now, on Typhon's whims, had been made to kill one another. At this, Terra wept.

"Well… of course. You were rather rude in your refusal of my advances before. But now that you've come to your senses, the fighting can end. Join me, my goddess, and I will make your name the greatest in the Kosmos!" Typhon roared insanely.

"Why… why won't you ever listen?" Terra cried, "Why are you like this?"

"You did this to me. Anything you hate about me is your fault." The demon's eyes flashed blood red as Terra's blue eyes began to water. The perverted demon couldn't help but admire her in this distraught state he had caused.

"My goddess, I love—" Typhon dared to try to say as he reached to touch fair Terra's face. Yet now, there was an impassible distance between them that he could never hope to cross again. Terra would not let him; he had been rejected again. The frenzied Titan grew angry and swung his sickle at Terra.

Without hesitation, Terra drew her legendary blade, the Sword of Dehmos. Just as soon as she began assuming a fighting stance, massive and gaping slash wounds tore open all over Typhon's body! By the time most saw her finish assuming the proper sword-fighting posture, more of the demon's blackened blood was outside his body than in. Just as soon as she'd taken it out, the goddess put her awesome weapon away: for she only needed the sword a moment to promise victory.

Typhon stumbled around, half dead after just that. He was completely incapable of putting up a fight any longer. And yet, the stubborn beast still refused to stand down. His dark Powers were dampened but not completely gone. Once more, Typhon focussed all his strength on regenerating himself so that he could continue the fight! If he had his way, it would go on forever like this.

Seeing this, Terra interrupted the demon by sending him flying into the air with a mighty palm strike! As Typhon was suspended in the air and looking up to the sky, he saw a great light open in the heavens above.

All eyes were lifted to the heavens and captivated by the otherworldly and breathtaking sight. Typhon, especially, was enraptured by this true beauty. A glowing Blue Marble stared down at him through a portal in space and time itself. Time seemed to freeze as the massive divine eye stared down at the helpless Titan. At that moment, the Kosmic giant felt completely overwhelmed and dwarfed by something much greater. In that instant, he felt true cosmic and primal fear.

"Smite: Earth." Terra's whisper ushered in an ear-piercing blast that shook the world.

Before Typhon could react, a massive beam of Power rained from the sky and blasted him down directly into Terra's raised blade. The impaled Titan melted away as the full weight of Terra's Power shone on him. Typhon screamed in agony as he was burned alive in the holy light. The light blasted through Typhon before being conducted and re-absorbed by the Sword of Dehmos that the goddess held aloft.

All were stunned at the display that seemed otherworldly and divine, even to the gods. Neptune and Jupiter, for their part, were horrified at the spectacle and stepped back nervously. Never had any of them unleashed their full power in this Kosmos. If not for mighty Terra's Sword of Dehmos being there to safely control the blast, its unleashed force would make the collateral damage of Jupiter's unrestrained lightning bolts look like firecrackers.

Finally, the rain of divine flames ended, and nothing was left of Typhon. Not even subatomic mist. In violation of

Lavoisier's assertions, his very matter had been destroyed. At this point, the entire battle had stopped. All eyes turned to the source of that awesome display.

Yet, after deleting his physical form, Terra did not wait for his will to usher forth a new one. With a wave of her hand, she expedited the process and reconstituted Typhon from nothing. The previously annihilated Titan's formerly fierce eyes had a thousand-yard stare as if he had seen infinity, and his mind had ceased all processes.

"Jupiter… Neptune… everyone… I'm sorry. I know we all agreed it was too risky. I broke our promise, but I'll make it up to you," Terra quietly said without turning to face them.

"Sure thing…" Jupiter awkwardly responded, still shaking from what he saw. He was glad that was not him.

"Right." Terra calmly exhaled. Then, while Typhon was still dazed, Terra delivered a powerful palm strike to his chest that blasted the rest of his Power reserves out of him in a magnificent flash of light! The powerless Typhon stood, hunched over with a strange symbol now carved into his chest.

"This Power is too much for you. You cannot handle it; may it never return." Terra said as the seared flesh was filled in not by regeneration but instead by a strange crystal-like substance. That seal deprived Typhon of his strength and left him as a mere powerless man. The battle was over.

Pan gave a great shout, and the victory cheer rang through all the Kosmos. The Titans trembled as now they were at the mercy of those they once lorded over. Tartarus Tower was torn down, and in its place, Olympus, the base of operations for the gods, shone over Graia ever after. For his great evil, Typhon was cast out into a banishment where he dwelt in a secret prison far from his servants. The war was won, the Titans had been defeated, and the great gods: the Olympians, now ruled.

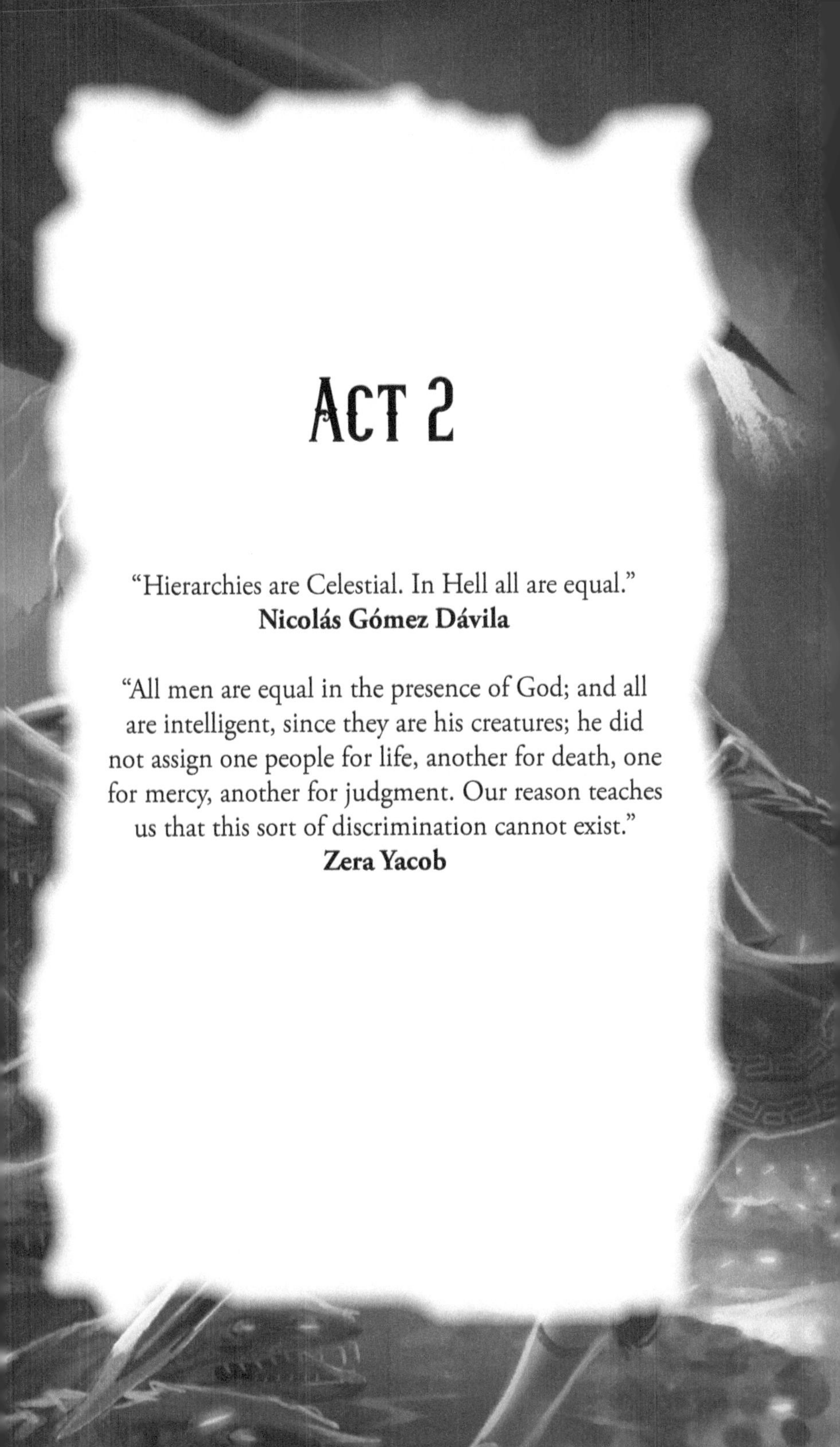

ACT 2

"Hierarchies are Celestial. In Hell all are equal."
Nicolás Gómez Dávila

"All men are equal in the presence of God; and all are intelligent, since they are his creatures; he did not assign one people for life, another for death, one for mercy, another for judgment. Our reason teaches us that this sort of discrimination cannot exist."
Zera Yacob

TALE 7

The New King

The glorious age of the Olympians was stable and enduring! For over a hundred years, the Kosmos knew order as humanity licked its wounds and progressed from the stone age to one of bronze. Under shining Jupiter's leadership, all of humanity was able to recover from the calamity of the Titans. The new king swore an oath not to rule as a tyrant in the same way that Typhon did; his regime was to be one of peace and justice.

Jupiter graciously agreed to restrict his domain exclusively to the region of Graia: the territory Ouranos once held dominion over. Within those realms, even though he was king of the gods, he was no Emperor. Each planet would have an independent ruler. Though Jupiter would keep order and coordinate pan-Graiac affairs, he did not interfere in local politics. He supported the rights and autonomy of the separated city-states known as poleis. Each polis would be left to their own devices. So long as they shunned the way of the Titans and revered the Olympians, they could do whatever they wanted.

However, as king, it was said that his work in the palace of Olympus kept him very busy. While he did not rule through politics, he instead oversaw the new economic system of Graia that held it all together: Mercantilism. People could hardly imagine how difficult it must have been to keep the whole Kosmos running. To be fair, Jupiter had no idea either. Like most kings, he left most of the actual work to other people while taking all the credit for himself.

Olympus was the floating wartime fortress of the Graiac pantheon, but now it was his personal playground. One hundred years after outliving its original purpose, the fortress had changed from its wartime stronghold days and was now a city-sized palace meant to host all Jupiter's parties. Unlike the rest of Graia, this divine abode was allowed to keep all of the advanced technologies that allowed the stone age barbarians to overthrow the Titans. Everywhere else existed only at the level of primitive bronze age technology, while the great gods existed in this blissful paradise. It was one of Jupiter's many retirement gifts to himself and those loyal to him.

But if most gods were perpetually absentee rulers, who kept things running? Not all the gods chose to check out the instant the Titans were overthrown. A small, dedicated few took their job as guardians of humankind seriously. They believed that with great power came great responsibility, and so acted on it. The foremost divinity that safeguarded this peace was the very one who'd helped bring it into existence: Terra Solaris. She just didn't care about collecting credit, and so Jupiter was ensured a passive income of new feats to take credit for.

Now, this wasn't to say that Terra was singlehandedly making the world run any more than her brother was. After all, the great man theory is more of a myth than Jupiter. No, on top of those few gods who cared, there were countless unappreciated and hardworking everyday people working alongside them to help the common folk. The King of the

Gods stole credit from them all. It was much simpler to say a single, great ruler was responsible for all the good or bad in the world. However, that isn't to say he couldn't contribute a lot of good if he actually wanted to.

Jupiter was far more interested in using his power to please himself selfishly. That was to be expected. That was easy. That was "believable." By contrast, many were suspicious of Terra. To most people, the most unbelievable thing about Terra wasn't her complete mastery over the laws of nature or even the unfathomable Power she could unleash; it was that she was nice. Power corrupted, so surely a being so powerful would be evil. Absolute power is corrupted absolutely.

Many viewed Terra with suspicion, and she didn't blame them. She viewed herself with suspicion, too. Always vigilant, always making sure she was on her best behavior. Resisting temptation and practicing self-control was the only task left for an omnipotent creature. People would always suspect her anyways, but that didn't matter to Terra. What mattered was holding herself to the standard only she could enforce.

Why wouldn't she just do whatever she wanted? Nobody could stop her. The answer was simple: Terra wanted to help people. And ironically, the very laws that kept her in line could stop her. Terra swore an oath that not even she was above the law; she couldn't be. Unfortunately, in many cases, those very laws kept her from helping more people.

But Jupiter convinced her this was a worthy trade-off. She didn't want to be completely unaccountable, did she? No, to avoid her desires corrupting her, she had to surrender to him and find peace. So it was; to avoid becoming a monster, the goddess placed herself under the yolk of Olympus.

Of course, she could overcome the monster Typhon, now the goddess Terra just had to ensure she never became like him.

But Terra served Jupiter and was restricted to only pursue goals that he approved. Throughout Graia, Terra did his will, and from high-flying Olympus, Jupiter took all the credit. That sounded like a fair deal. But curiously, on this day, Jupiter wasn't even on Olympus. On his desk, all that was left was a little sign that read, "On break. GO KNOW YOURSELF!"

He was far from Olympus, following Terra around for the day so he could take credit for more of her exploits. Their next stop was the planet of Dodona, which had been ravaged by a terrible storm. Jupiter couldn't have cared less about disaster relief but wanted some alone time with Terra, so he played along.

Jupiter didn't even remember that this realm was supposed to be under his protection. After all, the thunder god was the one who had liberated it from the clutches of the Titans and had a temple built there in his honor. His great battle defeating three Titans at once on Dodona was the stuff of legends!

The downside was that the northern pole of the planet had been destroyed in that great battle between the gods and the Titans long ago. This loss of the polar ice sheets created a massive change in the planet's climate. Most notably, the melted ice became water, and the wind patterns of the planet now changed. All this was the perfect recipe for worsened storms and flooding.

"That's a lot of damage." Jupiter whistled at the sight of his indirect handiwork.

"Exactly. This is why I warned everyone about using too much Power on a planet's surface. Dramatic changes to landscapes can be catastrophic for the powerless," Terra replied with sadness at the suffering before her.

The two deities descended into the ruins where the survivors had congregated. At the sight of their god Jupiter, they fell down and worshipped him. Ignorant Jupiter was confused by the welcome but nonetheless very pleased.

"What a miracle! On this day, we are graced by the presence of the king and queen of the gods!" the elder and local priest cried ecstatically. The crowd went wild as they two recognized the divine visitors. They looked just like all the propaganda statues Jupiter put up.

Seeing the two together was the greatest honor. After all, just as he said, they were the king and queen of the gods. Jupiter was the king of the gods, but "queen of the gods" was an odd title for Terra, considering that the two were never married.

"Why are they still calling us that? Shouldn't Metis be the queen since she's your actual wife?" Terra asked, feeling uncomfortable in the face of the cult-like praise.

"Remember, Metis is also an ex-Titan. For political reasons, it's best to minimize reminding people of that. I guess you were just second in line for the title," Jupiter whispered to her while smiling and waving.

"But we're brother and sister," Terra reminded him.

"True, but being a queen doesn't have to imply we're married. I'm the king because I am the highest-ranking male divinity, and you are the queen because you're the highest-ranking female deity. If a few people get the wrong idea, that's their problem." Jupiter hand-waved her concern. Almost everyone got the wrong idea. And as much as Jupiter would insist otherwise, it was by design.

Terra didn't want to be called the queen of the gods, but her wearing it served Jupiter well. Besides, since when did he care what she thought? On top of the title stating his questionable complex about his sister, Terra being called the queen was also a way of satisfying those ungrateful traitors who had pushed to try and make Terra the ruler of Olympus rather than Jupiter. Thankfully, she didn't want the role, feeling unqualified, so Jupiter got it. Unlike her, he would not foolishly overlook the benefits the crown yielded.

Nonetheless, as the two gods chatted amongst themselves, the elder priest rallied the assembled worshippers together to give the divinities a proper welcome. With one voice, they chanted and cried, "Hail, Zeus, hail! He frowns, and Olympus trembles; he smiles, and the sky brightens! Praise the name of Zeus. He is the Zeus Optimus-Maximus!"

Zeus was the most popular alternate name for Jupiter Solaris, the Master of Olympus and the loud-thunderer who saw far and wide. Zeus was Jupiter, and Jupiter was Zeus. In his capacity as king, he was Zeus. Only his friends could call him Jupiter.

The Thunderer couldn't help but flash a big old grin at the masses prostrating themselves before him. Sure, they had just survived a horrendous crisis, but pleasing Zeus was far more important than that. It had turned out that they were praying and sacrificing to his altar right before he arrived. The altar depicted Zeus singlehandedly slaying the demon Typhon, just as the legends said. Many felt their prayer had called him down to grace them. The people of Dodona had prided themselves on being among the most devoted to the cult of Zeus.

Despite the modern negative connotation, cults in ancient Graia were organizations run by certain divinities and their servants. Cults were primarily for standardizing worship of a deity as well as serving as primitive corporations and businesses that allowed a god to profit from their popularity and iconography as well as direct donations from their followers. They were the backbone of the new world's Mercantilism and also gigantic goddamned scams.

Coincidentally, a lack of centralized government meant a lack of any force capable of opposing the gods and their various financial adventures across Graia. Typhon's world was the age of the warrior, and Jupiter's world was the age of the charlatan. A few, like Terra, never got involved in the shady business of cults, but they were a slim minority. Most others gratefully accepted this other retirement gift Zeus' system prepared for them.

In response to the prayer offered by his loyal cult members, Zeus cleared his throat and prepared to address the crowd. As the head of all this, he had to instil confidence and reverence in his flock. If they thought their prayers had called him down, who was he to disagree with them?

"Of course. I heard your prayers and rushed over as soon as I could, my beloved children." Zeus lied as easily as he breathed. The people cried tears of joy and offered prayers even more ravenously. After finally finding a lull in their worship, Terra stepped in and offered to help them with the repair and recovery of their village as well as the recovery and burial of the dead. The villagers refused her help. Terra was shocked and said that to get their lives back together, they needed help. At that, the village elder politely rebuked her.

"We are to rebuild on our own as punishment from above." Though Zeus stood right there, the old man insisted on speaking for him. "It was our own impiety that brought the storm upon us. Zeus, the god of gods, demanded right action and truth. Failing to meet his standards led to this, so we are willing to accept his punishment."

Terra was baffled! In their minds, they were being punished for not worshipping the lord of storms nearly enough. How else were they to rationalize the seemingly random deaths of so many innocents? Zeus still had to be in control. If they could not negatively portray him… something must be wrong with them.

After the storm, the people planted a grove of oak trees that were sacred to the thunder god. It was a sign of his wise rule over them. After all, Zeus waited for the wicked to reach the pinnacle of their foolishness before punishing them. By contrast, he punished his subjects quickly so that they did not fall totally into degeneracy. Terra looked to her brother to correct the issue and clear them of this self-inflicted guilt. She was met only with a proud smile, for Zeus was pleased by all this.

"I congratulate you all for your steadfastness and fidelity. For keeping the faith even now, you have earned divine favor," Zeus declared before his flock. Disturbed by this, Terra pulled her brother aside for a quick sidebar.

"How could you be so cruel to obviously suffering people!?" Terra demanded. He was taken aback for a moment by her outburst. Nevertheless, shrewd Zeus, ever the politician, presented his spin.

"The dead are already dead. Even we can't bring them back, no matter what those villagers think. Instead, if this was the comfort that they chose, it is best to reassure them. It brings them comfort and us glory. It's a win for everyone." The politician charismatically argued.

"It's dishonest! In the long run, this can only lead to further harm." Terra cried. Zeus grew frustrated by her inability to be tricked as easily as his followers. Such pleasing illusions worked like a charm on her not long ago. The king prided himself on taking advantage of traumatized and vulnerable people. So, given that she was still Terra, Zeus calmed himself and put it another way.

"At least this reminds people of our power. The populace may get banged up a bit, but they'll never forget their true saviors. After the horrors of Typhon, they need comforting." Zeus tried to find the bright side.

"Jupiter Solaris, they're dead," Terra replied. She used his true name… not a good sign. Ignoring Zeus' will, Terra went back to the people and tried to address them.

"People of Dodona, please hear me. What happened to you was a tragedy and not your fault. You have not angered anyone, and Zeus would never punish you so harshly even if you had," Terra cried. Zeus snickered at that bit.

Confused murmurs arose from the crowd. The village elder, who had put this idea in their heads, was furious. Despite this, he held his tongue because even he knew better than to speak over a goddess. He was hoping to use this to further his control over the masses by interpreting the will of their god. Zeus' well-timed endorsement only solidified that. So why now did the fates conspire against him?

"While Zeus can create and use storms with his Power, storms can exist in nature outside his control. They are forces of nature, not the divine. This tragic natural disaster wasn't his wrath; it was a wind pattern beyond anyone's control." Terra tried to console them.

To Terra's shock, the people were horrified. It almost seemed like they preferred to be punished by some supernatural force rather than accept that bad things could just happen. The idea that someone was in control, even of forces against them, was preferable to living in a world where nobody was. They cried out and begged Terra to tell them that it was not so. She was just testing their faith, right? At this, Zeus stepped up and told them what they wanted to hear.

"Worry not. That was a test, one that you endured well, my believers. Just remember that if you pray and offer sacrifices at a temple to the king of the heavens, you will be saved from storms. Entrust all to me and find peace." Zeus reassured them. The pleasing illusion eased their hearts but unsettled Terra's.

"But what will happen when the next storm comes? What happens when storms keep on coming because of permanent damage to the climate?" Terra asked him quietly.

"We'll figure out the explanation then. Besides, most of these guys will be dead by the time it matters. The average life expectancy in this era is what? Thirty?" Zeus shrugged. "For now, the people's morale is raised, and the honor of the gods elevated. That's a job well done." he smiled.

The houses still lay in ruin, and the community was left vulnerable to the inevitable next storm. Yet, while Terra was conflicted, Zeus was content to have accomplished his usual amount of work for the day. He let out a loud yawn.

"So… are we done yet?" Jupiter asked.

"We haven't done anything! What was accomplished, if it can even be called that, was done with a lie. I thought you demanded right-action and truth?" Terra pleaded with him.

"Sometimes, it can be a noble thing to lie, Ter." Zeus patronizingly patted her on the head.

As they watched the villagers slowly and painfully rebuild on their own, the village elder approached Zeus and asked for a word. Zeus left Terra to discuss further collaborations with the noble soothsayer.

Terra was left alone with despair at the sight of the humans struggling with what she could have done for them in an instant. But by her strict moral codes, Terra couldn't just force them to accept new homes. As odd as it sounded, using her Power in ways people did not want would violate her principle of respecting free will. When people refused her help, she had to accept their wishes or else…

What was the point of all this Power if she couldn't use it to help them? What was the point of all the work she did if people still had to suffer? A hundred years in, and nothing was getting better!

However, as Terra silently despaired, a group of villagers approached the goddess. To her surprise, they thanked her for telling them the truth. They confessed that they were allured by the pleasing illusions people came up with, but that ultimately empty comfort was still empty. They much preferred Terra's helpful explanation and asked her if she had any more advice for predicting and warding off storms.

Terra complied with an overjoyed heart. She told them of the signs, such as the types of clouds to look for, temperature drops, sudden changes in wind direction, and so on. Natural disasters were almost impossible to predict more than a week ahead of time, but every second counted, and even a few days of foreknowledge could save countless innocents.

She returned the climate to a pre-Titan War state and ensured no future storm would be as severe as this one. Though Dodona was still a thunderstorm planet and though less severe, serious storms would inevitably come. During seasons where storms were more common, Terra advised the community to be on the watch for all these signs and have contingencies ready just in case.

Terra explained all this and more before creating a written file for them to refer to. She left this as a parting gift, and it was treasured by the Dodonans ever after. True to her word, with these warning signs, they could get to safety before the storms came rolling through. It was much more helpful than the empty promises of Zeus any day. By embracing the truth, many lives were saved.

There were some problems where humanity had to rely on divine intervention. But Terra much-preferred cases like these. Times when she could teach people how to fish rather than just feed them for a day. The goddess couldn't be everywhere at once, but by empowering people to fend for themselves, she felt that the mission could truly be accomplished. Meanwhile, Zeus was repulsed by the concept of loosening the gods' stranglehold on humankind.

Zeus and Terra left each content with the outcome in their own way. The contradiction between truth and lies was yet to resolve itself. And each had taken note of the other's approach.

Terra was disappointed in her brother's deception, and Zeus was terrified that Terra had openly defied him. She was nonconfrontational as usual, but… she brazenly defied his will in front of his face. She prioritized saving people over pleasing him. It sounded silly, but Zeus had gotten used to Terra letting him do as he pleased. This slight and indirect pushback was enough to make him internally panic. He still had nightmares remembering what she did to Typhon.

Terra, by contrast, couldn't get past seeing how Zeus acted as a god in person. Had he changed? Was she… losing her brother in the same way as Typhon? No. Terra did not allow that thought to continue. To the rescue came the usual thought-terminating cliché that ensured she never thought too much about it.

Instead, she thought of happy things. Then Terra began to smile again. The worst part was that she looked so happy; Zeus knew exactly why. Terra was known for her ever-radiant smile, but Zeus knew the truth. She had been forcing herself always to project happiness and positivity as if she owed the world. But that smile… that face she made whenever she thought of Hades… that was genuine.

Just then, Zeus realized it was almost time for her to go back to him as well. Supported by Hades and Demeter,

Terra negotiated her time working for Olympus down to two-thirds of the year. Now, she was made to waste a third of the year in his realm instead of attending to her Kosmos-sustaining duties. Outside those eight months, she wouldn't be where Jupiter could keep an eye on her- where he didn't have power over her.

She never would have done this before. Terra didn't like fighting with her brother. She wasn't allowed to fight with him, **ever**. Zeus liked it better when she never talked back. This whirlwind romance had raised rebellion in her. With moral support, she was beginning to dare to think and act for herself.

Hades… that man was just using her for his ambitions and power. He was taking her for granted! Each accusation was an admission. Nonetheless, Zeus swore that Hades would pay for this.

TALE 8

Speak of the Devil

Hades, the god of the dead, ironically enough refused to die. Back during the Titan war, he fought opponents out of his league, time and time again. Somehow, he always made it out in one piece. Like a cockroach.

"Like a cockroach? Ouch." Hades noted Terra's odd comparison.

"Sorry, I meant it as a compliment. Besides, cockroaches are cute." The nature goddess smiled as she finished healing Hades.

Terra had just saved him once again from a fight with Typhon. Working together, the two had liberated his homeland, Molossos. He was so exhausted after scrapping with the Titan king that his immortal body wasn't even able to regenerate on its own.

"Thanks Terra, you're literally a life saver. I feel good as new." Hades smiled.

"No problem, but we have to stop meeting up this way." Terra laughed after healing Hades.

"Well, given how many times you've bailed me out of trouble, I'm not complaining." Hades smiled back.

"After this is all over, we should meet up under better circumstances." Terra offered.

"Of course." Hades jumped at the offer.

He'd lost so many friends in the war that the few bonds he still had were the most precious things in the Kosmos to him. Though Terra had a special place in his heart, his pallid skin could hardly hide his blush at her offer.

But just as the war kept the two friends apart, even once they triumphed over the Titans, there still wasn't much time for them outside of work.

Terra was the sacred queen of the gods, the protectress of humanity, and the mother of nature. While many gods and goddesses saw this new era as one where they could retire and be rewarded for fighting in the great Titan war, Terra had to step in for them.

While most divinities spent their time among the wealthy and successful in society, somebody had to look out for the little guy. After all, with great power, there must also come great responsibility.

After a hundred years, the work never ended. Day in and day out, Terra was solving the same problems. Many others who once fought the good fight alongside her despaired and gave up hope. They either gave in and went with the flow of the other decadent gods, or they retired and despaired in isolation. Only a precious few stayed on with Terra, just barely holding the Kosmos together.

With great power, there must also come great responsibility… right? What was the point? Terra tried everything within her power, but these problems were not of the kind that one could punch away. She had to keep trying, but inside, she too began to despair and give up hope. As Terra worked day in and day out, it was just her and her thoughts, reflecting on all the mistakes that led her to this point.

The age of Zeus was supposed to be better. If she just worked harder and played by the rules, she could eventually fix all this. Every king was determined to abuse Terra's goodwill for their advancement, but Terra could not bring herself to hate anyone else, so she could only… no.

Even though the kings worked against her, eventually, they would learn, and… this world could become the one everyone had fought for. Terra had to believe that; she didn't know why, but she forced herself to believe that.

"This… is not the world we fought for." Hades declared nearly a century after the new regime had been ushered in. Terra looked at her old friend with her eyes wide. The two had kept in touch since the time of the war. Hades was a lowly miner and Monster hunter, and she was the queen of the gods.

After the war, the two often crossed paths on their common mission to help those in need. It was nice to have a kindred spirit for backup and support. However, even beyond that, Terra liked to visit Hades whenever she was feeling down or stressed. She visited Hades a lot.

The glorious golden age of Zeus was well established, and yet it was still hard times in the world of men. Not much had changed in the grand scheme of things, and Hades wasn't afraid to say it. That was, of course, why he'd been banished from his homeland of Molossos. Even as a god, he was not allowed to oppose the new superstructure.

"The new world of Olympus is just like the world of the Titans. Not in every sense, but at its core, the same problems remain. Some things seem similar but are, in fact, contradictory, and some things seem contradictory but, upon closer inspection, are the same. The world is filled with equals and opposites. These two worlds are opposites yet equal." Hades posited.

"How so?" Terra asked.

"Think about it: all we've done is replace the love of Power with the love of money! This obsession with the accumulation of drachmas is the root of all kinds of evil! But the coins are not the problem. It is not the people that are the problem. It's the foundation and the superstructure of the system itself. We've replaced the people wearing the crown but neglected the inherent corruption of the crown!" the radical god of the dead declared to his audience of one. He was normally a quiet man, but Terra always said he could tell her anything. She was just surprised by how much he had to tell.

"Just think about it! All the time we spend patching up symptoms of the much bigger systemic faults is time we spend avoiding addressing the root causes! That's why the work never seems to end. It's completely illogical. We feed the poor instead of solving poverty for crying out loud! What sense does that make? This isn't working, and this isn't stable. The contradictions of this world must resolve themselves! There has to be a better way!" Hades cried out.

Terra was left speechless. She wasn't alone. She wasn't crazy. She wasn't naïve! Hades said everything Terra had been suppressing. He said exactly what she needed to hear. Even though it had cost him everything, the unseen one had never given up in his quest to fix it.

Hades did not walk away in surrender or wallow in doom or despair. He fought on and inspired others to do the same. Many said Hades was a naïve dreamer, but big results required big ambitions. Most called him an idiot, but Terra found it admirable.

Hades maintained his optimism and drive in the face of impossible odds because the last time everyone called him a fool, history proved him right. After Typhon destroyed his village, he became one of the earliest anti-Titan rebels. Most called him a fool for thinking that a powerhouse like Typhon could ever be defeated. Yet, Hades kept fighting the good fight. Eventually, the perseverance paid off.

With his last foe vanquished, Hades set his sights on a new one. As long as there was injustice, he had the drive to help humanity overcome it and achieve an ever-more-perfect world. He was an eternal activist, and to Terra, no goal was nobler. His hope became hers, and his efforts redoubled hers. All this time, he never abandoned her, so Terra held fast to him also.

As for his struggle against Zeus' corrupt new system, Hades could go on and on about it and how things could be made better. He was a problem solver, after all. Rather than Terra's old dreams of holding out for reformation, Hades concluded that things had to become better by any means necessary. The only constant thing was change, and so if the system refused to do so, it had to be replaced.

"The problem is too much power consolidated into too few hands. The alienation from the public that gods and kings have is an impenetrable barrier to true progress. As long as there is a ruling class, there will be no true order; that is, order founded on justice rather than coercion. Only the people can solve their problems!" Hades stood up.

"A distinction without a difference was meaningless; the patina of a benevolent monarch over an openly tyrannical one was nothing but a pleasing illusion. Only after a nation was by the people and for the people could justice overtake fabricators of lies and false witnesses." Hades valued nature over names.

"But… it's impossible. A rule by the public… a rule by the demos has never existed." Hades deflated, "What would that even be called? Instead of a kingdom, it would be a demo-dom? Replace a monarchy with a demo-archy? Substitute autocracy with… never mind."

Terra froze up. There was something she wanted to tell him so badly, but she couldn't. It was a thousand years too early for that.

"Besides, beyond the problem of precedent, there are many other issues I haven't worked solutions out for yet. The new country would have the baggage of whatever nation it came from. Old enemies, political hangups, debts, etc., would hold them back from focusing solely on progress. There wasn't exactly any uncontested land out there to build on, so some conflict would arise just to secure a location. The established political elite of whatever chosen land would infiltrate and ruin the attempt to reform their lands. Without divine endorsement, the land would have no legitimacy, and the people who created the monarchal system weren't likely to aid a challenger to it. I'm a god, but a minor one: the project would need a massively prominent figure backing it, and if they had that much sway in the current world order, why would they move to replace it?" Hades thought out loud with lightning speed.

Terra listened to him go on and on for hours at a time. It was honestly a bit repetitive and preachy… but it was genuine. She learned a lot about him just from how he spoke about it. Hades was rarely so emotive about anything, but the sheer conviction behind each word, paired with the articulate way he explained each gripe, showed he'd thought a lot about this stuff. When he got fired up, he could go on for a while, but Terra didn't mind; that was more data for her.

Hades continued his passionate soliloquy until, eventually, self-awareness overtook the passionate radical. He'd been talking at her so long that the sun was starting to set.

"You're a busy goddess. Are you sure you should be wasting your free time listening to me rant at you?" Hades awkwardly asked.

"Hades… I'm intrigued by your ideas. If I made you king of the world, would you bring them to fruition?" Terra asked, much to his shock.

"No," Hades replied quickly. Now it was Terra's turn to be surprised, pleasantly surprised. She couldn't help but smile.

"I don't want to be king. As I said, a just society can only be ruled by the people who live in it." Hades declared, "Everyone lives in society, so everyone should have a say in how society is run. I just feel like it's one of those things that can't properly exist outside a group. By its nature, the kind of ideal leadership I desire can't exist in isolation. You know what I mean?"

"It's like color confinement, got it." Terra nodded.

"What it is, is the main reason why the world I envision can't happen. Not without some kind of miracle." Hades sighed.

At that, Terra smiled. She wasn't good for much, but miracles she could do. Terra snapped her fingers. In the sky above them, Terra teleported septillions of pounds of iron into view before crushing it down with such force that it threatened to liquefy and become molten. Around this core came all sorts of materials to form a molten mantle and then a thin crust of silicon stone. Hades was amazed by this miraculous sight. Terra created a planet and set it in orbit around a habitable star at the edge of Graiac space, beyond anyone's domain. She teleported herself and Hades into orbit around the new world.

The goddess of nature could do a lot more than grow plants. This was Terra's true power of nature at work: complete control over natural forces, elementary particles, probability, and quantum phenomena. To everyone else, it looked like a miracle.

"So, what do you think, Hades? The land seemed to be the biggest obstacle to your dream. I respect your refusal of the crown… but you don't need to be king to create the future you envisioned. What do you say?" she asked.

"I am not worthy to lead something so important. I'm just a working man. I'm just a soldier. I cannot lead." Hades shook his head.

"In the world you wish to create, the workers and the soldiers will be the leaders, will they not?" Terra asked, "Thus, you must be the change you want to see in the world."

Hades sighed. She had such unshakable faith in him; in everybody. If she believed in him so readily and offered such heartfelt encouragement… Hades just couldn't say no. So, rather than push back any further, he accepted Terra's words.

"Well, you already made the planet. So, I guess it's too late either way." Hades couldn't help but chuckle at her doing things out of order.

"Don't feel forced into the decision. This is your choice to make. If you don't want it, I can get rid of it." Terra casually pointed at the planet, ready to erase the new world in an instant if Hades said the word.

"No! No! I'll take it. You're right. This does resolve most of the issues." Hades laughed.

Terra was glad. She couldn't afford to let him give up hope like she had. He had a dream, and Terra knew that if there was anyone who could make it possible, it was him.

"I fear the uncertainty of this project… but Terra, you can see the future, can't you? I don't need to be nervous about anything. Couldn't you just tell me if this succeeds?" Hades asked.

"I'm afraid that isn't how it works. Looking any further into the future than a few minutes is completely unreliable. Even if I pushed my analytical ability to the limit with as much data as I could get my hands on—" Terra began before catching herself, "—let's just say that fate is a fickle thing."

"But don't worry about that! This is it, Hades! This is your spherical cow traveling in a vacuum," Terra said in one of her usual odd analogies.

"...why would the cow be a sphere?" Hades tried picturing it.

"What I mean is, you have the perfect conditions for the experiment." Terra cheered, getting excited at the prospects.

"Experiment?" Hades asked, continuing to be confused by her verbiage.

"That world you wanted to create; we can make it right here," Terra excitedly remarked.

"We?" Hades was surprised.

"Well, you said you needed a strong divine endorsement for this to work, right?" Terra reminded him, "Hades, as Goddess of the World, I swear that I shall do everything within my power to ensure that the future you envision comes to pass." Terra declared with an otherworldly glow. Hades accepted her oath.

Many complained about the status of the world, but Hades was different. Hades' analytical skills broke down Zeus' system just as it did any other enemy. Hades had a plan; Hades always had a plan. That's why Terra chose him and exchanged that sacred oath.

It was not good for Hades to be alone; now he wasn't. He and Terra were partners and grew closer than ever. As the two worked together towards their common goal, it was not long before they also exchanged oaths as husband and wife.

TALE 9

Goddess of the World

At the beginning of the bronze age, humanity began to settle down into sedentary zones and lose contact with other groups of their kin. The once-traveling gods became localized to specific regions. Not Terra, though. As the goddess of the whole World, the great goddess Terra continued to travel widely and stay in touch with foreign cultures, peoples, and gods.

On the one hand, at times, this could make her feel a bit homeless. But on the other hand, it allowed her to keep in touch with all her friends. Besides, one of the great morals the past nomadic society taught was that home is where the heart is. Terra was a citizen of the world.

Thus, far away from the lands of Graia, Terra had business in the lands of Caucasia, where the Nart gods of old reigned. These divinities from beyond Graia's borders were dear to Terra, who kept in touch across the ages. Upon her arrival, Terra's Nart counterpart, Setanaya, had prepared a grand feast in her honor.

As the matriarch of the Nart pantheon, she welcomed her Graiac peer into her home. The hundred children of Setanaya were the greatest, strongest warriors of the region:

the Nart warband. In honor of their divine guest, they displayed many feats of strength and athleticism. Their display for the assembled deities was a sight to behold.

As the guest of honor, Terra sat at the highest spot of honor with Setanaya and her husband, Warzameg, to review the festivities. The trio of old friends caught up and had a good laugh. However, when Warzameg excused himself to attend to other matters, Terra confided in her close confidant something that had been bothering her.

"Really? It's quite shocking that anything could trouble someone as mighty as you," Setanaya said.

"Power alone doesn't solve everything. This is more a matter of the heart. You remember Hades?" Terra asked with a smile as she lovingly grasped the beautiful diamond necklace he had made for her.

"The pale kid who had feelings for you since the two of you met?" Setanaya asked.

"Yep, that's the one." Terra couldn't help but laugh at the description, "We've recently been married."

"And he's giving you trouble?" Setanaya asked.

"No, none at all. He's the best." Terra blushed, "What I wanted your advice on was his daughter. He already had a child before our marriage. I know that technically makes me a stepmother and not a 'real mother', but… I do consider the girl to be my own. I'm just worried that the feeling isn't reciprocated." Terra sighed.

"Terra, let me stop you right there. Birth and biology have nothing to do with maternity. You are the child's real mother, as far as I'm concerned. All that is left is to wait for the child to accept you. It will take some time for the child to adjust, but I'm sure you'll make a great mom." The Nart mother goddess reassured her Graiac counterpart.

"Thanks. I know it's silly, but… I just wish she'd call me that from time to time. It's a minor thing, I know, but… I just wish to hear it at least once." Terra sighed.

"I know it's tough, my friend, but haven't you considered just talking to her about it?" Setanaya asked. Terra became flustered and admitted that it was just too embarrassing. The same being that could face an entire demonic army alone was too scared to do that.

"I see. Don't force yourself. Being a parent isn't playing a character. Do whatever feels natural and comfortable. But just to warn you, it is a lot of responsibility. A mother always has to protect her children." Setanaya smiled.

"Rather than focusing on just one family… I've always thought of the whole human race as under my protection." Terra smiled back.

"Really? Why did you let us die then?" Setanaya demanded in a sudden shift of tone. A sudden silence fell over the feast. Terra turned to her in shock, only to find her dear friend had been replaced by her rotting corpse! Terra recoiled in horror but bumped into the returning Warzameg, who now was so brutalized and decayed that he was an unrecognizable husk.

The entire pantheon of Nart gods was zombified horrors, closing in on the visiting Graiac goddess. All one hundred of Setanaya's children danced as mangled corpses while those that Terra had let down swarmed her. How dare she worry about such trivial matters after what she'd done! While she was fretting over such nonsense, she was failing countless of those she "cared about".

"Why did you let us die!?" the felled Nart divinities cried out at her. The Titans had come to Caucasia and slain every single one of them. Terra worried about what her child would call her; they had to watch theirs be put to the sword! How dare she.

"You were so quick to forgive those that killed us! Why do they get to live after everything they've done? Your weakness spits on our graves!" the corpse of Setanaya screamed. Terra had no reply. Every single pantheon outside of Graia had been massacred while Terra was on watch. If those under her "protection" could be killed that easily, then it could not have counted for much.

"You did this." The dead woman pointed accusingly at Terra. Terra was on the verge of tears as she accepted all their hatred and resentment.

"Don't give her all the credit." An ominous voice answered the screams of the damned. Terra was horrified to find Typhon smiling next to her. At once, the dragon emperor blasted Setanaya into ash with his flaming eyes. He walked over and stomped on her ashes with a smile as the entire Nart pantheon burst into flames as well.

"Come on. We both know I couldn't have done it alone, partner. But I did do the killing myself." Typhon turned to Terra with a toothy grin. The goddess got to her feet in anger.

"Ah… that hatred in your eyes. Before, such a thing would drive me mad. But now it makes me love you all the more. You don't want to hate anyone, do you? Love you give freely, but your hatred… is something I had to work very hard for." Typhon smiled.

"I don't hate anyone." Terra recoiled and restrained herself.

"Sure, you do. You hate yourself, my dear. And that is what continues to sadden me. A god need not feel guilt for the humans they trample underfoot. Does a human lament trampling ants? Come with me, and I can remove your guilt.

You made me a promise, didn't you?" Typhon chuckled as Terra looked away in shame.

"Or had you already forgotten our deal now that you're cheating on me with that pale corpse of a man?" Typhon scoffed.

Terra made a fist and trembled silently. She didn't even want to engage with her twisted admirer. She'd beaten him! In war, she'd triumphed over Typhon and his allies. But outside of battle, why did he always defeat her?

"My offspring still hasn't acknowledged you. You'll always be an outsider." Typhon grinned. Terra's heart ached. He always knew exactly what to say to torment her. He was able to spear her with every insecurity she'd tucked deep down.

"And that failure of a man who dares to call himself your husband… he doesn't even know what you really are. Surely, he'd flee in terror if he did. His love would evaporate and be displaced by disgust and fear. He is only a man, after all. He can't handle all of you. Only I can appreciate your true beauty." Typhon smiled. Terra at once grabbed Typhon by his throat and held him aloft.

"When you finally get bored of playing house with that fool, and you're ready for a real man… you know where you can find me." Typhon smiled.

But then Terra began crushing his neck! Typhon became exasperated as he continued choking. Terra squeezed so hard that her hand made a fist. But as the illusion faded, there was nothing there. She only heard Typhon's cackling echo in the silent night.

"Sorry, my dear. It isn't that easy. Unless you work up the resolve to actually come and kill me, your strength alone will never liberate your heart. Besides… I think there are others you need to put out of life first." Typhon's voice told her.

Terra had to ignore him. It was all in her head. But the snarls and roars of the beasts around her were not. After all, the real reason she had come to the Caucasus was not to feast with her old friends… but rather to put down the Monsters they had become after death.

When an Immortal god died, their remaining Power was reanimated into terrifying creatures that spread death and destruction wherever they went. Lacking any bodies of flesh and blood, Monsters existed only as raging infernos of Power given shape by a revenant will to consume more Power to maintain their existence. Stronger monsters could generate skeletons, scales, or armor made of Adamant that would crystalize in and around the Monster's flaming core to give them structure, weapons, and defenses.

Without a living form to contain their sacred heat, the beasts were constantly burning through that which maintained their existence after death: Power. Though they lacked sentience, basic survival instincts compelled them to venture ever onward to gain more Power to survive and escape a second death.

They ate humans to consume their Power, they hibernated in Adamant-rich regions to suck them dry of their Power, and if they became desperate enough, they'd even eat each other! With the Power of the gods, they once were behind them, Monsters could lay waste to entire worlds if left unchecked. It was an understood responsibility among Immortals to put down the Monsters their friends became before they could do harm to any of their loved ones. In that regard, Typhon had left Terra a lot of work.

Most people in Graia slept soundly. They were blissfully unaware of how close to Kosmic collapse their world really was. Fittingly, there weren't many bodies working the graveyard shift of hunting the undead. Sometimes it really did feel like Terra was the only thing keeping disaster at bay. If this army of the undead ever reached civilization, it was all over.

The over one hundred divine beasts surrounded the tiny goddess, far more powerful than they had ever been in life. The time for daydreaming was over: this was going to be a long fight.

Terra fought them all off with her bare hands, but at first struggled to punch through their thick Adamant armor.

"What is this!? Such foes should be beneath you. You've gotten much weaker since the war. Why do you restrain yourself so?" Typhon's voice echoed in her mind.

Terra tried to ignore him as she got out of a dire ambush from multiple enemies at once. To delete monsters of this strength, she needed to first puncture the armor that kept her powers out.

"If you still had the Sword of Dehmos, this would be child's play. I hate to see you in this pathetic state, my dear." Typhon's mental monologue continued.

Terra dodged past a Monster's claws before unleashing a barrage of punches on it that cracked its armor but did little more. The Goddess grew frustrated and had to leap back to avoid another attack.

"I've been defeated, so destroying your own weapon isn't keeping it out of my hands. Unless… are you also afraid of it being in yours?" Typhon continued his annoying commentary and broke Terra's focus.

"Shut up!" Terra screamed before punching that same Monster so hard that it shattered and was deleted from existence.

"That's more like it. Let loose!" Typhon grinned.

The other creatures recoiled in horror. They were supposed to be the Monsters… but Terra was the one scaring them. Behind her, a portal was sliced open in the sky, and the Goddess turned to face her foes, backlit by the Sacred Sapphire Sphere.

In a final desperate charge, the Monsters attacked her with all they had. Though, as mighty as those Monsters were, the ones that bore fangs at god would not triumph. Terra destroyed them utterly and left nothing but their bones to litter the arena.

Terra Solaris was all but invincible. In battle, she was without peer. But her Achilles heel was her heart. Not the physical organ that pumped blood… but rather her vulnerable feelings and psyche. Terra had that one weakness that her otherwise invincible nature could not defend.

"You know what your weakness is… gouge it out and throw it away. What's the point of holding onto such trivial things when all they do is bring you pain? You're holding yourself back… it's so much easier to just… give in." The voice of Typhon still refused to leave her.

Those demons within weren't the type of thing that could just be punched away. And those that absolute power corrupted had it easy by comparison. A perfect being that retained a good heart and had all that Power had to take responsibility for all the evils of the world. If they had the power to stop something and didn't… it had to be their fault. To Terra, all the world's evil was her evil.

It was so exhausting. Respecting free will while also punishing evil just meant that, in the meantime, the innocent would suffer. Even with unlimited power, there was no winning. Remaining uncorrupted meant not positioning oneself above the laws of others. But if those laws were themselves corrupted and evil… did not breaking them mean complicity? Was it worth risking the corruption of unaccountability if the law was truly heinous enough? It was such a pain.

Standing over the broken and dead skeletons of the defeated Monsters, Terra trembled. Maybe… Typhon was right. In her moment of desperation, she clutched the diamond necklace her beloved had made for her.

"Terra?" a gentler man's voice asked.

Turning around, the dark misery she was steeped in was pierced by the radiant grin of the Graiac god of the dead. Ironically, the lord of the dead was what brought light to her life now. It was Hades, her dear husband. When he was around, she didn't have to worry about any of the hateful voices in her head.

The voice of Typhon hissed in disapproval but was nonetheless driven from her presence. Terra gave Hades a giant hug and let it all out.

"So, even though you don't sleep, you can dream? Seems kind of dangerous," Hades said.

"Yeah. But most of them are more like nightmares than dreams." Terra sighed, which made Hades look with concern.

"Not this, though. It's good to see you again." Terra grinned as he wiped her tears.

"Of course, this is a dream too." Hades pointed out.

"I know. But I don't want it to end. I miss you." Terra admitted as she more tightly embraced the figment of her delusion.

"You know, it's sad that a lot of your friends are gone. I lost a lot of people to the Titans, too. But you don't have to be alone. You have a place to go, Terra." Hades began.

Terra looked up at him and all the people of the Land of Hades. All the friends and connections she made were right there.

"We'll all be waiting for you, Terra. The eight months are almost up, and we can't wait for you to come home," All her dear friends told her. Of course, Terra had a place to go. Hades was literally the man of her dreams now.

TALE 10

Home is where the Heart is

Terra, as the Goddess of the World, could not neglect her namesake. For two-thirds of the year, she was abroad, always traveling the stars and maintaining Kosmic order as she helped those in need.

After two-thirds of the year being away, she could finally return home to the land of Hades. Yes, Hades was the name of the country and the man who had founded the country. He didn't pick that name; rather, it had been put to a vote in the country's first Assembly meeting. After all, he had succeeded in founding the first democracy just as he envisioned it.

As the new land's founder, he had made the radical decision not to rule as a king. In the land of Hades, there was no king at all. There was no nobility and no rank conferred upon people by birthright. There were no rulers or subjects, just people. All adult citizens in the land of Hades were members of the Assembly: a citizen government that met in weekly meetings to discuss and vote on the community's problems. The Assembly ruled not by divine right but by popular will.

For more complicated or ongoing tasks, the Assembly would elect committees. That way, people had direct control over the affairs of their city while still having plenty of time to live their lives.

This new system wasn't perfect, but as a nation that prided itself on becoming an ever more perfect union, Hades' project was bound to progress and improve with time. Terra couldn't wait to get back to this little pet project of theirs. As a master of all skills, she instantly teleported herself to the land of Hades the second her eight months were up.

At once, she stood before the grand palace of Hades. The large and majestic palace was a rival for Olympus. Hestia, the goddess of the home, designed it herself.

While the beauty of Hades' palace matched Olympus, that beauty was of a different kind. Where Olympus was pristine and untouched, more like an exhibit than a house, the palace was much more homely and welcoming. After all, Hades wasn't the only one who lived there.

Hades' palace had many rooms to be filled with guests. Anyone who wanted to live in the palace could reside in one of the many guest rooms. The only catch was that everyone had to contribute to the maintenance of their big, shared home.

Tasks and chores were given out to the residents to keep their shared home homely in the absence of palace servants. This was the cooperative housing system they had arrived at. Hades thought the system worked out pretty well, and Terra loved getting to meet all the new people.

On that day, the crowded palace was even more crowded than usual. Massive preparations were underway for the festival celebrating her return. The entire land would be throwing a party to formally welcome her back to the land of Hades in their national festival: the Cornucopia! As the founding goddess of their nation, Terra was the greatest divinity in the land. Honestly, it made her a bit uneasy to be held in such high regard.

Nonetheless, she respected their efforts and played along with the festivities. More important than exalting her, Terra saw the value of social cohesion and fun that came from time for the community to get together and be merry.

People from all the cities across the land would gather in the capital for the grand event. The majestic palace sat at the heart of a floating capital city that hovered above a massive lake. The lake was fed by great waterfalls that the waters of the great rivers Styx, Phlegethon, Lethe, Acheron, and Cocytus flowed into. Mixing together, the five waters encircled Hades and kicked up the great mist the city became known for.

On the cliffs around the great falls were yet more human settlements that existed as outgrowths of the floating capital. One could still reach the floating city via any of the four great bridges that each led into it from each cardinal direction.

The city and palace were made in the typical Graiac style but with none of the gaudy glitter and gold that so thoroughly coated Olympus that it bordered on being visually offensive.

Beyond the city, a beautiful natural vista of fertile farmlands surrounded the city and kept its many residents well fed. Most of the land in Graiac Poleis was farmland anyways, with only about a tenth of the central area being for residential, metropolitan purposes.

Most poleis had wealth concentrated around a central palace, with prosperity decreasing the further out one got towards the rural farms. Yet, in the land of Hades, the diversity of architecture and style denoted local tastes rather than wealth, for in the land of Hades all knew prosperity. After all, it was a land designed with those farmers in mind.

Beyond the farms were ore-rich mounts, crystal clear waters, and yet unsettled continents abounding with further fertility and abundance. It was a paradise brought to life. As beautiful as the shining city was, some argued that the land itself was even more so. Honestly, it was some of Terra's best work.

Since the festival largely involved the people thanking her for all that, she humored them and played the part of the goddess in the event. It was one of the few times a year that Terra wore any elaborate dresses or decorative paraphernalia. She was more frequently seen in her warrior's armor or casual dress. But for that one day a year, she looked the part of a high goddess befitting her status as Zeus' female counterpart.

It was the one day a year when she was not just another member of the community (as Terra had asked them to treat her) she was their goddess. Terra was the sacred queen of the gods, the protectress of humanity, and the mother of nature. A year's worth of ritual and praise was compacted into a single day. It was exhausting.

The entire time, Terra yearned to be with her husband, who was so busy helping plan the festivities that she'd hardly seen him. It was a big event and the culmination of all their efforts. After all, this was the first anniversary of the land of Hades.

As the late night stretched into the early morning, Terra finally wrapped up all her ritualistic duties. Walking the halls of the palace, she heard voices coming from the kitchen and went to take a look.

Hades was in the kitchen with has adopted daughter Cerberus. The only reason he agreed to let her be up at that hour was because she helped with the festivities earlier and so earned a reward.

"Papa! One smart fellow, he felt smart!" Cerberus cried. Hades was silent a moment. He looked at his daughter in complete confusion. Was she expecting some sort of reply? Was that a coded message? He had no idea how to respond.

"Very good, Cerberus," was the response he decided on, just to be safe.

"No! Say it, papa. Say it!" Cerberus cried.

"You want me to say what? What was that again?" Hades asked.

"One smart fellow, he felt smart! One smart fellow, he felt smart! One smart fellow, he felt smart!" Cerberus repeated rapidly. Hades paused. This was obviously some kind of trap. He was one of the foremost tactical geniuses of the Olympian army who had impressed Terra herself. There was no way he was going to lose to an elementary schooler after that.

"Let's just decide on your midnight snack so we can get you to bed." Hades refused to engage.

"You can try to act all calm and collective, but you know you're just too chicken to try it!" Cerberus confidently misspoke.

"Collected," Hades corrected.

"What'd I say?" Cerberus asked.

"Collective. You said calm and collective, but the correct word is collected." Hades pointed out to try and educate her. Cerberus paused for a moment, considering how to react.

"No! It's collective!" Cerberus decided to be a contrarian. Hades knew she was just trying to start an argument now.

"Come on, Hades. You were the one who said correct language is whatever people' consensus is." Terra laughed as she entered the kitchen.

"Don't give her ammunition, she's going to repeat that now." Hades smiled to see her enter.

"Terra!" Cerberus cheered as she ran over and gave Terra a big hug.

The goddess bent down and hugged the pup back. Cerberus was an odd child: she had a set of dog ears on top of her head as well as human ears in the normal spot. Most people assumed she was just some kind of half-human, half-animal race of being like the centaurs, satyrs, or mermaids.

Terra liked Cerberus. She was a cute kid. There was the matter of her being Typhon's biological daughter, but she was a cute kid. When Hades first introduced the two, Terra instantly recognized Typhon's evolved DNA in the child. How was she able to examine the girl's DNA? Simple: she squinted.

Hades said he'd found an egg while he was out hunting Monsters, and Cerberus hatched out of it. That was odd: Terra knew that Typhon had evolved his body to go beyond human limits… but as far as she knew, he didn't lay eggs. She must've had an odd birth mother as well. Either way, none of that mattered. Terra didn't believe in punishing people for the sins of their parents. Cerberus was Hades' daughter, and that was that.

"You've gotten so much bigger in the last year alone," Terra excitedly told her.

"Yeah, just wait, Terra! I'm going to be taller than you are soon," Cerberus proudly declared.

"I'm looking forward to it." Terra smiled back.

"Oh yeah! While you were out, did you find any more clues about where my mom is?" Cerberus asked. There it was.

"Nope. Nothing still. But I promise, I'll keep looking," Terra reassured Cerberus with a smile. Hades could tell it was one of those smiles she forced.

"We missed you, Terra. It's great to see you again." Hades smiled genuinely. Hades went in for a hug, but to his surprise, she pulled him in for a kiss instead. Cerberus childishly covered her eyes to avoid the yucky grownup display, but Hades wasn't complaining.

"Papa, enough kissing! I'm still hungry!" Cerberus interrupted them.

"You're always hungry." Hades pointed out.

Terra couldn't help but laugh. When she was with them, her heart was warmed, and her soul was restored. With Hades, she was home. Not everything needed to be a grand adventure or legendary exploit. So, as the sun was rising, their first mission of the day was to cook up breakfast… before finally putting Cerberus to bed.

In ancient Graia, breakfast was a meal for the working poor and the warrior. Those who could afford to sleep in did so. For the others who ate it, breakfast was not a relaxing start to their day. It was the way to survive the morning. Hades and Cerberus used to have minimal breakfasts before heading out to go Monster hunting. They would eat on the go, just as Hades had learned from his time in the Olympian army.

Now, in the gigantic palace pantry, they had all sorts of food in stock. The trio huddled up and made their game plan. Cerberus wanted the Graiac breakfast known as Tiganites, a primitive form of pancake eaten with fruit or honey.

Even though he wasn't the best at it, Hades liked cooking because he was tangibly helping anyone who he helped feed. Terra liked cooking because it was structured, formula-based, and easily processed. Cerberus liked eating.

Terra led the other two in taking the dough and measuring it out. Terra, of course, had perfect mechanical accuracy, and each cake was perfectly equal in size and weight. Hades was pretty good at executing his orders and poured out each cake decently well.

Cerberus, by contrast, was dumping as much dough onto the stove as possible to make giant ones for herself. Her father tried explaining that whether she made ten small ones or one big one, it was all the same, but Cerberus was convinced that he was just trying to trick her so he could get more.

They fried the cakes made in pans to perfection, and Terra added the finishing touch, pouring out the condiment of choice: honey. With the meal completed, the three sat down and enjoyed the fruits of their labor.

Cerberus finished her share… and Terra's. Terra never ate, so it was fine. That was just another one of her weird quirks. She had intended for Hades to get some as well, but she could never say no to the little girl's puppy dog eyes. The problem came when Cerberus went on to try and haggle with Hades for his portion, too.

Despite a few tempting offers, Hades still wanted to eat his breakfast. The immortal gods didn't need food to survive, but they did still get hungry.

After enjoying their meal, Hades had to go and get ready for work. The Assembly had elected him the head of the labor credits feedback committee. Labor credits, Hades' prototype replacement currency for the drachma, had many odd quirks. One of which was the fact that they expired at the end of the year. The gift-giving festivities of the Cornucopia season were partially invented to deal with the rush to spend remaining credits at year's end but had produced several unintended consequences.

Hades oversaw analyzing the shortcomings of this prototype as well as preparing for their replacement with the new Power-based non-physical currency they would try next. Terra had invented an Adamant, Power-based device that could allow for labor-credit transactions while automating all the time-consuming and fallible paperwork that caused the land of Hades so much headache. However, she had done enough: Hades would take charge of the actual implementation of this alien technology.

"You seem overwhelmed with committee work this week. I'd be happy to help out—" Terra compulsively offered as she saw him getting ready for work.

"What makes you say I'm overwhelmed? Are you reading my heart rate again?" Hades asked.

"No, you fiddle with your hands when you're nervous." Terra pointed, making Hades stop in embarrassment.

"It's cute." Terra smiled genuinely.

"Either way, no need to worry. I'm just a bit excited because I'm nearing the end of the assignment. After that wraps up, I'll be freed up to relax with you and Cerberus. Just consider today your head start for resting." Hades couldn't help but smile back.

As Hades prepared to leave, Cerberus ran off to cause more mischief (since the land's public school was canceled for the week of Cornucopia), and Terra was left to do… well, she hadn't figured that out. It wasn't that she didn't have work to do; god, the work never ended… but she had been asked to take a break.

It wasn't much of an exaggeration to say that the community had an intervention for Terra. As laughable as it sounds, regular people convinced a god to take some time off. They were worried about Terra. The Assembly went so far as to appoint Hades, her husband, as an officer in charge of monitoring her.

These reactions seemed extreme, but drastic times called for drastic measures. A person could not last working 24 hours for a hundred years. Terra was supposed to take that time for herself, no more cheeky workarounds or loopholes. That meant no volunteering at the school or, in the kitchen, or on the farms. That meant no sneaking off to do leftover work abroad while nobody was looking. That meant actually taking time to enjoy her life for its own sake. They were desperately trying to avoid a repeat of last year.

In Zeus' world, Terra's drive to give all of herself for others was admirable; not for the altruism of helping others but rather because it allowed rulers to compel their servants to work harder for less pay. The idea of working tirelessly and freely, of course, had an appeal to those who lorded over such workers. Not to mention the idea of the "ideal woman" living a life entirely based on serving others also had its uses for Zeus and his ilk.

Nevertheless, again, Terra deferred to the will of others. If they so desperately wanted her to take time to herself, she had to oblige. But then… the question remained; what was she to do? She could just sit there, stewing in bad memories and painful regrets; but she could do that any time. A hundred years was a long time to let those feelings of hatred spiral; especially with Zeus' guiding hand. No, Terra had to find something to do.

That wasn't to say she didn't have anything she liked to do with her time. Terra had tons of hobbies and things she enjoyed, even outside of helping people. Terra loved gardening, she loved tending to animals, she loved planning and hosting events. Terra loved just being in town and being among people; she loved to catch up with all the land's inhabitants whom she knew by name, and she liked to hear what they were thinking about. Terra loved consuming human art and expression: appreciating sculptures and frescoes, plays, and athletics were fascinating to her. She loved philosophizing with those who would pass by the agora, just as was a popular pastime of wise men in those days.

Anything productive that didn't require Power was right up her alley. Especially if it involved creation or a better understanding of the human heart, she loved it all just as she loved all the people of the world. She just hated herself. And the stupid, endless pity party that this entailed made it so that she felt guilty whenever she did them. At the back of her mind, work continued to nag at her.

Do some gardening, watch a play, and hang out with Cerberus. She could, in theory, do whatever she wanted. But what did she want? Terra didn't allow herself to want; greed plus power was not a good combination.

"You helped me kill them. My Goddess, your Power is meant only for death. Succumb to desire and become the Titaness I've always imagined." Typhon hissed in one ear.

"Your powers are meant to hold up my world order. Every moment you waste is a moment countless innocents suffer and die. Forgo humanity and remain the goddess I know you are," Jupiter whispered in the other.

After the war, Terra only used her Power for others. If she used it for herself, she risked becoming one of the very tyrants she tried to stop. Even now, she was using her Power as a tool for Hades. No, it was worse: she was using him. Because their goals aligned, she could delude herself into thinking she was doing him a favor when, really, she was using him as a cover to pursue her own wishes selfishly!

"I love you, Terra." Hades casually waved as he was leaving for his work.

That was enough to snap Terra out of it. While her mind was going a mile a minute on such things, Hades still hadn't left yet. He was still there for her. All that darkness in her mind was instantly cleared away by that anchoring beacon in the real world. That four-word phrase was more powerful than any attack the Kosmos had ever seen.

"You once told me to do what you can, when you can, where you can *for as long as you can*," Hades emphasized that last part for Terra. "Burning yourself out doesn't help anyone."

"Remember… you need to rest and enjoy yourself too. There's no need to put the weight of the Kosmos on your shoulders, Terra. You don't have to be the one who does everything. All you have to be is yourself." Hades smiled at his wife. Terra genuinely smiled back; her heart was warmed by his words. They were exactly what she needed to hear.

TALE 11

Chthonic Deities

Many years ago, even before the rise of the Titans: Hades was working as a Monster hunter. Honoring the common pact among immortals to put down the Monsters they became in death, Hades went far and wide attending to the walking dead. For his many feats in this regard, he earned his position as god of the dead.

It had come to pass that a certain Monster had been wreaking havoc throughout Graia. Many Monster hunters had tried and failed to kill it. With each victory, the beast feasted on their Power and grew stronger and stronger. Thus, even though it was out of his usual region, Hades took it upon himself to finally vanquish this foe.

This beast was known for its frightening skeletal appearance and oddly developed combat abilities. At the time, many theorized that the Monster had been a great warrior in life. Later theorists suggested that it may have been a powerful deity who was among the first of Typhon's victims.

Nonetheless, Hades was prepared. As soon as he arrived in the region where the beast was last sighted, Hades transformed into his gigantic Monster form to fight his prey on even footing. Stomping around and looking for a fight, Hades was tense.

Then, Hades noticed that something was following him. It seemed the hunter had become the hunted, and Hades would not stand for it! After pretending not to notice his pursuer, Hades turned around and got the jump on his foe!

Hades, in his beast form, came face to face with a powerful monster: a gigantic skeleton clothed in a cloak of darkness that wielded a massive scythe! Hades generated a gigantic Adamant bident for his Monster form to wield. The monstrous weapons of the two clashed with terrifying force.

Hades' bident attacks were ineffective against the incorporeal cloak of the reaper. Likewise, the reaper's swirling swings of the scythe were inconsequential against Hades' invulnerable Adamant armor.

Neither beast could harm the other when suddenly a gigantic blast of Power hit the two of them while they were off guard. Hades was knocked over and barely conscious after that. Both Monsters looked up where a third creature hovered above with more blasts of Power ready to fire.

"Well, well, well… a two for one! Who would've guessed there were two skeleton Monsters for me to hunt." The three-headed witch creature cackled maniacally.

"That's my line! I'm not a Monster! I'm a human!" Hades cried. However, to his shock, he heard the exact same thing from the scythe-wielding Monster he was fighting.

"You can talk!?" the two cried as they looked at each other in utter confusion. Now, the three talking Monsters began to bicker and accuse each other of being the Monster they had come to hunt.

As the three Monster hunters bickered amongst themselves, little did they know that a massive skeletal Monster was stalking and hunting them!

It struck, but all three hunters reacted just in time and attacked in unison! They defeated the Monster and split the spoils between the three of them.

"And, since I got the last hit in, I technically won the entire battle," the witch Hecate, who was now Hades' good friend, finished recounting the tale in Hades' living room.

"Give it a rest, Hecate. Stealing the kill after I'd worn it down isn't something to brag about." The scythe-wielding Thanatos sighed.

"Aha! But you do not deny I killed it. Hades, back me up! I remembered it all perfectly." Hecate chuckled.

"I'll admit, you managed to stay shockingly accurate in this retelling. For once." Hades sighed, almost identically to Thanatos.

Hecate and Thanatos were among Hades' oldest (and only) friends. They were also the goddess of magic and god of death, respectively. Terra had met Hecate a few times in the past, but this was her first time meeting Thanatos. Everyone had a good laugh at the wacky Hecate's antics, but little Cerberus was confused about something.

"Aunty Hecate, in your story… how did you know about the parts you weren't there for?" Cerberus pointed out as she sat in Hecate's lap. The room went dead silent.

"Anyways, Hades, if I haven't said it before, a huge congratulations for actually managing to get with Terra. Who would've guessed your little wartime crush would pay off? Every time I visit, I still can't believe it." Hecate quickly changed the subject.

It was true Hades had a crush on Terra since not long after their first meeting during the war. Terra had saved his life many times on the battlefield. Like a stereotypical damsel in distress falling for the handsome prince who saved them, it was undeniable that the good old-fashioned suspension bridge effect sparked some of Hades' crush.

Many wartime crushes and couples began this way. The racing of one's heart caused by the stress and fear felt by those on the battlefield could easily be misconstrued as romantic arousal. Though, in this case, the word "misconstrued" may be incorrect. To Hades, Terra was legitimately the most beautiful woman he'd ever laid eyes on. In these types of stories, the handsome prince was generally still handsome after all. Rather than the stress being misconstrued as attraction, it was more accurate to say that those emotions... enhanced his feelings toward Terra. But through their friendship, their relationship became so much more.

"Well, it's kind of a long story, but..." Hades began. As all those fond memories came rushing back to him, he struggled to think of how to tell the tale properly.

"Wait! I've got this one, papa. I'll handle this." Cerberus confidently stepped up to play the role of storyteller.

Cerberus told the story of Hades and Terra up until now. However, it was extremely inaccurate and childish (most of it went over her head). Everyone looked skeptical as they noticed that even she was laughing at her own retelling.

"What? Don't believe me? Well, do!" Cerberus commanded her audience. She got a few chuckles out of that before continuing her retelling. In Cerberus' telling, Hades kidnapped Terra, and he had to insist that he didn't kidnap her repeatedly.

"I can't picture Hades doing that," Thanatos noted the implausibility.

"Hmph. Sounds like a skill issue. Don't bring down my story just because you lack *image-nation,*" Cerberus mispronounced as she scoffed at him.

Before Hades could interject, Cerberus got into how Hades would neglect her whenever the two had a date night. Worse yet, Cerberus had been made to do all the dishes afterward while Hades got all "kissy-kissy" with Terra.

"Hades, being a good father to your daughter is more important than putting the moves on your girlfriend." Hecate shook her head disapprovingly.

"First of all, she is my wife. Secondly, Cerberus is the one telling the story! Obviously, she's not a reliable narrator. Cerberus had to do the dishes because she pretended to be our waiter so she could eat the food that our neighbors were kindly bringing us for the date!" Hades pointed accusingly.

"Prove it." Cerberus put her hands on her hips.

"Besides, more importantly, as I've had to repeatedly say: I did not kidnap Terra. She came willingly," Hades cried. Thanatos and Hecate looked at each other and then at Cerberus.

"Fellas. Look at Terra again and then really consider, who's a more believable narrator?" Cerberus mischievously grinned.

"Cerberus! Lying isn't funny." Hades became genuinely panicked when his old friends began to glare at him with suspicion.

"It's only lying if you get caught." Cerberus winked (though she always winked with both eyes, thus blinking).

"But Cerberus… how did you know about the parts you weren't there for?" Terra asked.

"I made it up! I also made up the parts I was there for but still don't fully remember!" Cerberus shamelessly announced to the amusement of the adults.

"At least she's more honest than Hecate," Thanatos smirked.

"You endorsed my retelling. No backsies." Hecate turned to him.

Terra was excited to get to meet more of Hades' friends. They'd come to see Hades and were stunned by all that had happened. After inviting them into their home for dinner, Terra felt she got a pretty good feel for them.

After Cerberus went to bed, the divine quartet got the drinks out to celebrate their overdue reunion. Thanatos and Hecate were, after all, the closest thing that Hades had to family. Gods sometimes went decades without reuniting because with their long lives, it didn't matter. Thanatos was known for sometimes disappearing for half a decade at a time before just popping back in as if nothing had happened.

"C'mon! We've got to make this a party!!!" Hecate cried noisily.

"No, Hecate, you'll wake the neighbors." Hades reminded her that he wasn't the only one living in the palace.

"Fair enough. Arrow dodged, honestly. Have either of you ever seen Thanatos try to dance? It's even more frightening than he is normally!" Hecate laughed.

"Why did I even bother spending my night coming here to get mocked by Hecate? Being the god of death doesn't afford me much free time, you know." Thanatos sighed.

"That reminds me. Thanatos, your name means death. How can you also be the god of the dead when Hades already is?" Terra asked.

"God of death! Not god of the dead!" Thanatos and Hades cried in unison.

"Here we go." Hecate groaned.

In great and excruciating detail, Hades and Thanatos laid out how "completely different" their divine titles were.

Hades was the god of the dead, while Thanatos was the god of death. Sound confusing? It was, even after the endless insistence to the contrary by the two.

"These are the people I've been stuck with." Hecate sighed. She'd gotten bored listening to the two talking about how extremely different their titles were. In her boredom, Hecate began to create Adamant in the palm of her hand and shape it into various forms for amusement.

"Interesting ability. How did you learn to manipulate Adamant like that?" Terra asked after quickly losing interest in the boys' rambling, "I've been all over this kosmos, but your abilities are still an impressive rarity. Even centaurs, nymphs, and mermaids who have Adamant on their bodies lack the level of control that you three have displayed."

"I just figured it out by messing around," Hecate admitted.

"Mine just came to me during training." Thanatos shrugged.

"My ability just manifested in a life-or-death situation when I was younger." Hades explained.

Odd. The three didn't even have any animal or plant features like the aforementioned groups. Even Cerberus was less odd than this trio.

"We aren't like those other groups. I have a theory…" Hecate grinned at Terra's interest.

"Here we go." It was Hades and Thanatos' turn to roll their eyes.

"Here's my theory for what I like to call 'chthonic beings'. So, we all know that when Immortals die, they become Monsters. Yet even the first generation of Immortals remembers Monsters showing up very quickly. The first generation of Monsters were extremely powerful and, though fewer in numbers, were quite the menace. That's why I think that many of the most powerful Immortals wiped themselves out with their awesome powers shortly after they came into existence," Hecate explained.

"The more powerful beings that could not control themselves died and became that first generation of Monsters. The extremely powerful Immortals that survived this process became unopposed godlike warriors such as Typhon. So, the strongest either died and became the first monsters or lived and became leaders of their region as gods. But there was also a third group." Hecate cackled mischievously.

"I hypothesize that if an Immortal nearly died as they came into being, they would develop some Monstrous characteristics while keeping their lives. Being on the brink of death, these chthonic beings came back and kept the gifts normally reserved for the afterlife. That might explain why Hades, Thanatos, and I are so powerful compared to the average Immortal and have power over Adamant while still alive." Hecate concluded her lecture.

"How did all those first Immortals accidentally kill themselves? If they were the first Monsters, nothing else in the Kosmos would be strong enough to," Hades asked.

"What almost killed the Chthonic beings, and how did we supposedly come back? Why was this process exclusive to initial near-death experiences and not still observed in Immortals today?" Thanatos asked.

"Listen, I haven't figured everything out, but what I have is a start. I'm a monstrologist who studied Monsters and compares their features to our own and those of still-living Immortals. By identifying the differences and similarities, I can uncover how exactly we Chthonics got like this." Hecate countered.

"Amazing! There must be others like you, then! What fascinating sources of untapped data!" Terra giddily cheered.

Now Hades, Thanatos, and Hecate got to look at Terra as the odd one. "Sorry for getting distracted like that. Let's get to know each other better as people and leave the theorizing for another time." Terra nervously laughed as she noticed the strange looks, "After all, you are human beings not lab subjects."

"We know we are, but can we be sure about you?" Thanatos became serious as things became a bit tense.

"I'll be honest: I've always been suspicious of you and your family. I've seen members of the Solaris clan walk off what would kill even Immortal gods. Just like Typhon. You reminded me a lot of Typhon… as if you aren't even human," Thanatos said ominously.

Terra froze up at the accusation. For some reason, she remembered a question Typhon had once asked her.

"Thanatos, stop. You're making Terra uncomfortable." Hades stepped up.

"No, it's fine. This isn't the first time I've been asked that question. However, I can reassure you that despite all his unusual Powers, Typhon was indeed a human, just like you," Terra replied.

"Interesting answer." Thanatos became even more suspicious.

"I've also heard you have power over the minds of mankind; that you can bend us to your will… so you'll forgive my concern for Hades." Thanatos pushed further.

"I… I would never—" an exasperated Terra began.

"As his friend, I have to wonder if all his feelings for you are truly his own," Thanatos said.

"Thanatos!" Hades cried.

"Come on, Than. I thought that I was supposed to be the crazy one." Hecate broke up the tense situation with some levity, "She looks like her sister Venus; you don't have to be Athena to figure out why he likes her."

Hades blushed in embarrassment and nervously laughed as Terra smiled. Thanatos wanted to probe further but took Hecate's hint and backed off for now.

"The thing that I'm more curious about is, what made the highest of the goddesses fall for Hades of all people? For real this time, you've gotta tell us the secret?" Hecate interrupted, much to Hades' surprise.

"Of course." Terra smiled without hesitation.

Hades had his head in his hands with total embarrassment as Terra listed off all the fond memories that made her love him. Hecate was barely holding in laughter as she and Thanatos watched Hades' utter embarrassment.

So, things returned to their lax and festive attitudes. There were many tales and jokes to be shared, and the mystery of Terra was all but forgotten about.

Hecate and Thanatos stayed in guest rooms of the palace for the night, but the next day, the two got moved in as citizens of the community. Hecate became chief scientist, and Thanatos took over Monster defenses.

TALE 12

Terra Mater

Back when Terra and Hades were early in their romantic relationship, it was decided that Terra should finally meet Cerberus. Hades felt somewhat nervous about it, but Terra was excited. With the land of Hades nearly completed, the two would be moving in together there, and so it only made sense for Cerberus to become better acquainted with her.

"I'm so excited to finally meet the little angel I've heard so much about." Terra smiled.

"Little goblin is probably more accurate." Hades sighed.

While they had gone to do final checks on the palace to ensure it was ready to move into, Cerberus was tasked with beginning to pack what few possessions she and Hades had in their humble shack. Of course, when Hades and Terra arrived, Cerberus had a million and one excuses about how she was getting to it, but then she finally noticed Terra staring down adoringly at her.

"Papa, who is this pretty lady?" Cerberus turned to Hades and whispered extremely loudly.

"This is Terra, the goddess of nature and my fiancée. So, mind your manners," he awkwardly introduced the waving goddess. Cerberus' jaw hung open for a second.

"What? Why are you looking like that?" Hades smelled her mischief from a mile away.

"...did you kidnap her?" Cerberus looked at him skeptically.

"What!?" Hades panicked.

"She's way out of your league. Did you kidnap her?" the little goblin repeated.

"I did not kidnap her!" Hades cried. Terra burst out laughing.

"Sorry about her, kids say the strangest things... I swear, she's been spending too much time with Hecate." Hades panicked about this fumbled introduction.

"No, he didn't kidnap me. We decided that we were going to be husband and wife soon, so I was very excited to come and meet you." Terra bent down to talk to Cerberus at eye level.

"I see. Miss Terra... blink twice if he kidnapped you," Cerberus rather loudly whispered again.

A few years later, the trio was on their way to bring Hecate some housewarming gifts after she finished moving into their land. Hecate's witch hut was in the enchanted forest, an otherwise uninhabited wood at the edge of the wilderness.

Cerberus was happily skipping along to "Aunty Hecate's house." As the trio walked, scary noises and creatures filled the woods. Hecate had used her illusionary powers to make it seem enchanted and haunted, much to Hades' annoyance.

"If anyone else wants to move out here, she's going to have to take all this down." Hades grumbled after the fifteenth jump scare around a corner.

Cerberus was scared but excited by the haunted illusions. It was like they were on an adventure! Terra was horribly confused by their reactions since she was immune to any Power-based illusions that afflicted them. She felt a bit left out of the primitive haunted house experience they had. Finally, after following the correct path into the heart of the forest, they found a small witch's hut.

"Welcome…" Hecate playfully cackled as she opened the door for them. All the spooky decorations on her house activated to make her appear as ominous as possible. Hades rolled his eyes, but Cerberus thought it was cool. Terra could only see about half of them.

They all presented Hecate with their housewarming gifts. After letting them in, Hecate did magic tricks for Cerberus, which her goddaughter was always amazed by. Again, Terra was immune to her illusions and sleight of hand. Upon noticing this, Hecate was convinced to perform a magic trick that even Terra couldn't explain or see through. She could not.

But more important than that, during the visit, Terra did notice the natural rapport and bond between Hecate and Cerberus. It was almost as if they were mother and daughter. Terra couldn't help but feel a certain way about it. So, when Hades realized they'd stayed past Cerberus' bedtime, he dragged the little gremlin home to bed, but Terra remained behind. Hecate brewed tea for them, but Terra politely refused since she didn't drink.

"I see. Well, my magic rival, what was it you wanted to chat about?" Hecate playfully asked while reclining on her over-the-top monster sofa.

"I just… I've been with Hades for a while now, and I've been around Cerberus for a while now. I just feel like there's still some distance between us. I don't know if I'm being entitled, expecting her to treat me a certain way, but… I was hoping you could tell me how to get closer to her, and even if we can't be mother and daughter, at least have something like what you two have," Terra explained. Hecate, upon seeing Terra's genuine desire, dropped the silliness and engaged with her realistically.

"Listen, I'm going for the wacky aunt thing, not trying to steal your motherly role. I'm hardly the homemaker Zeus' world wants. I mean, I've never been into the whole sex thing from the start." Hecate shrugged.

"Oh, neat. You too?" the virgin goddess cheered at the discovery of a fellow asexual in the wild.

"You'd think it was a job requirement for the goddess of fertility and motherhood to have biological children..." Hecate noted.

"You'd think so. I've also been the goddess of marriage forever despite now being a newlywed," Terra seconded.

"Odd. Back on topic, if Hades is like a brother to me, that makes Cerberus my niece, not my daughter. What you want isn't what we have," Hecate explained.

"Well, what kind of relationship should we have then?" Terra asked.

"That's something for you and her to find out. But the first step is getting to know her better. From what I've seen, she likes you well enough, but you're making a few key mistakes if you want to get even closer. Cerberus may be adorable, but you can't baby her. She is attached to the idea of being a big kid. Hades complains about what I teach her, but this one is his fault. He's taken the old-school stone age approach to raising kids. After all, it's the only thing he knows." Hecate explained.

Terra could see what she meant. As a first-generation Immortal, Hades was essentially raised by other kids his age. The immortals in the tribe that would have been assigned his parents would be equal to him in age and thus his peers rather than his seniors. Hades wasn't completely lacking in discipline; it was just Hades' approach favored a lax attitude towards signs of respect in favor of ensuring fundamental character building. Hades cared less about Cerberus having all the right manners to appear polite and more about Cerberus having the moral fiber to not be mean.

"Not that he knows any of this himself. As you can probably tell, that man's mind is great with systems and strategy but… subpar with people." Hecate snickered.

"Very insightful observations," Terra noted Hecate's rarely seen intelligent side.

"Start with things like that. Your role as the new parent in town will have to sync up with what Hades has already established. From there, you find out how to proceed. I'd suggest finding things in common you can bond over," Hecate explained.

"Thanks, Hecate, you're the best." Terra grinned.

"Now… in exchange, tell me how to do an illusion even you can't see through!" Hecate immediately went back to being goofy.

The next day, Terra reflected on what Hecate had told her. Conveniently, it was Terra's first day off, so she had plenty of time.

The plan was to use the time to get closer to Cerberus. Step one! While Cerberus was at school, Terra went about gathering intelligence on the citizens' favorite pastimes for children. Part B! Terra coordinated with Hades and promised to handle all his parent-related routines on top of her own. She'd handle everything for the day, from picking Cerberus up to putting her to bed. The overworked Committee member happily agreed. Phase 3… profit?

Terra was so used to dealing with kids communally, as one of those village-appointed same-age "parents" Hecate mentioned. However, that role was more akin to a teacher or daycare worker than a modern parent. Now that she'd seen Cerberus open up to adults other than Hades, she had to give it her all.

So, when the time came, Terra was off to pick Cerberus up from school. Outside the school building, Cerberus and several other kids were playing a ball game as they waited for their parents. It was a game from all the way back when Hades was a child and a sort of primitive version of rugby. Cerberus was way too far from the goal but confidently declared to everyone in attendance that she could make the shot anyways.

She took the shot and missed by a mile. When all eyes turned to her in a mix of amusement and ire from her teammates, Cerberus just posed confidently as if she had actually scored the points.

Terra thought it was adorable, but her teammates, who had just lost the match, were not as amused. Seeing their impending anger, Cerberus looked around for any escape. Then she saw Terra watching with a smile and ran over.

"I have to go now. Good luck winning without me." Cerberus saluted her teammates playfully before heading off with Terra. The two went inside to retrieve Cerberus' school things as Cerberus told Terra all about her winning performance in the after-school ballgame.

But as they were retrieving things, Terra noticed another parent had arrived to do the same and was scolding their child for playing alongside Cerberus.

"You've got your dress all dirty. That was not very ladylike. Sports are for boys, my dear, you should have stayed inside and waited for me. What would Terra think?" the mother scolded her daughter just as she had been in her youth. Terra frowned.

Such ingrained social views from Zeus' worldview, unfortunately, didn't go away instantly. Many people brought old-world ideas, such as classism, sexism, etc., with them when they came to the land of Hades. That was why educating the next generation was so important.

The thing that always got Terra personally was the fact that those espousing such things would always shame women by comparing them to the "ideal" goddess. Terra was very feminine, or rather, much of Graiac femininity was molded around pressuring other women to look and act exactly like Terra. It was infuriating! Just because Terra was like that didn't mean she wanted to force others into a mold of herself. Even concerning her very identity, the rulers abused Terra for their purposes.

"Cerberus… you know that you're your own person, and you don't have to do anything just because you are a girl or anything, right?" Terra asked.

"Of course! Don't worry, papa already told me all that stuff. All that is just Zeus's mean control!" Cerberus cheered. She meant "means of control."

"Instead of focusing on any of that, papa says that just being a good person is what matters most. No matter your rates, gender, or creaks." Cerberus did her best to repeat Hades' lesson.

"Of course, he did." Terra smiled, genuinely thinking about him. They were in the bronze age, but Hades had already championed such ideals. Terra couldn't help but find it refreshing and admirable to know someone so ahead of their time. As she thought fondly of her husband, Cerberus read her reaction and was shocked.

"Oh my gosh! You have a crush on Papa!" Cerberus cried as her young mind finally recognized Terra's reactions by cross-referencing them with the intricate politics of her elementary classroom crushes.

"I have a crush on Hades? Well, I certainly hope so. We've been married for a while, after all," Terra noted.

"I've heard that tons of people hate their husbands and wives." Cerberus offered this as if it were fun trivia.

The two dropped Cerberus' things off in the palace's royal master bedroom, which the girl had claimed for herself. Hades and Terra ended up in the princess room that was made for Cerberus. After unpacking, Cerberus prepared to run off for her usual antics, only for Terra to stop her.

"Cerberus… I was wondering if today, you wanted to do anything… together? Just the two of us?" Terra asked.

"Fighting!" Cerberus cheered. Terra deflated a bit.

"Papa says you're super strong, but I've never gotten to see it! He's always so busy, so we haven't been able to spar or train lately. Will you do it?" Cerberus asked.

"I dunno. Is there anything other than combat you wanted?" Terra nervously laughed.

"Pretty please, Terra." Cerberus coated her voice in honey.

"Why do you like fighting so much?" Terra asked.

"Because it's fun!" Cerberus grinned.

"I wish I could relate," Terra admitted.

"Why don't you like fighting?" Cerberus asked, "If you aren't having fun, couldn't you just pick a more fun fighting style?"

"I wish it was that simple." Terra sighed.

"But wait a minute… your job involves a lot of fighting, doesn't it? Wouldn't it be miserable to do all the time? For all those years?" Cerberus innocently asked. Terra burst out laughing. She was laughing so hard she was crying.

"You're a funny kid, you know that?" Terra said as she wiped her eyes.

"Of course I am!" Cerberus declared.

"But, if you don't want to fight, I guess I could always ask Aunty Hecate." Cerberus thought out loud.

"Alright, let's go sparring!" Terra immediately changed her tune. She'd planned out all those other activities, but if this was what Cerberus wanted, maybe it would be a good bonding experience. However, before they could head out, Terra remembered something.

"Do you have any homework today?" Terra asked.

"…what's homework?" Cerberus answered her question with a question.

TALE 13

Hades' Guard dog

On the road out of town, Cerberus playfully jumped and skipped from one odd stone marker to the other. Etched into the roads leading in and out of town, each step was a list of planned reforms and quality of life improvements the society was striving towards. The completed stones glowed, and the uncompleted ones were just stone. Quite literally, the road to Hades was paved with good intentions.

"So, what have you and Hades gone over in your training so far? You know the basics of using Power for movement and increasing your strength and speed?" Terra asked.

"Of course! I'm basically a fighting genius!" Cerberus boasted.

"I see, Hades must've trained you well." Terra smiled.

"Yeah! He's great… but don't tell him I said that. He might get an ego about it." Cerberus grinned.

"Papa is pretty cool and working hard on all this stuff to make life better. I just wish he'd remember that all this was to give people more free time, not less." Cerberus' dog ears drooped. Seeing her become sad, Terra stepped in.

"Tell you what! We'll train you up, and then when Hades is done with his work, we can surprise him with what you've learned." Terra cheered.

Cerberus agreed, and so the two were off to a nice lakeside clearing where nobody would be hurt. After all, there was no fighting using Power allowed within city limits or too close to the surrounding farms (except in cases of self-defense).

Once they arrived, Cerberus did some warmup stretches before releasing a burst of her Power to fight. Even though she was only a child, she was as powerful as some gods! As expected of the biological offspring of Typhon, she was about as strong as he was at that age. Seeing that, Terra hesitated. She saw it, a little boy ready to spar with her and grow stronger just as this girl was now. Was she… repeating the same mistake?

"Before anything else, Cerberus, I need you to tell me something. Why do you want to be strong?" Terra asked cautiously.

"Well, I can't beat up bad guys if I'm weak. Papa says there are a lot of bad guys out there. Most people can't use Power to protect themselves, so I've got to be strong enough to fight for them! I'll be just like you and Papa when I grow up." Cerberus declared with gusto.

Seeing the girl's genuine altruism, Terra couldn't help but smile. Even if Cerberus was the offspring of Typhon, she truly was Hades' daughter. Pleased by this answer, Terra finally assumed a boxing stance to begin the spar.

"Hold on! Where's that cool sword everyone always talks about? I want to fight you with that!" Cerberus cheered.

"Oh. I kind of… destroyed it after the war so I can't use it anymore," Terra explained.

"Aw…" Cerberus pouted.

"But, I'm pretty well known for my boxing skills too. I think I can still prove a match for you with martial arts." Terra offered.

"I do boxing too so it's perfect!" Cerberus' eyes lit up, "This fight is going to be great!"

"Remember, Cerberus, this isn't just a fight. To improve, I'll be giving critiques and feedback based on your performance so you can learn." Terra reminded the little ball of energy of their compromise.

"Right!" Cerberus acknowledged before darting forward like a bat out of Hades!

Like a wild animal, she pounced and swung her claws at Terra. That was hardly the refined martial art Cerberus implied she practised. The goddess easily avoided the puppy's claws. Over and over again, Cerberus let out a relentlessly aggressive assault!

"Stop just running away! Fight back!" Cerberus demanded as her attacks continued missing.

Terra had to be careful with her Power; it was lethal to Typhon's and his spawn in high doses, and since the girl lacked his regeneration, that sacred heat would be curtains for the demon puppy. So, instead of exposing her to any direct Power, Terra decided to focus on a more grappling-based fighting style instead of punches or kicks.

Whenever Cerberus clumsily attacked and left herself open, Terra would place her in a restraining hold and force her to yield that way. She tried to use that to explain remaining balanced and focused during a fight, but Cerberus didn't like it.

"Hey! Stop babying me! I know you're supposed to be a good boxer, so actually fight back." Cerberus pouted.

"Technically, it isn't boxing. I use a mixture of martial arts from around the Universe. People just call it boxing because of what is familiar locally," Terra corrected.

"Either way, fight for real!" Cerberus cried.

Terra hesitated, remembering Hecate's advice. Then Cerberus rushed at her again. Terra dodged past her opening punch and retaliated with one of her own, lightly punching Cerberus in the face! Cerberus was thrown back and just barely landed on her feet.

"That's more like it!" Cerberus grinned before immediately rushing back in. Terra went about blocking and dodging the little dog's many attacks before returning a light tap of her own to make it seem like a real fight.

"You're strong, Terra… so now I can show you something special." Cerberus grinned and began to focus her Power. Terra raised her guard, wondering what to expect. Then Cerberus fired a thin, extending spear of Adamant from her body. The head of it quickly became a bident to try and pin Terra to a tree.

"That's Hades' technique!" Terra immediately noticed Hades' nonlethal move that had become the basis of the land's law enforcement officers and their dulled, man-catching bidents.

Terra caught the polearm and pushed back so that she wouldn't get pinned. She could've effortlessly snapped it apart but decided to play a bit and only push back enough to match Cerberus. Cerberus just grinned. While Terra was playing with her, the pup's shadow began expanding until it was right under Terra.

"Gotcha!" Cerberus cheered as, right beneath Terra's feet, a gigantic demon dog's head erupted from the ground! Terra leaped into the air to avoid being swallowed by its maw! Of course, she'd seen it coming. Terra could tell that Cerberus' extending shadow wasn't an ordinary one. It was telekinetically controlled Adamant she was sneaking across the ground to form into a weapon near her opponent.

While Terra prepared to fight the one dog head, she was attacked from both sides by two more dog heads. Each hellhound that extended from Cerberus attacked as remote-controlled Monsters under her control. Terra swiftly decapitated the dogs, but once they had been summoned, they no longer had to be physically connected to Cerberus via the shadow. The three autonomous attack drones followed Cerberus' commands and attacked Terra from all sides.

Then, Terra snapped her fingers, and the attacks from each dog deflected backward and annihilated them! She even anticipated and deflected the dragon tail Cerberus had hidden and tried to sneak attack Terra with. Cerberus was amazed by that deflection ability.

"Before we fight again, I want to learn how to make things hit themselves like you do! The defection move you have is so cool!" Cerberus mispronounced deflection.

"I see. Well, in that case, sure. I'm sure Hades will be impressed." Terra grew excited at the prospect of getting to teach again.

"Basically, to use this ability, you have to understand something about Power. Most people use Power to manipulate probabilities and exceed limits such as the strength of their muscles or the speed limit of the universe. For our purposes, it can also bend natural forces to one's will. In the case of this ability, the natural phenomenon you're dealing with is something called a reaction force. Whenever an action force occurs, its equal and opposite simultaneously comes into being. When you push against the wall, the wall pushes back," Terra explained. Cerberus looked completely lost, so Terra simplified it.

"When I deflect an attack, I'm making it so that any action against me becomes one with the kickback of the attack. If someone pushed me, I feel nothing while they would be pushed back with double the force." Terra simplified.

Cerberus was amazed; now she got it. She quickly connected the idea to how when she jumped by pushing off the ground, the ground pushed her up into the air. So, with Terra's ability, the ground would make Cerberus jump twice as high. Terra agreed and praised her little comparison.

So then, Terra showed Cerberus as an example: as she walked forward, she slid back! Cerberus thought that was the coolest and tried to replicate it, but she couldn't.

It took much trial and error, but eventually, Cerberus found herself able to reverse very small forces. In a single day, she was able to use a technique that most masters of Power couldn't have hoped to grasp. She had Typhon's skill for quick learning. Soon, Cerberus was backward, walking all over the place.

"Alright! I think I've got it, so then, Terra… why don't you try attacking me?" Cerberus requested. Terra obliged and prepared to flick Cerberus in the head as the little girl mischievously snickered. Terra obviously knew what she was up to but still flicked Cerberus.

As a result, Cerberus held her head in pain and yelled that Terra must have cheated. Despite Cerberus using the deflection move Terra showed her, she was still hit!

"Right. You reversed the force of my attack… and then I just reversed it back at you," Terra explained. That gave her an idea for a game.

Terra created a ball for them to play with out of thin air. Then she threw it to Cerberus, who easily deflected it back. Terra then double-deflected it back to Cerberus! Cerberus was shocked: it was true, Terra could send it back. Not to be outdone, Cerberus deflected it a third time. Back and forth, the ball went, slowing down from the lost momentum, before ultimately falling to the ground.

"Again!" Cerberus cheered.

The two played again, but the ball was faster this time. After a dozen or so deflections, the ball hit Cerberus square in the face after she missed a deflection! Terra asked if she was okay, to which Cerberus proudly declared she was.

So, they deflected it back and forth again. In only a day, Cerberus had all but mastered the technique. Though, she found deflecting pure Power to be much more difficult. So, ultimately, they went back to perfecting physical deflection. Terra showed Cerberus how to change the angle of what she deflected, and their advanced ball game became even more complex. The two played all day until sunset.

When Hades finished his committee work, he followed the direction people had last seen them going. When he found Terra and Cerberus sparring, he was impressed. Cerberus noticed him and ran over to tell Hades all about what happened. Mid-sentence, Cerberus jumped up to sneak attack, Terra. In the next moment, Cerberus was sent flying across the clearing by her own attack. Hades was shocked.

"Terra! Terra!!! How was that!? How many times?" Cerberus cheered.

"You deflected it nine times before getting hit. Very impressive for such a quick attack." Terra smiled.

"You can tell me all about it when we get home." Hades smiled.

"No! I'm having too much fun! You'll never make me! Mwahahaha!!!" Cerberus refused and ran about causing trouble now that she was mad with power.

"If you want me to go home, just beat me in a match, Papa." Cerberus smiled mischievously. Hades foolishly agreed, only to find himself thrown to the ground over and over again.

"Come on, Cerberus!" Hades grumbled, as he had to pick himself up off the ground.

"Never!" Cerberus cackled mischievously.

Beating Cerberus in her childish challenges usually worked to take the gremlin down a peg, but today, he was yet to beat her. Terra watched helplessly from a rock as the fierce god of the dead and veteran of the Titan War was getting beat up by a little girl.

It was all because of Cerberus' new deflection ability that she'd learned from Terra. Whenever Hades attacked, she'd send it right back at him! Even when he was holding back to not hurt her, the double damage really hurt him.

Terra gave Cerberus tips on how to mix things up and deflect the attack in different directions and spots that Hades couldn't dodge or block. Sure enough, Hades found a child that was less than half his strength, posing a humiliating challenge. Terra's power was next to invincible. If she was so willing to hand this out to Cerberus, what other monstrous abilities did she have stashed away to trump it?

"Terra, honey… how am I supposed to beat this?" Hades finally pleaded with his wife. He was a strategic genius, but for this… he had nothing.

"Oh. Just start with a weak feint and then hit with a delayed second attack after she's off balance from deflecting the first. Or just turn invisible. She can't deflect attacks she can't detect." Terra casually divulged the weakness of her signature move.

"Hey! That's cheating!" Cerberus cried.

Hades tried Terra's advice, and sure enough, it worked. Cerberus pouted that since it was cheating now, they had to catch her, but Hades did that instantly. With the little mischief monster defeated, the three went home.

That night, after Terra and Hades tucked Cerberus in, the couple discussed Terra's progress. It wasn't much in the grand scheme of things, but Terra was overjoyed. Cerberus still called her Terra instead of Mother, but all that mattered was that they had become much closer.

Tale 14

Double Date

In Graia, the goddess of love was the legendarily beautiful Venus. It was said that no matter the time or place, any who looked upon her would see the most beautiful woman they had imagined. This was how she was the prettiest woman in the world.

Befitting her status, Venus made every aspect of love her business. Need fashion and makeup to charm that special someone? Venus' cult produced it all. Looking for tips on how to charm one's crush? Venus' cult taught lessons. Inside and out, she was devoted to bringing out the beauty of every person who called upon her so that their relationships could themselves be beautiful. Venus was always most entranced by human bonds with one another: platonic, romantic, and familial, but in her mind, romance was the height of all three loves from which all others originated.

As such, even though it fell outside her domain, Venus wanted to use her position of authority to spread love in all stages of the relationship, including marriage. The idea that people would be married of their own free will was considered that of madness and a breach of social trust. True love was supposed to be for affairs. If there was supposed to be any "love," it would be something that the participants of the marriage learned to love.

But Venus remembered the bygone days before love itself was made political. Love was love, and the goddess worked night and day to ensure it stayed that way. So, the love goddess had made it her mission to bring this "true love" back into the world… while making a bit of money on the side.

As such, people of all colors, shapes, and sizes were welcome in Venus' house of love. Venus' house of love was a giant clam-shaped building on the beautiful beach of Lesbos that was partially submerged. The inside was soft and comfortable, with foamy, relaxing seats. It was as accommodating as any divine palace, but rather than keep it to herself, the goddess of love had opened this temple to love for the public.

The great structure was a center where couples could engage in a variety of pastimes—eating areas for courting, games for entertainment, bars for liquid courage, and sleeping areas for… sleeping. It even had rooms and appointments for couples counseling and classes on courtship etiquette.

All people from all walks of life and all socioeconomic backgrounds could be counted on to pay one of Venus' houses of love a visit.

Though the most exclusive part of the club was the divine suite: a room for high-end clients known to most only through legends. Befitting its name, the suite was like a room on Olympus itself. Venus had spared no expense in getting Hestia to replicate the halls of the gods perfectly. Normally, it was the prize of any romantic to take their date to this hallowed place. But for that night, it was going to host a nice family get-together.

Around the table were Terra, the goddess of the World and her husband, Hades, the god of the dead.

Also with them was their lovely host, Venus, the goddess of love and sex, as well as her husband, Hephaestus, the god of the forge. Venus looked remarkably similar to her sister Terra but had golden locks of hair instead of sky-blue ones.

Hephaestus, the god of the forge, was hideous and repulsive to lay eyes on, almost to the same degree as his stunningly gorgeous wife, Venus was beautiful.

He was also paralyzed from the waist down, a rarity for Immortals. Nonetheless, with his incredible ingenuity and forging skills, he overcame this disability with exoskeletal prosthetic limbs that he made himself.

Disappointingly, while many in the stone age were compassionate and did not let his physical disability affect how they saw him, times had changed for the worse. In Zeus' Graia, the physically disabled were looked down on as lesser.

In contrast, his brother-in-law Neptune was a paragon of ancient Graiac bisexual masculinity; unafraid to embrace the fancy finery and dress associated with the warrior class during peacetime. He had the beautiful nymph Amphitrite on his right arm and the handsome nymph Nerites on his left and stole the hearts of nearly any man or woman who laid eyes on him.

Here they were, Terra, Venus, and Neptune all in one place: the sheer amount of beauty was almost overwhelming! Indeed, the three sacred siblings were the most beautiful creatures in creation. It was almost as if their bodies were engineered to be the most attractive and comfortable specimens of humankind—especially their eyes.

Myths rarely give full physical descriptions of the deities they discuss. At best, there were only snippets here and there that sometimes contradict one another from tale to tale.

But one detail that was consistent across time was the description of their eyes. The Solaris family all had the same beautiful blue eyes. Not the paltry color humans developed when their iris' had low amounts of melanin or even the bland blue of the average Immortal's unnatural pigmentation. No, the eyes of a Solaris clansman were the blue of the sky itself. One could get lost forever just staring into those comfortable blue dots.

It was these eyes that let anyone be at ease around Terra and feel like they could tell her anything. It was also those eyes that lured many naïve maidens into the clutches of the radiant seducer: Zeus. Many a lost sonnet and poem was poured out to these marvels of supernature. Truly, no number of pages could contain the allure held by these greatest of the gods.

As the gods and goddesses caught up, Venus showed her guests around the divine suite, bragging of its storied history as the place where many gods and kings began their courtship process.

"Every single amenity needed to ensure total romance is at the occupant's disposal. Mood changes, customizable decorations, and even sounds and music are all controlled at your convenience." Venus presented as she showed off the small room control pad that projected an interactive holographic interface using Power.

Hades hadn't seen odd technology like that in a while. It was rare to see it anywhere outside the realms of gods after the war ended. After defeating Typhon, the gods had agreed that such strange things were too unnatural and dangerous to be trusted, so Terra turned it all over to Olympus.

The problem then was that Olympus saw fit to auction off the divine constructs to the highest bidders (often themselves). Since new advanced tools like these were impossible to create for the bronze age barbarians, each owner was assured of their purchase's uniqueness and value.

After all, if that technology was too available, the rulers' investments would lose their rarity and thus value. But then again, Terra had made those labor credit devices for the land of Hades in the same way. No! Hades had to snap out of it and stop analyzing everything he saw. He'd have time to think through and write his critiques when he wasn't on a date with Terra.

While Hades' mind wandered there, Venus moved on to the other main reward of her establishment. She changed the room control projection to a gorgeous menu displaying all the various foods offered by her prized chefs.

"A couple of friends mentioned how much they missed such and such dishes from other regions. Back in the old days, when you could visit other gods or even during the war when you were stationed in other lands, everyone had a foreign delight or two they wished they could try again. Well, behold! I have the best chefs money can buy on call to serve up authentic cuisine from all across civilization. Regional Graiac dishes, foreign exotic dishes, and even ancient forgotten dishes that only us immortal gods would remember. Pretty neat, huh?" Venus winked.

"Venus, I don't know why you're trying to sell us on this place; we're already here. You've been spending too much time with Mercury," Neptune pointed out with a laugh.

"I'm not selling you on anything. The point is, does anybody want food or drinks? When I said you can get it from anywhere, I mean anywhere." Venus proposed, presenting a menu that, for once, had drink options other than the Graiac staple of watered-down wine.

The Graiac gods were generally forbidden from interfering in the regions beyond their sphere of influence. The last Pantheon of Graiacs were expansionist imperialists, so naturally, the other regions wanted some assurances that the

Olympians weren't going to be the same. However, this little bit of cross-cultural appreciation was deemed minor enough to be allowed.

As they continued their party, the different couples (and throuple) shared stories of how they met and fell for each other. Everyone had a charming story to tell about falling in love, except for one who was oddly quiet.

"Terra… you know what that means. You're in the hot seat now." Venus stared at her sister from behind, steepled fingers.

"I don't know what you mean." Terra awkwardly laughed as all eyes turned to her and Hades.

"It's the question on everyone's mind… have you two slept together yet?" Venus directly asked.

Hades spat out his drink. Was this normal to discuss with everyone else around? Graiac culture was far more open with such topics and far less puritanical than many of the civilizations they would inspire. But still no. That was just how Venus, the goddess of love and sex, was. Everyone else was just used to it by that point.

"I think that's something that I'll keep between the two of us. I thought you were going to ask how we became a couple!" Terra cried in embarrassment.

"Dodging questions from your own sister? Fine then. If you won't give me the scoop on that, I'll accept you answering that other question on everyone's mind," Venus pointed accusingly.

Strangely enough, even Hades wanted to know. Up until that moment, it was a secret held only by the goddess of nature. Seeing the intrigued looks from everyone else, Terra gave in and finally told them the story.

Back when Terra was creating the land of Hades, she escorted Hades and Cerberus to one of her numerous natural paradises to help them choose what ecology their world would have. Grains, fruits, and vegetables of all shapes and sizes were planted in various climates. Cerberus ran through the fields, stuffing her face with the various foreign delights.

Terra gave Hades a tour through the different regions, doing her best not to gush about her work in organizing and planting everything. Each horticultural problem that she overcame threatened to spin off into an entirely new tangent, but the goddess of nature always caught herself to stay on topic. As they walked through, Terra gave Hades a rundown on the benefits, drawbacks, and requirements for each potential crop.

Hades even got to sample the edible plants that Cerberus had gotten to ahead of schedule. Terra made note of everyone that caught his eye and planned out the best corresponding plants to do soil remediation and crop rotation with. Hades had no idea what that meant, but Terra reassured him not to worry since, "It's just plant stuff."

After planning out the general vegetation setup for this new planet, Terra asked Hades if there were any other plants that he wanted in his new world that weren't in Terra's collection.

Hades laughed that he doubted any plant was outside the goddess of nature's collection. Terra pointed out that this was only one planet of a few hundred that she had like this. She was just asking to save time instead of visiting them all. Hades recalled a special fruit that used to grow on Molossos. It was his favorite childhood treat that he longed for the chance to have again. As far as he knew, though, the war wiped it out.

Terra asked to see it, much to Hades' confusion. Terra told him of her ability to see his memories, which would allow her to find the fruit most accurately. Though she always asked permission before peering in. Hades gave it.

Placing her hands on his temples, Terra looked into his memories. She saw Molossos in the past, before the war. Young Hades and his friends enjoyed peace and harmony. She saw a red fruit that was opened and revealed red jewel-like seeds inside that could be eaten.

Such happy memories quickly gave way to Hades' war flashbacks. All those friends who were put to the sword by Typhon's troops. His home burnt to the ground, with him being powerless to stop it.

When the vision ended, Terra began to cry, much to Hades' worry. She'd seen too much but reassured Hades that she was okay. Then Terra produced the plant of his memory by teleporting one to her hand from another one of her other distant planetary gardens.

The goddess presented the fruit to Hades and Cerberus. Hades felt a strange nostalgic happiness at the sight of it. After all these years, he could relive those happy memories as vividly as Terra just had. Seeing his reaction, she couldn't help but smile.

The moment was interrupted by Cerberus immediately trying to bite into the fruit's tough skin. Hades panicked and pried it from her fangs as he tried to explain that you don't eat it like that. Pomegranate was a rare fruit whose skin was dry and inedible but had countless juicy seeds inside that could be enjoyed.

Hades happily demonstrated his trick for how to peel it. Since he was much larger than the last time he'd done this, it didn't come out perfectly, but he did manage to extract a handful of the fruit seeds (known as arils) for the others to try.

Cerberus ravenously consumed them as quickly as they were given to her. Terra sampled them with a smile, saying she understood his choice. They were only supposed to have one, but after finishing the first, Terra brought more and more for them to have a snack break.

As the trio sat down and feasted on pomegranates, Terra was watching Hades' lifted expression with a smile. He had her now, even more than before. That loveable expression returning to one that was normally dour and downcast had Terra hook, line, and sinker.

It wasn't sexual attraction that drew her in. Terra just had to admit, that even more so than with other humans, when Hades was happy, she was happy. She'd always intended on helping see his dream through, but her conviction to stay with him grew stronger than ever. So, over a snack of pomegranate, Terra found herself unable to leave Hades.

The others in attendance were moved by the story. Even Hades was surprised by the tale. He remembered that day exactly as Terra described, it was just different from his perspective because he had been in love with her for many years before then. It honestly warmed his heart a bit to hear that.

Venus and Neptune were equally surprised. Terra hardly ever ate anything. The two smiled as they saw their Terra so happy with her chosen partner. The night of fun progressed from there, and a good time was had by all.

When the night was done, the gods prepared to head out. However, as they exited, Terra and Venus overheard some couples having trouble and once rushed to their aid! The two pathological matchmakers were ecstatic to freely lend their assistance as the ultimate romance goddesses. Hades couldn't help but smile, seeing Terra so excited.

"The real deal really does put all those forced ones to shame, doesn't it?" Neptune asked as he walked over to Hades. Hades was surprised. Though, it made sense that Terra's brother would be able to tell when she was really happy, just like Hades could.

"I'm relieved to see that you're just as happy as I am to see her truly happy as of late. You were the catalyst that started to bring her out of her shell so I could see the old Terra again. For that, I must thank you," Neptune explained.

"You think so?" Hades asked.

"Terra's internal battle is one she has to fight. But the fact that she doesn't have to alone is definitely helping. Even before you two got married, Terra always seemed a lot happier when she was around a certain friend she'd mention. So again, not to make it weird, but thanks for being there for her." Neptune grinned.

"After all she's done for me, it's the least I could've done. Besides, I didn't do it alone. Everybody's been pitching in," Hades replied.

"True. We all tried our best to be there for Terra, but you were the only one to make such progress. So just take the compliment and accept my thanks." Neptune smiled.

"I'd say no problem, but, honestly, I have no idea what I supposedly did. I learned as much about our relationship tonight as you did. Who's to say I even did anything special." Hades shrugged.

"You didn't give up like we all seemed to. I see now that is why none of us could reach her the way you could. So, while she may keep her reasons secret, know that every time she tells you how much you mean to her, she means it." Neptune took his leave as he patted Hades on the back. Yet, a few strides away, Neptune paused and turned back to face Hades.

"One more thing, Hades." Neptune smiled.

"Sure. What is it?" Hades asked as he turned around to face Neptune.

"Watch over Terra…" Neptune began with the same charming grin before becoming deadly serious, "And watch out for Jupiter…"

TALE 15

Hades and Aidoneus

Not all were happy with the success of Hades and his new land. The people there were happy and fulfilled: the foreign kings hated this. In the end, his success was their loss: he made them look bad and inspired their citizens to demand more from them. None was more bitter at his success than King Aidoneus of Molossos.

Aidoneus and Hades both grew up on Molossos. As fellow first-generation Immortals, they were conscripted into the warrior caste of the stone age tribe that adopted them. This warband was composed of the hundred strongest warrior adolescents from the community between the ages of twelve and nineteen.

It may have seemed odd to give such an important task to youths. However, it all made sense when considering that the first warbands were composed entirely of the many original Immortals brought in by the tribe. As thanks for being given a home, they made use of their supernatural Power to protect the powerless humans that raised them.

On account of being children, they were exactly as chaotic and immature with their Powers as one would expect. The worst cases became tyrants like Typhon. Slightly less awful specimens became tyrants like Aidoneus. Aidoneus wanted to be king before the concept even existed. As children, he bossed his fellow Immortals around as the leader of the Molossian warband and bullied Hades relentlessly. In truth, this was because he was jealous that Hades was always stronger than him, thanks to his weird, chthonic abilities.

During the war, Aidoneus prayed for Hades' death every time that fool went to fight Typhon himself. Unfortunately, since he kept surviving, he gained something of a reputation among the commoners and the troops. Fearing Hades may eclipse his standing among the future rulers, Aidoneus schemed to sabotage him.

After the war ended, Aidoneus swindled Hades out of his war boons and left the god of the dead destitute while enriching himself as the king of the newly liberated Molossos. While he felt no guilt for any of this, Aidoneus did have a growing sense of paranoia that Hades would one day come for his revenge.

Even after all this time, Aidoneus could only view Hades with the same suspicion and hostility that he did as a child. The king feared that by allying with the great unwashed, Hades was surely still trying to usurp his position. That or he was an utter fool for genuinely caring about those beneath him in the hierarchy, and his foolishness was equally risky. While insisting that Hades was taken in by childish ideology, it was Aidoneus who had refused to grow up.

All this was to say, it greatly amplified his material hatred of Hades that emerged from more worldly problems. Aidoneus' land had been hemorrhaging citizens ever since Hades started his own country. Without the labor of his serfs, there was no value or profit to give as tribute to his wealthy benefactors. They were not happy with the reduced earnings, and many began withdrawing their support for the king. Aidoneus' debts skyrocketed, and in no time at all his nation was on the verge of collapse. Better conditions drew away all the king's followers until the king had to impose a temporary ban on any further emigration. This was a hitherto unheard-of thing within the Kosmos.

Like so many others, he wanted Terra for himself and had hated Hades long before his rise to popularity. After all, the radical Hades had gotten his start as a thorn in the good king's side. He was an uppity and jealous Molossian native who coveted the king's power, at least in that king's eyes. Hades may have been a god, but Aidoneus did the will of Zeus, making him Hades' superior, at least regarding their conflict.

King Aidoneus' wrath burned against Hades! What had he done to deserve this? Sure, he'd worked his citizens to death and ignored their pleas. Sure, he'd placed profitability over safety, which caused a mining disaster that killed countless more people. Sure, he banished Hades for trying to help all those he abused in his quest for money and power…

But other than that, what had he done to deserve this? Why were they all leaving him!? Because Aidoneus hardened his heart and refused to concede anything the people asked, he was about to lose everything. Before long, it was Molossos, not Hades, that was going to become a ghost town.

That was why the king was horrified when he received word that Hades, his old foe, wanted to meet up to negotiate. Aidoneus hated Hades with every fiber of his being. Nonetheless, on the fated day, Aidoneus arrived in the land of Hades to negotiate with his hated foe of the parallel name. Following the swift reversal of fortune that he suffered after making an enemy of his subjects, the king arrived on the better shores they had all left him for. Aidoneus looked upon his rival territory with disgust. His nation was a kingdom in shambles, but in his eyes, that was still infinitely preferable to a thriving nation of equals.

Nonetheless, Aidoneus arrived in Hades' house and found him not on a bejeweled throne but rather on a common wooden seat, hard at work on his desk with Committee work. Hades had approached Aidoneus when he was at his lowest point and on the verge of ruin. The king suspected the lord of the dead had called him over to gloat. There he was with Terra on his arm, flaunting the woman Aidoneus coveted! Surely, that villain Hades was relishing this victory lap. Instead, the truth was far worse. Hades expressed sympathy and distress at the deteriorating conditions in Molossos. He asked how the people were faring in the face of such an economic downturn. Aidoneus retorted that Hades was to blame for all this.

By his account, only Aidoneus had spared the people from their hubris! Hades had angered those in power, and now Aidoneus' warnings had come to pass. Hades ignored him. Rather than fight like the king wanted, he got to the point.

"Aidoneus, if you step down and allow your land to become democratic, we are willing to take care of you and handle your debts. You'll be a free man," Hades offered.

"Nonsense. If I give up my power, what will become of my riches? What of my palaces?" Aidoneus scoffed.

"I've heard your properties are up to be repossessed by your creditors. So technically, you have already lost them." Hades corrected the king. Aidoneus grew angry at his retort. Hades was not wrong, and that made it even more infuriating.

"Your debts will be cleared and your properties transferred to your rescuers: the people at large. Whatever the population of Molossos votes to do with them would be done," Hades explained.

"Madness. This is madness spouted by a madman- a midday drunk and a traitor to the ruling class!" Aidoneus cried.

"Aidoneus." Terra only needed to speak the man's name to remind him who was in charge here.

Aidoneus bowed before the queen of the gods, remembering his place. As much as he lusted after her, he had to remember the main reason why none dared seize her, as was the whim of most kings in that day. This beautiful maiden could fight back, and fiends of Aidoneus' ilk knew full well that she could utterly annihilate them with a thought. Even though she was not one for violence, she could strip them of their powers and turn the public against them, given her high status.

Thus, for the rest of the meeting, Aidoneus was sure to mind his manners. He politely refused Hades' offer, but he suggested that the king take time to reconsider his offer, and he would ask him again at a later date.

Aidoneus left the land of Hades enraged, cursing Hades in his heart. When he returned to Molossos after meeting with Hades, Aidoneus was shocked to find a representative from Olympus waiting for him. Iris, the goddess of the rainbow and messenger of the gods, had come with good news. Aidoneus was invited to Olympus for a chance to meet with "the big guy."

The king was led to the most high place: the sacred abode of Zeus. In the king of the gods' throne room, Aidoneus bowed before the throne of Olympus and offered the prayer all kings were expected to offer up to the king of their gods, "Oh great Zeus! Hallowed be thy name. Deliver us from Kosmic evil, enemy armies, and from a bad harvest."

Zeus was pleased by the king's offering. The king of the gods declared that he had heard of Aidoneus' plight and took pity on him. The king of the gods was willing to wipe his debts and restore his former glory. Aidoneus' eyes lit up at the offer. If anyone was able to accomplish all this, it was Zeus.

"I would like you to do me a favor though." Zeus said with a twisted grin. Zeus revealed that Hades was a common enemy of theirs. His democracy made him an enemy to kings everywhere. But for political reasons, Zeus could not publicly move against him. That was why Aidoneus had been chosen to do the lord's work: destroy Hades.

Zeus was not explicit. His words always preserved deniability as every shrewd politician did. However, reading between the lines, Aidoneus knew what he was to do. Then, after undergoing the song and dance of indirect orders, Zeus dropped the façade and spoke directly.

"As a sign of my favor, I am giving you a small loan of one million drachmas. Use them in any way that will bring about the downfall of Hades," Zeus said plainly.

Aidoneus knew his mission: prevent any further converts to democracy and, furthermore, make an example of those that already existed. Using the money he received, Aidoneus at once amplified his anti-Hades rumors. He slandered the god of the dead by commissioning hit pieces, anti-Hades myths, and art to turn people against him.

Aidoneus spun his circumstances into the fault of Hades. In his retelling, Molossos' fate was what happened to any polis that negotiated with Hades. By giving a few alternative facts, now many more would see his near downfall as Hades' revenge for numerous slights.

Furthermore, by playing on Hades' role as the god of the dead, Aidoneus made Hades a boogeyman in the minds of Graia. Hades was the lord of the dead, surely those who went to his land would become dead themselves. Even if this were not literal, the fiend Hades would ensure that once people entered his realm, they could never escape. This lie was humorous, given Aidoneus' ban on emigration, but the irony was lost on him.

Beyond that, he attacked Hades' character. He mocked his pale complexion by calling him "white-armed Hades." This was an epithet normally reserved for goddesses in reference to the Graiac beauty standards' fixation with light-skinned women of status. He was calling Hades effeminate while also referencing his wife's epithet, implying that she was the real head of the household. Influenced by her defensiveness toward her husband, Hades was portrayed as a spineless failure of a man who could only hide behind his wife and only succeeded at all because of her. This insult was especially painful for Hades because, deep down, his insecurities made him question if that was true.

Though, the most aggressive and personal attack Aidoneus disseminated was the idea that Hades had taken Terra as his wife via underhanded means… the means Aidoneus would have gone about using if she wasn't so absolutely terrifying. It was a contradiction to the previous smear, but Aidoneus only cared about maximizing the number of insults he could throw at Hades.

With all this, Zeus was well pleased. Many poleis that were considering allying or negotiating with Hades' land to implement reforms all backed out of their dealings. Soon, even saying Hades' name was taboo, lest they bring misfortune upon themselves. Aidoneus was ecstatic. It was then that hubris overtook the man.

Aidoneus, going with the momentum of his previous victories, began to smuggle weapons and mercenaries into the land of Hades. He exhausted the last of the drachmas in stockpiling enough weapons to arm a rebel band of 10,000 men! Finally, he forced Hades' hand.

The scheme was quickly exposed, and Aidoneus' deeds were revealed to the Kosmos. Not just this latest scheme… Hades compiled numerous eyewitness accounts of Aidoneus' current and former citizens and published a laundry list of his many misdeeds to the Kosmos. The people of Graia at once saw Aidoneus for the cruel and neglectful king he was.

At once, many of his business partners fled from him just as soon as they were beginning to return. Aidoneus sank even further into debt and cursed Hades. Aidoneus called out to Zeus for more aid, but the king of the gods did not reply. He had failed. The king despaired at his sudden reversal of fortune. But things finally reached their lowest point when he received word that Hades, god of the dead, was coming to visit.

Hades entered Aidoneus' throne room and, without prompting, warned the king that he had brought all this on himself. However, Hades was still offering him an out. All would be solved if he simply held a vote among his population on whether they wanted to become a democracy. If they rejected the democratic change, Hades was still willing to render aid to Molossos, so there was no pressure.

Aidoneus rejected this. How could they hold a vote when Hades had just finished poisoning their minds against him!? Hades reminded Aidoneus that everything in the accounts was true. Rather than blame others, the king needed to do some soul-searching. Perhaps that was best accomplished with some time away from the throne. At this, Aidoneus' fury boiled over. Hades had come to see him alone. Without Terra to keep the king in his place, Aidoneus unleashed all his malice and hate.

"You almost ruin me and come when I am at my lowest? You are a fiend!" the king's wrath yelled.

"I beat you at your own game. It isn't very fun, is it? Losing in the same way that the people have for so long?" Hades asked.

To that, Aidoneus had no reply. Words failed him just as he failed Zeus. But no… maybe he hadn't failed yet. His orders were to bring about the downfall of Hades, and there was more than one way to accomplish that. Aidoneus knew that where words failed, violence was always the answer!

"As a king, I still have my pride!!!" Aidoneus screamed in a rage and attacked Hades.

Just like Hades, Aidoneus wielded a bident: his trusty spear with two spikes instead of one. The two veteran warriors clashed their polearms together. Dancing through the palace with planet-shattering clashes, the two laid waste to many of the king's prized possessions. Though notably, Hades only used his weapon to defend himself as he tried and failed to talk Aidoneus down.

The unseen king only grew angrier and angrier as the reuniter talked rather than fought while easily blocking and dodging any matter of attack thrown out. Struggling to resolve this with words, Hades finally counterattacked. Dulling the blades of his weapon by covering them in dull Adamant edges, Hades extended his bident to pin Aidoneus against the wall in the same fashion as the nonlethal man catchers used by law enforcement within his land.

Aidoneus was pinned to a gorgeous mosaic made not of glass, stone, or shells but of many precious gemstones mined from his resource-rich realm. It was worth a fortune and the centerpiece of the entire room. As Aidoneus threw a tantrum in a struggle to escape, Hades warned that he was damaging his prized possession.

Still, Aidoneus refused to listen to reason. Since he could not break the spear that pinned him, he destroyed the wall that he was pinned against to free himself! Hades was so confused. Did Aidoneus hate him so much that he was willing to destroy the commodities and possessions that he prized so much? On that wall alone, beyond the mosaic, were many priceless antiques and pieces of art that were worth enough to feed all his subjects for years.

Behind that wall were many of the king's cowering subjects who cried out in fear at the sudden destruction. To keep them out of harm's way, Hades took to the skies and flew to the roof of the palace with Aidoneus in hot pursuit.

"Aidoneus! Listen to reason! Is destroying your kingdom worth it for this temper tantrum?" Hades demanded.

"I will destroy as many things as I have to as long as you are one of them!" Aidoneus screamed.

His wrath and frenzy had overtaken any logic. The king would rather destroy it all than subject himself to the humiliation of democracy.

A large crowd gathered to witness the rooftop duel. Hades continued to block and dodge as Aidoneus pushed him closer and closer to the edge. Ironically, when Hades pivoted around him to avoid being thrown off, Aidoneus tripped and toppled over his palace. The building's height was so great that the fall would be lethal. Many would see this as a fitting end.

At the last moment, Hades reached out and saved Aidoneus from falling. The King's wrath only burned brighter.

"Unhand me! I can fly, you idiot!" Aidoneus roared. His Power saved him as always, and he shook Hades off before flying above him. Hades was confused. With his extendable polearm, Hades was the one who held a range advantage. However, he understood as soon as Aidoneus revealed his trump card.

As Aidoneus loomed above, even higher in the sky manifested the divine authority of the king: the Sword of Damocles.

This was a binding system for kings in Zeus' employ. He would grant them a literal Sword of Damocles. As long as the blade was manifested, the ruler would have access to incredible Powers from their patron god. But if they ever failed or displeased the king of the gods, the sword would fall from the heavens and utterly destroy them.

If democracy ever conquered their world, the kings knew that the sword was sure to fall. Thus, they doubled their efforts: using the power of the Sword, they would oppose any democratic movements. Their motivation was also helped by the terrifying fear of the sword's string being cut. This was their mission from Zeus: Aidoneus was just the most direct about it.

In brandishing this sword, he had made clear that this battle was to the death. If he failed to kill Hades, Aidoneus would lose his authority as king and be smitten by the blade from above. With great power, there must also come great responsibility. Hades and Aidoneus both understood this but in very different capacities.

So, empowered by the Sword of Damocles, Aidoneus prepared for round two with his antithesis. The king of the gods' lightning coursed through Aidoneus' body and greatly amplified his Power. A terrible storm gathered above that was conducted through the Sword of Damocles that fired a hail of thunderbolts!

The people below cried and panicked. Many houses were burned down, and many innocents were nearly struck and killed. Hades went about using his Adamant manipulation to create shields for the people that protected them from the king's rampage. Aidoneus struck while Hades was distracted and hoped to overtake the god.

But Hades expected him and so turned around with a fiery and divine wrath. Swinging his bident, he shattered Aidoneus' weapon like glass! Aidoneus trembled. If Hades hit him that hard, there wouldn't have been anything left. While Aidoneus' warrior skills had been dulled since the war as he spent his days administrating or relaxing, Hades' instincts were as sharp as ever.

No sooner had he destroyed his opponent's weapon than he had repositioned himself to strike again and finish their battle. Aidoneus' hubris had overtaken him. His arrogance as king made him forget just how much stronger Hades was. The god of the dead had not employed his helmet of invisibility or transformed into his Monster form. This fight was nothing more than a professional boxer playing with a toddler.

As his wits returned to him, the king begged the god for forgiveness. Hades' divine wrath had not yet subsided. He'd given the king many outs before. But being merciful, Hades threw his bident away and only hit the king with a mighty punch to the face! Even that was enough to completely deplete Aidoneus' reserves of Power as the supernatural flames all fled him in a great explosion. Without the sacred heat of Power, Aidoneus was but a mortal man.

The King of Molossos fell to the ground in defeat, Powerless. The soldiers of Aidoneus rushed to the roof, but, upon seeing Hades, stood down. They knew that if Hades was angry, they wouldn't be able to make enough coffins. That was the difference between a king and a god.

Speaking of which, from above, the Sword of Damocles began to plummet down towards the failed king. When the system had no more use for him, he would be disposed of. It was nothing personal, just business.

The Sword fell, ready to pierce Aidoneus, but to his horror, once again, Hades moved to save his life. The god of the dead swung his bident at the Sword of Damocles. He couldn't even scratch it. After all, that was not merely Aidoneus' construct; it was the crystalized Power of Zeus and his system itself. When in crisis, the true horrors of that system revealed itself. Hades was a god, but he was only human, after all.

Aidoneus felt relief. He was going to die, but at least he didn't have to suffer the indignity of being saved by Hades. The frantic god of the dead watched helplessly as his futile attacks did nothing to stop the Sword of Damocles' catastrophic descent to wipe Aidoneus and much of his kingdom out with him! Hades, even as a god, was powerless to stop it.

If Aidoneus had one regret, it was that he was dying. But hey, if he was going down, at least he'd finally get to have a victory over Hades… even if it was a pyrrhic one. This was where Hades' silly philosophies got him; he spent so much time relying on others that he'd never be able to do anything himself! In the end, once the liberal patina was removed, in Zeus' world might still made right. Aidoneus, content to feel this pre-death delusion was a form of enlightenment, accepted his fate under the might of such a system.

And yet, all of a sudden, a great hole was rendered in the sky. Above Molossos, a Pale Blue Dot hung in the sky. A portal had opened above to reveal a blue, watery planet. Yet, the slit in space-time with a dot on the other side looked foreboding. The circle in the middle of a slit looked exactly like a giant human eye. It was as if the Eye of God itself was glaring down at the little man, like something much bigger- vast and unknowable- that had peered down and set its sights on him.

Hades continued swinging with all he had to try and even dent the Sword of Damocles. Then, all at once, it shattered like glass! Hades and Aidoneus were both shocked. Then, as the Blade disappeared, Hades noticed Terra looking up where it once was with her hand raised. Her eyes and body glowed blue like that strange orb in the sky as mysterious Power burst forth and did away with Jupiter's curse.

Aidoneus was shocked. That was right. Hades was a fool for relying on others… but occasionally, it paid to have friends. Under democracy, nobody needed to fear the pressures of the crown. Besides, even when one's job applied pressure, repaying failure with death was not Hades' way. Aidoneus could not understand him. Yet Terra, as Hades' goddess, understood him perfectly and executed his will.

That monstrous Power that backed Aidoneus now had a countermeasure. In that clash of divine patrons… it became frighteningly obvious that Hades' counter system now had a fighting chance. As Aidoneus watched the shattered sword of monarchy crumble into dust in the skies above, he saw Hades and Terra looking down on him.

"It isn't too late, Aidoneus. Consider my offer," Hades said before disappearing with Terra.

Unsurprisingly, after that little outburst, many more abandoned Molossos. His little travel ban didn't matter. Hardly anyone respected him as king anymore, anyway. On the verge of ruin, Aidoneus nearly considered Hades' offer, but distant thunder snapped him to attention. The king was horrified to find Zeus, the King of the gods, sitting on his throne. At once, Aidoneus fell down before his master.

"Aidoneus. You've done so well in keeping the faith up until this point…" Zeus glared into Aidoneus' soul. He felt it again: the Sword of Damocles above his head. Aidoneus begged for his life and reassured the shining god and all the other "generous investors in Molossos' mines" that he would never succumb to democracy.

"Good." Zeus stood up and took his leave. His presence alone was enough to remind the little man who was in charge.

This fool, Aidoneus, had proven himself very nutritious to his betters after all. After testing Hades' mettle on that test dummy of a man, Olympus could better assess the threat their enemy posed. Aidoneus was a failure… but Olympus did not want to grant Hades this very public victory.

To save face, they backed the bus right over Aidoneus and insisted that Hades hadn't won anything against Zeus' world order. The individual "bad apple" Aidoneus had acted on his own and thus also failed on his own. Even still, it didn't look good to have a monarchy lose to a democracy. Thus, while Aidoneus' debts were not fully forgiven, he was given enough support to not collapse.

"It seems I must begin to take our little Hades problem a bit more seriously. While she hasn't carelessly given him Powers as she did with Typhon, it seems that Terra is indeed bonded to him. If she's ready to come to his aid at a moment's notice, I'll have to be a bit more creative." Zeus flashed a sinister grin before looking to the skies as, again, a great gaping hole was torn into it. On the other end was not a small, serene blue world, but a massive and stormy one. Chuckling to himself, Jupiter disappeared in a bolt of lightning. Aidoneus watched the god vanish into that oddly spherical eldritch horror in the skies above.

In Graia, gods were a dime a dozen. Any sufficiently powerful human could earn godhood. But that thing… those Solaris beings were something even further beyond. Just what was the Solaris clan?

Act 3

"Pacifism is objectively pro-fascist. This is elementary common sense. If you hamper the war effort of one side, you automatically help out that of the other. Nor is there any real way of remaining outside such a war as the present one. In practice, 'he that is not with me is against me'."

George Orwell

"Non-violence is not inaction. It is not discussion. It is not for the timid or weak… Non-violence is hard work."

Cesar Chavez

TALE 16

Hydra

Zeus was the noble king of the gods and the god of the kings. However, he was also the god of many other things. Most importantly for this tale, he was also known as Zeus the Hospitable.

The Graiac concept of "xenia" was a moral obligation for all Graiacs to be hospitable to strangers in their midst. Hosts were expected to do everything within their power to ensure the comfort and safety of their guests. In turn, guests were supposed to be respectful and grateful while in another's home. Violations of this agreement on either side were seen as a direct infringement on Zeus' authority as the god of hospitality. So, for once, the king of the gods sought to lead by example, and the cult of Zeus provided professional hosts in Zeus' Houses of Hospitality.

The Houses of Hospitality were primitive hotels where guests would be offered shelter and accommodations befitting kings and gods. The biggest houses of Hospitality were set up in major poleis to provide a place for wealthy visitors to stay. Any of the good rooms were far too expensive for the average Graiac. Most people would live and die next to a House of Hospitality without once being able to stay there. By contrast, some well-to-do citizens would even stay in local Houses of Hospitality just for the luxury experience.

But the Cult of Hospitality had a problem. That being one of its rather inhospitable cult leaders named Procrustes. He had a secret hobby of randomly killing his guests by confining them to his horrendously torturous bed!

The iron Procrustean bed was a perfectly standard size that was burdened with different and diverse people. To enforce true uniformity, Procrustes would take to stretching people who were too small to take up the whole bed as well as chopping off parts of the bodies of those who were too big for the bed.

Hence, ever after a standard marked with arbitrary restrictions that were uniformly enforced without regard for individual needs was known as Procrustean. A fitting double-edged accusation that critics of Zeus could use. Many noted the irony that Zeus would so generously extend hospitality to people… as long as they fit his restrictive and self-serving standards.

Even Procrustes was a man who was made to fit in a restrictive society. In his case, he was a warrior through and through. He was quite fond of the war since it allowed him to kill with impunity. He was the ideal soldier and also the worst kind of civilian.

Why was he forced to "act normal" within society? He was a warrior with unresolved violent urges! Being forced into a civilian lifestyle didn't sit well with him. How could the gods at first demand remorseless killing from him and then punish the same actions once he was no longer of use? He believed that they were betraying all veterans.

No. He was projecting. Hades and many other veterans had some trouble adapting to civilian life, but their warrior past never manifested this way. Procrustes was just internally excusing his evil.

Nonetheless, many began to question why the king of the gods would put a known violent warrior in charge of his hospitality cult. The truth was that Procrustes gave generously to Zeus and asked for this position (specifically to set up his murder trap), but that wasn't the answer people wanted to hear. It was a PR nightmare that Zeus could not fully remove himself from, no matter how much he denounced the villain.

Worse yet, all these things were only found out after Procrustes had been killed and all his various abuses of power came to light. As soon as he died, every misdeed, every abuse of his employees, and every customer he murdered was released to the public by some mysterious party. Even worse yet, the prime suspect in who killed him was none other than Theseus, the Athenian hero!

Procrustes, a high-ranking leader of Zeus' hospitality cult, was found dead: stabbed. The only person in the room when he was found was Theseus of Athens! Theseus was found bound in a strange torture device (the Procrustean bed), begging for his life. Since he was in the room, he was the prime suspect; however, because he was bound, he claimed to be innocent.

Theseus claimed that he was ambushed by Procrustes and trapped in that awful bed. As Procrustes went off to finish preparations for the murder, Theseus heard him scream, presumably as he died but didn't know who did it. A likely story. Investigators were more focused on determining how Theseus would have been able to strap himself in to create an alibi after murdering Procrustes.

Zeus just wanted him to plead self-defense and get this over with, but the hero maintained that he did not kill his host, even as he was about to be killed. Zeus didn't like the look of arresting a hero (and a demigod to boot) as it would be bad PR. The king of the gods was indeed very powerful… but this wasn't the kind of problem that could be overcome with brute force.

Thus, he called a meeting of the gods to discuss what to do about the whole situation. The Olympians gathered with kings to discuss this.

"Thank you for meeting on such short notice. Gods of Olympus, we must deal with this Theseus incident as soon as possible so we can return to business as usual," Zeus said once everyone had been seated.

"Business as usual!? Business as usual is what led to this crisis. We need a serious investigation into major cults to ensure similar abuses are exposed and stopped at once." Hades stood up in protest.

Hades led a faction of deities that wanted to open investigations across the Kosmos to expose similar corruption to Procrustes. Just how many more villains were hiding in plain sight?

"Sit down, boy—" Zeus began before remembering that Terra sat by Hades' side and not his own.

"What I mean is, I am offended that you make such baseless accusations against all rulers just because of the evils of a single individual! I thought you were the one who said it was wrong to generalize, especially on mere hearsay and rumors," Zeus cried.

"You can't accuse your critics of being baseless while shutting down any attempts to investigate!" Hades cried, only to be shouted down by many of Zeus' supporters.

After all, the ability to be their worst without scrutiny was the payment the rulers received for serving their god. Zeus protected his own, and he was not willing to set the precedent of those in power being investigated for wrongdoing. After all, he had more skeletons in his closet than any of them.

"Anyways. Back to the question of what is to be done about Theseus. He is the son of a god, and I wouldn't dream of punishing one of our own too harshly. But he still did kill a cult leader. We must find a way to resolve this quickly while maintaining the esteem of Olympus in every regard," Zeus continued once Hades surrendered to the protests.

Unfortunately, things were too far gone to just sweep this under the rug. Theseus was the only one strong enough to overwhelm Procrustes, not to mention he was at the scene of the crime. It seemed pretty open and shut.

"You're the ones treating this as open and shut," Hades muttered.

Zeus' faction shouted him down again, but many gods who supported Hades spoke up in support of him. Back and forth, the different factions argued about what the take-away was: resolve this incident and move on or try to learn from it and prevent crises in the future. Terra tried to mediate between her brother and her husband, but suddenly, her attention was grabbed by something else.

"Of course, your corrupt bureaucracy can't get anything done. A hundred years of talk, talk, talk. But talk is cheap." A voice scoffed at them.

Only Terra and Neptune had even sensed him enter. When the others turned to see the source of the voice, they were horrified to be looking upon Typhon the destroyer!

"What's the matter? It looks like you've seen a ghost." The man chuckled at the gods' terrified faces. He looked exactly like Typhon and even brandished his iconic sickle!

Terra, in a panic, teleported away. Then she just as quickly returned and announced, "It's not him!". She had gone and made sure Typhon was still in exile on Etna. But then… who was this?

"You can call me Hydra. Congratulations, you found your killer." He confidently grinned and took a bow. Most in attendance didn't know what to make of him. They were still shocked by his resemblance to the king of the Titans. Zeus, meanwhile, was relieved. A fall guy had emerged! Now, he could avoid having to prosecute one of his own.

"And I intend on killing most of you just as I killed Procrustes." The man calling himself Hydra said with a deceptively warm smile as he pointed his sickle at them.

The room erupted into protest and shouting, but unlike Hades, their words alone wouldn't work on him. It suddenly dawned on Zeus: that was the actual murderer, not an eager volunteer to take the blame.

"Come now, do you really think a dog of the gods like Theseus would care about the kinds of things Procrustes was doing? He'd never risk making an enemy of his superiors just to save the common people. Besides, most of the people in this room have more skeletons in their closets than Procrustes ever did. Sometimes literally." Hydra cackled maniacally.

"Oh. I should also mention that I'm the one who dug the dirt up on Procrustes and released it to the public. That is another fate many of you will be sharing with that bastard." Hydra said as he casually approached.

Nobody in the room dared move to attack him. If he looked that much like Typhon, was he as strong as he was, too? It didn't even occur to those in attendance to call their guards.

"What do you want? Are you after money?" Zeus growled.

"Money? That's all you rulers can think of. No. It isn't about money. It's about sending a message. It's about starting something big. Consider me a prophet- an evangelist even. I may not have seen the beginning… but I will proclaim the end." Hydra grinned.

The gods were horrified. His absolute confidence and charisma commanded the room of literal deities and sent shivers down their spines. Seeing that he had absolute control over his audience, Hydra continued.

"When asked what he thought of the outcome of your revolution, the Oracle declared that the results were yet to be seen. My warning is this, Olympians: revolution is back on the menu. This is the beginning of the end, Olympus. And the people will cheer when you're all dead." Hydra pointed accusingly at Zeus.

Like that, the reaction of the room turned from shock to rage. The enraged thunderer hurled a divine bolt at the man and blasted him into cinders. But even as he exploded, his ominous laugh echoed through the room. Olympus hoped that was the last they'd see of that mysterious man.

"You just killed him!? As a god of laws, where was his trial and due process? Are you a god or a Titan!?" an outraged Hades demanded. The king of the gods scoffed at the notion.

"He isn't dead. Whatever he's planning… this is just the beginning," Terra declared as she knelt down and inspected the ashes.

They weren't human; they were Adamant shards. That Hydra they'd just seen was just a remotely controlled puppet of some kind. The real killer who had declared war on Olympus was still out there. All of Olympus trembled with fright at this ominous sign.

Elsewhere in Graia, the king of a polis had all his people present themselves and praise him on his birthday. One by one, they would go up and offer their king praise as well as a gift from them to him. He had no use for most of the trash those peasants brought… but he oh so loved the feeling of them having to give it. After all, he'd already taken everything of value from them, so only the immaterial was left to steal.

However, after a while, a rather tall man made his way to the front of the line. It was Hydra. With a single swing of his sickle, he decapitated the king before making his escape.

Another king burst his way into a private marriage ceremony. He reminded them of the hefty wedding fee they owed the Cult of Hymenaios for sanctifying the wedding.

Though… the king was generously willing to have the Cult waive the fee if he was able to claim the bride's first night. This was prima nocte. The family wasn't "forced" to comply. They would just be financially ruined and starve to death if they didn't. It was a deal the lecherous king worked out with his patron cult.

The king made a mockery of the wedding vows, "Any who objects to this union, rise now!"

Nobody dared stand as the king's guards stared daggers at all those in attendance. Then, one in attendance finally stood up to object. The king turned pale as he recognized the man. Hydra disposed of him before anyone else could move.

But it was not only the kings. It was often the case that Cult leaders were the richest families in town. Like Procrustes, they were often abusive of those beneath them. An extreme case saw a family of higher-ups in Apollo's cult of Justice use their legal connections to get away with murder.

They killed their slaves. They killed their employees. They even killed some of their "friends". But as rulers, who would hold them to account? Hydra did.

Over and over, Hydra struck and assassinated many of the ruling class' most prominent members. As if on cue, all their evil deeds would be released to the public not long after. The remaining rulers, both cult leaders and kings alike, were extremely unnerved by the growing sentiment that those who had died had it coming. For those who had never faced consequences before in their lives, the people's response was mortifying.

When Hydra attacked, there seemed to be many of him running around at once! If any were destroyed, not long after, two more would be sighted. When attacked, he'd shatter into pieces and split. He was like a nightmare: uncatchable and unstoppable.

Hydra's calling card was a threatening manifesto delivered to the people that he would kill their king or local cult leader. If the masses voted that their ruler was good and honest, Hydra would spare him. The votes were not taken on literal polls, but rather a genuine and overwhelming majority outcry of support for their ruler to be spared was a vote for their life, and anything else was a condemnation. Fake shows of support orchestrated by the ruler were instantly disregarded and punished with prejudice.

It really was simple. If Hydra said he would kill someone and their people overwhelmingly made clear they did not want him to, he would not. Yet, never had it ever occurred that a majority ever pleaded for their ruler's life.

The only other way for the monarch to survive was to willingly give up their crown and convert their nation to democracy or for the cult leader to retire their post and democratize their cult. If neither of these could be satisfied, Hydra would sink his fangs into the despot.

This doubly effective psychological warfare would make a ruler irrational and overreact right before their untimely deaths. Their lashing out would make them even more unpopular and see that their subjects welcomed their fate even more.

Many feared a succession crisis or power vacuum after the overthrow. Zeus would desperately try to insert one of his lackeys, but many were hesitant to put themselves up next on the chopping block.

In the meantime, very mysteriously, any local democratic organizations in the polis would take charge and stabilize governance, frequently converting the deposed monarch's legacy into a democratic one. This was also believed to be the work of Hydra and his organization: the Sinisters.

The realization that Hydra did not act alone was horrifying to the rulers. Their subjects and servants were assisting that madman. The rulers all at once became aware of the "invisible" workers that kept everything running. Hydra was the only culprit whose name or face was ever focused on, but everyone knew that he couldn't have done it without their help.

He took all the blame and ensured that the vengeful oppressed got their revenge on their otherwise untouchable oppressors. Paranoia gripped the ruling class of Graia, and the otherwise invincible façade they put up began to fade. Outside observers began to note that their rulers could be killed if they ever got out of line.

Plain and simple, this was a declaration of class warfare. Having done his very best to inspire class collaboration, Zeus was panicking and losing his mind. His competence was being called into question because he still could not keep this under control. Then, he noticed that none of Hades' people were being threatened and began accusing Hades of somehow being involved.

"I feel like we've been here before." Hades groaned as Zeus finished ranting at him.

"This time is different. The villain has repeatedly admitted to agreeing with your radical ideas. I have no doubt that you are to blame for this, either directly or indirectly!" Zeus cried.

"I have never called for anyone to commit murder for my causes. I've already disavowed his murders as you disavowed Procrustes," Hades said. That just made Zeus even angrier. That point was still rather sensitive for him.

"Make this right. I'm sick of having to clean up your messes!" Zeus had the gall to say before storming out. He was at wit's end. Coincidentally, Zeus' most loyal minions were among the evillest targets that Hydra had taken out. If he lost too many more of them, his regime would be finished!

TALE 17

Enemy of my Enemy

The Olympians defeated the Titans, and Zeus ascended Typhon's throne. The evil titan king was banished to the ends of the world where none could hope to find him. Most celebrated from the bottom of their hearts.

By contrast, Krius, Typhon's most loyal soldier, would not stand for this! In the immediate aftermath of the war, he attacked the goddess Terra, who had dared to steal Typhon away from him.

The pathetic display was ended by Terra with a single attack. Krius knew that he could not return his master with brute strength alone. He had to be smarter, so he decided to bide his time. So, Krius swallowed his pride when Zeus offered him a deal to become his executioner just as he had been in the previous regime. Krius, the servant of Typhon, became the servant of shining Zeus. For now…

After the war, many Titans went into an ancient equivalence of witness protection. They received new names and identities to start over. Krius now went by Leonidas, the founding king of Sparta. His partner in crime, Dione, now known as Gorgo. She had truly reformed and just wanted to live a peaceful life. But as a Titan, she was inseparable from Krius, and so now, out of habit, she stayed close to Leonidas.

The Spartans were famous for their military might and role as the enforcers of the Olympians. Their patron gods were Mars and Zeus, from whom they took their marching orders. Training, deploying, and even daily life were regimented and orderly extensions of their military lifestyle. The Spartans were a warrior race that carried on the kratocracy of the Titans.

After a century of serving as Graia's policeman, Sparta's wickedness did not escape the attention of Hydra. The rebel condemned them as the main enforcers of Zeus' wicked regime.

Then, one day, one of Hydra's dreaded manifestos arrived in the lands of Sparta, declaring that Leonidas' life was on the line. Leonidas did not surrender his crown. He was confident that his subjects would cry out to spare him. Then, when Hydra came for him anyways, he could reveal Hydra did not truly care about the people's will.

To Leonidas' shock and horror, though, Hydra considered all Spartans, including all their slaves who outnumbered the warrior citizens ten to one. As much as the warrior Spartans raised their voices in protest of Hydra killing their king, the helots did not raise their voices to defend Leonidas.

The Spartan King was enraged at his slaves for not coming to his defense. Once this Hydra situation was dealt with, he would punish them severely. As he grumbled to himself and thought of ways to make them suffer even more than usual, the king was shocked to find another man sitting on his throne late at night.

Leonidas was confused and, at first, mistook him for Typhon. As a warrior first and king second, he was not among the assembled when Hydra first attacked. He really did look like Typhon. Leonidas was so overwhelmed with emotion that he froze in a moment of utter surprise and joy.

"Krius..." Hydra began in a soothing voice, "you haven't changed."

Leonidas' heart skipped a beat. That voice... his lord Typhon was calling his name once again. At once, his composure shattered, and he was drawn in by the serpent. Seeing this, Hydra smiled.

In the next moment, Leonidas was thrown from his throne room into the palace courtyard. He'd just barely survived Hydra's opening attack. He was enamored by the figure of Typhon, but he was still a warrior. Even if just barely, his battle instincts were able to save him.

"I'm impressed, Krius. You're indeed just as strong as you were during the war." Hydra grinned.

"Stop pretending to be Typhon! Your tricks won't work on me, imposter!" the enraged Spartan king growled. Leonidas counterattacked by making use of his enchanted helmet. As a replica of Mars' own divine weapon, Leonidas' helmet was made of a special Adamant that could morph into any shape the king desired.

Leonidas called upon his trusty spear and shield to make war with the Hydra. Hydra responded with a humble farming sickle. Round and round, Leonidas went, leaping around and attacking from every angle as Hydra half-hazardly blocked and dodged.

As a student of Mars himself, Leonidas was a master of every weapon he'd laid eyes on. His shapeshifting helmet became any weapon of war he needed. A spear and shield, a sword, a bow and arrows, anything Leonidas imagined was his to command. And all of them were equally useless against the Hydra.

Despite looking exactly like the sickle-wielding Typhon, Hydra couldn't have fought more differently. His completely distinct fighting style continuously caught Leonidas off guard and nearly spelled his doom on multiple occasions whenever he would finally counterattack.

That infuriatingly casual fighting style… it lacked Typhon's aggressive ferocity. This arrogant and untouchable style reminded him much more of… her. Reverting to his default spear and shield weapon combo, Leonidas raised his fighting Power to its limit. Leonidas grew angrier still at this imposter and threw his spear at him!

Hydra simply leaned out of the way and dodged it. His feet still had not moved from where he'd landed in the courtyard. However, while he was already off balance from dodging, Leonidas sprung his trap! The king's shield morphed into yet another spear, and the king moved to skewer the man through the heart.

Leonidas' blade struck its target, impaling the pretender through his heart! Leonidas roared with victorious laughter! Even an Immortal god could not survive being impaled through his vital organs with Adamant. Then, shockingly, Hydra began laughing as well. He grabbed Leonidas' hand where it held the spear so that he could not escape.

"Nice try. My turn now." Hydra grinned. The snake swung his sickle to gore Leonidas, but the king sliced his own arm off with his free hand so that he could escape Hydra's grip. As he leaped away to avoid the slice to his stomach, Leonidas was filled with terror. That ploy was exactly like something Typhon would do. Only the king of the Titans could survive such a mortal wound so effortlessly.

While Leonidas was distracted by considering such things, Hydra took the opportunity to further remind the king of Typhon. His eyes began to glow a fiery red before blasting the king with his flaming eyebeams!

Leonidas was taken completely off guard and blasted off his feet by the demonic flames. The king of Sparta writhed in agony on the ground as the flames melted his armor and body while keeping him from regenerating. Truly, those were Typhon's eyes.

In the face of such power, Leonidas had no chance. Even the Titan powers Typhon had given him back during the war would not have been enough to close the gap between himself and this new enemy.

Hydra casually pried the spear from his own heart before crushing it down into a ball with his bare hands. Just as quickly, the hole in his chest regenerated as if nothing had happened.

Finally, the guards on duty began assembling to investigate, but Hydra snapped his fingers, and in a moment, black Adamant snakes appeared and ensnared them all. The soldiers fell over, restrained completely by the many heads of the Hydra. Leonidas was on his own.

"I was speaking as myself before, Krius. You really haven't changed since the Titan War. You're just as wicked now as you were back then. And for that, you deserve to burn," Hydra declared as his flaming eyes fired up again.

Hydra prepared to incinerate Leonidas with the very eyes that the king had loved so much. But, just in the nick of time, Gorgo arrived and punched Hydra's head clean off! At once, Leonidas' queen rushed to his side to check if he was okay.

Then, she felt chills down her spine as a familiar laugh filled the air. Leonidas and Gorgo turned around only to see a horrific, inhuman sight! Hydra's body remained standing, and where one head had been before, two identical heads now cackled at them, attached to the body via long Adamant snakes. That thing wasn't human!

"Dione… it really is a shame. You seemed so close to turning over a new leaf. If not for your devotion to Krius, perhaps you could have been spared." The Hydra heads hissed.

The two heads lunged forth with bared fangs to inject their venom into the power couple. Gorgo defended her husband by destroying each head with one of her mighty punches. From each destroyed head, two more emerged. As Gorgo kept destroying the heads, more and more swarmed about. The more she fought against Hydra, the more powerful he was becoming!

"Dione!" Leonidas cried. Gorgo turned around in horror to find that while she was distracted by the many-headed Hydra, an identical single-headed Hydra was looming above Leonidas with his sickle drawn! The many-headed version at once seized her, restraining Gorgo so that the single-headed Hydra could strike his true target!

Leonidas was barely regenerated enough to put up a fight. And what fight he did put up was quickly stamped out as Hydra planted his foot on the king's throat. The restrained soldiers of Sparta cried out powerlessly. Even the gorgeous queen was unable to save her beloved. But no… she refused to lose him.

Above the fight, a thunderstorm gathered. Gorgo called upon her very own Sword of Damocles to empower her! In most kingdoms, only the king received such a divine gift, but in Sparta, both king and queen were Zeus' warriors.

Leonidas refused to take the power of any god other than Typhon into himself, but Gorgo didn't care about such things. When it came to saving her Leo, she'd do anything.

The empowered Gorgo completely vaporized the many-headed Hydra that held her restrained! Her explosive flame of Power sparked with Zeus' divine lightning, and as every Graiac knew: dragons were rather allergic to lightning.

The single-headed Hydra (the true one) was alarmed that his decoy had been destroyed. He'd only created it with enough Power to buy him time to sneak behind Gorgo, however, it was no pushover. To destroy the entire thing so easily meant that Gorgo the Spartan was now on the same level as Dione the Titaness.

Gorgo leaped forward and punched Hydra through several wings of the palace! Hydra laughed with amusement to himself as he stood up. He hadn't expected this.

Gorgo leaped after him and tried to crush the snake with a punch. Hydra shattered into pieces, revealing that it was yet another double.

"Honestly, I figured that Zeus was too much of a misogynist to entrust any of his powers to you." Hydra chuckled from behind Gorgo. Gorgo turned around and shattered that Hydra as well.

"But I suppose that the survival of his system trumps even his hatred of women," two Hydras spoke with one voice from either side of Gorgo. Gorgo recognized this pattern: it was just like the heads from before. Frantically, Gorgo dashed away to get back to Leonidas' side. Sure enough, Hydra was again trying to kill the king by luring her away. Gorgo would not let him.

"Damn it. I keep trying to spare you! Are you really so eager to die for this man?" Hydra asked while blocking and dodging her many fierce attacks.

"You'd never understand what it's like. I love Krius more than I fear death," Gorgo declared before shattering Hydra's sickle with a punch. The snake looked at his destroyed blade with a nervous laugh. Gorgo prepared a follow-up punch for the helpless Hydra, only to be sent flying by a massive hammer!

"Yeah, he's too much of an idiot to ever get that." A small woman sighed as she walked over. Her hair was like a bumblebee, black with flashes of gold akin to lightning streaking across the night sky. Her black and golden divine armor looked like that of a honeybee, but her sting was that of lightning instead of a stinger. As she reached out her hand, the massive hammer that was crushing Gorgo returned to the woman's hand.

"Mel, what are you doing here? I told you that I could handle it." Hydra grinned at the woman with the hammer.

"You were taking too long. We agreed that she only gets to live if she doesn't get in the way. If the queen is so determined to die with her king, it is only fair to honor her devotion," the woman he called Mel replied.

"Fair enough." Hydra sighed. "It's just that… she reminded me a lot of someone I know."

"Stop being annoying and get your head in the game, Hydra." Mel scoffed.

While the two were chit-chatting, Gorgo had picked herself up and regenerated from the hammer blow. Rushing to attack Hydra again, she was intercepted when the hammer wielder met her fist with the swing of her weapon.

"Sorry, unlike that idiot, I'm not afraid to hit a girl." The hammer wielder grinned. She fended off Gorgo as Hydra casually strolled over to the still-wounded Leonidas, ready to finish the job. Gorgo shrieked in despair as she pushed past her limits but was still unable to rush to her husband's aid. Hydra moved to slay Leonidas again, only for his sickle to be deflected by some invisible force!

Hydra was confused before the invisible foe removed his cloak to reveal a gigantic bident-wielding Monster! It was

Hades, the lord of the dead, in his Monster form! Swinging his bident all about, the giant Hades tried and failed to hit Hydra. He tore up the terrain as all his missed blows failed to even approach their target.

However, while he could not hit Hydra, he did succeed in forcing him further away from Leonidas. Hydra retreated to the hammer wielder's side. Now Hades stood between him and Leonidas as Gorgo kept her from aiding him.

The giant Monster loomed over them. Mel threw her hammer, but Hades dodged so quickly that he seemed to disappear. Despite his great size, his speed was nothing to scoff at. Even in his giant form, he was able to make use of his powers of invisibility. Then, at once, he struck from behind to try and hit both Hydra and Mel at once.

Just in the nick of time, Hydra turned around and caught his gigantic bident with one hand. Everyone else was shocked! What was more, Hades and Gorgo noticed that the thrown hammer wasn't aiming at Hades; it was speeding toward the immobilized Leonidas. Hades was held in place by Hydra's vice-like grip, so it was up to Gorgo. Pushing her speed to the limit, Gorgo managed to intercept the hammer and knock it off course. Yet she only achieved this at the cost of great injury to herself.

Mel's hammer came back around from her throw so she could catch it. While Hydra held Hades in place, she jumped up and prepared to attack. With her great strength, she could shatter his Monster like glass.

Before she could, Hades ejected from his construct and detonated it in Hydra and Mel's face. As he landed safely outside the blast radius, Hades smiled that he owed Hecate for that idea.

But then, when the dust cleared, they saw that Hydra had blocked that attack with one hand as well. Despite that good showing, he assessed that the two versus three odds were not to his liking, especially as Leonidas was almost fully healed now and ready to join the fight, and other Spartan soldiers began arriving as backup. Grabbing hold of Mel, he teleported away!

Hades breathed a sigh of relief, but in the very next moment, Leonidas was in his face demanding an explanation.

"How did you get into my country, god of the dead!?" the King of Sparta demanded.

"I—" Hades began, only to be cut off.

"For all I know, you're a co-conspirator!" Leonidas roared.

"No, I heard of the assassination threat and wanted to help. After all, I'm tired of getting blamed by Zeus over and over." Hades finally managed to get a word out.

"How did you even know of the assassination? If you aren't working with Hydra, that should be impossible. The assassination threat has been kept under wraps in my country; nobody abroad should have known. Unless, just as I suspected, you must have spies in my court, meddling in Spartan affairs!" Leonidas roared.

"Why do you have spies skulking about in my land!?" Hades cried in response. After all, just as Leonidas theorized, Hades had only sent his in to figure out why Leonidas' agents were around even after Hades had cleaned up Aidoneus'.

"I'll have them purged." Leonidas fumed.

"This is getting nowhere. Look, if I'd had more time to prepare, I would've brought Terra with me. Then we might've had a chance to catch them." Hades sighed.

"Which is, of course, why you neglected to bring her!" Leonidas could twist Hades' words into the worst possible interpretation every time.

The king's pride was clearly hurt by having to be saved by others. However, when Leonidas wasn't looking, Gorgo thanked Hades from the bottom of her heart for helping save her dear husband. He didn't like Leonidas, but when he saw Gorgo's genuine thanks, he was given pause. Leonidas sucked, but even he had people that loved him.

Though, Hades' sympathies quickly evaporated. Hydra's assassination failed, but he still released all the dirt he'd gathered on Leonidas. It made what Hades' spies had found look like nothing. Sparta's past of countless military brutalities and slaughters based on false pretenses that boggled the mind was exposed. But most of note to Hades was the fact that info just so happened to include evidence that Leonidas had been drawing up plans of attack to destroy the land of Hades! When pressed, Leonidas' defense wasn't exactly reassuring.

"Sparta has battle plans drawn up for invading and destroying every single nation in the Kosmos. That fool Hades isn't getting any special treatment." Leonidas scoffed.

Yet shockingly, that was enough for the rulers, and they moved on as if nothing had happened. Hades was not convinced, but many other gods insisted that he drop it. Besides, Leonidas was not the enemy of the gods… Hades was!

At yet another meeting of the gods, instead of being upset at what had been revealed about Leonidas, almost everyone spent time pointing fingers at Hades. He was the one spreading hate against the rulers, and this was the result. Eventually, Hades stopped trying to defend himself. Whatever. He tried to help, and he got nowhere.

He'd just learned that some people at the table were probably (definitely) plotting to kill him. They were forcing Terra to go about investigating Hydra during what should have been her time off with him. Why was he bothering to try to help them? Hades stormed out.

When Hades returned home, he just wanted to lie down. All of this was so exhausting. The kings were making their problem his problem and distracting him from his projects. He was so far behind on his committee work… things couldn't possibly get any worse.

"Hey, Hades." Hydra waved at him casually.

"Hey." The exhausted Hades mechanically waved back. Then he stopped and had to process what exactly had happened. Hydra, the serial regicidal killer, was sitting in the palace living room, playing dice with Cerberus! When Cerberus won, he lovingly patted her on the head as if they knew each other.

"Cerberus! Get away from him." Hades panicked. Cerberus was confused.

"Don't worry, papa. I know this looks like stranger danger, but it's fine. He smells just like me." Cerberus smiled. Hades didn't know how to respond, but now was not the time for her usual antics.

"Even though we just met today, we recognized each other at first sight. It really is a surreal experience to meet a long-lost sibling after all this time." Hydra smiled as he stood up. What was he talking about? Was that why he looked so much like Typhon? His eyes were different from Cerberus' since she didn't inherit Typhon's demonic eyes… however, their jet-black hair did look pretty similar. Their wild raven hair was almost identical to their biological father: Typhon.

But there was no time for that! He was a serious threat; Hades needed to get everyone out and call for help.

"Calm down. I haven't done anything wrong. I've just been playing with this little one while I waited for you to return." Hydra grinned.

"Yeah, calm down," Mel said from behind Hades. She was just lounging and taking a nap on one of the publicly available sofas! They'd really just come in and made themselves at home.

Hades didn't like being surrounded by two enemies that were each as powerful as a Titan. Mel stood up and rubbed her eyes as Hydra casually stepped forward. The two now stood directly in front of and behind Hades.

"What do you want?" Hades demanded.

"To talk. But not here." Hydra grinned. What did he mean by that? Hades soon had his answer. In a flash of light, Hydra pulled himself, Hades, and Mel into his Microcosm: Lernia Lake!

TALE 18

Deal with the Devil

Hydra's Microcosm was a lake. That was it, really: a peaceful swamp that surrounded a large body of water. However, the ever-alert Hades noted that the water had many peculiar properties. Hades and Hydra were standing on the water's surface without needing to use Power to float. The god of the dead looked into the swampy water. Despite the bright sun above, it was oddly opaque and foreboding.

"Like the scenery?" Hydra asked, catching Hades' attention mid-analysis.

"This is where I grew up in Lernia. Ever been before?" Hydra asked.

"Can't say I have..." Hades replied as he occasionally glanced back down at the water.

"No need to be so on edge. Your opponent is right in front of you." Hydra pointed at himself.

"You'll forgive me, but all the other Microcosms I've been trapped in have had some hidden dangers to be wary of," Hades noted.

"I'll tell you what. If you impress me enough, I'll show off this realm's hidden features. But unless you can prove yourself a threat, I'm the only thing you need to worry about." Hydra grinned.

Hades was skeptical of that promise but had to accept that against such a powerful foe, he couldn't afford to have his attention split. Hades prepared his bident and faced down the Hydra.

"Does that promise include her?" Hades asked as he looked at Mel. Despite her petite size, Hades could tell that she was Hydra's peer. Hades was a god, but he concluded that he stood no chance of defeating both the hammer and sickle.

"No need to worry about that. I'm staying out of the fight. Killing rulers is hard work, and I'm exhausted. You boys have fun." Mel said as she set her hammer down on its side and casually sat on it to watch the fight. The hammerhead was so massive and heavy that the handle that stuck out horizontally served as a stable seat for her. Even with all her weight on it, the hammer did not tip. Hades was glad he didn't have to worry about getting hit by that, at least.

But still, across from him stood Hydra. Even beyond his ominous resemblance to Typhon, Hades felt nervousness at his massive Power. The god of the dead couldn't help but feel like this was just the tip of the iceberg.

"I take it you're here for revenge since I interrupted your last assassination?" Hades tensed up.

"Well, you did ruin it. Those things take a lot of effort and planning to pull off, y'know," Hydra casually responded.

"Well, as sad as that is, I can't say I'm sorry. Though you claim to have admirable goals, I don't like resorting to violence. That's why I want to be certain off the bat… are you sure there is no peaceful solution to our conflict?" Hades asked.

"Hades… no. Fight as if you intend to kill. I want to see you at your best, god of the dead!" Hydra cackled before leaping forward to attack with an axe kick. Hydra fought with both hands behind his back as his barrage of killer kicks kept Hades on edge.

Hades did his best to block and dodge the blows but couldn't help but notice how casually and effortlessly Hydra was attacking. He was clearly unimpressed with Hades: after all, he wasn't even as strong as Krius. However, the god of the dead figured he could use this to his advantage.

After seeing an opening, Hades diverted all his Power away from his bident into generating his Monster. Rather than attacking, he manifested the giant, horned skull of his Monster and bit Hydra's lower body off! Hydra and Mel were impressed by how quickly Hades brought it out.

Hydra abandoned his swallowed half and instead used his Power to yank his upper body away, but Hades wouldn't just let him escape. Generating the rest of the Monster, Hades pressed the advantage and swung his bident down at Hydra. Hydra caught the blade with his bare hands as he regenerated his legs. Hades was shocked! Mel smirked.

With his incredible strength, Hydra shattered Hades' giant bident with his bare hands! Then, he created his iconic sickle (and a loincloth to cover up) with a thought.

As soon as Hydra leaped at Hades, his Power blazed out and clearly revealed that he had hardly tried at all before! Even the jaws of his Monster wouldn't be enough to do damage now.

Hades used his Monster form and was unable to defeat Hydra. If he really was Cerberus' brother, that meant that he could also increase his Power with a Monster form of his own. If that was the case… Hades didn't even want to imagine how strong his final form would be.

Hydra cackled wildly as he battered Hades. The tiny man was breaking apart the giant Monster with his bare hands. With each punch, he could launch the giant as if it were light as a feather. Smacking him around the arena like a rag doll, Hydra had clear control of the fight. Hades tried to grab Hydra with his massive hands, but he easily evaded. Instead, Hydra fired his flaming eyes right at Hades!

Hades surprised him by intentionally opening a hole in his Adamant construct so that the flaming beam would pass through and not hit him. While Hydra was still reacting to that, Hades fired back a massive beam of his own.

Hydra swiftly evaded and appeared behind Hades. Hades moved swiftly and repositioned himself behind Hydra. Hades struck, thinking he'd get a sneak attack. Hydra instead swiftly repositioned himself behind Hades and punched the Monster into the ground, shattering it into pieces. Hydra landed atop the pile of rubble with a confident grin.

He was waiting for Hades to come crawling out of the ruins, but nothing came. It was pure silence. After a few seconds, it was obvious: he was hiding using his power of invisibility. Mel, who was otherwise unimpressed, suddenly became very alert and stood up, grabbing her hammer.

"Don't worry. He isn't the type to take hostages." Hydra reassured her, "He's going to come after me." The two waited in quiet and tense anticipation.

Then, out of nowhere, Hydra punched at the air! Hades fell over with a bloody nose! How was he hit!? Hades was certain that he was still invisible. Even the light of Power's sacred flame should not have been able to see him.

"Sorry. The same trick won't work on me twice," Hydra warned before firing his flaming eyes at the downed Hades. The ground exploded, but there was nobody left. Hydra grinned. To Hades' horror, Hydra suddenly disappeared from his view! Could he copy abilities like Typhon?

"No. You're just too slow to follow my movements." Hydra snickered from behind Hades. Hades turned around just in time to be punched in the stomach and sent flying across the sky. Hades disappeared again, only to once more be hit before he could sneak attack Hydra.

Hydra grabbed Hades by the throat and, from high in the sky, crashed him down into the bottom of the lake! They'd smashed down from such a height that the force had blasted all the water in the middle of the lake up into a massive splash, revealing a giant hole in the bog with massive walls of water on all sides.

Hades screamed in agony at the painful blow as he sank into the solid stone of the lakebed. Then, all the water came crashing down on him, filling in the space.

Hydra flew back up to safety, leaving Hades to float in the drink helplessly. Then, the god of the dead saw it: what dwelt in the opaque lake. All around him floated a swarm of countless ferocious sea Monsters. They all lay in wait, patiently stalking him from afar. Seeing their gleaming eyes, Hades knew that if they all attacked, he was done for. That was the secret of the Microcosm. Even if, by some miracle, he was able to triumph over Hydra, there was no way he stood a chance against all of those beasts.

Hydra waited patiently as Hades pulled himself out of the water. The god of the dead looked to be half-dead himself, desperately panting for breath against this foe. However, even still, he could not give up.

"Well… if you have any secret divine attacks to throw out, now would be the time." Hydra grinned.

"Afraid not." Hades panted.

"Then… since defeating me is impossible, will you yield?" Hydra demanded.

"Never!" Hades declared. His eyes were filled with determination. He'd been in worse spots before. He'd fought Typhon himself! Hades was not the sort of man to give up, even in the face of impossible odds.

Hydra was impressed and let out a bellowing laugh. Mel sighed as she walked over to Hydra while dragging her hammer behind her. Hydra laughed and laughed until Mel bonked him on the head with her hammer. Hydra was, of course, just fine.

"I think that's enough; you win." Mel sighed.

"Don't write me off just yet! I can still fight!" Hades cried.

"Forgive her. She isn't referring to our fight. We just had a bet about your perseverance. Mel here gravely underestimated you, Mr. Hades. But just as I suspected, you passed the test." Hydra laughed again while casually lifting Mel's hammer off his head.

"I assume you've had enough fun, so let's get serious already," Mel grumbled before reverting her hammer into its seat configuration. Hades became nervous, but Hydra reassured him it was fine. The fight was over. He even helped the injured Hades limp over to some soft grass to sit on. Setting him down, Hydra began to treat Hades' wounds.

"I must apologize for all that. Mel here doubted your mettle, so I wanted to show her that you were a man who we could trust," Hydra explained. Hades was horribly confused.

"Even against an overwhelming foe, you never gave up. Your reputation as head of the democratic movement is well earned." Hydra smiled. It felt odd for such a friendly tone to be coming out of someone with Typhon's face.

"You could've killed me effortlessly if you wanted to, couldn't you?" Hades sighed. Hydra just began to laugh and patted Hades on the back.

"Yes, and this idiot could've also killed Leonidas and Gorgo if he wasn't so annoying," Mel complained. As soon as she said that, Hades remembered: he was talking to serial killers! They were acting friendly now, but they'd nearly killed him, Leonidas, and Gorgo not that long ago.

Seeing Hades' change in temperament, Hydra became serious and said, "Do not forget that Leonidas, that dog of Olympus, was making plans to have you and the people of your land killed. Sicking Aidoneus on you has failed so now those in power are preparing the more direct approach of Leonidas. Look how readily the rulers have turned on you when given a chance to villainize you." Hydra explained.

"Thanks for the heads up. I'll keep it in mind." Hades pulled away from them.

"No! You don't get it. Our methods may be different, but our goals are the same," Hydra declared. Hades was shocked.

"I'm a child of Typhon, just like your daughter. I was raised by an evil group of Typhon cultists that wanted to reclaim Typhon's Empire as my birthright," Hydra began to Hades' shock.

"...however, I began to notice that by their own logic, they would suffer in the world they were grooming me to create. They all had 'peasant brain' for lack of a better term. They worked against their own interest, and I felt pity for them. Then I noticed Graia at large has befallen a similar fate. People working hard to support a world that abuses and exploits them. Such a thing cannot stand. That is why I must fight for everyone and bring about a world that supports them just as much as they support it!" Hydra declared rather dramatically.

"That sounds noble on paper—" Hades began, only for Hydra to cut him off.

"That makes us comrades, Hades! You've made a lot of progress peacefully but have now hit a wall. As the current world order resisted you with all its might. Keep doing what you're doing. I fully support you. Just let me handle the rest. I'll be your shadow and handle everything you cannot." Hydra grinned.

"My shadow?" Hades asked.

"You must continue to do what is right. Your incorruptible spirit and peaceful nature shall form the base of public support. Meanwhile… I'll handle all the things that should never be done but nonetheless must be. You will be the revolution's light as I am its shadow," Hydra declared.

"I never agreed to work with you," Hades said.

"That is irrelevant. As long as your goal is a better world, we are allies. No matter what you tell Zeus or even what you tell yourself." Hydra smiled.

"But violence should only be used in self-defense," Hades cried.

"Poverty is violence. Imperialist wars for resources are violence. You know that. I've read your writings; you know how many people die to line the pockets of the rulers," Hydra declared. Hades paused.

"If we rely on force to win, we are giving in to those that say might makes right," Hades pleaded.

"Even to those who say that might makes right… what is mightier than people working together? The Titans outnumbered the gods: the warriors outnumbered the rulers. But the common people triumphed over them both! It was the people, the demos, that won that war. Even the mightiest warrior and holiest god trembles at this truth: when people worked together, nothing they planned to do was impossible for them," Hydra cried.

"But a violent revolution is risky... what if it fails? What if it goes astray and is overtaken by a sense of vengeance rather than justice?" Hades asked.

"The results speak for themselves. The deaths of those evil monarchs unquestionably improved the lives of their subjects. I will give my all to keep the revolution's path straight, but even if it strays, know that the end result of liberation trumps all. Even evil acts can bring about good outcomes," Hydra retorted.

"But if you admit they are evil, should anyone so readily use them? Shouldn't such things be saved only as a last resort?" Hades pleaded.

"Zeus' regime has crushed Graia for a hundred years. How much longer should the people be made to suffer before a 'last resort' is justified? Should an obsession with comfort and order put a timeline on another person's freedom or subject them to inhumane conditions because we feel they haven't suffered enough yet? I think they have. They have suffered more than enough, and the time to change is now! You agree with me, so why are you resisting?" Hydra demanded.

"Because... I don't want to bring about change that way..." Hades sighed.

"Do not let the perfect be the enemy of the good. You are letting emotions cloud your judgment," Hydra warned. Hades froze up. He knew he was right. His logical mind was nodding along, but Hades' rigid morals and personality made him hesitant.

Hydra had an answer for everything. Unfortunately, he wasn't as vapid or emotional as Hades' former foes. This Hydra had thought about all this just as much as Hades... maybe even more. On many points, the two had concerningly similar conclusions.

“Until the contradictions in the current world order were resolved, the people’s revolt against their rulers would never end. If they cut off one head, two more would grow to replace it,” Hydra repeated Hades’ thesis at him just differently enough so as not to be plagiarism. It was chilling.

“But still, I’m not with you…” Hades felt obligated to say.

“You’re not with us. You’re not in our way. You couldn’t stop us, even if you wanted to. So don’t delay what we both know is inevitable. I’m not asking for anything else from you,” Hydra reassured the hesitant god.

Hades felt a bit uncomfortable. He didn’t know if he was fully with them. But they made some good points… some that he had suppressed in his own mind. It was almost too good to be true: Hades could wash his hands and leave all the dirty work to them. They were going to do things that he knew were wrong… that he didn’t want to do… but that needed to be done. Was he betraying his pacifist nature by joining with them? Hydra saw Hades’ look of inner conflict but stopped him.

“Hades, let me reiterate: you don’t need to feel guilty. We aren’t asking you to join anything. My one request is that you stay in your own lane and focus on what you have always done. That was better than wasting everyone’s time and trying to get in our way. Besides, even if you wanted to, there isn’t anything you could do to stop me,” Hydra summarised.

Given their ordeal of a battle, Hades couldn’t help but agree. As of late, he felt rather powerless. He couldn’t do much of anything, it seemed.

“However, this is not a free ride. As payment for this, you have to do one thing: actually, pull this off.” Hydra gave a friendly smile.

“I know I… I just hoped the world’s contradictions could be resolved another way. I always intended to pull this off; I thought once I showed everyone the better alternative, they would come of their own accord. Then, maybe the rulers would heed my warnings and peacefully allow the transition to occur," Hades explained. As soon as Hades said it out loud, he felt like a fool.

"You don't want to admit it, but we all know that they would never willingly give up their hold on power," Hydra said plainly.

"Probably not…" Hades reluctantly agreed.

"And they resist change violently. Do you not remember your run-in with Aidoneus? Or the revelations of Sparta's scheming? Who knows who else is preparing to bring harm to you and those you care about? Think of them, Hades. If those who challenge the status quo are not defended, let's be honest: everyone but your wife is as good as dead. You see us as aggressors, but really, we are defenders." Hydra played on Hades' fears.

Hades felt uncomfortable. He didn't like what Hydra was implying. Like Terra, this natural conclusion was one he didn't want to admit. Just as the last change could only be made via violent overthrow, so too did democracies require revolutionary action against monarchies.

"How would the transition to another world be made otherwise?" Hydra demanded an answer. Hades had none. He didn't want that to be the case, but he also knew that he couldn't think of an alternative. He felt sick. But then, Hydra put his hand on his shoulder with a reassuring smile.

"Hades, I know you're a gentle soul. You're doing all this to help people and make the world a better place. Violence is the last thing you want." Hydra smiled.

"That is why… we shall become your shadow. We will do the dirty work needed to change the world," Hydra declared.

Hades felt relieved. Secretly, he'd always wished someone would say those exact words. Then, he felt even more sick than before. What was he thinking!? Was he genuinely happy that someone would kill on his behalf? Great guilt fell over Hades.

"Don't worry. There's no need to feel guilty. We would've done this with or without you. Whatever actions we take are our own burdens. We'll each stay in our lanes. That is all," Hydra explained.

Hades felt relieved again and then sicker still. No matter how he sliced it, Hades had to accept these thoughts that had been at the back of his mind. He didn't want to kill anyone… but he wanted people to die. He didn't hate them; he'd spare them if he could, but… ultimately, they were just in the way.

Such thoughts were the thoughts of villains… right? Everyone said they were evil, but now that Hades knew what they actually believed, he found a great deal aligned with his own ideals. What did that mean? Seeing Hades' wavering resolve, Hydra reminded him.

"Hades, changing the world is not taking a stroll in the park or watching a play or any other thing that can be done casually and carelessly. It is not casual or careless- or gentle or temperate or restrained; it cannot be. To force the world to change is an act of aggression and violence. It is to spit in the face of the very gods that established the firmament of our current world order. It is to pray for their downfall and bring about that overthrow by any means necessary. One's personal feelings can never get in the way of that paramount goal. We cannot let the perfect be the enemy of the good. A bloody yet successful violent revolution is better than a tepid and failed peaceful one," Hydra declared.

Hades was left speechless. Truly, with his charisma, if Hydra sought to be king of the world as Typhon or Zeus had, he would have been a shoo-in. Hades told him as much, nervously laughing that he should lead the movement.

"No. And put any fears of me co-opting this revolution out of your mind. I will not live to see the new world. As your shadow, I shall take all the bloodshed and evil that must be done onto myself. When the revolution is over, I will die and violence with me," Hydra said without hesitation. Hades was shocked. At that, Mel bristled.

"Murder is evil. And a murderer cannot reign in the era of peace that is to come after. But it is the role of the warrior to resolve the conflict between the rulers and the people." Hydra smiled.

"I shall become the villain that the world needs so that when the democratic revolution succeeds, I can have all the revolution's sins put on me and then die. That way, you can remain the blameless hero and take over once it is finished," Hydra explained. Hades didn't know what to say. They'd never met before, but he trusted him that much. Mel became upset at those words and grabbed Hydra by his cloak.

"You mean we! You aren't doing this alone, you idiot! We're both accepting that burden together! Stop talking like you have to do everything yourself!" Mel cried. Hydra looked surprised for a moment before smiling tenderly at her concern.

"Of course," He replied before taking her hand.

After the two talked it out a bit, they returned their focus to Hades, their new partner in crime of sorts. They didn't agree on everything, but ultimately, the three formed an odd semi-alliance. Even if they wouldn't directly coordinate or help each other, they knew not to get in the other's way. This was their diversity of tactics.

Then, the very Microcosm began to shake and creak. Something big was hitting the entire mini universe from all sides and causing ripples and shockwaves through it. The fierceness and rabidness of the attack were unnerving, like a swarm trying to force their way in. Then, the attack that was coming from everywhere suddenly stopped. Odd.

Then, a single, thunderous shockwave that was far more violent than the others combined punched a crack into the Microcosm! That one sent shivers down the spines of everyone who had been forced to endure it. Less than a punch rocking the plane, it felt as if some kind of bloodcurdling scream from some eldritch horror echoing through spacetime itself.

Whatever caused such a phenomenon was too terrifying to imagine. The cracks, in reality, began to widen as that terrifying something continued forcing its way in.

"What is going on!? It's impossible to interact with a Microcosm from the outside!" Mel cried in utter terror.

As soon as the word "impossible" was uttered, Hades knew who it was. Not a moment later, Terra burst into the Microcosm. She forced open the slice in reality with her bare hands, growling with fury as her sacred Power flooded the Microcosm, and its very presence began to disintegrate everything and erase all of existence in her wake.

"What do you think you're doing to my husband?" The most terrifying voice boomed from the otherwise sweet and pleasant goddess. Though Terra, the woman, stood before them, her roar was an overwhelming noise that came booming from their insides and simultaneously from all directions around them. From every direction came every voice in every tongue, both known and unknown to mankind. It was as if the world itself was shouting at them. That very angry lady was just a thin slice of something very big and very scary that they'd just pissed off.

Behind her, in the infinite void outside this artificial universe, there was yet another dimensional fissure that could be seen. On the other side was a Great Ball of Land and Sea. The dot in the middle of the slit formed the appearance of a massive Divine Eye just looming and observing the puny humans from afar. It was as if some giant monster was looking through the peephole at its weak, defenseless prey.

However, upon spying that Hades was still alive, it could calm down. As Terra exhaled and calmed herself down, both slits in reality closed. Now, the small, harmless-looking woman stood before them as if none of that had just happened. Hades, Hydra, and Mel were still too shocked to move.

"I said, what do you think you're doing to my husband?" Terra angrily repeated herself, this time with the voice of a human. Finally, Hydra's ability to think and act returned to him. At once, he pounced and sucker-punched Hades! Hades knew it had to be convincing, but it still really hurt. Hydra paused as he pretended to only then notice Terra. But when he turned to look at her furious glare, he felt another shiver down his spine. Hydra gave a genuinely nervous laugh as he backed off.

"Looks like time is up. Lucky you, Hades, it seems you get to live." Hydra smirked before leaping back. Terra teleported behind him and shattered Hydra-like glass with a single punch.

Terra didn't even flinch and instead turned to find that while Mel had vanished, there was an army of Hydras all mockingly laughing at her. With the snap of her fingers, she turned them all to dust. None of them were the real deal.

"He got away," Terra growled. The stress and fear of losing Hades had turned the goddess of nature into a truly terrifying thing. After all, while most associate Mother Nature with the nurturing and life-giving aspects of nature… in ancient Graia, she was revered as embodying all of nature's fury. From the calamitous power of storms to black holes, she was not to be messed with. The sunny disposition of the life-giving goddess could easily be turned into the fiery wrath of a supernova when truly angered.

But all that melted away as she cradled Hades in her arms and cried tears of joy that he was okay. Hades embraced Terra as well. Terra tore down the Microcosm around them as the two were returned to the real world safe and sound.

Cerberus ran over and hugged him as well, relieved that Hades was alright. Hades held the two he cared about most close. For a second, he thought about telling them everything but stopped himself. He was still feeling too conflicted. Normally, all he would be able to think about was how happy he was to see them again. But Hydra had left him with much to think about.

TALE 19

The Mycenaeans and Minoans

Melisseus was one of the many human warriors that served on the side of the gods during the Great Titan War. He was the leader of the Kuretes: elite warriors that worshipped Terra and served as the defenders of her champion, Zeus. Despite his mortal powerlessness, he was a mighty warrior with the blessing of the goddess Terra. As a native Cretan, Zeus granted him dominion over his homeland as his reward for liberating it from the Titans.

Under Melisseus' rule from his palace at Knossos, Crete flourished. They were wealthy traders who exported goods and culture across Graia. The Cretans were peaceful. Not a single weapon was to be found among them. Their national defense and protection from Monsters were handled by mercenaries who could be hired with their great wealth.

Such foreign mercenaries were the Mycenaeans, the various Graiacs not from Crete. Chief among the warriors that served them were the Spartans. However, unlike most mercenaries, the Spartans shunned payment in coins. Instead, they wanted access to Cretan craftsmen and workers to supplement all the things a civilization needed but that warriors could not provide. It was a symbiotic relationship. For a time, this relationship existed in a balance.

With the nation's security handled, Melisseus turned inward to further amplify the prosperity of his nation. The king was a follower of Terra and one of the few fools who became kings because they genuinely wanted to use their authority to rule as Terra would have wanted. Ideologically, he was a child of Ouranos rather than Zeus.

The good king tried to rule as ethically as a king could within the system. Since there was no concept of democracy yet, he did the best that he could. Melisseus' goal was this: to transform his position into that of a representative rather than a ruler.

He listened to his people and ruled on their behalf rather than their foreign masters. He abolished debt slavery and established strong labor protections. He valued protectionist economics to grow local merchants rather than have them bought out by big cults. Wealth was brought in and kept within the nation for a change.

For a time, they were prosperous… too prosperous. Zeus normally did not mind prosperity, but the means upset him. What was worse, the pacifistic people of Crete became critical of their support for Zeus' war machine: the Spartans. Lamenting that they were aiding in evil conquests, the people moved Melisseus to cut off any aid for nations that were conquering others or enslaving people.

Melisseus had fought to defeat the Titans and would not aid their ideological descendants in continuing their evil. Zeus was displeased by this. He needed the Spartans as his enforcers to solidify his control of the region. So, he decided to punish Melisseus and send a warning.

Crete was not a democracy, but they were the closest things ever got before the land of Hades. Before his sworn enemy was Hades, Zeus had seen Melisseus as the greatest threat to his beloved system. He devised a plan to get the Cretans back under control and so paid a visit to Crete. A grand celebration was held to greet the divine king, but Melisseus grew worried.

Zeus sat across from Melisseus during a private audience over dinner. Though things were casual and friendly at first with reminiscence of the war on Typhon… things soon took a turn.

"After the war, you've made quite the name for yourself. Though I hear your name often, I am afraid it is not often in the best light," Zeus said after finishing his food.

"I assume the Mycenaean warriors we worked with are upset at our conditional business?" Melisseus answered without skipping a beat. He figured this conversation was coming.

"Yes. All the other Graiacs who surround you will not provide their services for free. From one king to another, it isn't wise to neglect to pay your troops. Their previous defense contract is nearly up, and if Crete does not continue paying its tribute, I worry you might find yourselves defenseless," Zeus indirectly threatened him with a smile.

"Crete is not withholding anything. We expect that by the time it comes to renewing our contract, the Spartans will review our conditions and implement them accordingly. Crete is not trying to sever ties with the Mycenaeans; we are trying to help them change for the better. That is to say, for example, we want the Spartans to stop invading their neighbors and overthrowing their fellow poleis in unprovoked wars of expansion," Melisseus explained.

"Mel, old friend, I wasn't aware you'd become king of Sparta." Zeus let out a hearty laugh as if he'd heard a gut-busting joke.

"Great Zeus, I do this for the sake of the others also. Many other poleis that we deal with adhere to our conditions and fight wars only defensively. We readily offer military aid to them if they are ever attacked. However, if Sparta does not cease their attacks on their fellow, we may one day find ourselves as their enemy. We wouldn't want that." Melisseus explained. He then realized too late that it could be misconstrued as a threat.

"Melisseus… be careful. Graia is a decentralized land of liberty. It was established in this manner to promote freedom and independence for all poleis. No other poleis should be allowed to tell the Spartans how to operate. In fact, you picking favorites and meddling in foreign nations sounded an awful lot like the empire of the Titans," Zeus declared. Melisseus paused; that was a conundrum.

"Melisseus, consider all these things before being too hasty. Do not let the whims of the masses tarnish the prosperous land you've built. After all, you are the king. The final decision comes down to you," Zeus assured his 'old friend' as he saw his wavering resolve.

"That is where I must respectfully disagree, sir. Just as you said, all poleis are to be run in a manner they see fit. Consulting the people was the way of Crete; I am king only by their consent," Melisseus countered. Zeus did his best to contain the disgust rising from within him.

"Yes, I noticed your incessant use of the word 'we'. But if you must outsource rulership to the unwashed masses, you are broadcasting your failure as a king." Zeus scoffed.

"This isn't just about me. In our view, this community rule is the best guard against the old ways of the Titans. If the people of Crete have not changed their minds, I will not either." Melisseus stood his ground.

"I see. How regrettable," Zeus said before taking his leave.

As soon as he left, horrible news came in: a swarm of Monsters were attacking Crete. When Melisseus called upon the Spartans for aid, they refused. If they were not receiving their end of the bargain, why would they help? The same came from all their other usual clients. Almost as if they were coordinating.

The Mycenaeans did not move, but the fleet of man-eating beasts grew closer and closer. In a moment of desperation, Melisseus raised an army of veterans from the Titan War to go fend off the Monsters. The problem was, without a warrior god to grant them Power, they were just mere mortals.

They prayed to Mars, but Zeus, issuing orders to all war gods under his control, withheld his blessing. Terra's establishment of a temple could have been the solution, offering a source for them to receive her divine Power and fight as they once had.

So, Melisseus and all the men went to war as Crete was being evacuated, all according to plan. They would be ruined. It was a fitting punishment whenever the productive workers withheld their services from the warriors. On the battlefield, Zeus expected them to die, but a savior emerged at the last moment. Terra Solaris, patron of the common producers, slew all the beasts that threatened Crete.

She'd heard of their predicament and beneficently offered all those who had come with Melisseus her blessing. Since those brave Cretans were willing to risk their lives even when they had no chance, their courage was rewarded. Terra granted them divine protection and Power, just as she had during the war with the Titans.

Now, the Cretans could protect themselves without needing to rely on outsiders. The army that had set out for certain death returned triumphantly. The blessings expanded further, and Crete became an even greater thorn in Zeus' side.

Even more than defying the military-cult complex, Crete's good standards of living were beginning to inspire people abroad to seek better conditions. Crete became a shining example pointed to by a certain rabble-rouser on Molossos who advocated for his fellow workers' rights.

The people of Crete were workers of great repute largely because the king of the bees saw that they were properly compensated. Listening to their plights, he did everything he could to maximize their happiness and safety. What was more, key industries were nationalized and done collectively rather than handled by private cults. The fact that this succeeded was not a good look for the rulers who sought to exploit their people.

On top of such ideological issues, Crete's good domestic conditions came at the expense of foreign profits. To ensure that Cretan workers were well paid, the price for their services was extremely high. Zeus and the rulers saw this as an infringement on their powers and an attack on their control. An independent common people was blasphemous!

Zeus' wrath boiled against the Cretans. He was supposed to be their patron god, yet in their hour of need, they looked elsewhere. He had delivered them from the Titans, and yet now they schemed against him! He had redefined the economy of the world, and yet they went their own wicked way. How dare they! The thunderer returned to Crete, this time with Leonidas in tow. Negotiations quickly broke down in the same vein as last time.

"The will of the people is final. Sparta, given your refusal to change your wicked ways, it seems we must cut ties. It pains me to do this. I really did hope you could change, Krius,"

Melisseus said with genuine sadness. Leonidas growled, but Zeus spoke over him.

"It is adorable to see your renewed confidence given your better position, Cretan. However, as king of the gods, I must warn you against hubris." Zeus smirked and then spoke no more.

It turned out that doing business ethically in Zeus' system was very difficult indeed. While they no longer needed foreign defenders, trade with other nations began to dry up, and Crete's prosperity with it.

Furthermore, Zeus spread propaganda attacking the Cretans. They were seen as pretentious and arrogant. Trying to rule justly without divine approval was seen as hubris. The humans were doing what was right in their own eyes without considering the will of the gods. All these simultaneous attacks ruined what Melisseus had built. Crete became a pariah state on the verge of ruin. This was a problem that raw might alone could not defeat.

As hard times came to Crete, they became the recipients of aid from the countries they had helped raise up. Unbeknownst to most, those nations were also the same ones bringing about their downfall.

At Zeus' direction, they induced hyperinflation by flooding Crete with counterfeit Cretan drachmas. A weaker currency did not help things. What was worse, those that Terra blessed began to grow old and die. The old Kuretes of Crete died, and the blessing of their goddess died with them.

Now was the time to strike. Melisseus was an old man, and Zeus' agents had turned the people against him. He had no male heirs to inherit his throne. Olympus had convinced the masses that the foreigner Minos would be a good ruler.

Minos was a young warrior and also a demigod son of Zeus himself. Of course, Zeus endorsed him to take over from Melisseus. So, Minos declared Melisseus to be a tyrant who was to blame for his people's bad living conditions. He invaded Crete as a "liberator" and, as the master of a coalition of Mycenaeans, dragged Melisseus from his throne and executed him. Minos was treated as a liberator and a hero for finally bringing Crete under the complete control of Graia.

Zeus used his executive power to induce a condemnation of memory. All records of the Cretans under Melisseus were to be destroyed so that they would be completely forgotten through the process of *damnatio memoriae*. Just as would later be practiced in Reme, the ruling class had the power to literally rewrite history. Now, Minos ruled over the Cretans or, as they would now be called, the Minoans.

However, the princess of Crete, who was Melisseus' daughter, remembered all. Princess Melissa inherited her father's will and cursed Zeus for what he had done. Though they hadn't concluded all their investigating before his overthrow, Melisseus had more or less pieced together how Zeus and his cronies had coordinated this downfall.

He passed this secret to his only child, Melissa. Her wrath burned against Zeus and his whole society! She cursed the gods, especially Zeus, for what had happened. Then, Melissa's mother begged her to stop. There was one more secret that her father had not yet told her. Melisseus had loved and raised Melissa, but he was not her birth father. While her father was away, Zeus, the king of the gods, assumed his shape and forced himself on Melisseus' wife to beget Melissa.

Melissa was horrified. It was true that she was born with the divine strength of a demigod, but she had always assumed that it was because of the blessing of Terra. Her mother reassured her that Melisseus knew but never held it against the girl.

Melisseus was her true father. He loved her, raised her, and taught her right from wrong. Zeus had done nothing but hurt those Melissa loved. He'd led to the death of her father and assaulted her mother! There was nobody under heaven that Melissa hated more.

Of all the gods, Zeus was the most prolific bearer of demigods on account of his tendency to pursue anything that even resembled the female form. He also had a habit of siring heirs without the consent of the mother.

It was not an exaggeration to say that Zeus was something of a serial offender; a shameless and endlessly evil one at that. Typhon had taught him that a real man took what was his. In emulating him, Zeus had become a monster of equal caliber. Melissa only grew to hate Zeus all the more. That beast had harmed her dear mother, and that was the last straw. Now, Melissa began to plot her revenge.

When Minos left the safety of Crete to get revenge on his royal engineer Daedelus (it was a long story), Mel followed him. She tracked him down and effortlessly defeated him in battle. Her otherworldly strength was truly worthy of her divine origin. Now, Minos begged for his life, just as Melisseus had begged for his. Minos appealed to Mel as a fellow child of Zeus, but even mentioning that name made Mel's anger boil even hotter.

She struck him with a divine thunderbolt and blasted the villain to ashes. Now that the dirty deed was done, Mel fled into the night. However, little did she know she was being watched and followed by an interested party.

When Mel detected that she was being pursued, she decided to fight rather than run. She attacked the pursuer and nearly defeated him! Only then did her foe reveal his ultimate form as a monster that could overwhelm her demigod strength.

Rather than kill her, this mysterious foe explained that he found her extremely interesting. She had killed his prey before he had the chance to. Melissa told him that whatever reason he had to kill Minos paled in comparison to hers.

"You're right. It wasn't personal. I've never met the man. It is just that I have made it my mission to slay all the evil kings of Graia. Simply put, I'm on a mission to destroy Zeus' world." The man smiled.

He was Hydra, the son of Typhon, who had been making plans to accomplish that very goal for years now. Mel had no real plan to back up her quest for revenge. But meeting a like-minded soul, she swore herself as an ally to his cause. Thus, the son of Typhon and the daughter of Zeus formed an unlikely alliance.

TALE 20

Contradiction

Hydra left Hades with much to think about. However, the thing was… could he even trust Hydra? He said just about everything that addressed Hades' fears, but those were just words. What if he had some kind of ulterior motive? Hades could not let Terra in on this until he was certain of these things. No, that was not it. Hades knew the truth… he was too ashamed to admit what he had done.

Meanwhile, over the next several months, Hydra and Mel had slain a great many more kings and cult leaders. Terra was often dispatched to protect the victim, but because they feared her uncovering their dark deeds if they got too close, she was always kept at a distance.

They knew that if she discovered what they'd done in collusion with Zeus, they were dead either way. This fear was their undoing, as Terra was unable to protect them when the time came. Then their misdeeds would be released anyway.

Terra was yet to comment on the implication that Zeus knew of, turned a blind eye to, or even solicited their evil acts. Hades had suspected as much, but this confirmed it. Though he never publicly agreed with Hydra, he did redouble his efforts to criticize a system in which such abuses would be so rampant.

The embittered gods were suspicious that Hades alone had survived an encounter with Hydra. Seeing an opportunity, they tried to pit the two against each other. If he finally wanted to clear his name, Hades would have to protect his old foe, Aidoneus, from assassination after he had been named Hydra's next target. Hades agreed, much to their shock.

Aidoneus still hated Hades but nonetheless knew not to start anything. He refused to even be in the same room as Hades, making the bodyguard job much more dangerous. However, Terra refused to lose another person on her watch. While Hades guarded the perimeter, Terra was always with Aidoneus. Aidoneus, still in the throes of hubris, attempted to flirt with the goddess. Terra was not pleased.

"Aidoneus, remember that Hydra himself fled when faced with the consequences of trying to come between me and my husband," Terra said with a terrifyingly sweet smile. Aidoneus knew to back off.

The king stayed with Terra in a safe house until the day of the assassination passed. People began to notice that even with the king gone, the country operated just fine. At this, Aidoneus began to panic and insisted he return to his throne so that he could appear to be busy. It was then that Hydra's band attacked, using the strategy of setting fires and damage all around Molossos to tempt Terra to leave Aidoneus' side.

"We must stay put! This is an obvious trap! My protection is more important than any—" Aidoneus panicked as he saw Terra itching to spring into action. Aidoneus couldn't even finish squealing before Terra grabbed hold of him and teleported to a disaster area to help.

Using her powers, Terra put out all the fires and reversed all the damage. She was relieved that nobody was hurt. How convenient. Terra gasped as she suddenly realized something.

"Great goddess, I'm very happy for you. The peasants are all fine. Now then, can we please return to the safety of the palace?" Aidoneus pleaded while trying to pull Terra back toward his fortified home.

"How typical. The king literally had to be dragged out to attend to his subjects' suffering." Mel scoffed from one of the rooftops. Terra calmly assessed the situation. All around her, Melissa, as well as several other powerful fighters, had her in their sights.

"The palace! We must return now to mount a defense!!!" Aidoneus cried.

"It makes no difference. Your guards won't be much help against fighters of this caliber," Terra rebuked him.

"She's right. Besides, that palace isn't as secure as you think. Honestly, you're even more likely to die if you go back there." Mel smirked.

Terra released her Power to intimidate her foes. Instead, they all just eagerly laughed and released their Power. Just like Cerberus and Hydra, their Power felt a lot like Typhon's.

"It probably feels a bit familiar. Yes. We are children of Typhon as well." One of Mel's backup fighters politely introduced himself and his siblings.

"We're big fans of yours. It may sound odd, but it's an honor to get the chance to fight you," they all said before transforming into their ultimate Monster forms.

Terra looked around nervously as the monstrous lion, boar, horse, and bird all roared at her from all sides. As soon as the goddess took her eyes off Mel, though, the hammer wielder dashed in to make her attack. Mel swung her hammer at Aidoneus, but Terra kicked it with great strength to keep the weapon from hitting the king.

"That hammer is a high-quality divine weapon. I can recognize Hephaestus' handiwork anywhere. If you hate the gods so much, why would you trick them into commissioning weapons for you?" Terra demanded.

"We intend to win by any means necessary. Besides, our grudge isn't against all of your kind. Just your evil brother and his cronies. We aren't trying to kill you, are we?" Mel asked.

"You are! Right now!" Terra cried while barely keeping herself and Aidoneus out of Mel's warpath.

"No! We're trying to kill Aidoneus!" Mel growled as she pulled her hammer back to strike again. The beasts all pounced to join her. None were as strong as Terra had heard Hydra was but were nonetheless a great deal stronger than Cerberus.

But Terra's main concern was Melissa. Her lightning powers proved that she was a daughter of Zeus. Her divine Power wavelength had a destructive wave interaction with Terra's. Whenever members of the Solaris clan fought, their Powers interfered and suppressed each other's. It wasn't too big of a deal, but Terra wasn't keen on dealing with those negative effects at all. How could a mortal human so strongly radiate with sacred heat and Zeus' divine spark in particular?

Terra knew that none of her siblings were capable of naturally reproducing with humans. All of Melissa's genetic material did, in fact, come from Melisseus and his wife. Instead, Zeus had implanted some of his Power within women as a form of "blessing" their offspring. Terra had no idea why he would do this. Perhaps he was trying to sire a generation of heroes to protect the world?

How naïve. Terra couldn't comprehend the horrific reasons he had. It was that twisted pervert's way of "thanking" his victims, seeing it as doing them a favor by stamping all of their children as his own. Zeus would be their spirit father, and their true parents would never be able to forget or ignore what he did. But Terra would never suspect Zeus' twisted reasons for doing such an irresponsible thing. Either way, that was definitely Zeus' divine lightning.

At first, Terra thought that Zeus was handing out his divine powers too haphazardly. Then she noted the irony and went back to silently hating herself. But there was no time for that, Melissa darted at Terra like a bolt of lightning! Terra, of course, dodged. But Melissa used the momentum of her swing to spin round and round as a tornado!

Terra dodged all around the spinning lightning storm while pulling Aidoneus around with her. The king screamed in terror while the Queen of the gods narrowly pulled him out of harm's way over and over again. Terra liked dodging at the last second for the sake of efficiency, but every time she did so, Aidoneus' heart felt like it was going to stop!

"Why!? Why do you save such an evil man when you left my father to die?" Mel asked as she repeatedly swung her massive hammer at Aidoneus. Terra blocked and dodged each attack on his behalf. The goddess smiled. She was used to Mel's type and immediately prepared her go-to response.

"Killing Aidoneus won't bring your father back." Terra began a cliched hero speech. Melissa only grew angrier. Her swings became notably swifter and fiercer as Terra began to panic at her obvious misstep.

"Do you think I'm an idiot!? Of course, I know that. I'm not some one-dimensional villain from the myths that you gods indoctrinate the masses with. My father's death isn't why I hate Aidoneus; it's just why I hate you!" Mel growled and made Terra flinch.

Mel reared back and smashed the ground, shaking the entire town! The point of impact was vaporized on contact, but of course, Terra evaded it. Terra leaped away to get some distance as her attacks were hitting a bit too close now. They were so fast that the other combatants couldn't even keep up.

"I'm sorry, Melissa. What happened to your father was a tragedy. He was a good friend of mine, and I must offer my condolences." Terra caught Mel off guard with words rather than violence. Of course, she recognized her.

"I never forget a face. And you are your father's daughter." Terra reassured Mel, "But killing Aidoneus is not what Melisseus would have—" The goddess went back to the overused hero speech.

"Don't you dare finish that sentence!" Mel thundered as a bolt of lightning struck from above! Aidoneus shrieked as Terra just barely avoided the bolt and Melissa's simultaneous attack.

"Like I said, I'm not here to avenge my father. I'm here to change the world into one where he never would have died in the first place! With my own hands, I'll change the system so that people like my father can be happy! Under Zeus, that just isn't possible. My father's death was a tragedy but not an accident! Are you so dense that you don't realize I'm trying to save your husband's life!?" Mel screamed after another series of missed attacks. Those last words caught Terra off guard and made her freeze up again.

Seizing the opportunity, Mel put all her strength into a max power swing of her hammer! At once, Terra let go of Aidoneus and clashed with Mel's hammer using a punch! The hammer and fist created a massive shockwave that echoed across Molossos. Aidoneus was only saved from annihilation by Terra putting up a protective barrier to save him.

The shockwave died down, and Terra took hold of Aidoneus' hand again. Mel grew frustrated. She'd just hit her with everything she had. Mel was definitely stronger, so why was she able to stand against her? If Terra was this strong, how could she allow evil to persist? Mel only grew angrier, and the thunderstorm above grew worse.

While Terra focussed on Mel, the other Monsters finally caught up and positioned themselves to be useful for a change. As the Nemean lion threatened to swallow them whole, Terra had to take to the air! Just as they planned. Several of the Monsters all fired the flaming eyes of Typhon at Aidoneus. With a wave of her hand, Terra redirected all the flames so that each Monster shot one of the others instead!

While Terra was distracted, Mel leaped up and tried to smash Aidoneus. Terra, of course, dodged, and the momentum carried Mel past her. However, this time, while Terra's back was turned, the bee woman threw her massive hammer at Aidoneus! Even though her back was turned, Terra teleported away so that Mel missed again. Then, just as momentum was carrying Mel up, it also saw the hammer zoom down towards a group of innocent civilians who had gathered to watch.

At once, all combatants realized in horror that the hammer was going to kill those bystanders and sprang into action. Terra threw Aidoneus away and teleported over to the hammer, grabbing hold of it with both her hands. The goddess pulled it as hard as she could to try and cancel out its momentum.

To her surprise, Melissa as well used her telekinetic control to pull on the hammer and slow it down. The other beasts also instinctively lent their aid, and eventually, the gigantic hammer was stopped from causing unintended civilian casualties.

As the hammer was stopped, Terra released one hand and teleported Aidoneus closer so she could again grab hold of him. The Monsters all nervously backed away as they saw Terra holding Mel's powerful weapon.

Even Mel was worried. She could stop her throw remotely, but even she didn't know if the hammer could be pried from Terra's hands. But then, to her shock, Terra casually tossed the hammer back to her. Her enemies were very confused.

"I know it's stupid, but… I just… really wish you all were just evil." Terra sighed, feeling conflicted. She could have both stopped the hammer and saved Aidoneus if they'd attacked him. But none of them did. Even on their mission, their first priority was protecting the innocent. Why couldn't they just be evil?

"Evil? You want evil?" a frustrated Mel asked. The children of Typhon quickly got back into the formation surrounding Terra. All Terra's foes pounced at her at once as Aidoneus let out a terrified shriek. Terra steeled herself and prepared to fight.

However, in a flash, Melissa pulled both Terra and Aidoneus into her Microcosm: Beehive. True to its name, the arena had changed to look like the inside of a beehive. But something was off. The material wasn't wax… it was metallic. Electricity coursed through the entire hive with enough voltage to kill just by touching it.

Terra hovered above the ground while holding Aidoneus aloft. To let him touch the walls or the ground was to let him die. Mel casually strolled up to them while swinging her hammer around. The longer she stayed on the ground, the more she was being charged up. Aidoneus grew terrified as Mel's level of Power continued to rise.

Then, Terra heard a buzzing noise coming from behind her. Coming right at them was an army of lightning Monsters in the shape of bees. They were speeding over to back up their queen. Letting Aidoneus touch any of them, even for a second, was certain death too.

"How's that for evil?" Mel asked with a grin as she prepared to attack with this unbelievable home-field advantage.

TALE 21

Rematch

As Terra and Mel's battle continued, Aidoneus' palace was under attack by Hydra. The battle didn't last long at all; in short order, Hydra had arrived and effortlessly defeated all the king's troops.

"Warriors of Graia! Why do you fight your fellow at the demands of your wretched masters? You have more in common with the common workers of Graia than you do with those who produce nothing on their own. Reject Zeus' corrupt hierarchy so that you may cast off your chains with everyone else!" Hydra decided to lecture his defeated opponents rather than kill them.

"Agreed. What you say sounds admirable. It's what you don't say that makes you suspicious. If these soldiers… if the workers you're moving to liberate refused you, I have to wonder if you'd still let them live," Hades chimed in as he removed his helmet of invisibility.

"Your powers of invisibility are of no use." Hydra stood up and faced the god of the dead. He could tell he was there from the start.

"Let's go somewhere else. I don't want anyone getting hurt in the battle to come," Hades said.

"Of course." Hydra chuckled. The two flew a great distance away from the palace to avoid collateral damage.

"This should be a nice and isolated spot." Hades said.

"I agree," Hydra said out loud, but mentally, he sent Hades a different message via Power-based telepathy.

"Even though this is an isolated location, we can never be too careful. There may be unwanted listeners about." Hydra told him via silent mental communication. As they spoke out loud, the two communicated mentally in secret.

"When last we fought, something you said didn't sit right with me. We have a common goal but different methods. However, I intend to show you that my methods are not weak. People who oppose Zeus my way are no less devoted to the cause. So, let me make this clear: I intend to go all out this time and change your mind. We are in this fight just as much as you are!" Hades explained.

"I see. Though your view is rather black and white, I meant no disrespect back then. So long as you recognize Zeus to be more opposed to you than I am and stay focussed on him, we'll get along handsomely." Hydra grinned.

"I am not master of anyone else's life or death." The god of the dead said without a hint of irony, "The only person I can choose to sacrifice for the greater good is myself. Thus, even if they are my most hated enemy, I must save them from death. I must find another way!" Hades declared both aloud and privately. He truly meant that.

Hydra smiled. Hades was such a fool. His paragon's morality had no place in the cold, dark reality they lived in. But that was why Hydra admired him so much. Hades was the best of them. To maintain his purity of heart, Hydra simply knew he had to redouble his efforts and do the dirty deeds a man like Hades never could.

"I don't approve of your methods… but we have a common enemy. But while I can't bring myself to help you directly, I'll allow you to pursue good via your own tactics," Hades said.

"You'll let me? How nice of you." Hydra couldn't hold back laughter. Hades was right. Hydra admired Hades, but he didn't respect him, not really. Hades would change that.

"After this battle, I will focus on the bigger threat. I will leave you to your devices, but it is of my own free will and my fault when I do so. For the sake of this old soldier's pride, I need to prove to both of us that you were wrong when you said I couldn't stop you. I'm not a weakling that needs protecting; I'm not taking that easy way out. We're both strong enough to protect the people. I'm not your pawn that couldn't stop you if I wanted to. We're partners in crime in this devious deal of ours. To fully accept the responsibility for that, I have to know for sure," Hades declared in a message only for Hydra.

"Then I accept your challenge. To be sporting… I'll give you time to get your Monster out. It's only fair." Hydra happily accepted his challenge.

"No need." Hades grinned.

He seemed to have an undue amount of confidence for someone who had lost so badly last time. Little did Hydra know that Hades had a plan. Hades always had a plan.

Hydra noticed a thick mist had filled the battlefield. Curiously, even while looking with Power, the thick mist was obscuring Hydra's vision somewhat.

"We can drop the acting now. There's no way that any outsiders can see or hear us now," Hades explained.

But the Power signal containing his words was somewhat muffled and distorted. Hydra began to see where this was going.

So, he'd finally managed to pull it off? Had Hades finally created his Microcosm? No, that wasn't it. Hydra could tell he hadn't been transported into any pocket dimension. At first, he had intended to see what Hades' little Microcosm could do before displacing and destroying it with his own. If a stronger Microcosm were generated within a weaker one, it would overtake it.

However, Hades' limitation of not being able to create a Microcosm had actually worked to his benefit. Now Hydra couldn't just break his way out. This was getting interesting.

Was the mist poisonous? Hydra kept his Power covering his body to stop any of it from entering or even touching him. All that Hydra knew for sure was that it was hard to find his way around. In fact, he'd completely lost track of Hades in the fog.

Hydra simply began to walk toward where he'd last seen Hades standing. He couldn't see much, but using his depth perception, he thought he could pace out how many steps it was to Hades. As he approached, he put out his hands. He managed to actually touch Hades. The mist cleared a bit, revealing that Hades was indeed standing exactly where he was before this cloud cover came.

"Kind of missing the point of this cover, aren't you?" Hydra asked.

"Not really. Now that I'm ready, I have no need to hide." Hades smiled. Then Hydra saw it.

Looming behind Hades was a massive, demonic skeleton! It looked a lot like the upper half of Hades' usual Monster form, but its spine was planted into the ground. The beast had no legs: rather than invest in generating the bottom half, Hades had doubled the size and thickness of its upper body.

As all of this dawned on Hydra, Hades donned his helmet of invisibility. At once, the mist closed in, and Hydra could hardly see anything. Hades' regular power of invisibility had no effect, but there was more than one way for the unseen one to live up to his name. Rather than make himself invisible, the black mist of Adamant dust made it so that his foes couldn't see anything.

Knowing that he was right next to Hades, Hydra tried to strike his exposed body before his giant Monster could attack. But Hydra was horrified that movement through the thick and viscous air not only obscured his vision but also slowed him down significantly.

Hydra, nonetheless, hit something. Unfortunately, it was the layered blades of the four-armed death demon. All four spears' blades had been overlayed to form a shield for Hades. Then, the arms swung all four blades at Hydra and sent him flying.

Hydra landed a great distance from Hades. The attack still wasn't enough to hurt him, though. Even with all these tricks, Hydra was far stronger than Hades. Besides, if Hydra couldn't see Hades, that meant that he couldn't see him either. All he had to do was remember Hades' fixed position relative to himself, and then he could sneak attack from any angle.

While Hydra was sitting there and trying to think of a counterplay, one of the Monster's four massive spears came crashing down on Hydra! It seemed that the lack of vision only went one way. Hydra deduced that the shadowy mist he was in must have been a light powder made of Adamant that Hades produced from his body. Hades must have been able to feel distortions in his mist cloud by retaining some kind of connection to all the particles in the air. Whenever Hydra moved, Hades would know exactly where he was and where he was going.

Then, Hydra noticed that the powerful attack he was hit by didn't cause him to sink into the ground. Hydra felt the ground and was shocked to find that it was entirely covered in Adamant. That was right… if Hades' mist was light enough to float in the air, being exposed to the wind might blow his entire cover away. That meant he must have contained the area somehow.

Hydra began to laugh. When Hades' raw power fell short of being able to create a Microcosm, he really did just find an alternative. This trap accomplished all the benefits of a Microcosm on a budget. Even though it fell short of the true thing, Hades saw fit to name his pseudo-Microcosm: The Grave.

It was a contained area where Hades could use his powers to their fullest in an environment completely under his control. He couldn't create a Universe, but anyone caught in this area of effect was still trapped in Hades' world.

Hades was a problem solver by nature. His incredible talent for understanding systems to deconstruct their weaknesses was what had made him the foremost critic of Zeus' world order. But that same analytical eye had also served him well during the great titan war. He had an eye for strategy. Second only to his sheer perseverance, this problem-solving intellect was what had allowed Hades to stand among the greatest gods despite his relatively unimpressive level of Power.

While most fighters would train to increase their brute strength, Hades saw winning a fight as a matter of changing one's approach. His level of Power had long stopped growing, but his techniques' growth was only limited by his imagination.

Another spear hit Hydra, this time sending him flying with a vertical chop! Those things really had incredible reach. Hades often liked to use his polearm's reach advantage to give him an edge against faster opponents. This scenario just dialed that up to eleven.

Hydra was flung so far that he hit a wall of some kind. It hurt like hell, but at least he'd confirmed his theory. If he had to guess, Hades had trapped him in a solid Adamant dome with a radius just long enough that the four spears could hit him no matter where he was.

Hydra had to stop and consider his predicament. The best option was to just smash his way out. Hydra prepared to punch the wall, but in turning his back on Hades, he'd made a grave mistake. With his back turned, one of the four spears smashed him into the very wall he was trying to punch.

The instant he lowered his guard to attack the wall, the Monster would punish him. Hydra was hit so hard that he bounced off the wall and landed closer to his foe than he had been before. Despite things looking bad for him, Hydra just began to laugh. He was so powerful that this was the first time he'd been faced with a challenge in a while. In terms of brute strength, he could destroy Hades, but by using his head, that weakling had managed to prove once again that might did not make right.

But Hydra couldn't afford to be defeated that easily. As he got back to his feet, Hydra released a massive burst of his Power. Pushing the divine flames of his sacred heat out, he managed to displace a solid few meters of the mist away from him in all directions. It wasn't enough to blow it all away, but now, at least, he could see in a small area around him.

Closing his eyes, Hydra began to focus. When the next strike from one of Hades' spears came, Hydra felt it enter his own bubble of Power and was able to dodge it!

Hydra was ecstatic! He had successfully dodged the swing of Hades' spear. But at that very moment, a cluster of the dark nebula condensed into yet another spear and, after puncturing the already broken bubble around Hydra, skewered him from behind! Even if Hydra dodged the four main spears, the very mist he was surrounded by could form into an identical weapon and pierce him from any angle!

Hydra was running out of options. From all directions, he was being batted around inside Hades' domain. The attacks still weren't strong enough to do too much damage, but Hydra was beginning to feel dull pain and numbness throughout his body. If he didn't think of a way out, he was bound to lose.

All the launched attacks had so discombobulated Hydra that he had completely lost track of where he was relative to Hades. Judging by the angles he kept getting hit from, he thought he could more or less gauge his direction.

Hydra shot his flaming eyes in the direction of his best guess. Silence fell over the enclosed arena. Had he hit him? Hydra was smashed on both sides by two spears! Guess not.

Hydra fell to his knees but couldn't help but laugh. This desperation was a new sensation for him. He figured he'd have to go all out someday, but figured it wouldn't be until he faced Zeus himself. Hydra tried teleporting out of the mist, but that didn't work either. He should have figured. True to his promise, Hades had set this ability up to counter everything he knew of Hydra.

Hydra felt that he wasn't in danger of losing… but he also had no idea how to beat this either! It looked like he would have to use his trump card, too. Hydra created a bubble of Power around himself again to prepare his ultimate Power. But strangely, the mist was cleared away much more easily this time. In fact, he'd cleared several times the distance around himself that he had before.

Then, it finally happened. As that pressure pushed the mist out, all of a sudden, the mist cleared completely as the bubble burst. Hydra was shocked to find Hades on his knees, gasping for air in complete exhaustion. He'd run out of the Power needed to maintain all of that.

As his Power weakened, he couldn't keep the pressurized seal around the mist up anymore, and all of it exploded out from the built-up internal pressure. Hades' artificial Microcosm collapsed.

Tale 22

Equals and Opposites

It turned out that recreating the Microcosm system from scratch was rather taxing. Even without creating a pocket dimension to contain it all, it was a miracle that Hades held out as long as he had. But now he was spent. Hydra began maniacally laughing even more than before. Hades was truly a man worthy of his respect.

"You did much better this time, Hades. But you'll have to do a lot better than that to stop me." Hydra grinned.

"Damn… I was so close, too. Sorry, Terra. I failed." Hades sighed as he prepared to accept defeat.

"No way. You're incredible, Hades." Terra replied, much to the two men's shock. Placing her hand on Hades' shoulder, Terra smiled as she continued, "Let me handle it from here."

At once, Terra restored Hades to full strength and fussed over him as she checked for wounds.

"I'm fine. Hydra didn't hit me at all." Hades explained. Terra paused before getting the biggest smile on her face. Hades wasn't bragging about his fight performance; he was just trying to reassure his wife he wasn't harmed without considering how unbelievably impressive that statement was.

"You're amazing, you know that?" Terra smiled as she gave Hades a kiss on the cheek. The lord of the dead couldn't help but blush. Hydra loudly cleared his throat to remind them that he was still there.

"Right. Hades, take Aidoneus and get to safety. I'll deal with Hydra." Terra smiled as she handed the king of Molossos to Hades.

Hydra threw his sickle at the king, but as Aidoneus flinched, Terra just swatted it out of the air.

"I trust you, Hades." Terra smiled without ever once taking her eyes off her beloved. With a nod, Hades grabbed Aidoneus and fled to safety. Once he left, Terra became serious and turned to face Hydra.

"I suppose this is the match that everyone's been waiting for. The gods' enemy versus their strongest warrior." Hydra chuckled. He assumed a fighting stance, but Terra just sighed.

"Don't bother. I know you're just a duplicate of the original Hydra. There is no use fighting." Terra sighed.

"Nothing gets past you." Hydra laughed as he lowered his fists.

"If I had to guess, you'd already broken your friends out of the cell I put them in?" Terra sighed.

"Of course. Thanks for not killing them. We both know that you could have." Hydra smirked.

"I don't kill people. Unlike you, I know that murder is wrong," Terra declared.

"That's neither here nor there." Hydra grinned, "We can't keep doing things this way. Typhon desired the past. Zeus desires this present… but Hades wants the future. And you know that's right."

"Hades is nothing like you; he's ten times the man you'll ever be. Don't insult him by even pretending to be associated with him!" Terra cried.

"If you can't endorse my methods, you better make sure his work. Otherwise, you can't avoid me picking up your slack. A dreamer like him needs reliable support," Hydra declared.

"You… don't have to tell me that," Terra half whispered.

"Great. Then, that means our goals align. Even if he refused my help, I still give it, and you should stay in your lane to give him yours. It also means you should stay out of my way." Hydra tried to convince her.

"I can't do that. I will stop you!" Terra passionately declared, yet she did not move to attack him. This was the disconnect brought about by the ideologically broken telephone from Terra to Hades to Hydra.

"So, what now? Not even going to fight this double for the fun of it? As Hades saw firsthand, it's about as strong as the real deal. Or are you still doing the whole I hate fighting thing?" Hydra asked.

"Your fighting style just involves tiring out your opponents using your special regeneration. So long as your brain is intact, all other attacks enemies hit you with are a waste of time," Terra explained.

"Wait, back up a bit… if my brain is destroyed, I actually die?" Hydra asked in genuine surprise. Terra paused.

"Darn, and here I thought my regeneration was as potent as Typhon himself. But that just goes to show: no enemy has ever pushed me to my limit yet. I am unstoppable." Hydra grinned.

"Nothing is unstoppable. If you've realized that about the gods themselves, then you should beware your own hubris." Terra warned.

"You have to admit, there's a good chance that I'm stronger than all the gods of Olympus." Hydra grinned.

"Perhaps." Terra casually responded. Her lack of fear in that answer was in itself intimidating.

"Well, that would happen to include you, too, wouldn't it?" Hydra asked as he pointed at the goddess. Terra was quiet for a moment before letting out a sigh.

"If you're asking if you could beat me in a contest of raw strength, then sure. You would defeat me in an arm-wrestling match. As could your father Typhon… but you know what happened to him. Even including all that Power you've been hiding, I can put you down, just like your predecessor." Terra explained. Hydra's eyes widened in surprise at her assessment. She was still cool as a cucumber, so the snake couldn't help but laugh.

"So that's a no then?" Hydra laughed.

Terra was waiting for him and Hades the second the barrier fell. She must have defeated Mel (his equal in strength) and the others a long time ago. The goddess was just giving Hades a chance to build confidence and prove his growth to himself. If she had stepped in as support, her ability to restore Hades' stamina would have made his new technique all but invincible but denied him the chance to measure his own growth. Out of respect for Hades as a warrior, she allowed the duel to play out. The fact that she didn't need to double-team with Hades to face him was all the answer Hydra really needed.

"Don't take it personally. Besides, I might be wrong. You could actually come here yourself and give it a try." Terra motioned for him to bring it on.

"No, it's fine. I trust your assessment. I hold your estimation of me in high regard. This may sound odd, but I'm a huge fan." Hydra grinned.

"Some of your allies said the same thing. But you could've fooled me. You've killed an awful lot of people for someone who claims to admire me." Terra rebuffed him.

"How many people had to die to overthrow the Titans again?" Hydra asked.

"That's been enough warring for the Kosmos, don't you think?" Terra replied quickly.

"Yet Zeus and his regime see fit to kill as many as they desire in wars of their own." Hydra bit back.

"Murdering murderers still makes you a murderer. But we aren't here to talk about them. We're talking about you," Terra very uncharacteristically said in defense of her brother. Hydra paused for a moment, noting the odd blip.

"If you kill a killer, the number of them at large remains the same," Terra warned.

"Then just kill two," Hydra quipped back. Terra was not amused.

"I like to think that I've cleaned up enough to justify one more murderer to the world." Hydra's eyes flashed red.

"As a rule, it is substantially more likely that killing people will cause harm in society. Thus, even if I were to agree with your goal, I would still have to oppose your method out of pacifistic principle. Powerful people like us must follow strict rules or risk becoming tyrants like Typhon," Terra explained.

"Like Zeus is?" Hydra asked, getting back on target.

"Name the so-called exceptional cases all you want. Hydra, if you break the restriction on killing for Zeus, where does it end?" Terra both answered and dodged his question.

"It ends when I run out of people that need killing. Everyone understood that during the Titan war. You didn't stop any of them. So, what changed?" Hydra asked.

"You want to talk about the Titan war? Hydra, if I killed like you did… if I crossed that line, when would it stop? The Titan war would've been over a lot faster if I snapped my fingers and turned every follower of Typhon into dust." Terra said before snapping her fingers for dramatic effect. "The world would be saved a lot faster… but it would now be a lot emptier."

Hydra flinched when she snapped. In that moment, he knew she was right.

"Or, in fighting Typhon, would you prefer if I became just like him? Is that what you want? Another unaccountable, unstoppable monster like Typhon or…" the Goddess's impassioned speech crescendoed before stopping short as she caught herself.

"…or Typhon." Terra deflated with that odd repetition. Yes, it was Typhon that she was afraid of turning into. Hydra was stunned by her outburst. But nonetheless, she was still weaseling her way past answering his questions. That was a very good distraction, but Hydra wanted an answer.

"Enough dodging talking about him, Solaris. Come on, I have to know… you know that your brother is evil, right?" Hydra asked flat out. Terra froze.

"By our common moral view, he is as repugnant as the one he usurped. So please confirm for me: your familial bond isn't the only reason you haven't turned on him, is it? I'd be very disappointed if it is." Hydra stared her down.

Terra didn't know what to say- how could she even answer that? Her heart was racing the entire conversation. The contradictions of her own mind almost collapsed her right there! She knew he was evil? Why didn't she actively fight against him!? Even she couldn't put the reason why into words. Was Hydra correct? Was she just covering for her brother?

"Though I suppose even you can't be perfect. But if that's true, it makes you almost complicit in all the evil he does?" Hydra began.

"That's not true!" Terra snapped.

"Then tell me- with your great powers: why do you allow Jupiter to remain on his throne? You cannot both be all powerful and all good. You can't be if you allow the Kosmos to exist in this state, Terra," Hydra asked.

"Trust me, I'm far from either of those things." Terra made a fist.

"But not so evil that you enjoy this messed up Kosmos we all live in. So, tell me. Why sulk about how bad things are? There is no one more fit to change them than you. I wouldn't need to kill anyone if you simply toppled this oppressive system yourself." Hydra demanded.

Terra was silent. She was clearly uncomfortable and didn't want to continue. Yet, for some reason, she was still having this conversation. As she stammered to try and delay for a response, Hydra just began laughing.

"You've been trying to track my real location based on this copy, haven't you?" Hydra asked.

"Maybe," Terra responded nervously.

"I'll save you some time. All you're tracking is the copy of a copy that spawned this one. If you still haven't found one, you're never going to catch my real body." Hydra grinned.

Terra gritted her teeth. He'd come prepared and under-exaggerated. Terra had traced the copy of a copy of a copy of a copy that spawned this one and still hadn't found the original's location.

"We aren't enemies, Terra. You already know that. I can tell. Play the passive bystander for as long as you can. Soon, everyone else will know what I know." Hydra grinned. Terra froze up before he continued, "People think you're all mysterious. What is she thinking? The truth is, even you don't know because you're fooling yourself. You're conflicted, but you're also in denial. You're a walking contradiction. But you really ought to listen to Hades' theories on inherent conflicts working themselves out. Put it off as long as you want… you'll have to face the facts sooner or later." Hydra assessed. Terra wanted to rebut him, but words failed her.

"I just hope you become conscious of that before the time comes." Hydra left Terra with those dramatic last words before his Adamant double disintegrated into dust in the wind. Terra just stood there in silent contemplation.

How could Typhon, who she knew since childhood be incapable of understanding her? How could this man who wore his face yet just met her see through the goddess so completely? They looked the same but truly were equal and opposites. Was she at risk of respecting the latter just as much as she pitied the former?

No! Terra's mind immediately shut down that train of thought. She quickly rejoined Hades and Aidoneus. Sure enough, all of Hydra's allies had disappeared with him.

Zeus breathed a sigh of relief that now Hydra had failed three times. He'd failed against the warrior Leonidas, the man of the people Hades and the servant of the gods Aidoneus. Surely, this was the beginning of the end for such villains. Zeus' system would weather the storm!

Aidoneus was spared… but became so terrified of the encounter that he abdicated. Just like that, Molossos was turned into a democracy. It was Zeus' worst nightmare. The king of the gods himself reassured Aidoneus that if he returned to the throne, he would be protected. However, Aidoneus was only relieved when Hydra publicly announced that Aidoneus would be spared because he made the right decision.

The villain's words were more trusted than the trusted god himself! Now, all the other kings began thinking twice about staying in their position and trusting Zeus to save them. Things were getting so bad that Zeus personally visited Aidoneus, now living as a commoner in the democratic Molossos.

"Aidoneus... I need you to return and reclaim your position as king! No- return, and I shall make you the god of Molossos!" Zeus declared.

"A tempting offer, Zeus... or it would be before. But now it's obvious to everyone... that you no longer hold a monopoly on violence. Without that... your regime's days are numbered. We had a good run, commander." Aidoneus saluted his old boss: no longer as a sovereign king but as a soldier in the fight for power. It was just as he had been a hundred years ago.

Zeus' wrath boiled over, and he cursed Hydra's name. But more than that, he cursed Hades for starting that accursed democratic movement. He would make him pay dearly for this.

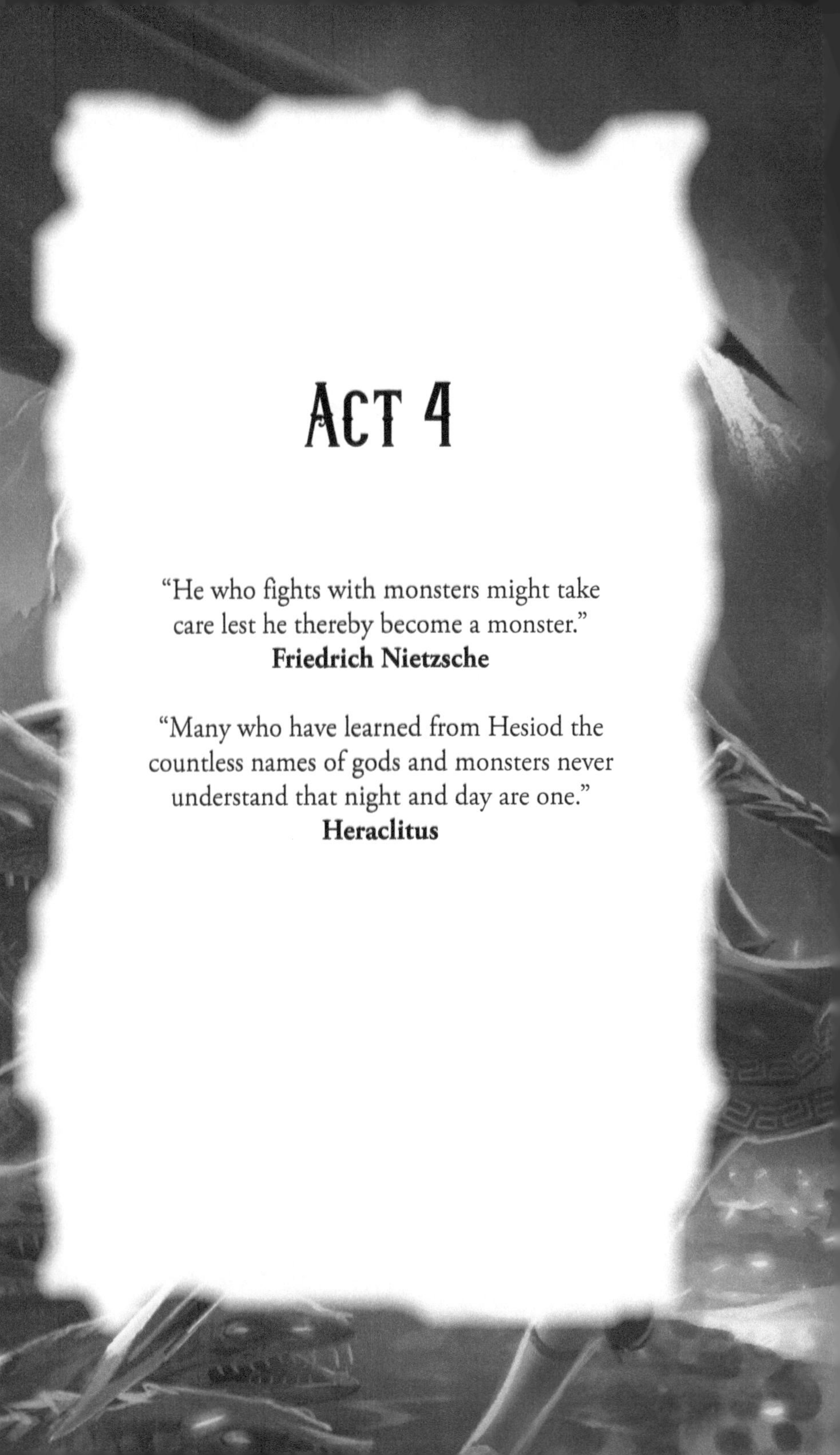

Act 4

"He who fights with monsters might take care lest he thereby become a monster."
Friedrich Nietzsche

"Many who have learned from Hesiod the countless names of gods and monsters never understand that night and day are one."
Heraclitus

TALE 23

Echidna

While Terra was away serving Zeus' regime, Hades and Cerberus missed her. She'd only been gone for a week, but still, they missed her. Those two-thirds of the year when she was away seemed to last forever. Terra wasn't going to return for several more months, but the two were already eagerly planning how to make the most of the time with her upon their happy reunion.

Cerberus was running around in the rain, splashing in the puddles. Terra made her a special cloak that was completely waterproof (it was also nearly indestructible, but Cerberus was more focused on being able to play in the rain without ruining her clothes).

It had been raining for the last few days in the land of Hades. While they were stuck inside, Cerberus and Hades made little boats to race in the streams that formed as water flowed down slopes towards drains. Cerberus raced after the boats, cheering hers on as if the little wooden box could hear her.

"Cerberus! No running. You might slip and fall!" Hades called after her.

Hades' boat won, and Cerberus insisted he must have cheated somehow. At that moment, the great rainstorm was parted, and the skies opened up to reveal the radiant sun from above. Something had fallen from the sky and touched down in the middle of town.

Hades and Cerberus were on their way to investigate, but as they approached, Cerberus smelled something. Instinctively, she perked up excitedly and started running towards the main agora of town as Hades followed after her.

Cerberus just kept excitedly cheering, "Mama is here!". Hades was confused. Terra wasn't due to return for several more months. What was Cerberus talking about? When they arrived, a crowd had gathered to see the crater. Standing in said crater was an odd woman.

This stranger was half beautiful maiden and half fearsome snake. She had the head of a beautiful woman with long white hair, yet within her soft lips, sharp and venomous fangs surrounded her forked extended tongue. She had the body, arms, and legs of a woman, yet a monstrous serpent's tail was attached to her otherwise attractive human form. She was naked, for instead of clothes, she was covered head to toe in black and grey serpent scales.

Her face was fair and her eyes alluring, but atop her head were horns. Her slender fingers ended in beautiful long nails, but at their tips were black, sharpened scales that could slice through steel. Despite all her beauty, on her chest was a single Adamant gem that was shaped like a terrifying red eye.

Nobody dared approach her as she looked around. However, before Hades could call out to her, Cerberus excitedly jumped down and gave her a big hug! The snake woman looked just as confused as Hades.

"Mama! It's you!" Cerberus cheered as she clung to this mysterious stranger. The woman smelled Cerberus in exchange and was shocked.

"Well, what do you know, we do smell alike…" the stranger noted what had tipped Cerberus off. The woman and Cerberus exited the crater to see Hades as the crowd watched eagerly.

"Welcome to the land of Hades. I guess that means you're Cerberus' birth mother. Is that what brought you here?" Hades asked.

"No, this is just a very odd coincidence. More importantly… is Terra Solaris currently on this planet?" the snake asked.

"More importantly?" Hades noted.

"Well, is she?" the she-viper asked again.

"I'm afraid you just missed her. However, if you'd like, we can prepare a place for you to stay and get settled in while you wait for her return," Hades offered.

"Excellent." The she-viper grinned.

As all this transpired, a young boy kicked his ball and went to go retrieve it. He excitedly ran to go pick it up and passed by the snake woman. The moment he took a step near her, his head was removed from his body with the vicious whip of her tail! He died instantly. The gore of his splattered brains splashed all over Cerberus.

"I suppose introductions are in order. I'm Echidna: the mate of Typhon," The she-viper said as her tail swung swiftly to get all the gore off it. The rainclouds she had parted filled back in as a monstrous thunderstorm began above the terrified land of Hades.

Screams and panic filled the city as people fled! Yet, next to Echidna, Cerberus was frozen in a traumatized silence. That boy was her friend from school, and now he was dead.

Hades prepared to leap in to get Cerberus away from Echidna, but the serpent locked eyes with him. Hades was paralyzed with fear as she just grinned. If he got any closer… Hades felt that she would kill him. But even if every cell in his body told him to flee, he had to rescue his daughter.

While Echidna's gaze struck primal fear in Hades, the dead boy's mother screamed and rushed over to his dead body. Hades was finally jolted back to his senses when, with the whip of her tail, Echidna splattered that poor woman as well! Echidna never took her eyes off Hades; she only smiled more widely as Hades reacted with horror at her second kill.

"Enough! I can't let you harm anyone else!!!" Hades screamed, more to rally himself than anything else.

"Anyone else? Ah, those weaklings. Look at them all run: those little bugs with no lives." Echidna pointed at the fleeing crowd behind Hades and charged Power up in her finger.

Hades took that moment to dive in and snatch Cerberus away from Echidna. Echidna swung her tail, but Hades just barely dodged away, landing with his head intact. Echidna smirked, interested in his skills.

"Nice. You should be a good warmup, at least." Echidna grinned as she turned around to face Hades again.

At that, she gave a great shout! The entirety of the land of Hades was then trapped within her dark realm: a Microcosm. Worse yet, her blood-curdling scream called down all sorts of hideous Monsters! These otherwise mindless beasts obeyed her every command and at once began to lay waste to the Land of Hades!

Hades wanted to stop them, but as the land's troops fought the Monsters, Hades had his attention squarely focused on the one that had called them. Hades could tell that she was more dangerous than all the others combined.

"Cerberus! Get as far away from here as you can. Go!" Hades instructed his daughter, but the poor girl was too shell-shocked to hear or respond. The blood of her friend that now coated her was still warm.

Hades looked back at Echidna with rage in his eyes. However, while he had his back turned, she didn't move to attack. Instead, she had bent down and started eating the mangled corpses of the boy and his mother. It was a horrific and disgusting display as she picked them apart and ate the raw flesh like a beast.

"Gross. They even taste weak." Echidna scoffed as she spat a wad of it out.

"Monster!!!" Hades roared at her as he was filled with righteous anger.

"You, on the other hand… look much tastier." Echidna grinned as she got back to her feet with a grin.

"You will pay for this! As protector of this land, I swear on my name as Hades that you will face justice!!!" Hades screamed as his wrath boiled over in a flash of his full Power.

"Hades?" Echidna's eyes widened in surprise. Suddenly, she was overcome with an insane and uproarious laughter.

"This is too perfect! You are Terra Solaris' beloved! I wonder how she will feel when she returns here to find her man already dead!" Echidna cackled. Of course, she wasn't looking for Terra with any good intentions.

Hades steeled himself, drawing his bident to do battle. Echidna's claws sharpened, and her fangs revealed themselves in a toothy smile. The gorgeous snake was showing her true colors: she was a monster worthy of being Typhon's mate.

"I haven't had a good fight in ages. Try to keep me entertained." Echidna stretched casually.

Then, Echidna leapt forward with a laugh and swung her razor-sharp claws at Hades! The lord of the dead dodged past with just enough room to survive. Yet, his cheek still bled from cuts by her grazing claws.

He landed behind her with Cerberus, but even with his great distance, Echidna's tail extended out and destroyed the ground where he was! Hades frantically dodged swipes and stabs by the extended snake tail. He knew that if even one of them hit him, he was done for! Echidna was amused by watching him dance around her. After getting far enough away, Hades placed the frozen Cerberus out of harm's way.

Jumping forward, Hades attacked with the swing of his weapon. Yet, as he approached and got closer to Echidna, the weight of her overwhelming presence terrified him. Hades froze up right before hitting her. Being that close made his entire body seize up with a primal flight response.

"What's the matter? Don't look at me like some kind of monster. You'll hurt my feelings." Echidna snickered.

Hades' anger grew. He had to attack again! This time, he wouldn't let fear get in the way! He'd faced down Typhon, and she was only… almost exactly as terrifying as he was! Aidoneus and Hydra paled in comparison to this absolute monstrosity, but Hades still wouldn't give up.

The god of the dead swung again at full strength, but this time, Echidna simply blocked it with her finger. Over and over again, Hades swung his weapon to kill, only to be foiled by Echidna's effortless finger deflections!

Using his power of invisibility, he tried to hit her with sneak attacks, but Echidna was adaptable and even quicker than Hydra found a way to detect the undetectable! Even against an invisible god, Echidna only needed a single finger to fight. After a while, she even mockingly yawned to show just how disinterested she was. Hades jumped back to try and strategize.

However, even while he was at a distance, Echidna just pointed at him and focused Power into her finger. Hades panicked and raised his bident to block whatever was coming next. Faster than Hades could even react to, Echidna fired a beam of pure Power that obliterated Hades' weapon and threw him back!

Hades fell to the ground, his ears ringing and his bident in pieces. He sat up, but Echidna was standing over him with a condescending grin. Unwilling to lose that easily, Hades threw her off with the creation of his giant Monster form. Hades now towered over Echidna and struck with great force. Echidna shattered his entire Monster with a single punch!

Hades was thrown out as all that Adamant shattered into pieces like broken pottery. Hades again fell to the ground as Echidna menacingly approached with sharpened claws.

Hades had no choice. He couldn't afford to waste any more Power on anything other than his trump card. He hadn't had enough time to perfect it, but the technique did well enough against Hydra. Maybe he could at least buy people more time to escape or contact Terra for help.

Hades released a fine powder of his Adamant dust into the air. The smoky mist that it created surrounded both him and Echidna. Echidna was surprised: she couldn't see anything at all. Hades wasn't even halfway through creating his four-armed Monster variant before Echidna let out a great shout and completely destroyed Hades' domain! He didn't even have a chance to finish setting it up. Not that it made a difference. Hades didn't have a chance of winning!

The lord of the dead could do nothing but panic and try to find a way out as the dragoness continued her approach with sharpened fangs. This was the absolute power that no strategy or perseverance could hope to overcome. Echidna was all but invincible.

However, from above, a massive Adamant bomb fell and exploded right on top of Echidna. Hades looked up with relief to see Hecate in her Monster form, having come to the rescue. Landing next to Hades, she exited her Monster to go help Hades up.

"Don't worry about me… that won't be enough to even hurt her," Hades warned Hecate. As if on cue, the serpent clawed its way out of the crater without a scratch on her!

Hecate fused back into her Monster and began firing dozens of Adamant bombs just like the last one! Echidna leapt through them unphased and sliced Hecate's Monster in half with her claws!

While she was in the air and still off balance from her last attack, Thanatos, in his Monster form, hit Echidna with a sneak attack! His scythe hit her at full strength and smashed Echidna down into the ground! She stood up as if nothing had happened.

Thanatos went in for another attack with his scythe, but Echidna shattered it with a finger! Seeing this, Thanatos desperately tried to dodge past her, but Echidna still sliced off one of his legs with her claws!

Thanatos fell to the ground, his Monster slowly regrowing the damaged Adamant. Echidna grabbed the Monster's leg and bit into it, chewing the Adamant chunks before spitting them out.

"How cute. It seems we're a lot alike. But it's a shame that your Adamant isn't as tough as mine." Echidna boasted as she presented her undamaged body.

While she was off guard, Hades swung his giant bident in Monster form. It shattered on contact with Echidna. Hades, Hecate, and Thanatos all teamed up against Echidna to little avail. The trio ganged up on her, hitting Echidna with all their strongest attacks. Their giant bodies batted her tiny frame around, and their perfectly synched teamwork gave her no reprieve from their onslaught. After enduring this routine and taking hundreds of attacks from her foes, Echidna just laughed at them.

Her counterattack destroyed all their Monsters with one blow. Echidna taunted and toyed with them, letting them regenerate their giant creatures to once again amuse her. Over and over, she would let them wail on her uninterrupted before returning a thousandfold damage with minimal effort.

Before long, they were too exhausted to generate any more Monsters. Echidna still hadn't taken any damage from their puny attacks. The three stood face-to-face with unimaginable terror and now had to desperately face her directly.

"How boring. Fighting you like this is a waste of my time." Echidna sighed. The trio grew worried. Was she going to finish them off now!?

"I know! This would be much more fun." Echidna snickered as she looked at them. Her demonic red eyes glowed ominously.

"Any ideas?" Hades asked as the three braced themselves.

"I've got one." Hecate smiled.

"Good, because I'm all out-" Hades began, but in the next moment, Hecate threw one of her Adamant bombs at him and blasted Hades off his feet!

Hades was writhing on the ground, coughing up blood as he turned around in disbelief. At that moment, Thanatos' scythe was inches from his face! Hades flipped back and avoided the attack just in time. Right after he dodged, another attack came from Hecate!

"What's wrong with you!? Guys! Stop!" Hades pleaded as he repeatedly dodged their attacks. Then he noticed their glazed-over, red-tinted eyes.

"Echidna! What have you done!?" Hades demanded.

When he turned to look, Echidna was snickering to herself as she sat down to pet the silently traumatized Cerberus.

"Don't look at me like that. If you lot can't keep me entertained by fighting me… perhaps I can get some enjoyment out of making you fight each other." Echidna hissed.

Hades was enraged and desperate to go save Cerberus; however, the instant he turned his back on Hecate and Thanatos, they turned their weapons on themselves! Hades desperately had to go back and stop them, only for his friends to attack him as he tried to rescue them!

Echidna laughed at the pathetic display! Hades struggled to get back to his feet. There wasn't any chance of winning this. He struggled in vain, but ultimately, Hecate and Thanatos brought him before Echidna. Now that he was defeated, Echidna was about to kill Hades but stopped short. She had a better idea. Just killing Hades wasn't nearly enough.

"Yes… I think I've had the perfect plan for revenge." Echidna grinned. After seeing all this, young Cerberus could do nothing but cry. She wanted her real mom.

TALE 24

Hell Hath no Fury

"Hades... have you ever felt that you'd been... too happy? Like, has it ever made you feel guilty?" Terra had once asked.

"What? No. I don't think that's normal... are you feeling alright?" Hades asked.

"What!? Me? But my question was if you... oh, never mind." Terra sighed. "Sorry for troubling you... I really am the worst."

Hades paused for a moment, doubly worried after seeing her force a smile as always.

"You're a strange one, Terra," Hades said, much to the goddess' confusion.

"Y'know, I've been wondering... if Narcissus had spent his days cursing his reflection as thoroughly as he is infamous for loving it... would his reputation of self-obsession be any different?" Hades asked.

"I suppose not," Terra conceded.

"Exactly. You're better than that, Terra. This sounds weird, but, I've never seen a more selfless person struggle so much with getting over themselves," Hades tried to explain.

"Getting over myself?" Terra thought, "I never thought of that. Though, surely, you'd agree that some degree of self-loathing would be in order?" Terra asked half-jokingly.

"That's up for you to decide. If you ask me, there are better things to spend one's time doing." Hades shrugged. He awaited a look of understanding from his friend, but instead, Terra only began to look sadder. She couldn't even muster a fake smile anymore.

"Terra… everybody has the right to pursue happiness. Your misery doesn't make anybody's day, so make sure you have time to make yourself happy, too. There's nothing to feel guilty about. You are still a person, after all." Hades comforted her.

Terra's heart was warmed. It was silly, but she felt as though she really needed to hear that. It was such basic advice, but from Hades, it was advice Terra would cherish forever. So, all these years later, as she worked for Olympus away from her family, she kept them in her heart to remain strong. She could finally pursue happiness in a place filled with people who accepted her.

Then, finally, it was time for Terra to head back to the land of Hades! She'd had a very exhausting year, but finally, after eight months, she could see Hades and Cerberus again. The second her time was up, she teleported home to see them! When she arrived, the land of Hades looked perfectly normal and peaceful. It was exactly how she left it. Terra walked through the streets towards the palace, giving friendly waves and greetings by name to everyone she passed.

Oddly, they didn't respond to her, but Terra figured they were busy. Besides, she wasn't owed their time or anything. It seemed like things weren't all that festive at all. She was surprised that the usual festival that welcomed her back was nowhere to be seen. She didn't mind. That just meant she could get back to Hades and Cerberus sooner. Terra just figured that people finally got over the novelty of having to throw such a big party for her every year.

"Hades! Cerberus! I'm home!!!" Terra cheered as she entered the palace of Hades.

There wasn't a soul in sight. How odd. The palace was a public building. On most days, people would be coming and going as they went about their daily business but none of the usual faces were there. Terra walked around, looking for anybody. She didn't mean to be vain, but maybe they were plotting some kind of surprise party?

As Terra turned the corner, she finally bumped into Hades. The goddess immediately gave Hades a hug and told him how much she'd missed him. Hades' expression was withdrawn and disinterested. Terra remembered that his resting face was often misconstrued and so knew not to take it personally. It was weird though… Terra thought he'd been working on that. Oh well, she was just glad to see him.

"You're back. Come. Dinner is nearly ready," Hades said as he simply turned and led her towards the dining room. Terra eagerly followed, holding his hand as she walked and asked him how things had been.

Hades didn't respond. Finally, the couple reached the dining hall, where Hecate and Thanatos were already waiting as they said around the table.

Pots were already boiling, and all the plates were set on the central table in the midst of all their couches. Terra saw the pots were boiling, eager to see what they'd cooked up. She could have easily peeked through them to see what was inside, but why spoil the surprise? It smelled like pork… sort of.

Before she could think too much about that, something else caught her attention. Things were perfectly silent despite

Terra's best efforts to strike up a conversation. They only spoke up when she prepared to take her seat next to Hades.

"Your seat is over there." Hades pointed at an empty couch at the opposite end of the table.

"Oh. I thought that was for Cerberus. Speaking of which, where is she?" Terra noted her odd absence.

"She will arrive when the last member does," Hades coldly replied.

"A guest? How exciting. Do I know them?" Terra asked.

"No. But I know you." Echidna responded from across the room. Terra turned to face her in surprise. Then she noticed Cerberus standing next to Echidna, holding her hand like a mother and child.

Echidna took her seat on the same couch as Hades with Cerberus in her lap, compounding Terra's confusion.

"Hello. I'm Terra- but you said you already knew that. Who might you be? Another friend of Hades?" Terra asked.

"You could say that. But more importantly, I'm Cerberus's true mother: Echidna." Echidna smiled as she lovingly patted her daughter on the head.

"Wow! I'm so glad we finally found you. Cerberus has been looking for you for a long time. Nice to finally meet you!" Terra smiled. As Terra and Echidna spoke, Hades stood up to fetch the pots and place them on the table. It was a stew of some kind.

"Hades, dear. I'm famished; serve the food." Echidna commanded him. Hades did as he was told, pouring out soup from the pots into each person's bowl, saving Terra for last.

"It's okay, dear. Remember, I don't eat," Terra reminded Hades with a smile. Hades ignored her and poured the food in as he was ordered to. When it splattered out into Terra's bowl, she stared at the meat in disbelief. That wasn't pork.

"By your expression, it seems that your keen eyes are more than just rumors." Echidna grinned.

Terra scrambled to her feet in a disgusted panic. She could tell that it was cooked human flesh! As she looked around in horror, she saw Thanatos and Hecate else digging in and eating as if it were the most delicious thing they'd ever tasted. Hades sat back down next to Echidna.

"Great work, my love." Echidna smiled as she pulled Hades in for a passionate, ravenous kiss before Terra's eyes. Hades looked to be enjoying it… maybe even more than kisses with Terra. As discomfort and despair came to Terra's face, Echidna grinned.

"I've stolen your man, Solaris. How does it feel?" Echidna smirked.

Before she could reply, the others at the table began to speak over her. Everyone talked as though Terra was an outsider and Echidna had taken her place.

What was going on!? Terra couldn't detect any mind control. That was because it had been so thorough that now their minds were permanently changed, and brainwashing was no longer necessary. There was no getting them back. Terra was frozen in sheer disbelief before Echidna's voice snapped her out of it.

"Dig in. It's stew a la King Aidoneus. You should be honored; I'm not normally one to share my food." Echidna grinned. Terra couldn't believe what she was seeing! The adults continued to eat the cooked man without batting an eye. Then, Echidna scooped up some of the stew for her daughter Cerberus.

At this, Terra snapped! Nobody was doing that to her daughter Cerberus. Jumping past Echidna, she snatched Cerberus away. Echidna was amused and simply ate the spoonful of Aidoneus herself. Hades, Hecate, and Thanatos stopped eating, and all turned to face Terra for daring to dishonor their Queen. It was torturous, just like Echidna wanted. Echidna hated her, and Terra didn't even know why.

"I don't know what you did to them, but you'd better undo it now! Whatever spell you have them under; release it!" Terra screamed.

"What spell? As you can tell, they aren't under any mind control. This is just how they are now. There's nothing that you or I can do about it." Echidna hissed.

"Liar!" Terra screamed even though she knew Echidna was right. They were lost to her forever. Terra was powerful... but some problems couldn't just be punched away.

"Now then, unhand my daughter." Echidna pointed at Cerberus. Terra trembled as she slowly looked down at the terrified Cerberus. Was she looking at Terra like that?

"It's okay, Cerberus! I'll protect you!" Terra insisted. That was it! The girl had to be afraid of Echidna, not Terra! The goddess was on the verge of mentally breaking.

"Well, Cerberus. Tell her how you really feel." Echidna grinned as she sat in Hades' lap and stroked his chin.

"You're not my real mom. Let go of me. I hate you, Terra." Cerberus said. It was like a knife in Terra's heart. She gently placed Cerberus down and just hunched over. She was mentally broken as Echidna grinned. Cerberus then ran back to Echidna's side, leaving Terra alone. Terra turned to the others, who took turns announcing their hatred and rejection of her. One by one, they spat insults and vitriol at their most hated enemy.

"You're a monster; even more dangerous than Typhon." Thanatos scoffed.

"Don't touch Cerberus as if she was ever yours. She never has and never will even think to consider you as her mother." Hecate cackled.

Terra tried to look away and ignore them. As always, she turned to Hades, the one refuge she could always rely on. But in the end, Hades joined in and said plainly, "How could I ever love you? You aren't even human." Terra collapsed to her knees, breaking down both inside and out.

"You know, before I thought of just stuffing their corpses in the meat locker for you to find when you returned home. However, this is much better. That is what they really thought of you. Underneath their friendly persona, they never accepted you as one of their own. Now, any love they once had for you is directed at me, and all that's left for you is their hatred amplified by my own." Echidna cackled maniacally.

"What do you want!?" Terra screamed as her sadness turned to anger.

"I want you to suffer, Terra Solaris. I want you to suffer just as you've made me!" Echidna screamed back. Terra froze up. All at once, Hades' kind words were forgotten, and she sank back into the depths of despair.

"But don't go despairing on me yet. We're just getting started. This was just the entrée. You are for the main course, Terra Solaris!" Echidna pointed at her! All at once, the others Powered up and prepared to attack Terra on Echidna's command.

"Now... should I kill you with my own hands... should I get your former friends to kill you... or force you to kill yourself?" Echidna sadistically grinned.

"It won't work. I can't die," Terra said plainly.

"I already heard from them. Your family has freaky regeneration like Typhon? No problem. Even he dies if he runs out of Power. I'll just keep killing you til you stay down!" Echidna cackled.

"No! You're not listening. No matter what you do, you can't kill me! Trust me: I've tried," Terra cried. The room fell silent again.

"I can't die… so please, don't make these innocent people suffer because of me," Terra pleaded. Echidna paused for a moment before regaining her snake-like smile.

"Well, I think you're lying. But if you actually can't die, even better." Echidna hissed, much to Terra's shock. "If I can't kill you, I'll just find different ways to torture you for as long as I please."

The dragoness let out an insane and terrifying laugh. Matching the explosion of volume was a burst of Power! The emanating sacred heat was so great that it almost blew everyone away. Then, in a flash, Echidna pulled everyone into a Microcosm. Not just that room, not just the palace or even the planet, but the entire star system was sucked into Echidna's Microcosm!

"Welcome to my Microcosm: Arima. It's a special place where Typhon and I could go all out. In here, there's nobody in and nobody out." Echidna smirked as her massive Power subsided.

It was true. Terra had lost contact with the outside world. She couldn't teleport herself out or teleport any backup in. Terra was on her own. Even Terra couldn't collapse or displace it with one of her own. Not to mention, she was trapped in there with a pretty nasty enemy. Even that flash of Echidna's Power hinted at a fighter on par with Typhon himself. This truly was a dire predicament.

"Do whatever you want to me; just let the others go!" Terra cried.

"Don't worry. I've decided I won't be doing anything. Your old friends will be the ones to serve you to me on a platter!" Echidna cackled as she sat back.

Out of nowhere, Hades lunged at Terra, putting on his helmet of invisibility. Terra still dodged every one of his attacks without moving her feet from where she stood!

Then Thanatos swung his scythe to try and decapitate her, but Terra leaned backward to avoid both attacks. Hecate threw an Adamant bomb, and Terra jumped out of the way! The entire room was destroyed as a massive hole was blasted through the palace!

Terra teleported to safety as she hovered above the Palace of Hades. At least she could still teleport within this "Arima" realm Echidna had trapped them all in. From a safe distance, Terra looked down at Echidna, who remained inside with a confident smirk.

As she was now suspended in the air, the goddess found herself being attacked on all sides by Hades, Hecate, and Thanatos! Terra managed to block and dodge the attacks from all of them, yet she couldn't bring herself to attack back. The whole time, Echidna watched from what was left of the dining room as she played with the docile Cerberus' hair.

A crowd gathered outside the palace, cheering everyone on as they tried to kill Terra. Terra looked down and saw all the people of the realm she had befriended and helped. All were turned against her. They weren't strong enough to hurt her physically, but those verbal attacks cut like a knife at her Achilles' heel.

As all of Terra's attackers converged on her again, Terra blew them all away with an expanding barrier of Power. The solid omnidirectional wall kept them away from her without harming them.

In response to this, they all transformed into their ultimate Monster forms! With their maximum powers, the beasts smashed through the barrier to get at the goddess within!

As the claws of her friends closed in to slay her, Terra closed her eyes and just wanted to accept the end. Then, in a flash, with pre-programmed instinct, she began to rip all the Monsters apart with her bare hands! They were utterly destroyed and fell to the ground as a disappointed Terra emerged victorious.

"Damn it… again. Not even if I wanted to," Terra lamented as she stood atop a pile of crushed Monsters. Crawling out of the Adamant wreckages came the attackers, still determined to kill her at any cost. Their minds had been permanently rewritten to serve only Echidna.

As they lunged to attack, Terra leapt into the air and took flight to once again get eyes on Echidna and Cerberus. Even if the girl hated her now, Terra had to be sure that she was safe.

"Come on… after that display back there, you can't go back to just dodging them. It's beginning to bore me." Echidna scoffed as she continued to pet the stoic Cerberus.

Everyone flew up to surround Terra again, but instead of attacking her, they turned their weapons on themselves! Even in the crowd, the entire population prepared to do the unspeakable to themselves!

"This is your punishment, Solaris. I ordered them to entertain me, and if they fail their master… they take it very hard." Echidna grinned. Cerberus began to panic as she saw this, too, but Echidna just laughed.

Terra screamed and at once used her Power to freeze everyone on the planet in place! Time itself, as a force of nature, ground to a halt the moment before any of them could do themselves harm. Terra was hyperventilating and going through a panic attack; however, she still heard Echidna's laugh.

"Well, isn't that interesting? You are a lot like Typhon, huh? Unfortunately for you, I've already learned how to deal with this trick." Echidna stood up with a grin during the frozen time.

"Echidna… release them. Then you can kill me yourself," Terra weakly said.

"You really are a bad listener, aren't you? Their minds have been permanently changed. They're never going back to the people you once knew." Echidna grinned.

Terra froze. Then she sighed. She floated over to Hades and hugged him. Time unfroze, but everyone was still frozen in place by a barrier of Power that restricted their movement. Terra just hugged Hades and cried.

Echidna was overjoyed. She was at her lowest point. Simultaneously, Cerberus continued to panic, acting completely differently from Echidna's other victims.

"You promised! You promised that if I played along, you wouldn't hurt them!" Cerberus screamed at Echidna. Terra snapped to attention and turned to face her.

"Pipe down, girl, they're all fine. Look, I knew they'd survive." Echidna grumbled.

"Cerberus! What's going on!? What do you mean by play along?" Terra cried. Echidna gritted her teeth. Cerberus turned around to tell Terra as her birth mother prepared to flick her in the head and, in so doing, kill her!

Yet, in the next second, Cerberus was teleported up to safety in Terra's arms. Echidna grew angry. Cerberus began to cry as she hugged Terra and begged her for forgiveness! Echidna had forced her to act like she was controlled in the same way as the others or else she threatened to hurt Hades.

"I'm so sorry! I don't hate you, Mom! I'm sorry!" Cerberus wept in Terra's arms. Then Terra realized: Typhon had made himself immune to all forms of mind control abilities. Perhaps that modification had been inherited by his children, just as Terra theorized his flaming eyes could be.

"Disobedient brat. I'm a woman of my word, so say goodbye to your putrid friends!" Echidna roared.

Down from orbit came Echidna's Legion of Monsters! Despite being beasts, they, too, followed her commands and began to lay waste to the land of Hades! The frozen population was just sitting ducks! But if Terra unfroze them, it was over. Terra was deep in thought about how to save everyone.

"It's over, Terra! I win!" Echidna pointed at her, "None of your little tricks get you out of this. There's no spell for you to break. Their minds are just like this now!"

She turned to Hades with a saddened expression and simply said, "I'm sorry, everyone. I wish it never came to this." Echidna grinned, thinking Terra had given up. Then, Terra released a massive wave of Power that directly hit the minds of everyone on the planet!

"Idiot! I told you that won't work. They aren't under the influence of mind control: their minds themselves were changed." Echidna growled. Yet when Terra released everyone from their restraints, they did not go through with Echidna's order to attack themselves.

Instead, they reacted to the chaotic Monster attack and began to flee. The soldiers among them at once sprung into action to slay the Monsters and save the city. Echidna was baffled. How was this possible?

Terra had found a way to save them. She used her powers to reset their minds back to before Echidna had mind-controlled them. They would lose their memories from after that point, but it would also undo the programming and return their brain states to being free agents.

"Terra!? When did you get back?" Hades asked in utter confusion. His last memories were from right before he was brainwashed.

At once, Terra sent a mental communication to them all and caught them up to speed without a word! She didn't like using her control over the human mind since she felt it infringed on free will. However, in this case, that normally untouched domain of nature was again brought under her control.

All the fighters turned to Echidna in united anger. They landed back in the crumbling palace and faced down with the serpent. Echidna was furious, cursing that she knew she shouldn't have overcomplicated everything with all that planning! Instead, she would just kill everyone the old-fashioned way! The others warned Terra of Echidna's incredible Power and durability, but to their surprise, that didn't change Terra's mind.

"If she was the mate of Typhon, she's no joke. All of you stand back. I know how to deal with her," Terra announced.

At once, Terra put out a mental call to her other six siblings of the Solaris clan. Inside Echidna's Microcosm, she couldn't send any signals out, however, her connection with her siblings in the Solaris clan was special. Their unusual nature allowed them to communicate from anywhere in the Universe.

Unfortunately for her, as soon as Terra put out the call, someone else shut it down. Her connection with the rest of Solaris was being jammed.

Terra was shocked! She had no idea what could have caused that. Was that the result of Echidna's powers? Surely, one of Terra's own wouldn't sabotage her like that. Terra's siblings were left confused. They couldn't tell which of them had initiated the call or what it was about. Maybe it was a mistake, and they just hung up. Either way… Terra was alone.

Without any backup, Terra had to steel herself. Echidna released her monstrous Power, which threatened to blow everyone but Terra away! Terra raised her own battle Power to counter Echidna's, and the two great forces pushed against each other, shaking the planet! It was incredible!

In a brilliant flash of light, Terra instantly donned her sacred armor just as she had during the Titan War. Echidna grew intrigued, noting the peculiar style of armament's resemblance to Typhon's own armor of darkness. Overflowing with more Power than she'd used since the war ended, Terra reminded everyone that she was a force to be reckoned with.

"Echidna! This ends now!!!" Terra screamed as she lunged forward to fight with incredible speed! Even Echidna was surprised by the goddess' swiftness and violent initiative. In a flash, Terra threw a powerful punch that could have defeated most Titans instantly!

Everyone cheered as Terra landed a punch directly in Echidna's face! Then their elation turned to horror as Echidna did not even flinch after that attack! Terra was as shocked as the others! Echidna, who was completely unharmed by Terra's attack, just flashed a toothy, evil grin. Even Terra couldn't defeat her!?

TALE 25

Echidnomachy

Blow after blow, Terra let loose on Echidna with fierce strikes all over her body. Echidna just stood there and took it, amused by how little damage Terra could do.

Faster and faster, harder and harder, Terra attacked Echidna with her full strength but could hardly even make the she-viper flinch in reaction! Even hitting Echidna with her harmonic fists, Terra couldn't penetrate her incredible snakeskin armor. Terra pulled back as she charged up her fists with even more Power to try and surpass her limits.

"They're Adamant scales, girl. I was tough enough to take blows from Typhon at his peak. You can't hurt me!" Echidna cackled at Terra's efforts.

Terra attacked Echidna with her charged-up attack. All she did was budge her a few inches. The powerless bystanders were filled with despair as even the great goddess Terra was seemingly unable to defeat Echidna. Had she really gotten that much weaker?

"Is this really the best you can do!? Why was Typhon so obsessed with a weakling like you!?" Echidna roared with laughter, "Aren't you supposed to be the perfect goddess even the gods worshipped!?"

At that, Terra stopped. She just stood there with a sad look on her face. Echidna flashed a toothy grin, thinking she was finally ready to give up.

"I'm not…" Terra responded much to the dragon queen's confusion.

"Everyone has these ideas about me in their head, but they couldn't be more wrong. I'm a person, and my name is Terra. That is the woman you're fighting against, not a goddess, not a larger-than-life idol you've heard about. I am who I am, nothing more, nothing less," Terra declared before Echidna.

Echidna scoffed at that nonsense. Who did she think she was, standing there in the middle of a fight to the death? Being off-guard during mortal combat was to be punished appropriately. In a flash, Echidna swiped with her claws to try and take Terra's head off with a maniacal cackle!

However, Terra effortlessly dodged Echidna's attack. Echidna stopped laughing. The she-viper attacked again with her tail, but Terra dodged that too. Echidna wasn't swinging haphazardly that time. It should've hit! A furious Echidna let loose with a ferocious flurry of clawing slashes and tail swipes, but none could hit their mark! As easily as Echidna could take Terra's attacks head-on, Terra could dodge Echidna's!

"Rules of Nature: Superposition. That's the ability that makes it impossible for you to hit me," Terra helpfully explained while instantly evading attacks that should have been too fast for her. Was she taunting Echidna by taking time to talk in the middle of a fight?

An outraged Echidna struck faster and faster with more and more ferocity but to no avail. Terra's body always seemed to move just out of harm's way at the last moment. It was as if she was in every single spot Echidna's attack wasn't!

Echidna was so angry that she threw a punch that knocked herself off balance and stumbled forward. She stood back up and turned around, seeing that Terra stood behind her with her back facing Echidna! Echidna snarled at her, swinging her tail to try and decapitate Terra. Terra's dodge was so swift that she seemed to disappear. While Echidna was distracted, trying to analyze Terra's strange movements, the goddess of nature teleported behind and kicked her in the head!

Echidna was sent flying into the wall! It didn't hurt, but Echidna was annoyed that she was launched off her feet by this nobody. She was determined to never be taken by surprise again. Getting back to her feet, the snake pointed at Terra with wrath burning in her eyes.

"Don't get smug. I'm still going to kill you!" Echidna cried as she began focusing Power into her finger. Hades and the others panicked! They recognized that attack from before. Desperately, they tried to warn Terra before it was too late.

Before a word could be let out, Echidna fired the deadly beam directly at Terra! Terra deflected it away with one hand. The room fell silent. Nobody was expecting that. As Terra's calm expression remained unchanged, the serpent grew angry. Echidna then let loose a machinegun volley of Power beams from her finger. Terra effortlessly slapped every single one away with one hand. She didn't just deflect them all. She also angled their trajectory so that nobody was hurt by the ricochet. Upon noticing this, Echidna growled.

"Wasting time to defend others in the middle of a fight will get you killed." Echidna smirked.

"I don't know about that. It's worked out pretty well for me so far," Terra replied calmly.

Echidna responded by unhinging her jaw like a snake! It was horrifying to look at as her cheek skin tore to allow her jaws to reach angles that were not humanly possible. But even more horrifying was that between her gaping jaws formed a massive ball of pure Power!

Hades and the others began to panic. That much Power was enough to destroy everything within Echidna's Microcosm, even if Terra deflected it. In the face of such destructive force, there was no minimum safe distance when it exploded.

Yet Terra remained perfectly calm. As the blast barrelled towards her, Terra simply swung her arm, and the second she touched it, all of its momentum completely reversed towards Echidna! Echidna panicked! She wasn't expecting that. The dragon of chaos was engulfed by her own attack and launched over the horizon! Terra had been waiting for just this moment. She knew that Echidna's armor was too tough for her to damage, but then the only thing strong enough to penetrate it would be Echidna herself!

Echidna was sent flying all the way to the distant continent of Tartarus. Terra teleported herself to the shore and looked into the boiling waters of Tartarus. Terra had made sure to reprogram the blast when she made contact. Instead of bursting out and destroying everything, the ball of Power was for a compact victim of one: Echidna!

However, Terra didn't need to worry about breaking her vow to never kill. Echidna's armor was tough, so while that should've hurt like hell, she knew the sea serpent would survive. As expected, Echidna pulled herself out of the water, but unexpectedly, she still didn't have a scratch on her! Terra was shocked! She expected at least a crack or two. Had she been too eager to deflect her attack? Maybe she should've waited until Echidna was angry enough to use more Power.

"Not to help you out… but you're wasting your time if you think you can hurt me with my own attacks. Typhon was a dear and pointed that weakness out to me. So now… as much of a punch as I pack, even I can't hurt myself. I've ensured that my defense is always one step ahead of my offense." Echidna grinned.

"Great. Winning this is going to be even harder than I thought." Terra sighed.

"Idiot, you aren't going to be winning at all." Echidna laughed before Powering up another mouth blast! Terra prepared to deflect it again, hoping Echidna was bluffing. Echidna simply aimed the blast down towards the planet of Hades!

Terra panicked and dashed forward to stop her. Echidna, predicting this, smiled. When Terra got close, Echidna stopped charging her blast and moved to try and bite into Terra's neck! Terra, of course, dodged past, and so Echidna bluffed at trying to destroy the planet again. Echidna knew that Terra had no choice but to react every single time.

Terra tried to trap Echidna in a Microcosm to avoid collateral damage, but the great snake would tear them down just as quickly as Terra could generate them! It was a no-go. Terra instead simply tried to teleport Echidna off the planet. She couldn't teleport outside the Microcosm, but thankfully, Echidna had made it large enough to give them room to fight in space.

Yet, Echidna was still there. Terra's teleportation didn't work. The goddess was horrified. This was impossible. She was certain she had teleported her.

"Sorry, girl… Typhon showed me that trick, too. I could never work it out myself, but I've had to deal with it enough times to work out a counter." Echidna snickered.

Terra then saw it: Echidna's Power blazing around her in an irregular shape. Echidna was no master of nature, but she was a fighting genius. She quickly discovered a weakness in Terra's teleportation: she could not draw a teleportation border in an area with Power present. When teleporting people, she always made the portal bigger than them to fit their Power inside. However, Echidna made her Power wild and erratic. Terra could never surround her with the teleportation area of effect without having it broken by Echidna's raging flame of Power.

"Shame for you… you fight just like the man I spent the most time sparring with." Echidna remarked. Echidna had seen all these techniques in her past battles with Typhon. Because of her ultimate battle instincts, she was able to counter them all. It was every fighter's worst nightmare. For the first time ever, Terra was at a genuine disadvantage.

"Is it finally setting in, Terra? You won't ever be able to defeat me." Echidna snickered.

She swung and missed again. Oh right. Echidna bit and clawed with great ferocity, but none of her attacks could land against the goddess of Nature. Terra, in exchange, let loose with ferocious mixed martial arts, but none of her attacks could even scratch Echidna's thick-scale armor. It was an unstoppable force versus an immovable object. Which of them was which was anyone's guess.

"How does she keep dodging me?" Echidna wondered as her most recent attack failed to meet its mark, just as all the others had.

Terra used her red-shifting ability to increase the space between her and Echidna and give her extra time to dodge. However, this tactic to aid in her dodging was canceled out by the sheer speed of Echidna. The speeds of universal expansion barely delayed her from catching up with Terra at all! She didn't even notice Terra was doing it.

Terra and Echidna battled in various locales, flying around and clashing with incredible power! With each clash,

Echidna still couldn't touch her, but Terra was running out of effective ways to block and dodge.

Her many tricks were having little to no effect. All the while, Terra couldn't find any weaknesses to exploit. As the fight dragged on, Echidna was also getting stronger and stronger. She also grew in speed and cunning, learning Terra's fighting patterns.

She wasn't very bright, but Echidna's fighting instincts were second to none. She discovered how to keep Terra from deflecting her attacks. Whenever she moved to strike, she would release a burst of Power that distorted the space around her and so kept Terra from calculating and reversing her attack.

After overcoming her limits, Echidna was cackling like a mad woman while swiping and slashing at Terra. In this duel to the death, the monster was having the time of her life!

"Why!? Why do you all love fighting so much?" Terra growled in frustration before punching Echidna square in the face and throwing her back. She recoiled at the outburst and ran over to check if Echidna was okay.

"That's why, you idiot!" an unharmed Echidna breathed hellfire all over the land once Terra was close enough. She still missed. Terra appeared behind her and kicked Echidna in the back of the head but still did no damage.

"It feels great to cut loose once in a while! Most of my opponents die before I even get warmed up! I feel like everything is made of straw! Admit it, nothing is more thrilling than getting to use your full strength, unrestrained! The results of my training and previous battles can finally bear fruit! It is a rare and beautiful miracle!" Echidna roared while pouncing after Terra.

"It's different for me. A sculptor taking years to hone their craft or a weaver whose fingers have bled to perfect their artform are impressive. Those are miracles. What I do… is just expected. It's just a thing I can do; I didn't work or train for any of this. It would be the equivalent of you getting excited about how well you can breathe." Terra sighed as she dodged each blow in kind.

"Don't look down on me; I also fight as easily as I breathe." Echidna grinned before firing dozens of deadly beams from her finger.

"Yes… perhaps you wouldn't mind accepting that an entire facet of your being was meant to destroy this beautiful world." Terra laughed weakly as she opened just as many portals so that each and every blast hit Echidna from a different angle!

Terra couldn't teleport Echidna, but any Power that left her body was fair game within that Microcosm. Again, the dust cleared, and Echidna walked out unharmed.

"Stop whining so much. Appreciate all that power you have. You're the one who defeated Typhon, aren't you?" Echidna asked.

"No. No one person defeated Typhon; it was a team effort. If Hades, Jupiter, and Neptune hadn't weakened him enough, I never would've been able to finish him off. If Metis hadn't sealed him away and restricted his strength going into that final battle, the three of them never would've been able to push him to the brink. If the countless brave soldiers of Graia hadn't given their lives to force him to craft such a weapon, to begin with, then she could not have weakened him. No one person wins a war, Echidna." Terra declared.

"Whatever." Echidna rolled her eyes before going back to fight.

Recognizing that blasts had no effect, Echidna just put all her focus on physical attacks as she darted around and attacked Terra from every angle in turn. Terra dodged each attack before just leaning out of the way enough to trip Echidna over her leg! Echidna rolled back up to her feet almost instantly. She stepped forward to attack again but then stopped with a smug grin as she put her hand on her hips.

"Please, just give up. I have an infinite supply of Power. Even if I can't harm you, eventually, you will tire yourself out. You can't hit me." Terra sighed.

"Are you sure about that?" Echidna asked as she pointed to the flowing fabric that hung at Terra's waist. The goddess looked down and, in disbelief, found that while she was unharmed, part of her outfit had the tiniest claw scratch from Echidna.

"Very soon, that will be you." Echidna ominously pointed at Terra. Terra hastily regenerated her clothing and assumed a fighting stance. But now, a bit of nervousness overcame her.

From far away, Hades and the others could feel the world-shaking battle. Even as they fought off her army of Monsters, even from afar, she was clearly a bigger threat. Having seen Echidna's strength up close, they didn't feel comfortable, even with her that far away. It was horrifying to know that such a creature even existed.

Hades could not just stand by! He had to go help Terra. She was his wife; he couldn't just leave her alone with that monster! So, as Hades told the others to watch Cerberus, he flew off to go back Terra up.

Back in the now flaming wasteland of Tartarus, neither warrior was capable of harming the other. Although Echidna's ultimate defense proved insurmountable, Terra was running low on nonlethal, combat-viable techniques. After overusing any ability against her opponent, Echidna found a workaround.

"Well… any more tricks to throw at me? Or can I finally get around to cracking the code for killing you?" Echidna grinned at the success of her strategy.

"I'm afraid I'm just about out. Unless… there's one technique I haven't used and one that I know Typhon didn't show you." Terra realized.

"Really!? You're so arrogant that now you even claim to know our intimate moments? How dare you!!!" Echidna snarled.

"That's not it. If Typhon ever used it, everybody would know. It's forbidden for a reason." Terra smiled.

"Forbidden? In our fights, Typhon laid bare everything for me! We both promised we were going all out!!! You're a liar!" Echidna screamed.

"I didn't want to do this… try not to die, Echidna," Terra said plainly. Echidna was confused.

"Smite: Earth," Terra said as a portal opened in the heavens. Down came Terra's raw, divine Power! Echidna's eyes widened in disbelief as she felt she saw infinite! This was the same attack that turned Typhon into atomic dust.

When the dust cleared, a massive crater was left in the landscape. The destruction saddened Terra, and even more so, she was worried. Had she used too much and vaporized Echidna? Just in time, Hades arrived.

"That attack… that's the same one you used to beat Typhon, right?" Hades cried in amazement.

"It is. But… as much as I tried to hold back… it might've just killed her." Terra began to cry. Hades went over to console her. He hated Echidna, but he knew that Terra never wanted to take a life, no matter how evil.

Then, Terra sensed it: Echidna's Power. She snapped out of it and turned to face the crater. Hades felt it as well and looked with dread. Echidna exited the crater and… still had no damage on her whatsoever.

"What was that!? It was so weak! If you're telling the truth about Typhon never using it, there's no wonder. I'd never let him hear the end of trying such a pathetic blast on me." Echidna cackled.

"Damnit… I held back too much." Terra sighed. That blast was far weaker than the one that took Typhon down. Her hesitance had overcorrected and compromised the divine Smite altogether. Why couldn't she do anything right!?

"Hit her again! With a serious one! Full power!" Hades cried.

"No… it isn't that simple. That attack… if I used its full power, then the entire Kosmos would be obliterated." Terra explained. Hades was shocked! Then he remembered what she had said to Jupiter before.

"I know we all agreed it was too risky. I broke our promise, but I'll make it up to you," Terra had quietly said long ago.

"Every time I use that attack, it has to be held back, but it's incredibly difficult to control. It's incredibly imprecise, often letting loose too much or too little. If I use too much, it kills the target, and too little… then this happens," Terra explained.

"But just one more time has to be okay!" Hades cried.

"No! You have to understand keeping it from going out of control is very difficult! Even a slight miscalculation and the whole Universe is destroyed! You have to understand that doing calculations to limit infinite is very difficult." Terra explained with a rare serious tone.

"Destroy the Kosmos? Oh, come on, give me enough time, and I could do that." Echidna rolled her eyes since she thought Terra was just trying to scare her. But after everything Hades had seen… if Terra said she could destroy the entire Kosmos, he believed it.

"Then… isn't there some way to focus it? A way we could have access to that power without risking the bad side effects?" Hades begged Terra. Terra gasped. There was one. But… every other time, she found another way. She always found an out without having to use it. But this was different; there was no other way.

"There is a way. I hoped I'd never have to use it, though," Terra said with a sad look.

"Another trick to pull out of your hat? Get on with it. I'm getting bored of waiting. But once this fails, I'm killing you both." Echidna said as she marched over to them.

"Alright. I'll use it. But I can't use it alone. I'm not worthy of it. A god cannot decide humanity's fate alone. So, I ask that you… use it with me. Please." Terra turned to Hades and smiled.

"Me? It's enough for me to beat Echidna?" Hades asked in surprise.

"Sure. But you won't have to. We'll defeat her together. Trust me," Terra assured him.

"Alright. I trust you. Let's do this!" Hades agreed.

"Then, reach out your hand." Terra put her hand out. Hades did as she said. Their hands were right next to each other. Then Terra began to glow.

A portal opened directly above Terra. On the other side, as per usual, was the Earth, ever distant and mysterious. But from the Mother Planet came a bright light not of destruction but of a bizarre, otherworldly substance—if it was a substance at all. The shapeless spirit of primordial Power flew at once to Terra's hands.

Closing her eyes, Terra took command of the formless chaos and began to give it shape. Echidna was unimpressed.

Terra's battle Power was rising as she worked, but it was still nowhere near Echidna's. But Terra wasn't charging an attack; instead, she was doing another trick of nature. A well-known one: $E = mc^2$. All that Power in one space was mass waiting to be given form.

The heavenly light became matter. That mysterious mist of Adamant quarks began responding and rearranging themselves based on the goddess of creation's thoughts. It was not a new artistic construct; it was a vessel. The new three-dimensional tether housed an aspect of the goddess and solidified its existence within the physical world.

With her powers over nature, Terra created it. From quarks to atoms to molecules and beyond, Terra created from scratch a weapon capable of defeating Echidna! Hades was amazed when, in their hands, he bore witness to the finished product: the Sword of Dehmos!

It looked like brilliant metal: a golden handle and sturdy steel blade. Carved into the divine metal was a single word that was written in the Greek alphabet: "Dehmos." It meant literally the people. Though most Graiac speakers would find the spelling odd. The word for "people" in Graiac was Demos. The 'h' inscribed on the blade was, in fact, an archaic and pre-Graiac spelling. This was, in fact, the original pre-Graiac spelling. Dehmos came from the ancient word "Deh" meaning to divide. Thus, it was a divine pun of sorts: it was a weapon that could divide any target in two on behalf of the people.

The Sword was sharp enough to slice apart an atom, and its sharp blade was rendered invisible by the otherworldly and divine light that coated the weapon's edge. The wellspring of Kosmic force was so overflowing that this lustre required no input of Terra: the blade's power came from within. All the power of a Smite attack focussed into a physical form, like a laser concentrating the light of the sun!

In fact, to Hades and Echidna's senses, it seemed as if a second Terra had appeared in the hands of the first. A blade-shaped and vastly more powerful Terra. She was a formidable warrior, capable of great destruction. However, like humans, a true god is best measured by their capacity to create rather than destroy. And in matters of creation, the goddess of nature was second to none.

Like every true master, she'd put a part of herself into her masterwork in a way that the witnesses of this event could never truly appreciate. This conduit- this sword of her spirit was the true warrior aspect of the Mother Goddess.

"This is our blade, Hades. With this, we can defeat her." Terra grinned as she held the handle out to be shared by her other half. Hades was left speechless as he held it. The weapon's Divine Power flowed through him! It felt... alive.

"Bored now. Let's get this started," Echidna roared as she lunged forward.

"Watch. This is our blade." Terra smiled.

In a flash, as Echidna swung to attack them, Terra disappeared and landed behind Echidna. Echidna stumbled forward, stopping right before Hades.

The dragon was confused. Hades was just standing there, looking at her in utter disbelief. Something had caught his attention to the degree that he wasn't even afraid now, even though she was within spitting distance. What could be more impressive than her!? Echidna was angry. She figured she'd just obliterate him with a punch.

Then she realized she couldn't feel her arm. Echidna looked down and found that there was nothing but a bloody stump where her arm used to be.

Slowly, she turned and saw the Sword of Dehmos, covered in her blood. Yet the sword's sacred heat quickly boiled the blood off it. Echidna looked and saw her severed limb on the ground, bubbling and disintegrating.

The Sword conducted Terra's divine Powers perfectly. If she were fighting Typhon, the sword's anti-Typhon properties would have vaporized him already. Unfortunately, since she had no connection to a Solaris, Echidna did not share his weakness with one's divine attacks. Against her, it was just a very strong sword. But it was still a VERY strong sword. Yet, instead of feeling anger, Echidna was ecstatic!

In the face of Terra's overwhelming power, it was clear that she was even more monstrous than Echidna. That *thing* in the sky was more dangerous than a thousand Echidnas!

"Finally! Maybe you were worth the hype, after all, Terra!" Echidna roared excitedly as her arm regenerated.

"Thanks. Here, Hades. Your turn." Terra smiled as she tossed the Sword of Dehmos to him. Echidna smirked, trying to snatch it out of the air as it passed her. But as she even approached it, the serpent recoiled in instinctual fear. Like a mischievous child stopping short of touching the stove… she knew that if she laid her unholy hands on the divine construct, she would meet a terrible fate.

As Echidna reluctantly let it pass her, Hades clumsily caught it, confused by what Terra intended for him to do with it. Echidna growled and lunged at Terra, nonetheless. Hades at once sprung into action to protect her and swung the sword at Echidna. Echidna felt great fear and, knowing what the blade could do, dodged rather than risk blocking it. She just barely avoided it, and still, the weapon sliced the end of her tail clean off!

Hades stumbled when he landed, but Terra caught him. He was shocked by how fast he was able to move with the sword in hand. Hades was used to spears, not swords. However, as he held the Sword of Dehmos, he felt all of Terra's sword-fighting experience flowing into him. Echidna was horrified: they were both monsters! He was just as shocked as Echidna: this was the strength of Terra's chosen one?

"Nice work. You'll get the hang of it soon." Terra smiled. Hades nodded excitedly.

"Now then… let's finish this, Echidna," Terra and Hades said in unison as they jointly pointed the blade at her. Each had a hand on the weapon and shared in its Power as they held it between them.

Echidna let loose her maximum Power and attacked the couple. Against her, Hades and Terra fought in perfect unison. They could block and dodge together: fight as one, or coordinate separately. They passed the blade between them, or both swung together; always switching it up to keep Echidna guessing.

Hades was more vulnerable when apart, but if he was ever in danger of being hit, Terra could teleport him away. Or the more fun option: Terra would use her teleportation to swap their location so Echidna couldn't even keep track of which of them was where!

Individually, the sea serpent was mightier, but united together, there was nothing that they could not do. Out of many, one: protecting one another, making up for each other's faults. That was the power that made the mightiest warrior and holiest god tremble.

Covered in slashes as her supposedly "indestructible" armor came apart, Echidna felt true fear in the face of Terra and Hades. As Echidna was still off balance from the last flurry of strikes, Terra and Hades both held the Sword of Dehmos high. With both their strengths combined, they brought the blade down. Echidna tried to flee but instead found herself sliced in half!

The Holy Sword had divided the celestial serpent in half with enough force to create the world! The shockwave of the attack was so great that it sliced the entire Microcosm known as Arima in half! Echidna's realm was shattered, and everyone was returned to the real world.

Echidna's divided body dramatically flew apart. Her lower half fell into the sea while her upper half launched to the heavens. As the momentum of the attack ran out, Echidna's upper body fell to the ground with only her right arm still attached to her.

"Echidna… you can't take much more, so I suggest you surrender now," Terra said as she pointed the blade at Echidna.

"Are you… mocking me!?" Echidna gnashed her teeth wrathfully.

"No. She's sparing you because she's a good person. A better one than me. You should be thankful you're getting this chance," Hades growled.

Echidna's wrath burned more violently than before! How dare those two weaklings look down on her. Echidna cursed them both, slamming the ground with her remaining arm as her body slowly but surely healed.

"How dare you! I'm going to kill you both!" Echidna screamed at the top of her lungs. Then her Power burst out into a pure, hateful inferno around her body. Her regeneration was completed in a matter of moments, but then her Power continued to grow.

Suddenly, her regenerated limbs grew in size massively! She attacked with those, but Terra and Hades easily blocked her using their shared sword.

Nonetheless, as the force of the attack sent them flying back, the two watched as Echidna grew as well. As much as her power grew, she did as well! She dwarfed the average

Titan as her features transformed from a snake-like human to those of a true dragon! From the waist up, she remained humanoid, complete with arms and waving long hair; however, any of her former outside beauty was replaced by the grotesque monster she was on the inside. Below the waist, she was a pure serpent, with no legs but instead a tail that seemed to extend forever!

The creature loomed above; the most dangerous beast Graia had ever seen! Hades was frozen in terror: this creature was leagues more powerful than Typhon himself had been in the final battle!

"Forget all these convoluted plans! Now I just want you dead!!!" the gargantuan snake demon Echidna roared before moving to crush them with the whip of its massive tail!

TALE 26

Typhon and Echidna

Long ago, before the war with the Olympians had begun, Typhon was bored. He had singlehandedly laid waste to an entire civilization on his own. But after fighting the likes of a true warrior god like Odin, no other enemy could compare. After the pure bliss of finally getting to use his full strength, everything else was an utter disappointment. It had been so long since the Titans had found him a decent opponent, so he just went out to raise some Hel on his own.

Typhon singlehandedly battled an entire Pantheon of gods and struck them down with a hail of his plundered weapons.

The only surviving god among the pincushions was the Pantheon's leader: Perkunas. The half-dead thunder god pried the weapons from his body as he channeled all his determination into regenerating so that he could strike Typhon. He couldn't let his comrades' deaths be for nothing. Yet his rush to recover before Typhon attacked again was interrupted when the god slayer spoke up.

"I'm going to give you one last chance to impress me. Hit me as hard as you can." Typhon smirked.

The desperate deity that faced him took the opportunity to raise his battle Power as high as he could. The rage for all that Perkunas had lost pushed him far past his limits. His face burned bright red, and his curly black beard caught on fire as his sacred heat was cranked up to the max. The already damaged planet they were on crumbled and broke apart in the face of this amazing force.

Then, the last standing god let loose all his Power in a massive cataclysmic beam of dragon-smiting lightning! The attack completely engulfed Typhon and illuminated the whole star system. The deity fell to his knees, completely exhausted after expending all his remaining strength. That was his ode to his fallen friends.

But of course, when the dust from the explosion cleared, Typhon didn't even have a scratch on him. The dragon emperor just let out a disappointed sigh before his flaming eyes began to glow and charge his counterattack.

However, before Typhon could vaporize the last remaining foe, a loud whooping shout caught both of them off guard. Echidna cackled as she dove down and crushed the poor god Perkunas underfoot before Typhon could kill him! Typhon was shocked. Meanwhile, Echidna looked down at the gory stain beneath her feet in disappointment.

"Aw… I got all excited when I sensed the big Power buildup… but I guess that was all he had." Echidna pouted.

"Hey. Who do you think you are?" Typhon demanded of the kill-stealer.

"And who do you think you are?" Echidna replied indignantly.

Growing irritated by the strange arrival, Typhon simply fired his flaming eyes at Echidna. The beams harmlessly deflected off her, doing about as much damage as the last attack did to Typhon.

"Hah! Looks like you're just another weakling." Echidna laughed at him. Typhon's wrath grew further! He'd held back on her before, but now—

Before Typhon could attack again, Echidna leaped forward and sent him flying across the vanishing planet with a mighty punch! Typhon stood back up and found that he was bleeding from that mighty blow! Instead of his anger growing, all of that feeling was replaced with overwhelming excitement!

Echidna flew towards him, ready to strike again, but Typhon began to power up! The shockwave of his massive Power pushed her back and forced her to dig her heels and claws into the ground to avoid being thrown back. Echidna began laughing excitedly, too: his Power level was as high as hers!

"Finally! A worthy opponent! Our battle will be legendary!!!" Typhon roared with excitement.

Typhon and Echidna did battle, destroying what was left of the crumbling planet they were on. In the end, all that was left was molten oceans of lava and a few islands poking above the surface.

They'd been fighting nonstop for almost a full day, growing stronger rather than weaker in the face of a true challenge. Now, Echidna loomed above Typhon in her massive monster form, breathing hellfire all over.

Typhon, despite the size difference, was still strong enough to dig his way through the beast and yank Echidna's true body out from the inside. She responded by breathing hellfire directly in his face. As the giant exoskeleton crumbled, Echidna and Typhon continued trading blows at heights of strength they'd never reached before.

Echidna's scales were cracked and chipped, but by comparison, Typhon's body armor was barely holding together at all. Typhon's unmatched regeneration and Echidna's unbreakable Adamant armor were perfectly equal in allowing each warrior to survive the world-ending attacks they hit each other with. Typhon had died and revived himself stronger and stronger several times now, and Echidna had molted and regrown a few sets of stronger and stronger scales.

Echidna was able to learn and adapt to all his tricks, so no technique ever worked on her more than once. Typhon was ecstatic! She was an opponent that grew in strength at the same pace he did!

After an especially vicious exchange of attacks, Typhon and Echidna were both thrown back by the explosion. Echidna's nigh-invulnerable scale armor remained but now Typhon's armor of darkness completely disintegrated. The two warriors stood back up, but Echidna stopped dead in her tracks, paralyzed by the sight of the god of destruction. Typhon stopped when he saw she had and realized that he was naked.

"Oh, come on, really!?" he said in near embarrassment.

"Nice." Echidna chuckled to herself now that she could see he was just as excited as she was. It seemed that the two couldn't separate their lust for battle from their more carnal kind. Echidna at once seized her scaly skin and tore it off to reveal her own naked human body underneath.

"If this is about making it even and fair, I can make a new set of armor, so you don't have to do that…" Typhon said while doing his best to stay focused on the fight.

"What? No, pause the fight right now. Something more important has come up, so let's take a time out." Echidna giggled as she playfully hopped and skipped towards him.

After the two finished up, Echidna returned to Tartarus Tower with Typhon. All the available Titans assembled as Typhon introduced them to their newest ally.

"Treat her with respect. Her strength is most spectacular," Typhon declared as Echidna sat in his lap, caressing his muscles. Everyone could tell that her Power wasn't the only reason she was there. Seeing her so openly lust after his beloved Typhon, Krius was overcome with jealousy and anger. Then Echidna stepped up to speak to the Titans.

"Hey, losers. I'm not part of your little Typhon fan club. I am my darling's equal and out of this sad little hierarchy of yours, so I expect you to treat me just as kindly as your master. Got it?" Echidna smirked.

"Such arrogance! We have one master, and that is Typhon! How dare you call yourself his equal- you barely even know him!" Krius screamed.

"Oh, trust me, I know him very well. Every inch of him. Which leads me to my next point. When darling and I are fighting or mating, stay out of our way. Unless you're invited to join either, I expect you all to make yourselves scarce. We don't need weaklings getting in the way." Echidna rolled her eyes.

At that, all the Titans were up in arms! Typhon shook his head; he should have expected this. Echidna was unamused as they all shouted and insulted this new temptress that had invaded their circle.

"You don't seem to understand that I won darling's heart using the arts of both love and war. Let me confirm the latter for you." Echidna grinned.

"Just try not to kill them. They handle all the tedious tasks for me." Typhon sighed.

"I don't remember asking you." Echidna scoffed before launching forward with a terrifying hiss to battle the Titans.

Not long after, Tartarus tower lay in ruins, littered with the mangled and unconscious bodies of the Titans. Typhon had sat on his throne the whole time and now the victorious Echidna returned to the throne room. She was dragging a half-dead Krius behind her, having defeated him without even taking a scratch.

"Darling! I'm back." Echidna excitedly ran towards him, while still dragging Krius behind her.

"Impressive. You defeated them even more quickly than I expected," Typhon admitted.

"Of course, silly. I get stronger every time we fight, so you were doing your little predictions off the old me." Echidna said before again throwing her arms around him.

From then on, the Titans begrudgingly allowed her to come and go as she pleased, visiting Typhon for their many engagements.

Strangely, after meeting Echidna, Typhon had all but stopped using his slave harem. He found her simple personality and equal viciousness to be charming. Before long, he even began to talk with her as an equal, learning more about her and growing ever fonder.

Soon, they were even going out and conquering civilizations together. The task of fighting weaklings was formerly tedious, but now, Typhon was more interested in spending time with Echidna than the murder and conquest of it! They had stories and inside jokes and so on. It was almost like… they were some kind of couple.

"Echidna… what are we?" Typhon asked one day.

"What? Darling, we're mates. You were strong enough to impress me, so now I've decided you're worth mating with," Echidna said plainly.

"…and what does that mean?" Typhon nervously asked.

Echidna paused. She didn't really know either. Typhon was rather fond of Echidna. She was amusing to be around. However, there was one thing he didn't like: her appetite.

"Have some Typhon! He was strong, so that means it must taste good!" Echidna eagerly tore a slab of flesh from one of her victims and presented it to Typhon.

"I'll pass." Typhon recoiled in disgust. After his apotheosis, Typhon didn't eat much of anything, and he definitely wasn't going to eat uncooked human!

Echidna childishly chased him around, playfully trying to get him to eat it while teasing him. They were in a field of corpses leftover from the civilization that they'd just slaughtered.

Ultimately, Echidna gave up and just ate it herself. She sulked and said Typhon was bullying her. Typhon countered by saying he wasn't a beast like she was, but Echidna joked that his "sleeping habits" would argue otherwise. Echidna took a bite of the dead warrior's flesh but was disappointed.

"No good, it's tough." She sighed before getting a smirk, "But then again, I guess a good soldier ought to be," she quipped. To her surprise, Typhon burst out laughing. He hardly ever did, so she was shocked.

"Hey, you don't have to tease me. It wasn't that funny." Echidna pouted as she threw the half-eaten meat slab away. Typhon kept laughing, and Echidna began to blush. Had she broken his brain?

"You're just laughing because you're trying to flirt with me. Isn't that right?" Echidna asked.

"Don't flatter yourself. That just caught me off guard, is all." Typhon sighed.

Even after he finished his laugh, Typhon couldn't help but smile at Echidna. He genuinely enjoyed being around her for some reason.

That smile… Typhon's genuine grin stuck with her. Echidna's heart was warmed, and her day was made. Even more than that big battle, he made her happy. She genuinely loved him (in her own Echidna way).

Another day, the two lovers reclined on top of Tartarus Tower, enjoying each other's company and developing a new ability for Echidna together. Echidna had heard that snakes could hypnotize and control their prey and so wanted that ability for herself.

"Snakes cannot hypnotize their prey. That is a myth," Typhon corrected her. Echidna was confused. She'd definitely heard that before.

"Of course. It's a common belief. One that I also used to hold until I learned better. I have gained significant insight into nature beyond what mere folk tales and superstition provides." Typhon grinned.

"And you know everything about every animal?" Echidna asked.

"…you could say I'm a diligent student. I have it on good authority that I'm correct. She's never been wrong before." Typhon smiled as he thought of Terra fondly. He was so excited to show her that he was able to figure it out on his own, even if she'd already taught him that such tricks were beneath the ultimate warrior.

Echidna was furious! The two of them were on a date; why was he thinking about other women!? Seeing her anger, Typhon quickly got back on the topic of their mutual interest: fighting. Even if it was nothing but a myth, Echidna still wanted that ability for herself.

Typhon helped her develop it without much difficulty. Echidna wondered why Typhon didn't use this ability himself, but Typhon said plainly that it didn't interest him. He much preferred to control others with fear and coercion. That feeling of domination that he got would be nullified if humans were mere puppets. He wanted to know he was forcing them to do something they didn't want to.

"Or perhaps… I want to make it so that they actually do want to do it." Typhon grinned.

As time passed, Echidna became viewed as the Queen of Typhon's Empire. She was beloved by him but hated and feared by his subjects. After all, if she was ever even slightly angered, Echidna was known to quickly dispatch her target of anger with the swift swipe of her tail. From there, she would disgrace them further by eating whatever was left of her victim. Though, to be fair, even among his subjects, Typhon would vaporize whoever upset him using his flaming eyes. The two were practically made for each other.

So, one day, Typhon woke up next to his queen horrified: he thought he was starting to fall in love with her! He thought he was "starting to" because, for all his great powers, he was horribly inept when it came to introspecting about his own feelings.

One day, as he sat on his throne hearing a report from Dione on the progress of their campaign into Mesos, Typhon's mind was elsewhere. Was he in love with Echidna? Was she distracting him from his one true love, Terra?

"We've finished slaying all the Mesos deities except for one minor warrior known as Sargon. All we need is your go-ahead, and he can be dealt with." Dione explained.

"Yeah, neat. We can deal with that later. Anyways, Dione, have you been… addicted to something that's probably bad for you, but you like it anyways?" Typhon asked, betraying an uncharacteristic unsureness in his voice.

"…is this about Echidna?" Dione immediately realized.

"Maybe," Typhon continued. "The point is… she refuses to worship me, acts as if she's my equal, takes up my time with unproductive distractions, and bites me in bed. But the problem is I think I kind of enjoy it—"

"Too much information, my lord," Dione cut him off.

"Focus on the first parts." Typhon sighed, "She is an excellent sparring partner that has accelerated my growth towards perfection. I am indeed getting stronger, but I need to keep my eyes on the prize. Terra is my Kosmos, I can't forget that."

"Well, I wouldn't want to be led on just to be dumped when you get the girl you've been aiming for. You should probably talk to her about this before it becomes an issue." Dione gave her thoughts but paused in disbelief that this conversation was even happening.

This was very strange. Typhon never talked to his minions this familiarly. Dione almost felt like they were back in the good old days as childhood friends. He seemed a lot happier recently... a lot more human.

"Damn it all... if I get too attached to another woman, what will Terra think?" Typhon fretted, much to Dione's shock. Then, the doors to the throne room came flying off the hinges.

"Darling. Remember how I was telling you about my impeccable hearing? It seems you could work on yours." Echidna growled as she stormed in.

"I heard just fine. Do you think I care if you heard me? You're a guest in my house, so behave yourself." Typhon immediately put back on his invulnerable, arrogant attitude.

"Terra this, Terra that... I've noticed you always bring her up. Are you saying that you are in love with her!?" Echidna demanded as she stomped towards him.

"Of course. She is my goddess. Once I am strong enough, I can make her mine," Typhon declared.

"Darling… is that why you sometimes call out her name instead of mine? You said not to worry about it! Were you thinking about her!?" Echidna's anger boiled.

"Of course. Whatever carnal pleasures you provide me are insignificant compared to the divine bliss I will receive from Terra." Typhon scoffed.

Dione felt horribly awkward. Typhon hadn't dismissed her, but she really didn't want a front-row seat to this.

"Darling? Are you trying to break up with me?" Echidna asked.

"And what if I was?" Typhon tried to assert his dominance.

The two fought again. They destroyed much of the Tower and tore up the lands around it. As always, they fought each other without holding back. However, while Typhon was merciless in battle, when he and Echidna tired each other out, they just… stopped fighting. For the first time, they'd each found someone they did not fight to kill.

Typhon just sat down and crossed his arms to sulk about being unable to overwhelm her. Echidna just walked over and kissed him on the cheek. After getting their anger out in a good fight, the two were back on good terms. However, while they were back to flirting and chatting, Echidna made one thing clear.

"If I ever find this Terra woman, I'll kill her where she stands," she said with a deceptively sweet smile.

TALE 27

Demokratia

"Forget all these convoluted plans! Now I just want you dead!!!" the gargantuan snake demon Echidna roared. She was now stronger than in any of her battles with Typhon. In fact, she may have been stronger than Typhon himself.

The tail of the giant Echidna was coming crashing down, ready to crush Terra and Hades. Hades was filled with fear and paralyzed where he stood. However, Terra took the Sword of Dehmos in hand and, with a mighty swing, repelled Echidna's attack!

The tail was knocked back, but Terra noted that while she could cut it, the blade was not powerful enough to slice the tail off! Echidna cackled and hissed at her ineffective attack.

"Fool! You should've killed me when you had the chance. My original body was covered in but a thin layer of my scales. This body is entirely composed of it! Layers upon layers of indestructible armor that even your fancy little blade has no chance of breaking!" Echidna taunted.

They were so close! Was their fate really sealed? Echidna let loose a gigantic blast of demonic fire from her gaping maw! Terra naturally deflected it back at her before it could even touch her or Hades! Yet, when the smoke cleared, there wasn't a scratch on her! Those flames were far more powerful than the last time! Echidna was on a complete other level now, what would they do!?

"Terra, her armor is tougher, but the Sword of Dehmos can get through that, right?" Hades asked, assessing the new situation.

"It can… but that's the problem. The only attack that can defeat her now would be a full Power Smite. It would completely destroy Echidna, and since she lacks Typhon's regenerative ability… she wouldn't come back," Terra despaired, "not to mention that I'd be risking the entire Kosmos to do it. I can't do it… I just can't."

Echidna swung her tail to crush the two puny gods. Hades prepared for battle, but Terra just stood, mentally defeated. There was a way out, she figured, but it made her despair more. She could not defeat Echidna… but she could easily kill her.

Fighting her this way; restraining her true, monstrous strength, was much harder than ending her foe's existence. But that restraint; Terra's naïve rule against killing, was a restraint on Terra, the person. That foolish safeguard, "Thou shalt not kill," was for mankind and not a god after all. To save Hades… to save everyone, she had to be willing to abandon that faux humanity.

But what would Jupiter think!? Who cared what Jupiter thought? Terra had brought Echidna here; she'd foolishly spared her and let the beast reach this true form, she had to take responsibility for all her failures. She should have done this back in the days of Typhon as well. Terra knew that if she surrendered herself to that Sphere and became even more monstrous than Echidna, she could destroy her. If she sacrificed herself to herself, the world could be saved.

"Yes, my Goddess… just as I ascended and became a Monster in your name, I eagerly await finally getting to see what kind of Monster *you* can become." Typhon's haunting voice returned. The window to the Heavens was thrust open wider than ever before, and the Alien World prepared to accept its sacrifice.

This was Terra's last temptation; the straw that would break the camel's back. Irredeemable, if her "rigid morals" could be discarded so easily, she should have just given up from the start. Yes, Typhon and Echidna were right: that monster of monsters was just waiting to cut loose. After all, who was going to stop her?

While Terra thought all this, the dragon's tail came slamming down, ready to crush her. What did it matter either way? In a few moments, Terra the person wouldn't matter anyways, if she ever did at all. Terra prepared to leave without even saying goodbye but was taken off guard when Hades swung their holy blade and defended his wife from the demon snake.

"Don't think like that, Terra!" Hades cried as he held Echidna's tail back using their Sword. What did he mean? She hadn't said anything… had she?

"You aren't fighting this alone! We can beat her if we work together!" Hades declared to his beloved.

It was such a simple and cliché sentiment. It was a meaningless, emotional appeals unbecoming of Hades' usual analytical style. But he believed it nonetheless and so motivated Terra to as well. Of course, as she clutched the necklace Hades had given her, Terra realized that was the key she'd lost. After all, when she was unable to defeat Typhon, she still knew what to do. Even the strongest warrior in the World couldn't do everything alone. Sometimes, collective action was required.

Everything fell into place for Terra all at once. Just in time, she placed her hands on the sword as well, and the couple repelled Echidna's attack together! Typhon's mate growled with fury as she saw Terra back in fighting form. The two of them working side by side was too much, even for Echidna to destroy.

"It's too soon to give up. Besides, I have a plan of attack." Hades grinned.

"You always do." Terra nodded back. Typhon's hissing faded into the distance as the light Terra and Hades' partnership illuminated all.

Hades normally based his strategies off what weaknesses he could find in his enemies. But Echidna didn't leave many of those to exploit. Instead, this time, he would focus on the strengths of his allies. Given what he could surmise from Terra, he had something cooking up. Besides, whatever he didn't know, he could just ask her. They were a team, after all.

However, Echidna had no intention of giving them time to strategize. The monster sprayed demonic fire all over as the couple flew around her, persistently slashing shallow wounds in the giant dragon that were quickly repaired by her scales.

"It's useless! You might as well give up now!!!" Echidna taunted them. But neither Hades nor Terra was listening to her.

"So, what do you think? Now that we've tested her durability, is it feasible?" Hades asked.

"Yeah! Her armor is way too tough!" Terra said in a confusingly excited voice after hearing Hades' plan.

Echidna grew angry and tried to crush them between her hands in a mighty clap. It took the beast a second to realize that the two had evaded by teleporting on top of her head. The couple stabbed the sword into the dragon's skull, making her stumble a bit, but still did little to no damage! Echidna roared with anger, but the two were long gone before she could counterattack.

"Alright! So, let's do it!" Hades cheered.

"A slight problem… the calculations and charging of the attack can take a while. I can't fight while I'm doing all that, so… can you buy me some time?" Terra asked with a nervous laugh.

"I'll try my best." Hades nervously laughed, "It was my plan, after all."

"Hades, don't be such a wuss. We're Monster hunters, remember." Hecate chuckled as she and Thanatos landed next to them.

"You're here even faster than expected. I guess that means the Monster cleanup in the city is done?" Hades asked.

"Of course, and everyone back there is ready on their end, too. Now there's just one more Monster left for us to defeat!" Thanatos concurred.

What the here were they talking about!? Was everyone on the planet in on this "plan" except for Echidna!? They were up to something, and she didn't like it. Hades, Hecate, and Thanatos stepped up, defending Terra and preparing to face down Echidna.

"Fights are about Power, you buffoons! Stop your pathetic scheming! Whatever it is you're doing won't work. I've beaten all of you before, remember? Since she has the Sword, shouldn't you all be cowering behind her?" Echidna pointed and laughed at the pathetic last line of defense.

Yet, Echidna hadn't even finished her taunt before Terra waved her blade in front of them and, with it, bestowed her powers onto them! Ever since the war ended, she refused to give it out. What if another Typhon emerged? But this was different: rather than concentrating Power in the hands of one individual, she was spreading the wealth to everyone who was able to fight.

The three Chthonic deities were overflowing with Power, unlike what they'd ever felt before. They had to be nearly as powerful as a Titan now! Even with all that, they sea monster just scoffed at them. Echidna grew tired of waiting for them to attack, and despite expecting that Terra would deflect this, too, she charged up another flaming breath attack.

Hades wouldn't let her and, in a flash, jumped up and kicked her head back so that blast was fired into space, away from everyone else! Echidna wondered where he had gotten that sudden burst of speed and strength.

Echidna furiously swiped her tail at him, but Hades just as swiftly dodged. Despite her great Power, Echidna's sheer size slowed her down. Hecate and Thanatos attacked her while she was confused. Echidna's size also made her a bigger target. Hecate showered her with a rain of exploding Adamant bombs.

Thanatos slashed her arm away from retaliating, and Hades pinned her tail to the ground with his bident. Then, all three deities grabbed hold of her tail and, with their strength combined, threw the snake over their shoulders and into the sea! Echidna was in utter disbelief! She'd beaten them so easily before with a fraction of this Power. After the shock wore off, the great snake rose from the chaotic waters with a haughty laugh!

"Fools! You may have gotten stronger, but none of those attacks could even scratch me! You'd be better off still using that silly little sword of yours!" the titanic Echidna boasted.

Then she noticed Terra hadn't been attacking her. Echidna looked and found that Terra was just standing back with the blade raised above her head. Echidna didn't know what she was doing, but she didn't like the looks of it. Terra had pulled out too many tricks for Echidna's liking already.

Then she noticed Terra was pointing the blade directly up towards that weird Planet in the sky. Unnerved by that ominous Celestial Sphere, Echidna fired an attack at it to try and destroy the Earth. It did nothing. Instead, the distant World responded by sending a shower of sacred light directly into the Sword!

Terra, the Sacred World, channeled Power into Terra's Warrior Sword, which was held aloft by Terra, Mother Nature. All three aspects aligned for their ultimate Smite attack, but this time, it was different. Where was the kaboom? All of the Power of a Smite attack was being contained in the sword and now… being aimed directly at Echidna!

Seeing this, the serpent of chaos leapt forth to try and crush her with its claws. Terra flinched, unable to move while her attack was still being prepared. However, just in time, Hades transformed into his gigantic Monster form and defended her. This time, he was larger and stronger than ever before. Hades grew to Echidna's size and sent her flying with the swing of his bident! Still, he couldn't cut her scale armor, but he successfully deflected her away. Thanatos and Hecate transformed as well, and the three stood between Echidna and Terra.

"Out of my way!" the snake bellowed as she flew towards them again. The four giant monsters had an all-out battle. Gigantic claws and slashes and tail whips tore up the landscape as gigantic explosions detonated with each beam attack hit or missed!

Hades and the others were much more agile than Echidna, though when they did get hit, they took far more damage than the indestructible serpent. Nonetheless, with teamwork and determination they successfully pinned the snake down. Hades, though he was crumbling and lost his bident in a clash, let loose with vicious clawing attacks directly in Echidna's face as Hecate and Thanatos held down her arms.

Echidna fired off a blast of flaming breath that knocked Hades off and had him crumbling. Then Echidna threw off the other two, before swiping all three away with the swipe of her tail! She was furious that the three weaklings had gotten in her way for so long.

Then, Echidna panicked. While she had been distracted, the mass of Power building in Terra had grown massively! Then Echidna sensed it, from all around the planet! All the souls of Hades were sending their Power to Terra! This was the new technique Hades had invented for her: Demokratia!

Those who freely elected to contribute to the Demokratia submitted a vote of confidence in Terra and their other representatives: Hades, Hecate, and Thanatos. Individually, they didn't have much, but combined, it was substantial enough to catch Echidna's notice. Worse yet, Echidna could tell that there was far more Power within the sword itself and that all this energy was merely reigning in and controlling or, rather… focussing it.

In a panic, the beast rushed towards Terra to destroy her. Terra gritted her teeth. The attack was so far along, but if she moved or got too distracted, it would all be lost! Hades tried to rush to her aid, but his crumbling Monster couldn't even stand up after that last attack. Echidna prepared to attack the immobilized Terra, but then, out of seemingly nowhere, Cerberus flew in her way.

"Cerberus! Get out of here, it's too dangerous!!!" Hades screamed as he clawed his way out of his now-dead Monster.

"Out of the way, brat!!! I don't have time for this!" Echidna screamed.

"No! I won't let you hurt my mom!" Cerberus screamed at Echidna. Those words alone almost brought Terra tears of joy.

Echidna was enraged and prepared to swat the child away. However, Cerberus channeled all the Power in her tiny body and transformed into a gigantic three-headed hellhound! Echidna's attack was then instantly deflected back at her by Cerberus, showing off the attack she learned from her true mother!

As the biological offspring of Typhon and Echidna, Cerberus had high Power at a young age and a talent for fighting. More importantly, as the daughter of Hades and Terra, she had the nurturing required to make the most of her natural talent. With the combination of this prime nature and nature, Cerberus was a force to be reckoned with. The hellhound leapt onto Echidna and began biting and clawing all around the snake's body!

Echidna couldn't get the dog off, panicking as she was unable to get her even as Terra was right there! Finally, Echidna pried the pup off her and threw Cerberus to the ground! She prepared to squash the little girl with her giant tail, but Hades flew in and saved her at the last moment!

Echidna was furious! She screamed and swore she'd kill them all! Then, all at once, everyone felt an overwhelming surge of Power. All eyes turned to Terra, who held the Sword of Dehmos aloft, fully charged.

Its power eclipsed even Echidna's! It was so massive that they couldn't sense the end of it! Hades, Hecate, Thanatos, and Cerberus had all given their Power over to Terra as well! Yet this attack was clearly more than the sum of its parts. The people's collective strength aiming this power was unmatched. It would have vaporized Echidna in an instant!

"Whoops. That's a bit too much… let's turn it down a bit." Terra awkwardly laughed as she brought the strength of her attack back down significantly! Now, it was far too low! It wouldn't have been enough to hurt human-sized Echidna, let alone her giant form.

"Oops. Darn, I thought I calculated this already… just a bit higher." Terra adjusted the output to try and get it perfect. Even with minor adjustments, now it shot back up to eclipse Echidna's! It wasn't as overwhelming as the first anymore, but the sheer mass of all that strength still terrified the serpent!

In a panic, Echidna swung her tail to try and kill Terra before she could use it! Terra blocked the tail with her sword and, in doing so, sliced it clean off! Echidna was horrified.

"That should be good." Terra grinned confidently. Then she leapt into the air! Echidna looked up in utter dread. That was true Power, the likes of which no titan could ever wield on their own. It was the ultimate revolt by the people against the rulers!

Not just the residents on Hades but everyone across the Kosmos was filled with awe. Instantly, they remembered why Terra was the only being in the Kosmos that Typhon respected and feared.

Across the Kosmos, Neptune looked to his brother and found Jupiter trembling with a silent, primal terror. Terra was back to full strength again, and every fiber of his existence feared that she'd aim that blast at him next.

Back at the fight, the attack was ready to be fired, and Terra looked to Hades with a grin.

"Hades!" Terra called out. Hades was confused, she wanted him up there too!? In the next instant, Terra teleported him up there.

"Here you go. I said I couldn't wield all this alone." Terra grinned as she held out the sword for him to take hold of. The two both held the blade, ready to attack.

Echidna wanted to dodge or attack or even move at all, but simply being in the presence of such a daunting force had paralyzed her with fright. She was finished. The slithering serpent demon writhed in the chaotic waves as the heavenly glow of divine order broke through the clouds.

"Thank you, everyone! And Echidna! This is what the strength of so-called weaklings really is." Terra declared as she readied the strike.

"DEMOKRATIA!" Terra and Hades screamed in unison as they let loose all the power of the Dehmos. The dragon, in a last desperate assault, fired the last of its Power in a monstrous display of destruction, yet it was a candle swallowed up by a much greater inferno. Echidna's attack was instantly overwhelmed, and the blast of the people hit her at full force. The gigantic, godly attack completely destroyed the gigantic Echidna Monster, and the battle was won.

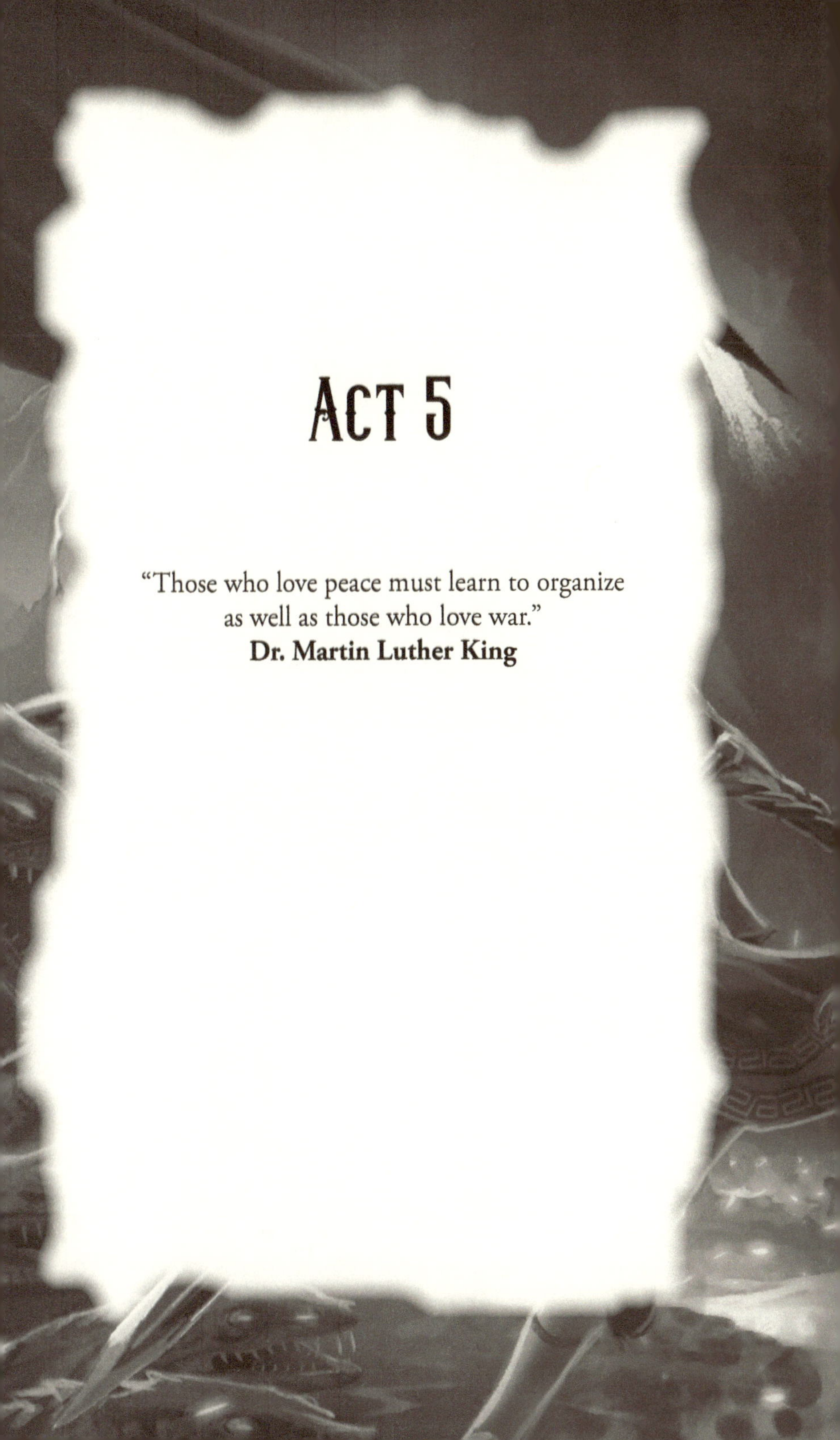

Act 5

"Those who love peace must learn to organize
as well as those who love war."
Dr. Martin Luther King

Tale 28

Redemption

A grand funeral was held for those lost in the fight against Echidna. After all that happened, Cerberus didn't speak to anyone for a week. Gloom filled the land as the season of grieving overtook the usual spirit of thanksgiving and togetherness that time of year was known for.

Even though she was bound and defeated, Echidna loomed large over all the land of Hades. People had nightmares reliving the attack. Families found themselves unable to reorient themselves in light of all those lost. An entire chunk of the past year had been stolen from them by Echidna. Though, many feared it would be even worse if they remembered what the snake had forced them to do while under her spell.

But after the time of mourning came the celebration. There was a grand feast to celebrate the triumph over Echidna. Yet, even after the gloom had left, many still didn't feel right.

The Cornucopia festival wasn't as cheery as it usually was. There was a feeling of artificiality to it. Everyone agreed to move on… but hated Echidna even more because, even now, they could not. During the paradoxically depressing party, Terra left to think. She still held the Sword of Dehmos. Terra looked at the divine blade in her hand. She was hesitant. Should she destroy it again?

Terra reared back, ready to throw the weapon into the sea. However, right before she did, Hades stepped up, letting her know that everyone was looking for her. Terra agreed that she'd be right back, but again, her eyes were on the sword.

"That sword is pretty strong." Hades nodded, "So much so that it begs the question of why you didn't use it earlier."

"It's dangerous, plain and simple." Terra sighed, "It might've been harder, but I always found a way without using it before."

"So dangerous that I reckon just throwing it into some water won't do much of anything," Hades smirked.

"Oh. Did you see that? This is embarrassing. I would've annihilated it properly after. If I worked up the courage." Terra nervously explained herself.

"It's your choice… but I'd have to side with the part of you that's against it." Hades put his arm around her for an embrace.

"It saved us… but I can't have this power," Terra said plainly.

"I thought you said we'd wield it together?" Hades asked and made Terra's eyes widen in realization.

"That's it! You hold onto it." Terra smiled as she shoved the weapon into Hades' hands.

Hades was so confused. She looked so relieved for some reason. Then he felt it: that portal in the sky opened again, revealing the mysterious Planet.

"Hades. I pledge all that I am to you now. Take that sword in hand and wield me as you see fit." Terra urged him. She was smiling, and Hades could tell it was genuine, but it was also so sad. Something about it felt off; like Terra was about to stumble right at the finish line. It would again be two steps forward and two steps back.

"Hades... take it. Take it from me... please," Terra repeated desperately as she noticed his hesitation.

"Terra, like I said... we wield it together. This is a partnership." Hades replied as he held the blade out for her to grab hold of. Terra felt uneasy and trembled as she slowly reached for it. She was so close to getting rid of it, so then why?

"It's okay. It's a big burden; nobody should hold it alone. Nobody: not you... and not me. But we both know that it's something we can handle together," Hades reassured her.

Slowly cautiously, Terra took hold of the weapon in truly equal partnership with her beloved. The blade of Terra began to glow as the body of Terra and the Planet Terra above resonated and did the same. She was not giving herself away as a mere tool of Power once again. She'd finally found someone to share her life with, after all.

Jupiter was too distracted by the ample curves of Terra's oblate spheroid to see her as a person. Typhon saw Terra as a means of gaining Power and pleasure, never a person distinct from that. Hades was different; it was a pathetically low bar to clear, but in bronze-age Graia, it was miraculous.

Jupiter desired Terra, the sacred planet; Typhon lusted after Terra, the Sword of Power, but Hades loved Terra, the person. He had chosen correctly. She was not a thing to possess but a person to embrace. And for choosing correctly, he was granted what his rivals for the goddess could only covet from afar. The Sacred World shone over him, and the sword empowered him while the woman of his dreams loved him.

Terra could not wield all that Power on her own... nobody, not even she, could be trusted with unchecked power. However, the solution was not to just blindly pass it off to others and hope they could do it better. Power could only be wielded together, not hoarded or monopolized by any one person or cabal. Zeus would not get the World, and Typhon would not wield the Sword, but Hades and humankind would work together with Mother Nature.

The trifunctional goddess could finally accept the three aspects of herself that had fallen out of alignment. Now, they had come back into harmony. Terra, the person who loved Hades, Terra the blade was now in worthy hands that could support her, and Terra the Planet had acknowledged this new champion. For the first time in a long while, the being Terra felt complete.

Yes. Now, when the time called for it, she could wield the Sword of Dehmos without hesitation. And if Hades ever had need of it, the blade was now just as much his as it was hers. This way, she could be certain that the land of Hades would be safe no matter if she was there or not.

On the flip side, as soon as the party was done, Terra returned to Tartarus prison to continue her work… trying to rehabilitate Echidna. Echidna had her Powers sealed. With her scales and other Adamant-generated animal features removed, she looked like a harmless woman one might see on the streets. She was so small and pleasant-looking: who would have ever suspected what she was capable of? Her horns, tail, claws, fangs, and even her serpentine tongue were all augments she added to her body with Adamant. Without all that, she was just a human being.

"How are you feeling today, Echidna?" Terra asked.

"If I still had my fangs, I would tear out your throat," Echidna hissed back.

It was just another day with Echidna. She was like the straw man of what the critics of Hades' rehabilitation approach would warn about. Echidna was a genuine villain who was completely lacking in any remorse. Even though she was defeated, all she would do was insult and try to guilt-trip Terra. Though she wasn't a physical threat anymore, she still wanted to make Terra suffer.

"Is this what you did to Typhon too? If he's here, do we get conjugal visits?" Echidna joked.

"No. Typhon's location is a secret. However, once I successfully rehabilitate you, maybe he can be brought in for the same treatment. When you're both better, you can see each other again." Terra replied.

"Better? I feel fine. I'd feel even better if I got my powers back. Doesn't this violate your precious freedoms?" Echidna asked.

"No," Terra replied.

Echidna wasn't like Typhon. He had mentally snapped after Terra's rejection. She wasn't mentally ill in any physical or chemical capacity. She was just evil. After all, evil and mental illness are hardly the same thing; perfectly sane evil people were far more common than the stereotypical "sociopath." Echidna wasn't born like this; she'd just developed a personality that had no room for empathy.

"We just had a funeral for all the people who died in your attack," Terra began.

"The people that you let die?" Echidna asked with a grin. Terra paused but calmed herself down. She knew that Echidna was doing it on purpose. Echidna didn't care about all those dead people in any capacity other than how she knew she could hurt Terra.

Echidna didn't care that she traumatized her daughter, she was just interested in how that might upset Terra. Everything she did and everyone she hurt was just a way of causing as much pain to her hated enemy as possible.

In fact, she would often (unprompted) go into detail on how she would lure people to the Land of Hades just so that she could enjoy hunting them down and eating them. When she ran out of foreigners to gorge on, she would release some of the land's citizens from mind control and then play the world's most terrifying game of hide and seek with them. Echidna always won. She gave names and gory details about every single person she'd killed who Terra knew and cared about.

Echidna could comprehend empathy in others and derive pleasure from their suffering, so she was more of a sadist than a sociopath. Though, Echidna grew frustrated any time Terra asked for her help in psychoanalysis.

Echidna readily volunteered details about her actions but rarely her thoughts. Echidna bristled at this: she didn't overthink things like others did. She was pure Id: focussed on her own pleasure and enjoyment. That was all.

"They're bugs. They're beneath us, so why would I care? In fact… why should you care?" Echidna smirked. She sounded a lot like Typhon since she'd discovered that was what upset Terra the most.

"I wouldn't be so eager for me to view people that were weaker than me as ants. After all, that would include you, too, Echidna," Terra replied, getting a snarl from the serpent. It was clear that they weren't getting anywhere.

Echidna was a tough nut to crack, and she noticed that Terra's mental fortitude had rather notably increased out of nowhere. Terra couldn't help her, and Echidna couldn't hurt her; it seemed that their annoying stalemate persisted even outside of battle. It was another unsuccessful day. The she-viper was like Typhon: completely unrepentant. Why?

What was a restorative justice-based society to do with a genuinely evil person? For now, she was to be detained indefinitely. However, other people were dissatisfied. There were grumbles about having Echidna executed. At that next Assembly meeting, someone finally stepped up and proposed what everyone else had wanted to say. A motion was put forward to execute Echidna for her crimes against the people!

When called upon to address the Assembly with a status report, Terra could not deny that she was not repentant. That predictable outcome, paired with how much suffering she caused, executing the villain was a popular sentiment.

However, before this could even be put to a vote, Hades reminded the rest of the assembly that not even the assembly could deprive anyone of their life except in the defense of someone. Echidna had been restrained and deprived of her powers. She wasn't a threat to anyone.

The Assembly was furious! Rules that they themselves had put in place now held them back from what they wanted to do most! Surely, an exception could be made for that demoness!

No. Democracy was a majority rule with minority protection. Executing prisoners for any reason was a slippery slope, and the passions of the mob were not enough to override the guiding principle that the Assembly was built on.

"A lot of people want to kill you. They're very upset by what you did," Terra explained to Echidna. Echidna hesitated for a moment before just smiling. She could tell that Terra didn't want that and so welcomed it with a laugh.

Terra was horrified! Did Echidna hate her that much!? She was willing to die just because she knew it would upset her. How could she be so petty and spiteful over such a little thing?

"You'll never understand! Typhon was the one person in the whole Kosmos I ever cared about, and you took him from me!" Echidna shrieked at Terra, incensed that she would downplay what she and Typhon had. Love was, after all, right up there with money and power for murderous motivations.

Echidna ranted and raved about how much she loved Typhon and how much that made her hate Terra. Then the snake stopped when she saw Terra's warm and genuine smile. Terra noted that they were making progress and thanked Echidna for opening up like that.

Echidna grew frustrated, and so instead began to list explicit and raunchy details of her relationship with Typhon as if to make Terra jealous. Echidna noted that giving birth to the hundreds of fertilized eggs over the next several years was the worst agony she had ever suffered and had her incapacitated for much of that time. Though, in the end, she thought it was worth it.

From the rant, Terra at least learned why Echidna was absent for the Titan war: she had intended to return but was physically incapable. While she was initially still traveling the Kosmos, looking for strong foes when she first started laying the eggs, it eventually got so bad that she couldn't even move.

Echidna's half-human and half-snake biology reached an odd reproductive compromise. After laying with Typhon countless times, it eventually stuck. Echidna conceived 100 offspring but would only lay about one per clutch. That, on the one hand, kept her from dying, but on the other, meant a long and drawn-out labor period that lasted years and years. Echidna had only just finished recovering from the ordeal.

When the eggs didn't turn into Monsters for Echidna's army, she just figured they were defective and moved on. This happened about one hundred times, at which point she had exhausted all the fertilized embryos she and Typhon had conceived.

That meant many of Cerberus' siblings were scattered across the Kosmos. They didn't hatch on their own and needed to be properly incubated, as seen by Cerberus and Hydra's age gap. That meant those unhatched young would be babies, while any who hatched shortly after being laid could be more than a century old. Terra was enthralled by the fascinating biology of Echidna that she was able to deduce from their conversation.

Echidna grew frustrated that Terra was still gaining valuable information from her and so began to growl. After that, Echidna would speak no further, and so Terra gave up for the day and left. When Terra left, she was surprised to see a group of people waiting at the entrance of Tartarus prison. Terra asked what they were doing there, and they simply asked to see Echidna. The courts could not kill her… but they were willing to do what needed doing. Terra refused.

Tartarus prison both kept the people safe from Echidna… and Echidna safe from the vengeful people. Yet, all this weighed heavily on Terra's heart. As such, the goddess called upon her trusted husband, Hades, to consult him.

"Are we acting like monarchs by keeping people away from what they want?" Terra asked as her resolve wavered a bit.

"The death penalty has been banned in this land since our founding. The level of majority required to overrule such a foundational law is next to impossible to reach, even with this climate. That's why they haven't called for a referendum." Hades shrugged.

"But Hades, beyond the law… the arguments that the Assembly had agreed to in regard to abolishing the death penalty was that even if some people deserved to be killed, it was unwise to inflict something so irreversible when mistakes could be made. It wasn't wise to render the power to violate human rights when even a single innocent person might lose their life in error," Terra countered. "But Echidna was in control of her own actions and undeniably the one to cause such harm to everyone…"

She was concerned since the above explanation was the main convincing argument in the assembly's vote. Her own reservations about killing functioned without that explanation; however, was this technically a circumvention of the people's will?

"Echidna is undeniably guilty and did every horrible thing she has been accused of. And for that, she has received the harshest punishment our society has to give. We all agreed to these terms beforehand, and justice is being fulfilled in perfect accordance with all that," Hades reassured her.

"The whole point of this democracy was to allow people to change their society if they changed their minds: irrespective of the imposed will of any god. Are we betraying that?" Terra asked.

"No. Because the point of this democracy is also to protect the people from themselves, fundamental rights cannot be taken away so easily, lest the majority rule with minority protections devolve into another kind of tyranny." Hades argued, "If the rights of murderers were rolled back today, how long before other groups lost their protections? It is best not to even introduce this precedent. Right now, in the grips of anger and despair, it sounds good, but most of humanity's bad excesses begin with justifiable measures. None can be deprived of their life except in self-defense."

Terra had no response and just stood in silent contemplation. Hades looked at her worriedly. She was doing so much better than before, but Hades was constantly on the lookout for potential backsliding.

"What's wrong? You knew all that, Terra. So why are you arguing against yourself?" Hades asked.

"I know. I just... don't want to ruin everything we've worked for because of my personal baggage. Sometimes, it's reassuring to hear you say it, even if we already agree," Terra confessed.

"It is painful right now. The outrage will subside, and the society will continue to function," Hades reassured her. "Vengeance does not actually calm the heart or remove people's pain in most cases. It will only give our society a horrible sense of lingering guilt that will be Echidna's true victory. Ultimately, in the future, people will understand that this was a painful and difficult choice, but ultimately the correct one."

"Thanks, Hades." Terra smiled back.

Ultimately, the death penalty was ruled out as Echidna's fate. However, next, a group of people figured that if she was unwilling to rehabilitate, she should be forced to undergo mental reconditioning in the same way that Terra was able to reverse their brainwashing. With the ability to alter minds, surely Terra could convert Echidna into an upstanding person via mind control.

Terra was hesitant. She had nearly never used her mind-altering abilities because she believed that they were unethical. After all, one of Echidna's many crimes was brainwashing. If Terra did the same to Echidna, at least on that charge, she would be equally immoral.

Many argued that mind control was merely speeding up the rehabilitation progress, but Terra felt that it still violated her rights as a human being. Was the government really to be trusted with the ability to alter the brains of its citizens on the chemical level against their consent?

Well, then, what was to be done with her!? The people of the land of Hades were still running around trying to uncover what they were doing during the time their memories were erased. Their international reputation was now sullied, and Hades was taking the brunt of the rage by the families of those who had been lured in and eaten from foreign countries.

The innocent victims had to go around and apologize to those they had harmed on Echidna's orders, while the puppet master Echidna got a comfy cell for the rest of her Immortal life!? She would be fed and clothed and taken care of in prison with conditions superior to most other countries' average living standards- on her victims' dime!?

Ultimately, Terra had to accept that, at the moment, there were just some people she couldn't rehabilitate. Nonetheless, she was still against capital punishment or mind control and instead resolved to keep Echidna away from others for the safety of the public as they tried to find a way to fix them.

Echidna had left Terra with an ominous warning that her kindness would get everyone killed. True warriors will NEVER change. But hopefully, someday, a better solution will be found.

When the question was asked about what to do with such people in a utopian society, it was not in bad faith. Maybe the solution was a long way away, but it was a thought-provoking and desperately sought one.

TALE 29

Revelation

Hades knew who Terra was. She was the beautiful, out-of-this-world woman that stood by his side. She had otherworldly sky-blue hair and eyes that were sometimes silhouetted by a literal other world in the sky.

She had her secrets, sure, but everyone did. Some saw her as a god, others as a monster… but Hades knew she was a person. Maybe not a human… again, she had her secrets, and it didn't matter to him either way. She was strong but gentle and invincible but hurting inside. Some might complain she was a walking contradiction, but Hades knew that contradictions would eventually resolve themselves and stabilize. Those were the aspects of Terra he cared about and thought of day and night.

The literal question of "what Terra was" mattered much less than its abstract counterpart. No, the real question was, "who Terra was?" Of these things, Hades was certain. They'd been through so much together, and he could tell that the biggest battles were still ahead of them. That was why they now wielded the Sword together.

But before there could be any future battles, the aftermath of the last one had to be dealt with. When the warriors' business was done, that was when the true work began. After the war, the much more difficult job of picking up the pieces started.

Armies left death and destruction in their wake. Every competent nation had a Ministry of War. What they lacked was a "Ministry of everything else" that could undo the horrors of war brought about by the former.

Hades had tried implementing such a group. Their introduction was a trial by fire: their first job was undoing the horrors of Echidna's rampage. As Terra was trying to reform Echidna, Hades was trying to help the recovery force undo Echidna's evils. To do that, first, he had to try to get to the bottom of what exactly Echidna was doing while in charge.

While she had everyone under mind control, Echidna had begun using the land of Hades' resources to try and reunite with Typhon. Yet strangely, she had also instituted a strict travel ban so that no gods or kings could enter the land of Hades. Any who tried would be turned away. That way, only Terra, who teleported in, would enter. Perhaps this was to keep her from getting backup?

Echidna only gorged herself on the masses of commoners who would come to see Hades' supposed paradise. Instead, they were met with a nightmare. Echidna spread the madness further; she took control of many other fledgling democracies that were aligned with Hades and repeated similar tragedies there.

Hades felt disgusted that so many of his allies and friends were taken advantage of. But their records were still incomplete. Nobody could remember what had happened after they were mind-controlled. Terra was going around, reverting Echidna's brainwashing in the same way she did in the Land of Hades.

Terra promised that while she had taken a copy of everyone's memories, she did not look at them. But Hades needed to know what happened during that time. Even outside the investigators, some people wanted access to their memories, and Terra restored them.

The information was edited so as to not revert their loyalty to Echidna. Now, these memories were more akin to a first-person movie: the experiences of another, evil version that would not affect their psyche. They were a different person in them, akin to a mature person looking back at a darker part of their life that they had evolved past.

Hades asked for his memories back to better help those who had suffered. As soon as he received them back, he vomited and had a panic attack as the PTSD of everything he experienced rushed back into him. It was awful.

But now they had all the information they needed. The families of all the people who had been invited to the land of Hades only to be eaten were contacted and informed of their loved one's passing. Hades offered condolences and any form of restitution he could offer.

Even at home, he apologized for allowing such evil to persist. Some chose to be angry at him, but others accepted the truth: there was nothing that could undo all the harm. No money or gifts could undo what had happened.

Worst of all, Hades now remembered the isolation that little Cerberus had to suffer all alone while Echidna was in charge. Ever since the incident, the once upbeat girl seldom spoke or left her room. The traumatic experience was just too much. Hades' heart ached.

Hades went on an apology tour across the Kosmos, trying to make things right. But outside the land of Hades, people were much more willing to blame him for everything. Overnight, public opinion turned against Hades. Of course, the god of the dead would lure people to a land of death from which they'd never return! Zeus and his allies were loving every second of it.

The bodies weren't even cold before Zeus' people started a "Victims of Democracy" organization meant to help those whom Echidna's rampage had hurt. The blame was not on the tyrannical demon but on all democracies collectively. Even all the democratic poleis where Echidna had no influence suffered a blow to their reputation because of her.

The death of Aidoneus was held up as a warning to kings that any who took a deal with Hades and stepped down would end up dead. This tragedy had been a great boon to Zeus and his people.

As Hades continued to help with picking up the pieces, he went to the dungeon to free those she might have been torturing or keeping for food. To his shock, waiting for him in the dungeon was none other than Hydra himself.

"Surprise." Hydra grinned and waved from his cell.

"Hydra!? What are you doing here?" Hades cried.

"Well, ironically, I was supposed to be the one rescuing you. Unsurprisingly, we were unable to defeat a monster like Echidna. The demon beat me within an inch of my life and had my powers sealed." Hydra explained.

"I see. Even if she's your family, I understand not being a fan," Hades replied.

"She ate half of my comrades in the rescue party and was going to eat me as a victory feast once she killed Terra," Hydra curtly responded. Hades understood.

"Wait… what about Mel?" Hades asked.

"She's fine. Don't worry. I got captured making sure she survived, not that she made it easy," Hydra smirked, "In the battle with Echidna, Mel refused to retreat with the others until I knocked her out. She had to be dragged to safety while I stayed behind to get obliterated."

"I see. I'm sorry for putting you through all that." Hades frowned.

"No problem, pal. Echidna did all the killing herself. You have nothing to feel guilty about. Don't apologize for her," Hydra reassured him. "Besides, it was reassuring to know that the land of Hades is so well defended. Even before Echidna personally joined the fray, you and your allies were a force to be reckoned with."

"That's a very odd way of looking at that." Hades noted.

"Even after our fight on Molossos, you've continued to grow stronger. Plus, with that… I don't know if anyone could stop you." Hydra noted the Sword of Dehmos on Hades' back. Even being near it made him feel uncomfortable.

"I'm strong, perhaps even stronger than Zeus. But I still know better than to fight Jupiter directly. As Terra showed, being stronger than a Solaris is not enough to defeat them. Their mysterious powers were not to be taken lightly. But with that sword… Hades, you might actually stand a chance of defeating the ultimate enemy," Hydra noted.

Hades looked at Hydra in confusion. Why was he staring so intensely at him?

Either way, Hades released Hydra and led him out of the dungeon. As he opened the door to exit, however, Hades was shocked to find Mel waiting for them. Mel looked furious… but also like she was on the verge of tears.

"I hate you," Mel growled as she physically pulled Hydra down to her level.

"Sorry about knocking you out back there." Hydra sighed.

"You're the worst." Mel released him and crossed her arms.

"Yeah. But it's good to see that you're alright." Hydra smiled.

"I suppose the others will be happy to see that you're alive too." Mel scoffed. Despite Mel acting tough, Hydra just went in for a big hug. At that point, she completely broke down and hugged him back. They were overjoyed to be reunited. Hades couldn't help but smile fondly. Oddly, he saw himself and Terra in those two.

"You're the worst..." Mel sniffled.

"Love you too, Mel," Hydra whispered to her before releasing the bear hug.

"Not to break up the heartwarming reunion, but you need to get out of here before Zeus finds out," Hades cried.

"Zeus already knows I'm here. Who do you think laid the trap?" Hydra asked. Hades froze. Seeing his reaction, Hydra just sighed.

"I think it's time we had another chat. Come to the place I showed you in our first fight. I'll be waiting for you there." Hydra grinned.

That swampy lake on Lernia... was the place where Hydra had based his Microcosm off. Hades went to Lernia in secret, tracking flying overhead to try and spot similar-looking lakes. It was a big planet, but using deductive reasoning, he was able to narrow down the spots fairly quickly. Then he saw them: abandoned ruins of Typhon's cult in Lernia. As he landed and entered into the abandoned site, Hades found Hydra and Mel waiting for him.

"It's about time you found us. If you kept us waiting much longer, I'd have had to put out a signal or something." Hydra let out a hearty laugh.

"There's no time for that, Hydra. I need answers: how is Zeus involved?" Hades cut to the chase.

"Hades, who defeated Typhon?" Hydra asked as he became serious.

"Terra." Hades, of course, replied.

"Correct. As a child, the Cult of Typhon taught me all about it." Hydra began, "But most children in Graia grow up hearing a different story, don't they? As far as everyone else was concerned, the one who defeated Typhon was..."

"Zeus." Hades had a horrifying realization.

"That's right. I've dismantled or converted almost all the remnants of the Typhon cult. The few stragglers that remained had no way of encountering Echidna, so then who else could have told her but Zeus or his people?" Hydra asked.

Hades finally put all the pieces together, and a look of shocked horror overcame him.

"When Echidna first arrived back in Graia, she must have heard the official story that Zeus defeated Typhon. In a rage, she'd gone looking for Zeus, but agents of his regime were quick to point her at Terra instead. They were just defending their master from this dangerous adversary. But even if unintentionally, they had diverted the tragedy to you and your allies instead." Hydra shared his theory.

"Now Terra is blaming herself for something Zeus did! It didn't matter if Zeus' people wanted Echidna's rampage to happen; they sent her and sat back as it all happened." Hades' blood boiled.

It was incorrect to say that all evil came from Zeus' regime. Echidna was an unaffiliated force of nature that came to be without them. However, even in times of crisis, Zeus' people could steer the chaos in a direction that was beneficial to them.

"We don't know for sure that bastard's government directly caused Echidna to attack, but they did allow it to happen and never alerted Terra. They even increased security around her so that Hydra and I couldn't contact her. Zeus' people ensured that several powerful gods loyal to him were always with Terra. They did everything within their power to ensure that Terra didn't learn about Echidna's invasion until it was too late." Mel added.

"Since every day wasted trying to recruit Terra was a day that more innocent people died, we began making plans to go ourselves and save the land of Hades. We even received word from our agents there that Echidna was going to carry out a huge slaughter soon. It was then or never. But it was a trap." Hydra made a fist.

When Hydra and Mel arrived, they were horrified to find that Echidna had control of their people's minds and used them as a way to lure the two into a fight they had no chance of winning. But why? Echidna had no way of knowing of them, and without knowing Hydra was her son, she wouldn't care. Someone must have told her about him.

"Zeus had interfered again. He told Echidna that I was her long-lost son and piqued her interest in a reunion. That also meant that Zeus' spies probably also know that we have agents guarding you." Hydra concluded his retelling.

It seemed that even though they had avoided direct conflict, Zeus was still working from the shadows. Hades was furious. Hydra shared other hypotheses about Zeus' work with Echidna. Hades was able to confirm a few.

"She told me that Zeus had asked for my head, but she refused. Even though I was immune to her mind control as a son of Typhon, Echidna sought to turn me into her loyal soldier. When she grew frustrated at a lack of progress, she decided to just eat me, reckoning that I was decently strong and thus probably tasted good. Ironically, it was that grim fate that saved me from Zeus' clutches." Hydra sighed.

The two radicals turned to Hades, eagerly awaiting his response. He was so overwhelmed as all this hit him at the same time.

"It's... so awful. Zeus was in direct contact with Echidna? Who knows if he had even helped direct some of her tyranny? This is insane! Everyone needs to know! Terra needs to know!" Hades cried.

"That isn't a good idea. It isn't time yet." A man rebuked Hades as he entered. Hades turned in shock to find the god of the sea, Neptune himself standing there.

"What is going on? Why would Zeus' own brother be here!?" Hades panicked at the arrival of Neptune.

"About time you arrived, boss-man." Hydra, the water snake, smiled as the true mastermind finally showed himself.

TALE 30

Gods and Monsters

The Sword of Dehmos had opened Hades' eyes. When Neptune entered the room, the god of the dead felt the weight of what he was now in the presence of. He couldn't fully perceive it, but even though Hydra was right there: Neptune was what shook Hades to his core. He looked like a man, or rather a god… but Hades could tell he was something totally alien. He'd put off asking the question but… what exactly were these Solaris beings!?

Hydra noted Hades' shock, but assumed it was only at Neptune being there. He snapped Hades' out of his trance with a casual explanation.

"When trying to overthrow the government, having an inside man always helps. Though he rarely graces us with his presence, he's had his hands in everything from afar, working behind the scenes to hedge his bets in the war against Olympus." Hydra explained while casually throwing his arm over Neptune's shoulder.

"Hades, I'm sorry that I couldn't reveal myself sooner. I wanted to go and save the land of Hades, but that ban on gods entering your land was not just one way. When I arrived to try and battle Echidna… it was Zeus himself who escorted me away. I shouldn't have been surprised; he watches us all like a hawk." Neptune made a fist.

"It's alright, I understand now. Of course, Echidna had some help pulling this off." Hades responded in kind as everything fell into place.

"I'm sure Terra has mentioned how busy and tiring her year has been. Zeus has a stash of difficult missions far from Graia saved up for Terra during situations just like these. She had no chance of sensing anything was amiss or even hearing rumors to that effect. Keep that in mind; if any of us Solaris are around, be certain Zeus' people are nearby, making sure we are staying in line," Neptune explained.

"Are we sure we can be safe right now then?" Hades asked while looking around nervously.

"For now, I've given them the slip. But I can't stay long. We have to be careful. Zeus… or rather Jupiter is already suspicious of me, and if he ever found out that I was working with Hydra, it is all over," Neptune apologized.

"I get it. This entire resistance would be destroyed." Hades forced a chuckle to try and add some levity.

"Not just the resistance. If any of us make too grave of a misstep, the entire Kosmos would be destroyed," Neptune explained.

"What does that mean!? There's no need for such hyperbole." Hades laughed, refusing to believe that things could get any worse. Mel, Hydra, and Neptune weren't laughing. They were dead serious.

"It is time…" Neptune sighed, "It is time that you finally understood why Jupiter is so dangerous and why nobody, not even Terra, has actively made an enemy of him."

Neptune then opened a portal through space and time. On the other side was a dark blue planet of some kind, similar to Terra's own. Yet, it was bigger and darker and of a noticeably different composition.

"That… is a source of infinite Power. I suppose it looks like a planet of some kind to you all. Each member of my family has one. We eight members of Solaris: Mercury, Venus, Terra, Mars, Jupiter, Saturn, Neptune, and Uranus, are this way. Saturn was stolen by Typhon and was the source of his infinite Power. But if used carelessly, any one of us could destroy all of creation. Infinite Power does mean infinite after all," Neptune explained.

Hades remembered the times that Terra had opened that strange portal. Just what was the Solaris clan? What were these Planets that had come into Graia?

"The power you speak of… that's the Smite attack," Hades said as he put it all together.

"That's right. We're only supposed to use it if our actual existence is threatened. If any of our siblings used it carelessly, our programming or… rather, our instincts would bring about mutually assured destruction. Terra is the only one that can use it consistently, thanks to that sword you carry," Neptune said while motioning to the Sword of Dehmos.

"Nonetheless, Jupiter, who is the least qualified, is also the most likely to use it. His instincts are completely eroded. He is so senile that he's as illogical as an actual human!" Neptune explained before angrily stabbing his trident into the ground. He had to calm himself down as he went on.

"As an… actual human? Neptune, what are you?" Hades asked before pausing. He knew what Terra was- no, he knew who Terra was. The "what" question didn't matter! Hades prepared to retract his question, but Neptune answered first.

"I understand your confusion," Neptune began.

To Hades' shock, his voice came not only from Neptune, the man, but also Neptune, the planet above, and Neptune, the trident between them.

"The superhuman arrogance that often accompanies Power did cause those with it to proclaim themselves gods. But hear this: the gods of this Universe are humans; they are human beings animated with the ability to manipulate probabilities and thus gain powers that appear divine." Neptune explained.

"Alright… but that doesn't explain what you are," Hades noted.

"Correct. I described what you are to define it as what we are not. You can think of us as beings from… beyond. Trying to explain it any further will be of no use to you. When I tried going more in-depth with Hydra and Mel it just made their heads spin. For simplicity, you can just call us Solaris as we do." Neptune grinned.

As Neptune spoke, the blackness of space from within the portal engulfed the room. Now Hades, Hydra, Mel, and Neptune seemed to float in the vacuum of space. Finally, Hades could see all eight of the mysterious Planets at once.

Each of the Heavenly Bodies seemed so massive and daunting and out of reach. But there! There was Terra, or at least the Planet she always called to her side. It was foreign to Hades' eyes but also the only one of the Planets that looked even remotely habitable.

"If you think those are impressive, just imagine what it would look like from a… higher vantage point." Neptune smiled as he looked and could see them for what they were.

"The people you meet: Terra, Jupiter, and I exist as thin slices, or perhaps aspects of those higher beings that can only exist partially in your Universe. We are the observational terminals that exist at the points of contact with your level of existence," Neptune explained.

Next to him, a dark blue sphere passed through a two-dimensional plane. As it did, most of the sphere was outside the plane, but the infinitely thin point of contact glowed brightly.

"That glowing part would be us. Just scaled up in dimensionality." Neptune motioned towards it but saw Hades was confused. It was a bit of an abstract visual aid, but it was the best he could think of.

"I get it. The nature of my kind's complete existence is alien, even to us. Are we part of the same being?" Neptune asked as the 3D sphere became a spiral, making contact with the 2D plane at eight points, each glowing a color that corresponded to a Solaris.

"Or are we all parts of different beings?" Neptune asked as the Spiral's mass split apart to become eight different spheres, making contact with the 2D plane.

"I can't remember, and unfortunately, neither can Terra. Her memory, while more intact than the rest of us, isn't perfect either," Neptune explained. The spheres and planes vanished, having completely failed to explain the higher concept to its intended audience.

"I apologize; this is all high-concept stuff. But beyond what I just explained, your guess becomes as good as mine. We have our theories, but that is about it," Neptune explained. "You're an observant guy. I'm sure you have plenty of your own."

"Give me some time to process this, and I'll make an attempt." The confounded Hades sighed.

"Right. There are many unknowns. But what we do know is that we are interested observers. Humans, powerless beings once confined to a single planet, are spread across the vastness of space. Myth and magic, once the domain of the imagination, are now real. Something strange happened in this dimension, and its aftereffects need to be studied. So, we came down to have a look. At least, that's how Terra tells it. The rest of us are too senile to remember anything from before our humanoid forms were created." Neptune shrugged.

"Senile?" Hades asked. Neptune seemed pretty sharp to him. Other than the usual immaturity observable in most gods, the Solaris siblings all seemed normal to Hades.

"Yes, we refer to our current state as senile. Perhaps a comparison to human adolescence would be more accurate, but senility won out." Neptune shrugged. Seeing that Hades expected more of an answer, Neptune decided to elaborate.

"To better blend in with humanity and observe you all, these third-dimensional avatars of ours began to take on your qualities. The closer we got to you, the more detached we became from our higher existences. After all, at one point, each and every one of us was capable of the same feats Terra is now. We just unwittingly traded such abilities born out of higher knowledge for raw Power more fitting of this world's beings," Neptune said while motioning toward the cold, distant Sphere in the distance.

"Basically, the more attached they are to our world, the stronger they get here, but the dumber they get too." Hydra laughed.

At once, all across the blackness of space, images of Terra as a young, emotionless child were contrasted with her as the loving and emotive woman she had become. As a child, she was strong by human standards but looked absolutely pathetic next to the unmatched Power she showed when she wielded the Sword of Dehmos.

"Terra's case is a bit special because her relatively low level of senility allows her to use her weapon to the utmost.

The rest of our divine tools are pretty pathetic in comparison," Neptune explained as he finally pried his trident from the ground. "Without her weapon, Terra's Power is no match for me or many other Solaris siblings."

"On the other hand, I'm sure you remember who the strongest and most dangerous Solaris is," Mel growled.

Then, the images of Terra were replaced by images of Jupiter wielding powerful storms. His simplistic abilities were far less impressive than Terra's kosmos-bending reality warping, but they were far more Powerful. Jupiter could destroy entire planets with massive cosmic storms! They were simple but destructive.

With his powers, Jupiter could effortlessly conquer the Kosmos just as Typhon did. However, as the destructive Jupiter laughed maniacally, he found himself surrounded by a condemning mob of his siblings. Hades was confused when he saw Neptune among them, even though, in reality, he stood next to Hades. This must have been a simulation of some kind. The simulated Jupiter began to panic, seeing the others ready to pounce on him and punish his evils!

"While my Mind has degraded to the point of harboring human emotions and forgetting much of my higher functions, at least my core instincts are intact. Don't overly interfere with humanity to avoid corrupting data, observe and collaborate with the others of my kind, and generally safeguard the life of this Universe. All three directives point to this rule: NEVER use the Smite," Neptune explained.

"But Jupiter no longer has those safeguards?" Hades asked as he saw the image of Jupiter's insane expression. Just then, the simulation of Jupiter called out to the corresponding Planet above.

"Jupiter's lust for power… that corruption he received from Typhon is now so important to him that he equates it to life itself. His central instincts have been overwritten. In the same way that Terra is willing to risk breaking the taboo to save others, Jupiter is extremely trigger-happy with using it to save his crown. If any of us prove a true threat to him, he is willing to destroy the whole Universe rather than lose his power," Neptune warned.

As Neptune said that Jupiter the man and Planet both began to glow brighter than a star. Then a massive explosion burst forth and vaporized all the other Planets before continuing infinitely, destroying the rest of the Universe in short order!

Hades was mortified as he watched the shockwave wash over him and eradicate all of existence. Then, all of that seemed to rewind as time itself worked backward to show the Universe as it had been before that collapse.

"If Jupiter did that, we other Solaris would have no choice but to respond in kind. Then, nothing would be left; just mutually assured destruction," Neptune ominously explained before the other Planets joined Jupiter in firing blasts this time. In this simulation, Jupiter, too was blasted apart by an opposing explosion from the reformed Planets. That time, all of them were mutually destroyed, and the Universe was left truly empty.

"As you can imagine, this is an outcome we would like to avoid," Neptune said as time within the simulation rewound again. "Most of us wouldn't even imagine pulling that trigger. If that doomsday scenario were to occur, it would be Jupiter that fired first," Neptune ominously warned.

"That is why… all of us, his siblings, have had no choice but to play along," Neptune began.

This time, the simulated Solaris siblings bowed before Jupiter and took oaths to him as gods within his Olympian regime. Jupiter was at first very confused but then very happy.

They were acting as if they didn't see any of the evils that he inflicted on the humans they were supposed to protect. The Planets above would not let the humanoid avatars below see the evils, let alone risk conflict with him.

"The worst part is, as a part of self-preservation, we are incapable of even thinking of defying him. After all, even now, I'm terrified that if this plan to defy him fails... we all die. It took me decades to break out of that spell and accept that risk. It was unbearable. Being forced to let him do whatever and never understand why. Deluding myself and ignoring all his evils for no good reason! It was like being a prisoner in my own body! I can't let my siblings suffer that fate any longer, and I can't let him trample the human race either!" Neptune cried.

His wrath was obvious to everyone. The simulated Neptune still bowed before the king, but his rage was betrayed by his shaking fists. While his programming said he could not openly fight Jupiter, the contradiction with his determination to protect the humans, he'd come to love resolved itself in this way: he would oppose Jupiter indirectly instead. The simulated figures all vanished, leaving Neptune with his last hopes: Hydra, Mel, and Hades.

"Hades... if you've ever felt an internal conflict within yourself... I need you to try and magnify that by a thousand. That is the turmoil Terra is in every day. Until the threat of Jupiter is done away with, she can never know peace. The World itself will never know peace!" Neptune explained while calming himself down.

"How? What can even be done?" Hades cried.

"Jupiter has his limits. He is restrained by his equivalent fear of us, especially Terra. That is why he tries to avoid being exposed or doing anything so blatant that it can no longer be ignored. We can use that to our advantage. Whether or not she did it consciously, Terra being so close to you ensures that Jupiter can't attack you directly." Neptune grinned. Hades paused for a moment. Was that really why she'd fallen in love with him? No. There was no time to consider that.

"Terra is strong… she's starting to awaken and defy him as I did, but the primal fear is holding her back. Consciously, she will never understand why she's afraid of Jupiter. She probably isn't even sure that she's afraid of him. But subconsciously, she knows the danger. Even Typhon wasn't so insane as to risk the destruction of the Universe with a Smite. Jupiter is. For as much progress as Terra has made, she will never be able to fight Jupiter as we do; trying to get her involved is a fool's errand." Neptune revealed.

"How can we stop him then? Are you saying we just have to sit by and do nothing?" Hades cried. It was horrifying: a bully on the world stage who was untouchable because of the looming nuclear option. Was there any way to stop such a nightmare!? Was this a doomed mission from the start?

"No, there is still a chance." Neptune shocked Hades, "Do you remember the Maw of Typhon?" Neptune asked.

"Of course. The device Metis trapped him with to weaken him. He'd made it originally to capture Solaris beings like you and steal your Powers… Terra most of all," Hades recalled.

"Precisely. When Typhon was captured by his own weapon, Saturn's connection to him was weakened. What was more, he lost his ability to use the Smite. These bodies are not human, but if we can disrupt the connection between Jupiter's three-dimensional form and his core, we might finally be able to defeat him. But until we find them, we cannot make Terra his enemy. There is nothing Jupiter fears more than that. But Terra is afraid of her own Power- likely because she doesn't want to risk triggering Jupiter's self-preservation instinct. We can't be too hasty. We must box him in, but the killing blow must come at the perfect time. The plan isn't perfect, but it's the only way to stop my brother," Neptune explained.

"Now... knowing all that, are you going to chicken out?" Mel asked. Hades made a fist and felt uneasy. Much more was at risk than he ever imagined.

"We've had no luck locating the device yet, so you'll need to keep stalling him out until we do. Plus, he likely knows you're working with us now. It's do-or-die from here on out," Mel cried. Hades gritted his teeth. Could he fight his own brother-in-law? His beloved wife's older brother?

"What do you say, Hades? Are you ready to fight the king of the gods himself?" Hydra asked as the celestial illusion fell, and they returned to the real world.

"Of course. The enemy is Jupiter, but we aren't facing him alone. Jupiter is not just our enemy but the enemy of the whole World!" Hades declared as he drew the Sword of the People.

www.ingramcontent.com/pod-product-compliance
Lightning Source LLC
Chambersburg PA
CBHW030340310726
48979CB00001B/123
* 9 7 8 1 9 9 8 7 5 3 3 0 7 *